Frostbite

Faith Webb

Published by Faith Webb, 2024.

This is a work of fiction. Similarities to real people, places, or events are entirely coincidental.

FROSTBITE

First edition. November 13, 2024.

Copyright © 2024 Faith Webb.

ISBN: 979-8230815518

Written by Faith Webb.

Chapter 1: The Encounter

His eyes were cold, calculating, like ice chipping away at every layer I didn't even know I'd built around myself. They held a spark of something dark, something I probably should've feared, but all I felt was the thrill. His coat hung loose on his frame, the collar pulled up against the late autumn wind that whipped through the empty alley, scattering papers and dust between us like some kind of makeshift battlefield. And even though every logical part of my brain was screaming at me to walk away, to get out while I still could, I couldn't shake the sense that this was the exact place I was supposed to be.

"Are you lost, little girl?" he asked, his tone a mix of amusement and something harsher, something that bit into me in a way I hated to admit I liked. There was a slight smirk playing at the corners of his mouth, like he knew exactly what he was doing, like he was used to people backing down just because he looked at them the wrong way.

I crossed my arms, tilting my chin up with a defiance that wasn't entirely genuine, but I wasn't about to let him see that. "Not lost. Just bored."

He arched a brow, taking a slow, deliberate step forward, and I fought the instinct to step back. "Bored," he repeated, his voice low and edged with something that sounded like mockery. "Then you're even more of a fool than I thought."

"Maybe," I shot back, not caring that my voice wavered slightly. "But at least I'm not the one hiding in alleyways, trying to scare off people who have better things to do."

That smirk widened, became something almost wolfish. He was close enough now that I could see the faint scar tracing his left cheek, the roughness of stubble across his jaw, and it struck me as almost absurd that a man who looked like he belonged in some dark, forgotten corner of the world could be so... captivating. He had the kind of face that you couldn't ignore, no matter how badly you wanted to.

"You think you know me?" he asked, voice dropping into a low, dangerous tone that sent a shiver down my spine. "You think you have the slightest idea of what you're getting into?"

I rolled my eyes, though my heart was pounding in my chest. "I think you're trying way too hard to be intimidating. It's almost cute."

For a moment, there was silence. Just the sound of the wind, the creaking of a loose metal shutter somewhere down the alley, and the two of us staring each other down, locked in some strange, inexplicable dance neither of us fully understood. He looked at me, really looked at me, like he was searching for something, and I felt a flicker of doubt twist in my stomach, a feeling I shoved down as quickly as it had surfaced.

"Tell me," he said finally, breaking the silence. "What exactly are you hoping to find here?"

I opened my mouth to answer, to say something sharp and cutting, something that would show him I wasn't just some naive girl looking for thrills. But the words stuck, caught somewhere between the truth and the lies I'd been telling myself for as long as I could remember.

"I don't owe you an answer," I replied instead, my voice firmer than I felt. I didn't dare admit that I wasn't entirely sure what I was looking for, that I'd spent so long chasing shadows I couldn't even remember where it all started anymore. But I wasn't about to let him see that. I wasn't about to give him the satisfaction of knowing he'd rattled me, even if only for a moment.

He laughed, a low, rough sound that echoed off the walls around us. "You're in over your head. But you're stubborn. I'll give you that."

"And you're awfully full of yourself for a guy who spends his nights skulking around abandoned buildings," I shot back, refusing to let him have the last word. There was something infuriatingly smug about him, the way he seemed to know exactly what buttons to push, exactly where to aim to make me feel like I was coming apart at the seams.

He took another step forward, close enough now that I could feel the heat radiating off him, close enough that I could see the faint twitch of a muscle in his jaw. "You think this is a game?" he asked softly, his voice barely more than a whisper. "You think you're ready for what's coming?"

"I think," I replied, refusing to look away, "that you're all talk."

His hand shot out, catching my wrist in a grip that was just tight enough to send a surge of adrenaline through me. "Careful," he murmured, his gaze flickering to my lips for the briefest moment. "You might not like what you find."

For a split second, I almost leaned into him, almost let myself give in to the strange pull that was drawing us together, despite every rational thought screaming at me to get as far away from him as possible. But then I yanked my hand free, stepping back and putting as much distance between us as the narrow alley allowed.

"I've dealt with worse than you," I said, forcing myself to keep my voice steady. "Trust me."

He watched me for a moment, his expression unreadable, and I could almost see the wheels turning in his mind, calculating, assessing, deciding whether I was worth the trouble. And then, without another word, he turned and walked away, disappearing into the shadows as silently as he'd appeared.

I stood there, breathing heavily, my mind racing with a thousand questions I knew I wouldn't get answers to. But even as I told myself it was over, that I'd seen the last of him, a part of me knew that this was just the beginning. Because something in his eyes, in the way he'd looked at me, had told me that he wasn't the type to just walk away.

And, truthfully, neither was I.

Two days later, I was back in the same alley, hoping to pick up the pieces of the lead he'd nearly wrecked. The wind had turned bitter, gnawing at my cheeks and slipping icy fingers down my collar, but I wasn't about to let a little discomfort stop me. I'd barely set foot in the alley when I noticed the faint outline of something sprayed across the wall in front of me, words scrawled in black paint that dripped down the cracked brick like blood.

Keep digging, and you'll end up buried.

I snorted, more amused than intimidated. If he thought a little spray paint was going to make me pack up and go home, he clearly didn't know me at all. I took out my phone, snapping a quick picture of the message before moving on. My informant had mentioned a hidden entrance, an old basement door hidden behind the abandoned laundromat at the end of the block. It sounded like a scene straight out of a B-movie, and I half expected to find nothing but mold and rats down there. But I wasn't in the habit of ignoring leads, especially not the kind that came from someone with as many scars and secrets as Vance. If anyone knew how to find the darker corners of Keldorn, it was him.

I made my way down the narrow path between the laundromat and a building that looked like it had been empty since the last century. The place reeked of mildew and regret, and the flickering streetlight overhead cast everything in a sickly yellow glow that made my skin crawl. There, behind a stack of rusted metal crates, was the door. It was heavy, industrial, with a layer of grime so thick I doubted anyone had touched it in years. But the dust around the handle was smudged, smeared in the way that only fresh fingerprints would be. Someone had been here recently.

I took a deep breath, bracing myself as I wrapped my hand around the freezing handle. Just as I began to turn it, a low voice spoke from the shadows.

"Curiosity killed the cat, you know."

I didn't jump—I'd learned a long time ago not to give people the satisfaction of seeing me flinch. But I turned slowly, keeping my face neutral as I met his gaze. He was leaning against the wall, that same infuriating smirk playing at his lips as if he'd just been waiting for me to stumble onto his trap.

"Good thing I'm not a cat," I replied, my voice as steady as I could make it.

His smirk widened. "No, but you're just as reckless."

"Reckless?" I scoffed, trying to ignore the slight chill that settled over me as he stepped forward, his shadow stretching out until it nearly touched mine. "I think that's a little rich coming from the guy who leaves cryptic messages on alley walls. What's next, anonymous notes in cutout letters?"

He chuckled, a low, rough sound that sent an uncomfortable thrill through me. "You're the one digging through places you shouldn't be, sweetheart."

"Sweetheart?" I echoed, raising a brow. "You don't know me well enough to be calling me that."

"Fair enough," he said, his tone nonchalant, but his eyes glinting with something far sharper. "But I'd say we're well past introductions at this point."

"Funny, I don't recall asking for one," I shot back, keeping my stance as steady as I could. But he just looked at me, a look that told me he saw far more than I wanted him to.

"You're looking for trouble," he said softly, almost as if he were talking to himself.

"I'm looking for answers," I corrected, refusing to be baited by his half-truths and veiled threats.

"Is that what you tell yourself?" His gaze flicked over me, appraising. "That you're just here for answers? Because from where I'm standing, it looks like you're here for something a little more… dangerous."

"Or maybe you're just seeing what you want to see," I countered, folding my arms as if I could block him out with sheer willpower.

He laughed again, that low, rumbling sound that was starting to get under my skin in ways I didn't care to analyze. "Tell me something, then," he said, his tone turning almost conversational. "Why'd you come back? Surely you got the message loud and clear."

I hesitated, just for a fraction of a second, but it was enough. He saw it, of course he did, and his smirk widened, that maddening glint in his eyes growing sharper.

"Maybe I don't take orders from graffiti on a wall," I said, trying to sound as unbothered as possible.

He took another step forward, his gaze never leaving mine. "Then you're either braver than most, or stupider."

"Depends on who you ask," I muttered, my pulse pounding louder than I cared to admit.

His gaze darkened, and for a moment, the teasing glint in his eyes faded, replaced by something colder, more dangerous. "Then maybe you should think about who you're asking."

I swallowed, but held my ground. "And maybe you should stop trying to scare me off, because it's not going to work."

For a long, tense moment, he just looked at me, his eyes narrowing as if he were trying to see right through me. And then, without a word, he stepped back, holding up his hands in a mock gesture of surrender.

"Fine," he said, his voice dropping to a low murmur. "You want to play in the dark? Be my guest. Just don't say I didn't warn you when you find yourself in over your head."

With that, he turned and walked away, leaving me standing there in the cold, empty alley. I watched him go, my mind spinning with questions and possibilities I wasn't sure I wanted to examine too closely. But one thing was certain—whatever I'd stumbled into, it was bigger than I'd expected. And for the first time, I felt a flicker of something I hadn't in a long time.

Excitement.

It was dangerous, and it was reckless, and I knew that I was probably setting myself up for a fall. But I couldn't help myself. The thrill of it was intoxicating, pulling me forward even as every sensible part of my mind screamed at me to turn back. I took a deep breath, letting the night air fill my lungs as I steeled myself for whatever came next.

After all, curiosity may have killed the cat, but satisfaction had always brought it back. And right now, I was determined to find out just what kind of satisfaction was waiting for me at the end of this twisted, winding path.

I don't know what possessed me to go back the next night, but there I was, creeping through the same alley as if it held some promise only I could decipher. A fog had rolled in, thick and cold, curling around my legs like smoke and swallowing up the flickering streetlights. The whole city felt eerily quiet, as though it were holding its breath.

My boots scraped against the broken pavement, each step sending echoes down the deserted alley. This time, I kept my eyes open for shadows that didn't belong, glancing over my shoulder every few steps. But there was no sign of him, no graffiti messages, no mocking voice from the darkness. Just silence.

I turned a corner, and there it was: the same industrial door I'd tried the night before. It loomed in front of me, its surface scarred by rust and neglect. I glanced around once more, feeling an odd mix of relief and disappointment that I was alone, then reached for the handle, cold and unyielding beneath my fingers. With a creak that seemed loud enough to wake the dead, I pulled it open and slipped inside.

The air was damp, thick with the smell of mold and stale cigarette smoke. It was pitch black, and I fumbled with my flashlight, the narrow beam cutting through the darkness just enough to reveal rows of crates and rusted metal shelves, all coated in a thick layer of dust. There were stacks of paper scattered on the ground, some of them torn, others so faded they were unreadable. I crouched down, holding my flashlight between my teeth as I sifted through them, looking for anything that might give me a clue as to what this place was—or why he'd been so determined to keep me out of it.

I was so focused that I didn't hear the footsteps behind me until they were almost too close. I froze, my heart leaping into my throat as I slowly turned, half expecting to see him standing there, arms crossed and that insufferable smirk on his face.

But it wasn't him.

A man I'd never seen before stood in the doorway, his face hidden in shadows, but I could make out the gleam of something metallic in his hand. My fingers tightened around the flashlight, the beam wavering as I tried to keep my breathing steady.

"Well, well," he said, his voice a rough rasp that sent chills down my spine. "Looks like we've got ourselves a little trespasser."

I straightened, forcing myself to meet his gaze, though my mind was racing with escape routes and backup plans. "And it looks like I'm not the only one," I replied, my voice steady, though I felt anything but.

He took a step closer, and I caught a glint of silver—the unmistakable shape of a knife. My pulse spiked, but I held my ground, refusing to give him the satisfaction of seeing my fear.

"Funny," he murmured, tilting his head as if studying me. "The boss said someone might come snooping around. Didn't think it'd be you, though."

"Didn't realize I was that predictable," I shot back, though my mind was racing, trying to piece together who his "boss" might be.

He laughed, a low, humorless sound that echoed off the walls. "Oh, he was very specific. Said you'd be trouble."

"Well," I said, forcing a smirk I didn't feel, "trouble's my middle name."

Without warning, he lunged forward, the knife slicing through the air in a flash of silver. I ducked, my flashlight clattering to the floor as I stumbled back, my hands finding the edge of a crate that I gripped for balance. The knife missed by inches, the man's face twisting into a scowl as he steadied himself for another strike.

My heart pounded, adrenaline surging through me as I scrambled backward, my fingers brushing something cold and heavy—a metal pipe. I didn't think; I just swung, the pipe connecting with his arm with a sickening crunch. He let out a yell, staggering back, and I took my chance, darting past him toward the open door.

But he was faster than I'd anticipated, his uninjured arm reaching out and grabbing my wrist in a vice-like grip. I twisted, yanking my arm free, but he blocked my path, his expression darkening as he raised the knife again.

"Should've listened to the warnings, sweetheart," he sneered, and I had a momentary flash of déjà vu, hearing those words in a voice far more familiar.

I had no choice. I lunged, ramming my shoulder into his chest, sending him stumbling back just enough for me to slip past him and out the door. I didn't stop to look back, my footsteps echoing off the walls as I sprinted down the alley, my breath coming in gasps that burned in the cold night air.

When I finally slowed, my legs trembling and my heart racing, I ducked into a side street, pressing my back against the wall as I struggled to catch my breath. The alley was empty, no sign of my would-be attacker, but I knew better than to let my guard down.

I could still feel his grip on my wrist, a dull ache that served as a reminder of just how close I'd come.

And that's when I heard it—a slow, deliberate clap coming from somewhere nearby.

I turned, my heart sinking as I saw him standing at the edge of the shadows, arms crossed, watching me with that same infuriating smirk.

"Well," he said, his voice dripping with mock admiration, "looks like you've got a bit of fight in you after all."

I glared at him, my pulse still racing. "Did you know he was going to be there?"

He shrugged, his eyes gleaming with something that might've been amusement. "Maybe. Maybe not. Consider it a lesson."

"A lesson?" I spat, my hands clenching into fists. "What, that you're perfectly happy to let someone else do your dirty work?"

He took a step forward, his gaze unflinching as he looked down at me. "No, that you're playing a game you're not ready for."

I wanted to scream, to hurl every insult I could think of, but I forced myself to stay calm, meeting his gaze with as much defiance as I could muster. "And you think you get to decide that?"

He smiled, a slow, dangerous smile that sent a shiver down my spine. "I'm just trying to save you from yourself," he said, his voice dropping to a murmur. "But if you're so determined to keep digging, well... don't expect me to come to your rescue next time."

He turned to walk away, but I wasn't about to let him have the last word. "Maybe I don't need rescuing," I called after him, my voice sharper than I'd intended.

He paused, glancing back over his shoulder, his expression unreadable. "Then I guess we'll see just how deep you're willing to go."

And with that, he disappeared into the shadows, leaving me alone in the alley, his words hanging in the air like a dare, one I knew I couldn't ignore.

Chapter 2: Shadows of the Past

His shadow slipped around the corner, disappearing into the haze of the city lights, and I followed close, my heart pounding in that uneven way it does when you're teetering on the edge of a bad decision. The night air was thick with the scent of exhaust and damp concrete, a blend that always made my pulse quicken in some primal way, like I was thirteen again sneaking into places I shouldn't be. Keldorn wasn't the type of place that offered comforting scenery—it was more about sharp edges, hidden traps, and alleys that seemed to swallow up the unwary.

I kept my distance, blending into the shadows like a habit. The dampness seeped through my shoes, making every step a silent, squelching reminder of how far I'd come—or maybe how far I'd fallen. He moved with the kind of confidence that could either mean he was dangerous or simply foolish. And I couldn't decide which was worse. His coat flared as he rounded another corner, disappearing briefly under the flickering neon lights of a bar sign that proudly declared it served "the best drinks on this side of morality." Keldorn's humor, if you could call it that, was in its small touches of irony, unspoken but felt in every corner, every crack of the city's bones.

A few moments later, I slipped through the door after him, and immediately, the oppressive hum of bad jazz hit me. It clashed with the smell of stale beer and unwashed bodies—a sensory assault that somehow made me feel right at home. The dim lighting cast hazy halos around everything, giving the people an almost ghostly look, blurred but not entirely unrecognizable. The bartender eyed me with a glance that was half suspicion, half indifference. Perfect. I wasn't here to stand out; I was here to observe, to listen.

And there he was, sitting at the far end of the bar, hunched over like he was nursing his sorrows or secrets in the form of whatever liquid courage he'd ordered. I slid onto a stool a couple of seats down from him, pretending to peruse the laminated drink list as if it were a sacred text. But my eyes, and all my attention, were on him, and not because of some spark of attraction or curiosity. No, it was the way he held himself—rigid and ready, like he was expecting something to jump out of the shadows. His shoulders were coiled tight, his gaze darting to the door every few seconds. It was the posture of a man hiding something. Or of someone running from something. Maybe both.

"What'll it be?" The bartender's gravelly voice cut through my thoughts, his eyes not leaving mine. He was older, graying at the temples, with hands that moved slower than they probably used to. But his gaze was sharp, assessing, and it was clear he'd seen more secrets pass through this place than drinks.

"Whiskey. Neat," I replied, mirroring the man's order without even glancing his way. It was a calculated move; I wanted him to think I wasn't paying attention to him. People like him, people who lived in shadows and secrets, they noticed when you noticed them. They slipped away the second you got too close.

The glass clinked onto the counter in front of me, a faint amber liquid sloshing around in the bottom. I took a sip, feeling the burn as it traced a path down my throat, warm and slightly bitter, grounding me in a way I hadn't realized I needed. The man still hadn't looked my way, which was both a relief and a little annoying. I had to be careful, though. Too much attention, and I'd spook him. Too little, and he'd think he had the upper hand.

"You look like someone who doesn't drink whiskey," he said suddenly, his voice barely above a murmur but carrying enough weight to stop my heart for a beat. He hadn't even looked at me when he spoke, still hunched over his glass, his eyes fixed somewhere in the middle distance.

I shrugged, letting a hint of a smirk play on my lips. "I look like a lot of things. Doesn't mean any of them are true."

He finally turned to face me, his eyes catching the dim light, sharp and almost curious. They were the kind of eyes that saw too much, that held layers of stories no one else would want to tell. "Fair enough," he replied, but he didn't offer any more. He just watched me, silent, with a gaze that seemed to peel back layers I wasn't ready to share. I wasn't even sure I had those layers anymore, not after what Keldorn had taken from me. But he looked at me like he knew, like he saw something in me even I didn't recognize.

"Why are you here?" he asked, his tone sliding between bored and suspicious.

I let out a low laugh. "Funny. I was about to ask you the same thing."

He raised his glass in a silent toast, a slight smile playing at his lips. "Then I guess we're both here for answers." He took a sip, his gaze never leaving mine. There was something unsettling in his steady attention, a kind of challenge hidden behind those dark eyes. Like he was daring me to dig deeper, to pull at the threads of whatever secret he was hiding, fully aware that unraveling it might come at a price I couldn't afford.

I decided to play along, at least for now. "You seem like someone who doesn't ask questions without knowing the answer first."

He shrugged, that slight smile still lingering. "Maybe. Or maybe I'm just someone who likes seeing how far people are willing to go for what they want."

I raised an eyebrow, more amused than I probably should have been. "And what do you think I want?"

His eyes flickered, just for a moment. "Answers. Or maybe just a good story to tell yourself."

The words hit me in a place I didn't expect, a reminder of all the stories I'd told myself to justify every bad choice, every risk I'd taken. It was easier to believe in the story than to face the truth, easier to pretend that this was all some kind of adventure rather than the mess it really was. But I wasn't about to let him know that. "Stories are just answers dressed up in fancy words," I replied, keeping my tone light but my gaze steady.

He laughed, a low sound that was almost a growl. "Touché." He set his glass down, fingers lingering on it for a moment before he leaned in closer. "But sometimes, the answers are uglier than the stories we tell ourselves. And not everyone's ready for that."

In that moment, something shifted between us—a quiet understanding that I didn't quite understand but couldn't ignore.

The silence stretched, taut and humming like a live wire, broken only by the faint jazz buzzing from the bar's ancient speakers. I could feel the weight of his gaze on me, a tangible presence prickling my skin, even as he turned back to his drink, his fingers tapping an erratic rhythm against the glass. If he was as calm as he pretended, he wouldn't be fidgeting. But then, maybe that was his game—to look like he wasn't playing one. It was hard to tell with people like him. Harder still when they knew enough to keep their secrets buried deeper than my own.

I leaned back, feigning nonchalance, and traced a finger along the rim of my glass. "So, are we just going to dance around each other all night, or are you planning to give me something useful?" I said, letting a smirk tug at the corner of my lips. A flicker of amusement crossed his face, brief but unmistakable. Good. If there was one thing I'd learned in Keldorn, it was that humor—especially the sharp, biting kind—was as good a weapon as any.

He tilted his head, studying me with the kind of interest that felt unsettlingly precise. "Useful," he repeated, almost testing the word on his tongue. "What exactly are you looking for, then? Something useful for your 'case'... or something else?" He lifted his glass, pausing just before it reached his lips, waiting.

The way he said "case" made my spine tighten. I hadn't mentioned anything about a case. Not to him, not to anyone in this city. Not since I'd started poking around the warehouse two weeks ago, when the trail I'd been following went ice cold. I'd taken precautions, kept my movements careful, my questions subtle. And yet here he was, sliding that single word into conversation like a blade between ribs. It hurt, sure, but the real damage was the kind that stayed hidden, festering. He'd just told me, without saying anything outright, that he knew more about me than he should. And now he wanted to see how I'd react.

I forced myself to laugh, soft and casual. "Everyone in this city's looking for something useful," I said. "For most people, it's just enough to get them through the next day." I watched him closely, noting the slight twitch at the corner of his mouth. It was the kind of expression you could almost miss if you weren't paying attention, the kind that said he recognized the bluff and was choosing to play along—for now.

He leaned closer, elbows resting on the bar, his gaze drifting to the bottle-lined shelves behind it. "If that's all you're after, you're not half as interesting as I thought." His tone was light, but there was a razor-edge to it, a challenge I didn't fully understand yet. He had a way of talking that was deliberately vague, like he was drawing me in and keeping me at arm's length in the same breath.

I rolled my eyes, feeling a spark of irritation flare up. "And what do you think is interesting, then?" I didn't expect an answer, not a real one, anyway. Men like him, the kind who played with shadows for fun, they thrived on mystery. They used it to keep people off-balance, to keep themselves hidden. But I wasn't about to let him control this conversation—not entirely, at least.

He tapped a finger against his glass, slow and deliberate. "People who know what they want, and why." He paused, letting the words hang between us, heavy with meaning. "People who aren't afraid to admit when they're in over their heads."

I snorted, refusing to let his words needle me. "Please. The only people who aren't in over their heads in this city are the ones who left long ago." I took a sip of my whiskey, letting the warmth spread through me, a grounding sensation in a place that felt anything but solid. His gaze stayed fixed on me, sharp and unyielding, like he was waiting for me to give something away.

"So why are you still here, then?" he asked, his voice low, soft in a way that felt almost dangerous.

I raised an eyebrow, not missing the bait in his question. "Maybe I like the view." I gestured vaguely at the room, filled with its hazy light and smoke-stained walls. "Nothing like the charm of sticky floors and broken dreams."

He laughed, a sound that was equal parts genuine and mocking. "You're a terrible liar," he said, his eyes glinting with amusement.

"Maybe," I replied, meeting his gaze without flinching. "Or maybe you're not as clever as you think." The words slipped out before I could stop them, a little too bold, a little too close to the truth. I didn't know why I was pushing him, testing his patience like that. But there was something about him, something that felt like an itch I couldn't scratch.

His expression didn't change, but there was a flicker of something darker in his eyes, something that made the hair on the back of my neck stand up. "Cleverness is overrated," he murmured, almost as if he was talking to himself. "Sometimes it's better to know when to leave things alone."

A chill settled over me, the kind that wasn't just from the stale air and dim lighting. He was right, of course. I'd learned that lesson the hard way, too many times. But something told me he wasn't just giving advice—he was warning me, subtly and deliberately, to stay out of whatever tangled mess he was involved in. And if there was one thing I knew about myself, it was that I never could resist a challenge.

"Funny," I said, keeping my tone light, almost playful. "I'd say the opposite. Cleverness is what keeps people like you and me alive." I watched him closely, waiting for a reaction, any sign that I'd hit a nerve.

He didn't flinch, but his gaze sharpened, cutting through the dimness like a blade. "People like you and me?" He repeated, voice low and dangerous. "Don't flatter yourself. You don't know the first thing about me."

It was a jab, designed to put me in my place, to remind me of the distance between us. And maybe he was right. But if he thought a few sharp words were enough to scare me off, he didn't know me nearly as well as he thought he did.

"Oh, I know plenty," I replied, leaning back with a smirk. "Enough to know that you're not half as mysterious as you think you are." It was a lie, of course. I didn't know anything about him—not really. But I wasn't about to let him have the upper hand.

He chuckled, a low, dangerous sound that sent a shiver down my spine. "Keep telling yourself that," he said, his tone laced with just enough amusement to be unsettling. "But don't say I didn't warn you."

With that, he slid off his stool, leaving his glass empty on the bar. He didn't say goodbye, didn't even look back as he disappeared into the shadows. I watched him go, feeling a strange mix of relief and disappointment. I'd gotten under his skin, sure, but he'd done the same to me. And that was a problem—one I didn't have the luxury of ignoring.

The bartender cleared his throat, pulling me out of my thoughts. "You know," he said, his voice gruff but somehow softer than before, "sometimes the ones who don't look back are the ones with the most to hide."

I nodded, more to myself than to him, feeling the weight of the bartender's words settle over me. He was right, of course. But knowing that didn't make it any easier to ignore the nagging feeling that this man, this stranger, was just the beginning of something far bigger than either of us could understand.

The alley outside was a different world from the cramped dimness of the bar, colder and somehow even quieter. A faint drizzle had started to fall, misting the air and giving the street a kind of surreal shine under the neon lights. Keldorn's glow, all harsh edges and mismatched colors, was deceptive; it could make even the ugliest parts of the city look like they held secrets worth keeping.

I'd barely made it halfway down the street when I saw him again, leaning against a crumbling brick wall, his coat collar turned up to shield against the rain. The sight of him, standing there as if he'd been expecting me, made me hesitate. He looked up, catching my gaze, and that half-smile from earlier crept back onto his face, a mix of amusement and something darker, something challenging.

"You're persistent," he remarked, his voice carrying easily over the soft patter of rain. "Most people would have given up by now."

"Most people aren't me." I kept my voice steady, meeting his gaze with the same level of calm. I wasn't about to let him see that every instinct in me was screaming that this was a mistake, that whatever lay ahead was dangerous, something I should walk away from. But that part of me, the part that listened to reason, was drowned out by the sheer curiosity he had stirred up in me—a pull stronger than caution, stronger than sense.

"Clearly not." He pushed off the wall, his steps slow and deliberate as he approached me. "So, let's settle this. You're following me, and I'm letting you. Call it mutual interest, if that makes you feel better." He shrugged, his expression casual, but there was something calculating in the way he watched me, waiting for my reaction.

"Mutual interest?" I echoed, crossing my arms. "You don't seem all that interested to me. Or maybe that's just an act you're putting on. Men like you are good at pretending they don't care."

He chuckled, a low, dark sound that rolled through the air, mingling with the rain. "And you think you know what kind of man I am?"

"No," I replied, stepping closer, "but I know you're hiding something." I let my words hang, watching his reaction. His expression didn't change, but there was a flicker in his eyes, a glint that told me I'd struck a nerve. "People don't spend their nights in bars like that for no reason. So tell me—what exactly are you running from?"

For a moment, he didn't say anything. He just looked at me, his gaze so intense it felt like he was peeling back layers, searching for something. I held my ground, refusing to flinch, to give him any hint that he might have intimidated me.

Finally, he laughed, the sound more genuine this time, but tinged with something bitter. "Maybe you're right," he said softly, his tone almost contemplative. "Maybe I am hiding something." He paused, letting the words settle between us. "But the real question, the one you should be asking, is why you care so much."

He was good. That question cut right to the core, catching me off guard. I didn't have an answer—not one I wanted to say out loud, at least. Because the truth was, I wasn't entirely sure myself. It was more than the case now, more than whatever mess I'd convinced myself I was unraveling. There was something about him, something that felt... unfinished. Like I'd met him before, maybe even trusted him once, though that didn't make any sense.

Instead of answering, I took a step back, putting a safe distance between us. "You're deflecting," I said, forcing a steady tone. "You're hoping if you make this about me, I'll back off."

"And are you?" His voice was soft, laced with a hint of a challenge.

I narrowed my eyes. "Not a chance."

He tilted his head, as though studying a puzzle he couldn't quite solve. "Fine. Then let's cut through the games." He leaned in, close enough that I could see the faint scar near his temple, a thin line that almost vanished under his dark hair. "I'm not a good guy," he said, each word precise, as though he wanted them to sink in. "You should know that now, before you get in over your head."

"I figured as much," I replied, keeping my tone casual. "Men who warn you away usually have the most to hide."

He looked almost surprised by that, and for the first time, I saw something that looked like real hesitation in his eyes. He opened his mouth as if to say something, but then his gaze flicked over my shoulder, and his entire demeanor shifted. His face hardened, and in a split second, he was all business, the softness replaced by an edge I hadn't seen before.

"Get down," he hissed, grabbing my arm and pulling me into the shadows of the alley.

I barely had time to react before he shoved me against the wall, his hand clamped over my mouth. Any protest I might've had died in my throat as I caught the look in his eyes—sharp, focused, and deadly serious. I knew better than to fight him, so I stayed still, listening to the faint sounds of footsteps approaching from the other end of the alley.

He kept his gaze trained on the entrance, his body tense, every muscle coiled like a spring. Whoever it was, they weren't bothering to be quiet. The footsteps grew louder, closer, and then, just as quickly, they stopped. The silence that followed was heavy, oppressive, pressing down on us like a weight.

I could feel his heartbeat, fast and steady, as he kept me pinned against the wall, his body shielding mine. He shifted slightly, just enough to glance down at me, and in that moment, I caught a glimpse of something raw in his expression—a flicker of vulnerability that vanished as quickly as it appeared.

He removed his hand from my mouth, but his finger went to his lips, a silent command. I nodded, barely daring to breathe as we waited, every nerve on high alert. Seconds ticked by, stretching out into what felt like an eternity, until finally, the footsteps started up again, receding down the alley and back into the night.

He let out a breath, stepping back, his gaze still scanning the street as if he expected someone to jump out from the shadows. When he finally looked at me, his expression was unreadable, but there was a hint of frustration in his eyes, as though he was regretting ever letting me get this close.

"Are you done playing hero?" I asked, keeping my voice low but unable to hide the note of irritation.

His jaw tightened. "I'm trying to keep you alive. If you'd listen to me for once, maybe we wouldn't be in this mess."

"Listen to you?" I shot back, my voice rising despite myself. "I don't even know who you are. You think you can just drag me into alleys and play the knight in shining armor when it suits you?"

He clenched his fists, his face a mask of controlled anger. "Believe me, I don't want to be here any more than you do," he said, his voice tight. "But you're not the only one looking for answers, and if we're going to get them, we'll need each other, whether you like it or not."

Before I could respond, a sharp crack echoed down the alley—a gunshot, unmistakable and too close for comfort. My heart slammed against my ribs, adrenaline surging through me as I instinctively reached for the wall behind me, trying to steady myself.

He grabbed my hand, pulling me further into the shadows, his eyes blazing with a mix of fear and determination. "Run," he whispered, his voice barely audible but laced with urgency. And just like that, he took off, dragging me with him into the darkness, the sounds of footsteps and voices closing in around us.

I didn't have time to think, to process what was happening. All I knew was that he was right—whatever game I'd started, I was in it now, and there was no going back.

Chapter 3: Trapped Together

The first thing I noticed, after the dust settled, was his laugh. Low, sardonic, and so utterly amused that it made my fists itch to connect with his jaw. I hadn't known laughter could sound so grating, each chortle like a claw scraping over my nerves. I shot him a glare, but he just leaned back, studying the crumbling walls as if they held some private joke, one I was clearly missing.

"You think this is funny?" I demanded, brushing dirt from my knees and trying to ignore the sting of a scrape across my hand. It was a useless endeavor, though; grime streaked up my arms, and I probably looked as desperate and dusty as I felt. But I wouldn't give him the satisfaction of seeing me defeated. I forced my shoulders back, lifting my chin defiantly, even as my heart hammered with an unsettling mix of frustration and fear.

"Oh, absolutely," he said, lips twisting in a smirk as he glanced over at me. "Of all the people in this city, I had to get trapped underground with you." His eyes held a flicker of amusement, mingled with something else, something that made me want to look away. But I didn't. I wouldn't give him that either.

I crossed my arms, ignoring the ache blooming in my shoulder from our unexpected tumble into what felt like a cavern beneath the city's foundation. "Well, you're welcome. Consider it your lucky day," I shot back, voice dripping with sarcasm. I let my gaze wander the walls, studying the jagged, peeling bricks and the shadows that clung to the corners. There were no windows, no doors. Just four walls and us, trapped like misfit rats in a cage.

He tilted his head, watching me, eyes sharper than I cared to admit. "Is that what we're calling this? Luck?"

The glint in his eyes was infuriatingly knowing, as though he saw through the bravado I wore like a shield. He was probably right; I wasn't exactly thrilled with our predicament, though I'd sooner chew glass than admit it. Instead, I huffed and took a slow, deliberate step toward the opposite end of the chamber, pretending to search for a way out. I traced my fingers along the wall, hoping for a secret door, a loose brick, anything that could be our ticket to freedom. My hands brushed rough stone, catching on jagged edges and ancient dust, but found nothing.

"Great. Just great," I muttered under my breath, too low for him to hear—or so I thought.

"You're mumbling again," he said, his voice infuriatingly close now. I felt his presence at my back, his warmth creeping in despite the chill that clung to the underground air. I tensed, willing myself to ignore it, focusing instead on the wall as if my sheer determination could summon a passageway to materialize.

I shot him a sidelong glare, but he didn't flinch. Of course, he didn't. Instead, he watched me with an expression that was part amusement, part... something else. Something I couldn't quite place, nor did I want to.

"So," he said casually, as if we were in some café instead of a subterranean pit. "What do you think they used this place for? It doesn't exactly scream modern architecture."

I rolled my eyes, unable to resist the sarcastic response bubbling up. "A secret underground lair for people who like terrible lighting and damp walls? Probably some forgotten storm shelter." I paused, looking around as my voice softened, surprising even me. "Or maybe it's one of those places where the city's secrets end up. Lost and buried."

The words felt strangely heavy in the quiet, and for a moment, we just stood there, surrounded by the weight of the past, of stories we'd never know. He didn't respond, but I felt his gaze linger on me longer than I wanted. I shook it off, focusing again on the cracked bricks.

Then his voice cut through the silence, low and cautious. "Think they'll notice we're missing?"

His tone was light, but there was an undercurrent of something—vulnerability, maybe? It was gone before I could pinpoint it, though, replaced by his usual smirk.

"Doubtful," I replied, shrugging. "You and I? I'd wager most people would be thrilled to have us out of the way."

He snorted, half-amused. "Well, they can throw a party when we get out of here. Assuming we do, of course."

I gave him a look that was pure exasperation. "We will. You might be happy to waste away down here, but I've got things to do. Life to live."

"Ah, yes. Such important things," he drawled. "Like what, exactly? Breaking hearts? Ruffling feathers?"

I rolled my eyes, hoping it hid the slight twist of guilt his words stirred up. He had a point, though I'd die before admitting it. I'd built walls as high as the city skyline, insulating myself from everyone and everything that didn't serve a purpose. Or maybe, deep down, I was just as trapped in my own maze of emotions and half-kept promises as we were here, in this physical prison. I wasn't about to let him know that, though.

"Breaking hearts and ruffling feathers is what I do best," I said flippantly, lifting my chin. "I'm sure it's why the universe decided to give you the honor of being trapped with me."

He snorted again, but there was a flicker of something more in his eyes, a softness that slipped through the cracks for a fraction of a second. "Yeah. Lucky me."

We lapsed into silence again, the weight of it pressing down on us like the stone walls themselves. I kept my gaze fixed ahead, unwilling to let him see the way my hands trembled slightly, or how my heart was racing with a strange mix of fear and something I couldn't quite name. Something that felt a lot like curiosity, or maybe even hope, buried somewhere deep under layers of pride and stubbornness.

When his hand brushed mine as he moved past, his touch was unexpectedly warm, grounding. My heart did an infuriating little flip, which I immediately scolded into silence. This was him, after all—arrogant, smug, insufferable him. And yet, somehow, here we were, caught in this moment, in this place that held more secrets than either of us could probably ever uncover.

I squared my shoulders and turned to face the darkness ahead, each step I took echoing in the silence, the weight of unspoken words hanging heavy between us. We would get out of here, somehow. And when we did, maybe—just maybe—things wouldn't be exactly the same as they'd been before.

The stillness around us was unnerving, broken only by our own breaths and the occasional scrape of a shoe against the rough stone floor. I had given up pretending to search, leaning back against the damp wall, arms crossed, watching him as he paced, frustration pinching his brow. I was finding a twisted kind of satisfaction in his inability to keep calm. For once, his composure had cracked.

"Any brilliant ideas yet, or are you waiting for inspiration to strike from above?" I quipped, tilting my head and letting a slow smile spread across my face.

He shot me a look that could've curdled milk. "I don't see you doing anything helpful, except, of course, holding up that wall with your unparalleled attitude."

I chuckled, feeling a strange thrill at getting under his skin. "Maybe if you were a bit less insufferable, I'd feel inspired to assist. But honestly, I'd rather wait it out down here than give you the satisfaction of agreeing on anything."

He rolled his eyes, muttering something under his breath that I was fairly certain wasn't complimentary. Then, as if a thought had just struck him, he paused, looking around. I watched him, skeptical, as he tapped the stones, testing them for any hidden mechanisms, any hollow sounds that might indicate a passageway. His fingers moved with surprising patience, and I felt an uncomfortable pang of admiration for his focus. I quickly brushed it aside.

"Careful," I teased. "Wouldn't want to strain that single brain cell you're working with."

He didn't look up, but I saw the corner of his mouth twitch. "You're hilarious," he said dryly, still moving his hands along the wall with frustratingly slow precision. "Keep going—I'm sure one of us is laughing."

I huffed, deciding that sitting around wasn't going to cut it for me anymore, either. I moved to the opposite wall and began to tap and press on stones with my own set of fingers. They were cool and gritty, and I couldn't help but notice the eerie sense of permanence, of old stories embedded in this forgotten space. Places like this didn't get discovered; they were simply ignored, waiting for accidents like ours to unearth them, like a message in a bottle waiting decades for someone to pick it up. The idea of secrets lingering just out of reach made my skin prickle.

"What do you think this place actually is?" I asked, almost to myself.

He shrugged without looking at me, but his voice softened, like he was indulging in the mystery, too. "A forgotten part of the city, maybe. Places like these... they're everywhere if you know where to look. Abandoned bunkers, forgotten subway stations." He paused, glancing at me. "Every city has a skeleton or two buried under its skin."

I raised an eyebrow, intrigued despite myself. "Didn't peg you as the poetic type."

"Don't get used to it," he muttered, running a hand through his hair, clearly regretting the momentary lapse into vulnerability. "Places like this make you think weird things. Must be the dust."

I hid my smile, letting silence settle again as we continued our search. But it didn't take long before I felt the unease creeping in, an itch at the back of my mind that grew with each passing minute. I could feel the walls closing in, the air thickening, heavier somehow, as though it, too, had been waiting for someone to disturb its centuries-old stillness.

"Do you think..." I hesitated, unsure if I wanted him to have an answer. "Do you think they'll actually find us?"

He stopped, turning to face me with a look that was unexpectedly direct. "Honestly? I don't know. If anyone notices we're missing, maybe. But this city isn't exactly known for caring about people slipping through its cracks."

I swallowed, hating how his words hit too close to home. This place was filled with people who disappeared, who drifted into the shadows and were never seen again. I'd spent so long clinging to its edges, trying not to be one of them, and now here I was, literally buried beneath it all with the last person I would've chosen.

"And yet," he added, almost as if he could read my thoughts, "I have a feeling you're the type that doesn't go quietly."

I looked up sharply, but he was already turning away, back to his meticulous examination of the walls. It was a strange sort of compliment, one I wasn't sure how to respond to, so I let it linger, swirling around like dust in a sunbeam. For a second, the silence between us felt less hostile, more like the pause between breaths.

Just as I was considering asking him about himself—an uncharacteristic curiosity tugging at me—the silence shattered with a soft crack and a sudden rush of air. His hand had found a small stone that moved, ever so slightly, and with it came the unmistakable sound of a mechanism stirring to life. We both froze, listening as the gears ground together, ancient and reluctant, until a small section of the wall slid aside, revealing a dark corridor beyond.

"Well, look at that," he murmured, a glint of triumph in his eyes as he straightened, wiping his hands on his jeans. "Guess I still have a few brain cells to spare."

I rolled my eyes, but I couldn't help the surge of relief flooding through me. I walked to the doorway and peered into the darkness, feeling the weight of whatever lay beyond pressing against me like a dare. He joined me, and for a moment, we stood shoulder to shoulder, gazing into the unknown.

"Ladies first?" he offered, with a mockingly gallant gesture.

I snorted. "If you think I'm going to trust you at my back in there, you've got another thing coming." I stepped aside, gesturing for him to lead the way.

He smirked but didn't argue, and as he took the first tentative step into the corridor, I followed, feeling an odd sense of partnership, of shared adventure, tinged with the unmistakable tension that seemed to spark and dance between us.

The corridor was narrow, our footsteps echoing in the cold, damp air. I kept my eyes trained on the back of his head, half-expecting him to make some snarky comment, but he was unusually quiet. It was almost eerie, the way the silence swallowed every sound except our breaths, quick and shallow. My senses sharpened, each drip of water, each shift of shadow adding to the mounting suspense.

Just as I was about to whisper something snide to break the tension, his voice cut through the darkness, low and guarded. "Don't suppose you've got a flashlight in that bottomless bag of yours?"

"Wouldn't you like to know?" I shot back, pulling my phone out with a small, triumphant flourish. I clicked on the flashlight, illuminating the narrow path ahead. The beam of light sliced through the dark, revealing walls lined with faded graffiti and old posters, remnants of a past that had long since been abandoned.

He raised an eyebrow, surprised. "Well, well. Didn't take you for the prepared type."

"Survival instincts," I muttered, moving the light across the walls, searching for any clues about where this corridor led. My hand brushed his arm accidentally, and I felt the tension spike again, crackling in the air between us like static. But neither of us moved away.

We pressed forward, step by step, and for the first time, I felt a strange, stubborn glimmer of hope—maybe, just maybe, this wasn't where our story ended.

The corridor stretched before us, narrowing with every step until we were forced to walk single file. Shadows clung to the walls like cobwebs, darting in and out of the flashlight's thin beam, and the air was thick with the stale scent of forgotten things. I tried not to breathe too deeply, unwilling to taste the dust and secrets that had gathered here over years, maybe decades. Every so often, my foot would kick against something—a loose stone, a rusty can, once even what looked suspiciously like a small bone. I didn't point it out; no need to add to the growing sense of dread coiling tight in my stomach.

The silence between us was less comfortable than it had been before, each of us caught in our own thoughts, no barbed jokes to act as shields. He moved steadily ahead, his shoulders hunched slightly, as if he could feel the weight of the earth pressing down on us. For a split second, I considered reaching out, if only to anchor myself to something tangible, but I quickly pushed the thought away. The last thing I needed was to give him the impression I was leaning on him for support, in any sense of the word.

"So," he finally said, his voice startlingly loud in the oppressive quiet. "Do you think this ends with a miraculous escape or a tragic obituary?"

"Depends," I said lightly, though my heart skipped a beat at the thought. "Are you planning to be my tragic end?"

He chuckled, a sound as dry as the dust under our feet. "Depends on how long we're down here. Give it another hour, and you might start looking like a prime suspect."

I rolled my eyes, though I knew he couldn't see it. "Please. I'd hate to give you that satisfaction. You'd probably make an entire career out of whining about it."

"Oh, I'd definitely milk it for all it's worth," he agreed, his tone amused, as if he were picturing it. "Tragic widower vibes—very poetic. And I'd get so much sympathy, you wouldn't believe."

His words hung in the air, and I felt an uncomfortable tug, as if he'd exposed something raw without even realizing it. There was a vulnerability lurking under the joke, one he hadn't meant to show, and I found myself at a loss for a clever retort. Instead, I looked ahead, letting the silence settle over us again.

The corridor soon opened into a larger space, a sort of crossroads where several paths diverged, disappearing into the dark. I shone the flashlight around, hoping for some kind of sign, something that could tell us which way led to the surface and which would send us spiraling deeper into the bowels of this place. But there was nothing—just more dust, more shadows, more silence.

"Left or right?" he asked, his tone too casual, like he was pretending not to care which path we chose.

I weighed the options, my gaze flicking between the paths. I couldn't explain why, but something about the left path seemed... wrong. There was a chill to it, a darkness that felt somehow heavier, more claustrophobic. The right, while just as uncertain, felt like it held the possibility of something else—maybe not freedom, but at least not dread.

"Right," I said, forcing confidence into my voice.

He raised an eyebrow, a half-smile quirking at the corner of his mouth. "What makes you so sure?"

"Just a gut feeling," I replied, shrugging. "Besides, I trust my instincts more than yours."

He snorted. "Big words, coming from someone who thought it was a good idea to walk down a crumbling alley with me."

I rolled my eyes, though I couldn't help the small smile that slipped through. "One of my few regrets in life."

We started down the right path, our footsteps echoing in a rhythm that felt oddly comforting. It was strange, the way our bickering had become less a battle and more... familiar. Like a dance, each barb and retort timed perfectly, keeping us both on our toes. And for the first time, I felt something other than resentment curling in my chest—something warmer, though I quickly shoved it aside.

We walked in silence for a few minutes, the only sounds our breaths and the soft scuff of our shoes on the stone. My mind began to wander, drifting over the things we hadn't said, the secrets we both seemed to be keeping. I couldn't help but wonder what he was hiding—what had driven him to wander dark alleys and forgotten ruins like these. There was a story there, I could feel it, one he would never tell willingly.

Just as I was about to break the silence, a faint sound echoed from somewhere up ahead—a soft, almost rhythmic tapping, like someone... knocking. I froze, holding my breath, my grip on the flashlight tightening until my knuckles turned white. He stopped beside me, his posture tense, listening.

"Did you hear that?" I whispered, my voice barely audible.

He nodded, his expression unreadable. "Sounds like it's coming from up ahead."

I swallowed, glancing at him. "Do you think... someone else is down here?"

"Could be," he replied, his voice low. "Or it could be the sound of something dripping, or rats, or who knows what else."

Despite his words, there was a flicker of something in his eyes—hope, maybe? I realized I felt it too, a strange thrill at the thought that we might not be alone down here. It could mean danger, yes, but it could also mean an exit, a way out. We shared a look, a silent agreement passing between us, and I stepped forward, leading the way.

The tapping grew louder as we moved closer, the sound echoing off the stone walls in an eerie, rhythmic pattern. It felt both familiar and unnatural, like something I'd heard in a dream. My heart pounded, each step taking us deeper into the unknown, the flashlight casting long, flickering shadows across the walls.

Then, just as we rounded a corner, the tapping stopped. I froze, the silence somehow more terrifying than the noise had been. My flashlight beam swept across the darkness, illuminating empty space and more of the same cracked, ancient walls. Nothing. No one.

"Maybe we imagined it," he murmured, though his voice held a note of doubt.

"Or maybe," I replied, my voice barely above a whisper, "they're just waiting for us to get closer."

He shot me a look, half-amused, half-wary. "Trying to scare me now, are we?"

But before I could respond, the tapping resumed, louder this time, so close it felt like it was coming from just around the next corner. My pulse quickened, every instinct screaming at me to turn back, but something else—a curiosity I couldn't shake—compelled me forward. I took a step, then another, and he followed, his presence steady at my side.

We edged forward, until the source of the noise came into view—a rusted, iron door set into the wall, the paint peeling, the hinges thick with years of rust. I could barely make out a faint outline of letters scratched into the metal, too worn to read, but unmistakably deliberate. My heart hammered as I reached out, my fingers brushing the cold iron. The tapping had stopped, but a low, shuffling sound came from beyond the door, something heavy moving on the other side.

I glanced at him, my breath catching. He nodded, a flicker of anticipation in his eyes, and together we leaned closer, pressing our ears to the door.

And then, from the other side, a voice whispered, so faint I could barely make it out. But the words were clear, chilling in their simplicity.

"Are you there?"

Chapter 4: The Spark of Magic

The light flickered like a dying ember, casting shadows that danced along the stone walls. The air was heavy, carrying an ancient scent of dust and something sharper, almost metallic. My pulse quickened as I tried to decipher the symbols that glowed faintly on the stones surrounding us. They looked like they'd been carved centuries ago, each line worn down by time yet somehow alive, as if they thrummed with a heartbeat of their own. For a fleeting moment, it felt as though the walls were watching us, and I resisted the urge to reach out and trace my fingers over those strange markings. Maybe I thought if I touched them, I'd understand, or maybe I was just curious—or foolish.

My companion, whose name I still didn't fully trust, shifted closer, his face half-lit in the dim glow. There was an intensity in his gaze that made me shiver, and not from the cold. This wasn't the face of a casual adventurer; it was the face of someone who knew more than he was letting on. But for now, I needed him, and maybe he needed me too, though he'd never admit it.

"Do you feel it too?" I whispered, as if speaking louder would shatter whatever fragile magic held us here.

He didn't answer immediately. His eyes were trained on the symbols, studying them with the kind of reverence that bordered on fear. "Feel it? Yes," he murmured, his voice almost a reverent whisper. "Understand it? Not even close."

His fingers grazed mine as he reached out, a light touch that sent a ripple of electricity skittering up my arm. I fought the urge to pull back, caught between the strange sensation and the strange man. Despite myself, I was drawn to him, like the magic in this place had tethered us together in some inexplicable way.

"Are you always this cryptic?" I asked, hoping sarcasm might shake loose some truth from him.

He arched an eyebrow, a slight smirk pulling at the corners of his mouth. "Only when it suits me," he replied, and for a brief moment, I saw a flicker of warmth beneath his guarded expression.

Rolling my eyes, I focused on the task at hand—or at least tried to. There was something about him that kept pulling my attention back, and it was maddening. Every look, every carefully chosen word seemed to hint at secrets he was determined to keep buried. And I couldn't decide if I wanted to pry them out of him or let them lie untouched.

"Well, it doesn't suit me," I replied, pulling my hand away from the wall. But I could still feel the tingle in my fingertips, a reminder of that strange energy. "If you know something, now would be a great time to share with the class."

His smile faded, and his eyes grew serious. "I don't know as much as you think I do." He hesitated, glancing back at the symbols. "But I do know this: whatever power lies in this place, it's been waiting. And now we're here, it's...awake."

Awake. That word settled over us like a shroud, as if the shadows had deepened, and the temperature dropped. I wrapped my arms around myself, trying to shake off the chill. Part of me wanted to turn and run, to leave this strange chamber and never look back. But something rooted me in place, a pull I couldn't explain. Maybe it was curiosity, or maybe it was the undeniable sense that leaving now would mean I'd always wonder what we might have uncovered.

I took a deep breath, mustering whatever courage I had left. "Alright, so we're stuck here with some ancient force that has a penchant for eavesdropping and mood lighting. How do we get out?"

He laughed softly, the sound dry and a little bitter. "You think I know that?"

His laughter faded, replaced by an expression that was almost vulnerable. Almost. He reached out and lightly brushed a stray lock of hair from my face, his fingers lingering just a fraction too long. I froze, caught off guard by the gesture, feeling the warmth of his touch against my skin. For a moment, the magic in the air seemed to intensify, thickening until it was almost palpable, as if the chamber itself held its breath.

"Maybe," he said quietly, "the only way out is through."

There it was—the puzzle, the challenge, the idea that the chamber was more than just stone and shadows. There was a purpose to this place, a reason we were here together, and I could feel it humming beneath the surface, like a thread waiting to be pulled. And as much as I hated to admit it, I wasn't sure if I wanted to leave without understanding what lay at the heart of this place.

"Fine," I said, stepping back to break whatever strange connection had formed between us. "But if we're going through, we're doing it my way."

He chuckled, a low, rough sound that sent a spark of irritation through me. "And what exactly is your way?"

I squared my shoulders, lifting my chin defiantly. "The way that doesn't involve cryptic half-truths and creepy ancient magic."

He tilted his head, considering me with a look that was both amused and impressed. "You have a death wish, don't you?"

"Only on special occasions."

He shook his head, that slight smirk returning. "Alright, fearless leader. Lead the way."

I took a deep breath, facing the room that now felt alive in ways it hadn't before. There was a part of me that wanted to retreat, to go back to safety and leave the mysteries for someone else to solve. But another part of me, the part that had dragged me here in the first place, wouldn't back down. I glanced back at him, noting the way his eyes glinted in the faint light, and steeled myself.

I took a step forward, reaching out to touch one of the glowing symbols, my fingers hovering over the worn grooves in the stone. I could feel the energy pulsing beneath the surface, waiting, almost as if it recognized me. And for the first time, I wondered if maybe, just maybe, it did.

The silence stretched, thick and taut, as though the room itself was holding its breath, waiting for us to make the next move. My hand hovered just above the symbols, the sensation still thrumming through my fingers, alive and sharp. It was exhilarating, terrifying, and, if I was being honest, more than a little addictive. I could feel his gaze fixed on me, his presence so close I could feel his warmth despite the icy air that wrapped around us. There was something about him—a magnetism I didn't quite trust but couldn't pull away from.

"So, fearless leader," he murmured, his voice low and rough, carrying that infuriating hint of amusement. "Are we just going to stand here and commune with the wall, or do you have a plan?"

I arched an eyebrow, glancing sideways at him. "Well, if you have any suggestions, now would be a good time. Unless, of course, sarcasm is all you've got up your sleeve."

The corner of his mouth lifted in a smirk, and for a fleeting moment, I thought he might actually laugh. But then his expression shifted, and something darker, more intense, flickered in his eyes. "You think I'm here by choice?" His tone was as cold as the room around us, any trace of amusement gone. "Believe me, if I could get out of this, I would."

I wanted to ask him more, to pry into whatever it was he was so desperate to escape, but the words caught in my throat. For all my bravado, I couldn't shake the feeling that this place was watching us, listening, waiting to see if we'd be worthy or foolish enough to delve deeper. And there was something in his expression that told me he wasn't ready to offer answers, not yet.

Instead, I took a steadying breath and looked back at the symbols. They seemed to glow a little brighter, as if responding to the touch of my gaze. The energy was pulling at me, tugging me forward like some unseen force wrapping itself around my wrist and leading me deeper into the unknown. I could feel its pulse echoing through my veins, a rhythm that was both foreign and familiar, and with each beat, my hesitation faded just a little.

"Alright," I said finally, more to myself than to him. "Let's see where this leads."

Without waiting for him, I pressed my palm against one of the symbols. The stone was cool and smooth beneath my skin, yet the energy that surged through me was anything but. It hit me like a lightning bolt, flooding my senses with light and sound and heat, as though I'd stepped into a storm and become part of it. I gasped, barely managing to keep my hand steady as the chamber around us shifted, the walls melting into new shapes, new symbols, new mysteries.

When the light dimmed, I blinked, trying to adjust to what lay before us. The chamber had expanded, stretching out into a vast hall that seemed to go on forever. The air was warmer here, tinged with the faint scent of something sweet and intoxicating, like crushed wildflowers and damp earth. Torches lined the walls, casting flickering shadows across the floor, and at the far end of the hall stood a door, ancient and heavy, its surface covered in runes that pulsed faintly in time with the beat of my heart.

I glanced over at him, half-expecting to see the same awe I felt reflected in his eyes. But instead, his expression was unreadable, a mask of cool indifference that only made me more determined to crack it.

"So," I said, trying to keep my voice light despite the adrenaline still racing through me. "Still think this place has nothing to do with you?"

He looked at me, his gaze sharp and unyielding. "I think it has everything to do with both of us," he replied, and there was something in his tone that made my skin prickle. "The question is whether we're here to unlock it...or be consumed by it."

I swallowed, the weight of his words settling over me like a shroud. There was a challenge in his eyes, a dare that I knew I should resist. But I couldn't bring myself to turn away. "Well," I said, forcing a smirk, "I'm not exactly the consuming type. So I say we unlock it. Worst case, we get a few nasty scars to tell the story."

"Bold words," he murmured, his gaze lingering on me with something I couldn't quite place. "Let's hope you're as fearless as you sound."

I didn't bother to answer. Instead, I started toward the door, each step echoing in the stillness of the hall. The closer I got, the stronger the pull became, the magic in the air growing thicker, more insistent. By the time I reached the door, my heart was pounding, the beat so loud it almost drowned out my thoughts. I could feel him just behind me, a silent presence that was both reassuring and maddening.

As I raised my hand to the door, the runes pulsed beneath my fingers, their energy crackling through my skin like wildfire. I took a steadying breath, half-expecting some ancient trap to spring the moment I pushed it open. But instead, the door swung inward with a slow, creaking groan, revealing a staircase spiraling downward into darkness.

He stepped up beside me, his gaze fixed on the stairs. "After you," he said, gesturing with an exaggerated flourish.

I rolled my eyes, but couldn't help the small smile that tugged at my lips. "Chivalrous, aren't you?"

"Only when it suits me," he replied, that familiar smirk returning.

I took the first step, my fingers brushing along the cool stone wall for balance. The air grew colder as we descended, the scent of flowers and earth fading into something sharper, tinged with the faint hint of metal. The darkness seemed to press in around us, thick and almost tangible, as though it were a living thing, waiting for the right moment to close in.

"Don't suppose you have a flashlight?" I muttered, half-joking, though part of me wished he'd produce one from some hidden pocket.

"Afraid not," he replied, his voice low and steady behind me. "But I do have a knack for finding my way in the dark."

I shot him a look over my shoulder, catching the glint of mischief in his eyes. "Of course you do."

As we reached the bottom of the stairs, the darkness seemed to recede, replaced by a faint, eerie glow that seeped up from the floor, casting long shadows against the walls. The room before us was smaller than the hall above, but no less imposing. Strange, twisted symbols covered the walls, spiraling toward the ceiling in a chaotic web of lines and curves. And in the center of the room stood a pedestal, its surface smooth and polished, as though untouched by time.

A strange feeling washed over me, a sense of déjà vu that made my skin prickle. I took a step toward the pedestal, my heart racing, and reached out, my hand hovering just above its surface.

The air was thick with tension as I hovered above the pedestal, my fingers tingling with the memory of that strange spark. The faint glow coming from the walls seemed to pulse in time with my heartbeat, like the entire room was alive, waiting for me to make the next move. Beside me, he shifted, his gaze fixed on my hand as though he expected—or feared—that I'd touch the pedestal.

"So," he murmured, his voice a low rasp in the silence, "is this where you activate the ancient curse that locks us in here forever?"

I shot him a look, but his eyes didn't leave the pedestal. "You're awfully confident about that, considering you followed me down here."

"I'm a glutton for punishment," he replied with a smirk. "Or maybe I just enjoy watching you stumble around in the dark."

I rolled my eyes, fighting the urge to push him just for the satisfaction of seeing that smug expression disappear. "If you're so sure of yourself, why don't you take the lead?" I said, folding my arms and stepping back to give him an exaggerated gesture toward the pedestal.

For a moment, he looked like he might actually do it. His hand twitched at his side, fingers flexing as if testing the feel of the energy in the air. But then he shook his head, a tight smile pulling at his lips. "Ladies first," he said, his tone smooth, though I could see the tension flickering behind his eyes. "I'd hate to steal your thunder."

"Convenient," I muttered under my breath, but there was something in his hesitation that made me hesitate, too. It wasn't like him to be cautious—not with the way he'd practically dragged me into this mess in the first place. His confidence was usually infuriatingly unshakeable. But now, it wavered, just slightly, and that unnerved me more than I cared to admit.

With a deep breath, I reached out again, my fingers hovering over the pedestal's surface, tracing the faint patterns etched into the stone. The symbols seemed to shift beneath my gaze, like they were alive, curling and twisting into new shapes that I couldn't decipher. My hand trembled, and I forced myself to steady it. If there was any way out of this place, it was tied to whatever magic lay in this pedestal.

Just as my fingers brushed the stone, a surge of heat shot through me, sharp and fierce. I gasped, stumbling back as the room shifted, the air filling with a low hum that grew louder, vibrating through the walls and the floor until it seemed to echo inside my very bones. The light grew brighter, flooding the chamber in a golden glow that chased away the shadows, and I had to shield my eyes against the glare.

"Well," he said, his voice tight with something that sounded suspiciously like awe. "You certainly know how to make an entrance."

I squinted at him through the blinding light, catching the hint of a grin before I turned back to the pedestal. The symbols were shifting again, faster now, morphing into something sharp and jagged, like they were trying to form words but kept changing their mind. My heart pounded as the light swirled around us, taking on shapes that seemed to reach out, curling and twisting like tendrils of smoke.

"What is this?" I whispered, half to myself, half to him.

He didn't answer right away, his gaze transfixed by the shapes that danced around us. Then, finally, he spoke, his voice low and unsteady. "It's a binding spell," he said, his eyes darkening as he looked at me. "This place... it's trying to link us to something. Or... someone."

A chill ran through me, sharp and cold, cutting through the warmth of the light. "Link us?" I echoed, trying to ignore the way my pulse jumped at his words. "To what?"

He shook his head, his jaw clenched as he watched the swirling light. "I don't know," he admitted, and for the first time, I heard a trace of fear in his voice. "But whatever it is, it's not something that wants us to leave."

I opened my mouth to respond, but the light pulsed, brighter and more intense, until it felt like the room itself was spinning. I stumbled, my knees buckling, and he reached out, steadying me with a firm grip on my arm. His touch was warm, grounding, and for a moment, the spinning slowed, the light dimming to a soft glow. I glanced up at him, surprised to see the concern in his eyes, and for a second, I forgot the pedestal, the symbols, the whole terrifying situation.

Then, just as suddenly, the warmth vanished. His grip slipped, and his expression changed, shuttering into that guarded mask I'd come to know too well. He released me, stepping back as if he'd been burned, and I felt a pang of something that I didn't want to name. I didn't have time to dwell on it, though, because the light was fading, sinking back into the pedestal until only a faint glow remained, barely illuminating the room.

As the last of the light vanished, the room fell into a heavy silence, the air thick with the aftermath of whatever strange energy had been released. I swallowed, my throat dry, and looked back at the pedestal. The symbols had stilled, settling into shapes I didn't recognize but felt drawn to, as if they were calling to me, whispering secrets just out of reach.

He cleared his throat, breaking the silence. "So," he said, his tone carefully neutral, "any brilliant ideas about what that was?"

I forced myself to shake off the lingering haze of the spell, crossing my arms as I regarded him with as much composure as I could muster. "Just another day in paradise," I said, flashing a smile that felt more brittle than confident. "But if you're done letting me do all the work, maybe it's time you shared some of that endless knowledge you're hoarding."

He raised an eyebrow, looking unimpressed. "I told you, I don't know much more than you do."

I held his gaze, refusing to let him off the hook so easily. "You know enough to know this isn't normal. You recognized that binding spell. So unless you want to stand here and play coy all night, I suggest you start talking."

He hesitated, his jaw working as though he was fighting some internal battle. I could almost see the calculations flickering in his eyes, the debate between keeping his secrets and trusting me with whatever he knew. Finally, he sighed, running a hand through his hair with a frustrated huff.

"Fine," he said, his voice barely more than a growl. "There are... stories. Legends of places like this, hidden pockets of magic that act as conduits between worlds. They're rare, and dangerous, but they have a way of... attracting people who don't quite fit in anywhere else."

"People like you?" I asked, the words slipping out before I could stop them.

He looked at me, something unreadable in his eyes. "Maybe," he said softly. "Or maybe people like us."

A shiver ran down my spine, and I opened my mouth to respond, but before I could, the room shifted again. The floor trembled, a low rumble that grew into a steady vibration, and the walls around us began to close in, the stones grinding together with a sound like bones cracking. I stumbled back, my heart racing as the space around us shrank, the air growing thick and suffocating.

"What's happening?" I gasped, my eyes wide as I looked to him for answers.

He grabbed my hand, pulling me toward the pedestal, his expression grim. "We've worn out our welcome," he said, his voice tight. "Whatever magic was holding this place together, it's coming apart. And if we don't move, we're going down with it."

Before I could argue, he pulled me forward, his grip strong and unyielding. The room was collapsing around us, the walls closing in, and there was no time for hesitation. We had to run—straight into the unknown, hand in hand, as the ancient magic crumbled to dust around us.

Chapter 5: Uneasy Allies

The night air was crisp as we stepped out from the underbelly of the ancient ruins, a biting breeze snapping at the edges of my coat. I stole a glance at him, hoping to catch even a flicker of something familiar—a hint of a smirk, a twitch of an eyebrow, anything to make this strained silence more bearable. But his face remained unreadable, shadows clinging to his cheekbones like they belonged there. I couldn't tell if he was brooding or just miserably cold, but then, he'd probably tell me it didn't matter anyway. He was built for this—stone, steel, and secrets. The kind of man who looked at a full moon like it had stolen something from him.

"Try not to lag behind," he said without looking at me, his voice low, almost lazy, but with that serrated edge I was beginning to recognize. He moved quickly, each step calculated, as though he was aware of every pebble, every shift in the ground beneath his feet.

"Lag behind?" I snorted, ignoring the scrape in my knee that reminded me I wasn't nearly as well-built for this as he was. "You're not exactly the picture of grace yourself, you know." I saw his mouth twitch, just a fraction, and a small burst of satisfaction warmed my chest.

We walked in silence after that, weaving through the twisted trees and underbrush that loomed around us like skeletal hands reaching for something they could never quite grasp. The forest was darker here, almost unnaturally so, as if the moonlight was too afraid to filter through the canopy. Each step felt like an invasion, a reminder that this place held secrets it was reluctant to share.

"So," I said finally, trying to break the tension that coiled between us like smoke, "where exactly are we heading?"

He stopped abruptly, turning to face me with an expression that was just short of annoyed. "You didn't listen back there, did you?"

"Oh, I listened," I replied, folding my arms across my chest. "But you seem to have a habit of saying a lot without actually saying much of anything. So I thought I'd try my luck with a straightforward question."

"Straightforward," he repeated, like the word itself was foreign to him. "Fine. We're heading east, toward the Ashen Crag. There's an old contact of mine—if she hasn't skipped town or, you know, died—who might have information on the relic." He turned on his heel and started walking again, clearly expecting me to keep up.

The Ashen Crag. I'd heard stories about that place, the kind that got whispered around taverns late at night when the fires burned low and everyone's drink was a little too strong. Something about the air there wasn't right, the locals would say, as if every breath you took drew something dark and ancient into your lungs. But of course, he didn't seem fazed by any of that. If anything, he looked like he was heading toward a familiar friend.

"Just so we're clear," I said, catching up to his long strides, "this contact of yours—she's not about to stab us in the back the second she sees us, right?"

His chuckle was dark, humorless. "Depends on how much I owe her this time."

I rolled my eyes. "Comforting. Really."

The night stretched on, the forest gradually thinning as we made our way toward what I could only assume was the fabled Crag. Exhaustion began to settle into my bones, but I kept my head high, refusing to let him see how drained I was. He'd already saved me more times than I wanted to admit, and the last thing I needed was to show him any sign of weakness.

As the trees began to thin, revealing the faintest hint of a mountain range silhouetted against the horizon, he stopped suddenly, his posture stiffening like a predator sensing danger. I reached for my blade instinctively, every nerve in my body lighting up with adrenaline. It was too quiet. The kind of silence that made the hairs on the back of your neck stand on end.

"What is it?" I whispered, edging closer to him, my voice barely louder than a breath.

"Listen," he said, and I could hear the tension laced in his voice.

I strained my ears, but there was nothing—no rustling leaves, no distant hoots or howls. Just an oppressive, suffocating silence that seemed to press down on us from every direction.

Then, a faint crack—a sound that echoed like a whip through the stillness. I spun around, searching for its source, my heart pounding in my chest.

"Move," he hissed, grabbing my arm and pulling me into a run. His grip was firm, unyielding, and I could feel the urgency in his stride as he pushed me forward. "We're being watched."

We stumbled down the slope, ducking under low-hanging branches and dodging rocks that threatened to trip us at every turn. I didn't dare look back, didn't dare slow down, even as my lungs burned and my legs screamed in protest. Whoever—or whatever—was behind us, I had a feeling it was no ordinary tracker.

Finally, he pulled me into a small crevice between two boulders, pressing a finger to his lips as we crouched in the shadows. My heart hammered against my ribs, each beat echoing in the silence. We stayed like that for what felt like an eternity, barely breathing, listening for any sign of pursuit.

After a long, tense moment, he finally exhaled, his shoulders relaxing just a fraction. "Looks like we lost them."

I let out a shaky breath, leaning back against the cool stone. "Remind me again why I agreed to this?" I muttered, more to myself than to him.

He chuckled softly, a sound that was almost...human. "You didn't. You just didn't say no."

I couldn't help the reluctant smile that tugged at the corners of my mouth. "Touché."

For a moment, we just sat there, side by side, the weight of our exhaustion settling over us like a blanket. The danger hadn't passed entirely, I knew that much, but for now, we had a brief respite. And sitting there in the dark, the rough stone pressing into my back, his shoulder a warm, solid presence beside me, I felt a strange flicker of something I hadn't felt in a long time.

Maybe it was just the adrenaline wearing off, or maybe it was the quiet between us, a fragile truce in a world that seemed intent on tearing us apart.

The dawn crept in quietly, turning the edge of the sky a muted purple as we picked our way through the narrow path that led to the village below. The night had worn on, stretching our nerves thin and leaving us both silent, though not exactly in peace. He had this way of walking beside me without actually being there, a practiced trick of making himself small enough to blend with the shadows even in broad daylight. I wondered if that habit ever tired him out, or if he was so used to retreating from the world that the idea of stepping forward and just being was as foreign to him as... well, as not speaking my mind was to me.

"Would it kill you to walk a little louder?" I muttered, side-eying him as he ghosted along beside me.

He raised a brow. "You prefer your allies clomping through the underbrush like a herd of oxen?"

"Ally is a strong word."

He smirked. "And clomping would suit you so well."

I bit back a retort, unwilling to give him the satisfaction of knowing he'd poked at my ego. The morning mist settled around us, softening the edges of the world, and the path ahead twisted like it wanted to lose us. Part of me wondered if it was a warning or an invitation. The other part of me, the part that had been ready to face whatever waited at the Ashen Crag, took it as a challenge.

The village appeared like a patchwork of smoke and stone, huddled against the forest's edge as though the trees themselves had pressed in, forcing the small collection of houses to huddle together for warmth. It wasn't welcoming, exactly, but it wasn't hostile either. Just... wary. A place that knew to look twice at strangers, especially those who arrived at the break of dawn with dirt-streaked faces and eyes that held more shadows than light.

He slowed his pace, glancing around with a practiced eye. "Stay close," he said, his voice low, almost an afterthought. As if I needed a reminder that every stranger's gaze held a potential threat.

I matched his careful, calculated steps, feeling the weight of the villagers' eyes on us even before we entered the main square. Women carrying water paused mid-step, and men with carts angled their bodies slightly, one hand always close to a makeshift weapon. They all watched us with a blend of suspicion and curiosity, as though they could tell we weren't just passing through but were also not here to cause trouble—not intentionally, anyway.

"Here's the plan," he whispered, his voice a soft thread beside me. "We'll go to the tavern, lay low until my contact arrives. She's a little... unpredictable, but she owes me one."

"I'd like to meet the person who doesn't owe you anything," I replied under my breath.

"I'd like to meet the person who owes you anything," he shot back, a flicker of amusement coloring his words.

We stepped into the dim, smoky tavern, the kind of place where the floorboards creaked with secrets and the air was thick with stories no one cared to tell. A few pairs of eyes flicked toward us as we entered, sizing us up, then quickly dismissing us as just another pair of travelers with a tale best kept to ourselves. He led me to a table in the back, one that gave a good view of both the door and the exit through the kitchen, and we settled into a silence thick enough to match the atmosphere.

A tall, wiry woman with sharp eyes and even sharper elbows approached our table, her apron stained and her gaze unimpressed. "What'll it be?"

I opened my mouth to order something safe, but he beat me to it. "Two ales. And whatever's hot."

She looked at him like he'd just asked her to juggle flaming swords. "Hot? At this hour?" She scoffed. "You're lucky if it's lukewarm."

"Lukewarm's fine," he said smoothly, flashing her a grin that had no real warmth to it but was charming enough to ease the woman's scowl a notch. I watched him with a touch of fascination; it was like watching someone try on different faces, each one more convincing than the last.

The woman shuffled off, muttering under her breath, and I leaned in. "Lukewarm ale and stale bread—your idea of laying low?"

"Laying low," he said, tapping his fingers rhythmically against the table, "is about not drawing attention, not about indulging your taste buds."

"Oh, I'll remember that when I'm starving in some ditch next time," I replied, feigning an air of complete agreement.

The ale arrived in chipped mugs, sloshing precariously as the woman set them down, and I gave the cloudy drink a dubious look. He took a long swallow without hesitation, setting the mug down with a thud, his gaze scanning the room as though he could already sense his contact's arrival.

"Subtle," I muttered, taking a tentative sip and regretting it immediately as the taste of something vaguely sour hit my tongue. "Could we not have waited outside, where at least the air doesn't taste like disappointment?"

"Patience," he murmured, barely paying me any mind as he continued his quiet surveillance of the room.

Just as I was about to throw a few more biting remarks his way, the tavern door swung open, and a figure slipped inside with a grace that matched his own—sharp, feline, and just as likely to bite. She was tall, her eyes quick and calculating, and she moved through the room like she was born to slip between spaces without being seen. But she didn't come straight to us. No, she lingered by the bar, ordering a drink with a nod toward the innkeeper. Her gaze flicked briefly in our direction, and though she didn't make a show of recognizing us, there was a spark of something dangerous in her eyes.

I looked at him, arching a brow. "Is that her?"

"She has her moments," he said, his tone light, but his eyes narrowed with something close to caution.

The woman slid into a nearby table, settling her drink in front of her with the ease of someone who owned the room. Slowly, she lifted her gaze to meet ours, and I could feel the weight of her appraisal, cool and razor-sharp. She gave the faintest tilt of her head, and he, without a word, got up and motioned for me to follow. We crossed the room and took the seats opposite her.

"Long time, no see," she said, her voice a smoky rasp, her eyes flitting to me with a curiosity that held the slightest edge. "I thought you'd given up on this little hunt of yours."

"Could say the same for you, Mara," he replied, his tone just as smooth, but his posture taut. It was clear there was a history here, the kind that held both loyalty and betrayal close, like two sides of the same coin.

Her gaze settled on me, and her lips quirked in a small smile that didn't quite reach her eyes. "And this one?" she asked, her tone dangerously pleasant.

"An investment," he replied, his voice steady, though his fingers curled slightly, as if bracing for something. I could feel the tension coiling tighter around us, sharp as a blade and just as unforgiving.

Mara's smile hovered between amusement and calculation as she leaned back, crossing her arms, the leather of her coat creaking slightly in the dim light. "An investment, hmm?" She let the words roll off her tongue with a soft lilt, her eyes flicking over me as if I were a curiosity she couldn't quite categorize. "She doesn't look like your usual fare."

I tilted my chin up, meeting her gaze with a steady look of my own. "I'm right here, you know," I said, my tone as sharp as a blade. "Feel free to talk to me directly."

Her grin widened, a wolfish smile that barely touched her eyes. "Oh, I like her. Fire suits you, darling. But you might want to be careful. People who burn too bright don't always last long around here."

He shot me a warning glance, as if to say, Let me handle this. But I was tired of being the shadow at the edge of someone else's conversation, especially when that someone looked at me like I was a gamble not worth taking.

"So," Mara continued, settling back in her chair and swirling the dregs of her drink with one idle finger, "what's the game this time, hmm? You've got that look about you—the kind you get when you've gone and thrown yourself into the middle of a mess that you think you can charm your way out of."

He sighed, his eyes cutting toward me for a fraction of a second before locking back on her. "The relic's resurfaced. Word is it's somewhere near the Crag."

Mara's gaze sharpened, losing the glint of amusement. "The Crag?" Her voice dropped a note, her posture straightening. "You're both either brave or foolish. Maybe a bit of both." She leaned in closer, and her voice dropped to a near whisper. "There are things in that place that make nightmares look like child's play."

I felt a chill prick up my spine, but I masked it with a scoff. "We're aware of the risks," I said, though I wasn't entirely sure I meant it. "Seems like they just come with the territory."

Mara's eyes narrowed on me, as if she was assessing just how much I understood the weight of those words. "So you're in this for the thrill, is that it?" she asked, cocking her head slightly. "Or maybe you're just here to play hero?"

"Neither," I replied coolly. "But I'd be lying if I said I wasn't looking for answers."

"Oh, answers are never the problem," she murmured, casting a sly glance at my companion. "It's the questions that get you into trouble."

A flicker of something I couldn't quite read passed between them—a shared history, perhaps, or the ghost of a regret. I wasn't sure, and part of me didn't want to know. But I also couldn't shake the feeling that Mara held more knowledge than she was letting on, like she was dangling just enough in front of us to keep us both on edge, yet never quite within reach.

He leaned forward, lowering his voice. "Mara, if you know something, now's the time to share it. We don't have the luxury of games."

"Ah, but what's life without a bit of mystery?" she countered, her tone playful but her eyes hard. "Fine." She drew in a long breath, her expression becoming grim. "There's a map. Or rather, there was one. It was torn apart centuries ago, scattered across regions and locked away in places that most sensible people avoid. Rumor has it that each piece carries a curse, a little 'gift' for those who think they're clever enough to outwit the past."

"And you know where to find this piece?" I asked, watching her carefully.

She raised a brow, glancing between us. "I might. But knowledge like that doesn't come for free. Not from me, anyway." She pushed her drink aside, folding her hands neatly in front of her. "The Crag is a maze, and without that map piece, you'll be as good as blind in there. The only thing waiting for you is your own funeral."

"Typical Mara," he muttered under his breath, shaking his head. "Always generous to a fault."

She laughed, a sound that was far too cold to be genuine. "Generous? Darling, if I were generous, you wouldn't be sitting here, breathing in this particular moment." Her gaze settled on him, her expression darkening. "If you want my help, it's going to cost you. And I think you know exactly what I want."

His jaw tightened, and I caught a flicker of something raw and unguarded in his eyes—a hint of vulnerability that he quickly buried beneath that usual mask of calm. "I don't have it," he said, his voice steady but taut. "And even if I did, I wouldn't give it to you."

"Then maybe you should rethink how badly you want this relic," she replied, her voice dripping with challenge.

I watched him, a question simmering on my lips. But his eyes were fixed on Mara, a silent standoff that hung thick and dangerous between them.

"What exactly does she want?" I asked finally, cutting through the tension like a knife.

They both turned to me, Mara with a look of dark amusement, and him with a hint of warning. "Some debts," he said, his voice rough, "aren't paid in coin."

"Wise words," Mara murmured, her gaze settling on me. "Your friend here owes me a favor. One I don't intend to forget." Her tone softened, but it carried the weight of iron. "I need a certain... object recovered from a place not too far from here. Consider it my insurance. You help me with this, and I'll give you the map."

I glanced at him, searching for a hint of what lay beneath his stoic exterior. But he offered nothing, just a hard stare that spoke of things he wasn't ready to say.

"Fine," I said, feeling a reckless thrill buzz through me despite my better judgment. "What's the object?"

"A pendant," Mara replied, her eyes gleaming. "It belonged to someone I... knew. It's not far, but getting it won't be easy." She gave me a look that was somewhere between pity and admiration. "The thing is guarded, and if you're not careful, well... let's just say the Crag's maze will seem like a stroll through the park by comparison."

I swallowed, feeling the weight of her words settle over me, a quiet dread mingling with my resolve. There was no going back now; whatever this favor was, it was our only chance. I looked at him, but his gaze was already locked on Mara, his face a careful mask.

"Then we have a deal," he said, his voice colder than I'd ever heard it.

Mara leaned back, looking entirely too pleased. "Good. I'll be waiting here when you get back... if you get back."

As we rose, the weight of what we'd just agreed to settled over me like a shroud. But he didn't wait for hesitation to creep in; he was already at the door, his eyes dark and unreadable. I trailed behind, each step drawing me further into the unknown, and as we slipped out of the tavern into the fading morning light, I couldn't shake the feeling that I'd just walked into something far bigger than I'd bargained for.

We'd barely taken a few steps before he turned to me, his face as impassive as stone. "Are you ready for this?"

I met his gaze, feeling my heart hammer against my ribs. "Are you?"

He didn't answer, but there was something fierce and unyielding in his eyes. The morning was still, the village slumbering beneath a shroud of mist, but in that moment, the silence around us felt like the calm before a storm. And as we set off toward the looming darkness beyond the trees, I couldn't shake the feeling that whatever lay ahead was watching, waiting for us to make the first move.

Chapter 6: A Dangerous Game

The alleyways of Keldorn's underbelly twisted like a maze, walls slick with damp and echoes bouncing from stone to stone. Shadows moved, some human, some harder to name, shapes that flitted along the edges of vision and vanished before they could be fully seen. I stepped over a puddle, the muddy water reaching high enough to splash my ankle. Lovely. The last thing I needed was to be drenched in Keldorn's finest street sludge. I spared a glance at my so-called partner, who was, predictably, striding through the narrow pathway as if it were some grand parade. Unbothered, untouched. Immaculate, even here.

He shot me a quick look, smirk stretching lazily over his face. "Having trouble keeping up?" His voice dripped with the kind of arrogance that would usually make me want to trip him, or at the very least roll my eyes. But this was an act. A game we were both choosing to play. In Keldorn, the city thrived on masks and deception, and the two of us were no exception.

"Just savoring the ambiance," I replied, trying to keep my tone light but still sharp enough to cut through his charm. The words hung between us, sharp as broken glass, and he laughed—a low, rumbling sound that somehow blended into the night, as if it belonged here more than we did.

We entered a bar—if it could even be called that—lit dimly by a handful of flickering lanterns that seemed to want nothing more than to snuff out completely. Inside, it smelled of stale beer, smoke, and a bitter tang that I didn't want to guess the origin of. People hunched over tables, talking in quiet voices or casting wary glances our way. They were used to seeing strangers here, but strangers usually didn't walk in like they owned the place. I let him lead, trying to mask my wariness with a disinterested expression as I took in the surroundings. Every single detail mattered.

A towering man with scarred knuckles manned the bar, his gaze hard as he tracked our every move. My partner, ever the performer, nodded at him as if they were old friends, and the barman inclined his head back, just enough to acknowledge without conceding anything. I stayed silent, aware that one wrong word could unravel everything. We were here for information, after all, and in a place like this, that information was sold dearly, in more ways than one.

We settled into a booth in the corner, the seats peeling with age, and I watched as he ordered two glasses of something amber and suspiciously murky. When the glasses arrived, I eyed mine warily. "Is this supposed to poison me?" I murmured, holding the glass up to the light—though I didn't have much hope of actually discerning what it was made of.

He gave me a wicked grin. "Only if you're lucky." He lifted his own glass and tipped it back in one smooth motion, as if he drank questionable liquor in seedy bars every day of the week. Maybe he did. I wasn't foolish enough to ask. Instead, I took a careful sip, wincing at the burn, which tasted less like whiskey and more like regret.

"Why this place?" I finally asked, keeping my voice low. Our cover story was flimsy at best—just two faces in a crowd, playing at a business deal—but it was the sort of flimsy that could hold, provided I didn't tear it apart with too many questions.

He leaned forward, his voice dropping even lower. "Because here, no one cares who we are. They care about what we're willing to trade." His gaze met mine, and I could feel the intensity of it, sharp and unyielding. "You can handle that, can't you?"

"Of course," I replied, trying not to let his words get under my skin. He enjoyed testing me, pushing to see how far I would go. There was a game within this game, and he was playing it with unnerving ease.

Just then, a figure slipped into the seat across from us—a wiry man with a twitchy gaze, one that darted from the doorway to the bar and then settled on me, with an intensity that sent a shiver down my spine. He looked like he hadn't slept in weeks, skin pale and stretched over sharp bones. The air around him seemed to vibrate, tense as a coiled spring. It was as if he was expecting something to explode at any moment.

"So you're the new players," he said, his voice a rasp that barely reached us. "Thought you'd be taller."

My partner laughed, low and confident, and leaned back, one arm resting casually over the booth. "Funny, I thought you'd look a bit more... well-fed."

The man's lips curled into something resembling a grin. "In this line of work, you get by with what you need." He reached into his coat pocket, pulling out a worn scrap of paper and sliding it across the table. "Here. As promised."

I reached for the paper, but my partner's hand closed over mine, firm and unyielding. "Not so fast," he said, voice smooth but with a hard edge that made me pause. He looked up at the man across from us, his eyes narrowing. "Why are you so eager to hand this over? What's the catch?"

The man's grin widened, showing teeth that gleamed faintly in the dim light. "No catch," he replied, but his eyes flickered, just for a moment, betraying something. "Just a warning. The kind that comes with a price."

The silence stretched between us, thick as fog, and I felt a prickle at the back of my neck. This wasn't going to be as simple as we'd thought. My partner's hand was still on mine, and for a second, I didn't mind it—until I realized the point. It was another layer of the act, a quiet signal to stay sharp.

I watched the man's twitchy gaze flicker over us, calculating, weighing, as if he was trying to decide just how far he could push us. And in that instant, I saw it—the faintest flicker of fear. It was brief, gone in a heartbeat, but it was there, clear as the smirk on my partner's face. Whatever game we'd stumbled into, we were in deeper than I'd thought. And if this was a warning, I had a feeling it was one I'd better not ignore.

The man across from us hadn't moved since sliding the paper over. He just sat there, his gaze flicking between us as if daring one of us to flinch. I held his stare, barely breathing, while my partner's fingers remained on my hand, warm and solid. I wanted to shake him off, tell him I could handle this myself, but I'd learned the hard way not to push too fast in situations like this. In a room like this, one wrong word or gesture could turn a deal sour in an instant.

With a casual, practiced air, I leaned back, pulling my hand free and letting my fingers trace the edge of the glass. "Your warning," I said, my tone deliberately light, as if we were simply discussing the weather, "does it come with a reason? Or do you just enjoy scaring off potential clients?"

The man laughed—a harsh, grating sound that seemed to draw the attention of a few nearby patrons. He waved them off without a glance, his focus still pinned on me. "A reason?" he echoed, his voice low, almost conspiratorial. "What I have is more valuable than that scrap of paper you're holding. I thought you two looked smart enough to understand that." His gaze flickered to my partner, a slight sneer on his lips. "At least one of you does."

My partner raised an eyebrow, his expression calm, unaffected. "Then enlighten us," he said smoothly. "If there's more to this than just a piece of information, we're listening."

The man leaned forward, lowering his voice. "There's a bounty out. Word has it that someone's looking for trouble in Keldorn, and there's a price on anyone who gets too close to certain names, certain... secrets." His gaze shifted to me, a quick, assessing look that made my skin crawl. "So if you're here for a 'deal'—I'd start watching your backs."

My partner chuckled, the sound a mix of amusement and dismissal, and I almost admired his composure. Almost. "We'll manage," he said, his eyes flashing with that sharp, challenging glint I'd come to know too well. "But we appreciate the concern."

The man smirked, the twitchiness returning to his expression as he slid out of the booth. "Just remember—you've been warned." He shot me a lingering look that sent another chill down my spine before turning and vanishing into the crowd, blending seamlessly into the shadows. As he disappeared, the air in the bar seemed to release, like the room itself had been holding its breath.

I glanced down at the scrap of paper in front of us, running my thumb over the faded ink. "Do you think he was serious?"

"He's a player in this game, just like we are," my partner replied, his gaze fixed on the paper. "They all are. It's just a question of whose hand is stronger."

"Yours or his?"

That earned me a small, crooked smile. "Ours," he corrected. He took the paper, folded it neatly, and slid it into his coat pocket. "Shall we?"

I forced a smile, slipping out of the booth and following him toward the exit. Outside, the chill of the night air hit me hard, banishing the stuffy warmth of the bar and clearing my head. The streets were quiet, the noise of the city subdued at this late hour. I couldn't shake the feeling that every shadow was watching us, that every silent alley held some hidden threat. I kept my voice low. "Do you think he knows?"

"Knows what?" he asked, his voice equally soft, as if he understood what I was getting at without me needing to elaborate.

"What we're really here for."

He shrugged, his steps steady as we moved through the narrow streets. "He probably suspects. But he won't know for sure. And that's to our advantage."

There it was again, that casual confidence that both irritated and reassured me. "You make it sound so simple."

"Because it is," he replied, a smirk tugging at the corner of his mouth. "You just have to learn to see it that way."

Before I could reply, I heard the scrape of footsteps from behind us. Instinctively, I stopped, my hand going to the knife I kept hidden beneath my coat. My partner caught my movement, his expression shifting instantly from amusement to alertness. He grabbed my arm, tugging me forward and down a side alley before I could protest.

"What are you—"

"Trust me," he whispered, pressing a finger to his lips as we crouched in the shadows. We waited, tense and silent, as the footsteps drew closer. The figure passed by, oblivious to our hiding spot, a dark-cloaked figure with a sharp, purposeful stride. I let out a breath I hadn't realized I was holding, and my partner released my arm, glancing down at me with a grin.

"See? Easy."

I glared at him, though I could feel a reluctant smile tugging at my own lips. "You're impossible."

"That's why I'm here," he replied smoothly, straightening and offering me his hand. I ignored it, standing on my own, but the smile refused to disappear.

As we emerged from the alley, the tension lingered, crackling between us like a live wire. The city felt different now, each street and corner charged with a strange electricity. Every instinct told me to turn back, but there was something intoxicating about it all, a thrill I couldn't quite name.

He must have sensed it too, because he shot me a sidelong glance, his expression almost... amused. "Nervous?"

"Hardly," I replied, though I wasn't entirely sure it was true. The lines between fear and excitement had blurred, and I wasn't sure where one ended and the other began.

He chuckled, but there was a note of something serious beneath the laughter. "Good. Because if we're doing this, we can't afford nerves."

"And what exactly are we doing?" I asked, the question coming out before I could stop myself. It was something I'd wanted to ask since we started this whole scheme, something I was afraid to put into words.

His gaze held mine, steady, unflinching. "We're playing the game," he said softly, as if that explained everything. "And if we play it right, we just might win."

The words hung in the air between us, thick with meaning, and I realized, with a thrill that was both terrifying and exhilarating, that I didn't want to stop. Whatever this was, however dangerous, however unpredictable—I wanted to see it through.

The air grew colder as we walked, the quiet settling heavily around us. Street lamps flickered above, casting pools of weak light that felt almost reluctant to reach us. I could hear the low hum of the city beneath the silence—the faintest hint of music from a nearby club, the laughter of strangers, the sharp murmur of conversations held just out of earshot. It all blurred together, creating an atmosphere that felt equal parts thrilling and foreboding. I kept my steps light, senses alert, every instinct screaming that we were being watched, though I couldn't say by whom.

My so-called partner walked beside me, an infuriatingly casual figure who looked as though he hadn't a single care in the world. Hands tucked in his pockets, gaze focused forward, as if he were just out for a pleasant midnight stroll. I wanted to shake him, demand he take this seriously, but then again, I was starting to suspect that he was always serious—just in a way I couldn't fully understand.

A quiet, low chuckle escaped him, and I scowled. "What?"

"Nothing," he said, but his grin remained. "Just wondering if you were about to start whistling 'Jaws.' You're wound so tight I can practically hear your heartbeat from here."

"I'm not wound tight," I shot back, glancing around us, my voice sharper than I intended. "I'm just... aware."

His grin softened, the kind of smile that almost felt real, though I'd seen enough of his tricks to know better. "Good. Awareness is... useful." He spoke the words slowly, as if savoring each syllable, and I had to resist the urge to roll my eyes.

"Is that supposed to be encouraging?"

"Take it how you want," he replied, giving me a wink that felt far too casual, especially given the tension crawling through me. "But a little fear's a good thing. Means you're still human."

"Good to know you're confident in my humanity," I muttered, shoving my hands in my pockets to keep them from trembling. "Should I thank you for the reassurance?"

He didn't answer, just nodded toward a narrow alleyway ahead, barely visible under the dim glow of a single, sputtering streetlamp. "In there," he murmured, and all traces of his earlier levity vanished.

I followed him, my pulse quickening as we moved deeper into the alley, stepping over trash and dodging puddles. The sound of muffled voices reached us—a low, rapid exchange that echoed off the stone walls. I felt my partner's hand on my shoulder, a light touch that surprised me with its gentleness, and he leaned close, his breath warm against my ear.

"Stay here," he whispered, his tone commanding in a way that left no room for argument.

"Excuse me?" I whispered back, turning to glare at him. "I'm not some helpless sidekick you can just tuck away until it's safe."

"This isn't about you being helpless," he replied, his voice barely above a murmur. "It's about keeping you alive. So unless you've got a better plan, stay put."

Before I could argue, he slipped around the corner, blending into the shadows with an ease that left me feeling strangely exposed. I watched him disappear, his figure swallowed by the darkness, and I fought the urge to call after him. Instead, I crouched down, pressing myself against the wall and straining to hear any sound that might give me a clue about what was happening.

The voices grew louder, though I couldn't make out the words, only the tone—a low, dangerous cadence that made the hairs on the back of my neck stand on end. I shifted slightly, trying to catch a glimpse around the corner without giving myself away, and froze at the sight before me.

Three men stood in a circle, their faces partially obscured by the shadows, but their postures unmistakably hostile. One of them, a broad-shouldered man with a face like a stone carving, was speaking, his words clipped and cold. My partner stood opposite him, his stance relaxed, hands still tucked in his pockets as if he hadn't a care in the world.

"Look, all I'm saying," my partner was saying, his voice carrying a lazy, amused tone that only seemed to make the big guy angrier, "is that if you wanted to make a point, maybe you should've picked a target with more cash. Or at least better taste."

The man's fists clenched, and I saw a flicker of something dangerous pass over his face. "You think this is a joke?" he growled, his voice like gravel scraping across glass. "You think you can walk into my territory and start making demands?"

My partner shrugged, his expression maddeningly calm. "Not demands, exactly. Think of them more as... suggestions. Friendly ones, at that."

The man took a threatening step forward, and I tensed, my fingers curling into fists as I fought the urge to step in. But my partner just smiled, unbothered by the proximity of danger, as if he thrived on it. "You know, I'm actually a little hurt," he said, his voice dropping to a smooth, dangerous purr. "Here I thought we were getting along. Guess I misread the signals."

The man sneered, reaching into his coat, and I felt my heart leap into my throat as he pulled out a blade, its edge glinting in the faint light. My partner's gaze flickered briefly to the weapon, but his expression remained cool, unfazed. I felt a surge of panic, the instinct to act warring with the knowledge that I'd be outnumbered and, likely, outmatched.

And then, without warning, he moved.

It happened so fast I almost missed it—a blur of motion, a flash of silver, and suddenly, the man's knife was on the ground, clattering against the cobblestones as my partner twisted his arm, forcing him to his knees with a swift, brutal efficiency that left me breathless. The other two men took a step back, their bravado wavering, but they were clearly sizing him up, calculating the best angle to attack.

"Now," my partner said, his voice low and deceptively soft, "I'll ask once more. Are we going to play nice, or do we have to make this... uncomfortable?"

For a moment, no one moved. The big guy on the ground glared up at him, his eyes blazing with a mix of hatred and fear, but he said nothing. And then, with a grunt, he nodded, his body going limp in surrender.

Satisfied, my partner released him, straightening as he stepped back, the faintest smirk tugging at his lips. "Good choice," he murmured, casting a glance at the other two men. "Anyone else feel like testing their luck?"

The silence that followed was answer enough.

He turned, catching my eye, and the smirk widened, a silent acknowledgment of the thrill we both felt in that moment. But as he began to step toward me, something shifted in the shadows behind him—a figure moving with eerie silence, cloaked in darkness. My breath caught, a warning on the tip of my tongue, but it was too late.

The figure lunged, a glint of steel flashing toward him, and I felt a scream rise in my throat as I saw the blade arc downward, its path aimed directly at his back.

Chapter 7: A Whispered Secret

The light in the room was thin and sharp, slipping through the crooked blinds in jagged stripes, painting a cracked road map of shadows across the cheap laminate floor. The air was stale, tinged with the faint smell of cigarettes and something else, something sweet and cloying that made my skin prickle. I'd been to a lot of terrible places with him by now, but this might just have taken the crown. The kind of place that collected secrets and sadness in its carpet fibers, that held onto the ghosts of people who left and never quite came back.

He was sitting at the small table by the window, half-turned away from me, his fingers drumming out an uneven rhythm against the plastic cup in front of him. His face was half in shadow, a dark slash of cheekbone and narrowed eyes. It was strange, watching him like this, so still, as if he were unraveling himself in a way he usually fought against with that arrogant tilt of his chin and the defiant glint in his eyes. For once, there was a weariness there, a crack in the iron exterior he always wore like armor.

"Do you ever wonder," he began, his voice low, almost as if he were talking to himself, "what it would be like to just... stop?" He paused, his fingers stilling against the cup. "To walk away from all of it? This life, the chase, everything that's out there waiting to eat us alive?"

I shifted, pulling my knees up onto the lumpy bed, pretending not to notice the springs groaning beneath me. "Can't say it hasn't crossed my mind," I said, keeping my tone light, though his words pried at something deep in me. "But running doesn't really seem like your style, does it?"

He gave a short, humorless laugh. "You'd be surprised."

For a moment, silence stretched between us, thick and tangled, and I was tempted to leave it there, to turn away and pretend I hadn't seen the way his shoulders sagged, the way he was gripping that cup as if it were the last real thing he could hold onto. But there was something about this side of him, raw and exposed, that made my chest ache in a way I didn't like to think about. Against my better judgment, I found myself asking, "Why do you do it, then? If you hate it so much?"

He didn't answer right away. Instead, he reached into his pocket and pulled out a small, worn object—something I'd never seen before. It looked like a piece of jewelry, a pendant maybe, dull and scratched from years of wear. He held it between his fingers, staring at it like it was both his curse and his salvation.

"This," he said, his voice barely more than a whisper. "It belonged to someone I lost a long time ago. Someone... important."

His words hung heavy in the air, and I felt the weight of them settle into my chest, cold and unyielding. "Who was she?" I asked, my voice softer than I intended.

He shook his head, a shadow flitting across his face. "Not 'she.' He. My brother."

The admission was like a key turning in a lock, one I hadn't even realized was there. I'd known he had his secrets, known that there was more to him than he let on, but I'd never expected this. It was as if the man I thought I'd known had been peeled back, layer by layer, revealing something fragile, something real beneath all the bravado.

"We were close," he continued, his gaze distant, as if he were seeing something beyond the cracked walls of this dingy motel room. "Closer than anyone would have thought. He... he looked out for me when no one else did. Taught me everything I know about surviving in a world that doesn't give a damn about you. And then..."

He trailed off, and I could see the struggle in his expression, the battle to keep his emotions in check. It was a look I recognized all too well, that need to keep everything locked away, hidden behind a wall of indifference and sarcasm. And yet, he was letting me see it, letting me in, and I felt a pang of guilt for every time I'd thought of him as nothing more than a means to an end.

"When he disappeared," he said finally, his voice rough, "I searched for him. For years. Did things I'm not proud of, made deals I shouldn't have. All to find some trace of him, some clue that he was still out there. And then... one day, I found this." He held up the pendant again, his gaze fixed on it with an intensity that made my skin prickle. "It was in a pawnshop, half-buried under a pile of junk. But I knew it was his. I could feel it."

I watched him, my heart aching with a sympathy I hadn't felt in a long time. I'd been running from my own ghosts for so long, I'd almost forgotten what it felt like to care, to feel something other than anger and bitterness. But here, in this desolate place, with him laying bare the wounds he kept hidden from the world, I felt something shift, something fragile and terrifying in equal measure.

"So that's why you're after the relic," I said, the pieces finally clicking into place. "You think it can bring him back."

He looked at me then, his gaze steady, unwavering. "It's not just about power. It's about redemption. About finding a way to make things right."

The room fell silent again, but this time it was a different kind of silence, one filled with an understanding that went beyond words. For the first time, I didn't see him as my enemy, didn't see him as the obstacle standing in the way of my own goals. He was just a man, broken and scarred, fighting his own battles in a world that had stripped him of everything he'd once held dear.

I could have walked away right then, could have let him bear his burden alone. But something held me back, something stronger than fear or caution. Because in that moment, I realized that his fight was mine, too. We were both searching for something lost, something that felt like it could heal the gaping wounds inside us. And maybe, just maybe, we could find it together.

Without thinking, I reached out, my hand resting on his, a silent promise that I was with him, that I wouldn't leave him to face this alone. And as his fingers curled around mine, I felt the faintest flicker of hope, a fragile spark in the darkness. We were two people who had been broken by the world, but maybe, just maybe, we could find a way to put the pieces back together.

The silence between us felt like a held breath, each second drawing us further into some strange new understanding. He glanced down at our intertwined hands as if he couldn't quite believe it, his thumb grazing the back of my hand with a gentleness that didn't fit the hard-edged person I'd come to know. It sent a shiver through me, not entirely unpleasant, and I found myself wondering what lay beneath all that practiced indifference, all those quick comebacks and wary glances.

"I always thought you were doing this for the thrill," I said, my voice barely above a whisper, afraid to shatter the quiet. "That you were just...in it for the game."

He smirked, but it was tired, lopsided, a shadow of his usual cocky grin. "That would be simpler, wouldn't it? If I was just some thrill-seeker, a greedy jerk out to snag the relic for himself." His eyes met mine, and there was a spark in them, something dark and wounded that sent a pang straight to my heart. "Believe me, it's a lot harder to hate someone when you find out they're just...stuck. Trying to make up for all the things they got wrong."

I looked away, feeling exposed under that gaze. "Believe me, I know something about that."

A low chuckle escaped him. "Yeah, you do, don't you? Miss 'I Don't Need Anyone's Help.'" He softened the words with a wry smile, and I couldn't help but roll my eyes, fighting a smile of my own.

But then he turned serious again, his gaze dropping to the pendant still dangling from his fingers. "I know this might sound...stupid. Like I'm reaching for something that's gone. But that relic? If there's a chance it can help me find him, bring him back, even..." He trailed off, his voice tight, and for the first time, I saw how desperate he was, how deeply he'd buried this part of himself. He looked up, his expression raw. "Wouldn't you do the same?"

His words hit like a blow, breaking through the wall I'd spent years building brick by bitter brick. I knew exactly what I'd do if I thought there was a chance, any chance, that something could fix what I'd lost. But I'd spent so long convincing myself that nothing could heal the scars, that it was pointless to even try. And yet here he was, putting all his faith, all his hope, into something that might very well be nothing but a mirage.

"You're not the only one who's lost people," I said quietly. "But hope like that? It's dangerous. It's..." I hesitated, searching for the right words. "It's like playing with fire, knowing you're going to get burned."

He tilted his head, studying me with that unsettling intensity of his. "Sometimes, getting burned is better than staying in the dark forever." He leaned back, folding his arms with a hint of defiance, like he'd already made peace with whatever price he'd have to pay.

That was the problem with him. He never stopped pushing, never let himself give up, even when it would have been easier. And somehow, without realizing it, I'd started to respect that. I'd started to feel something that terrified me, something that made me want to take his hand and promise him that I wouldn't let him fall. But that wasn't me, was it? I didn't do loyalty, didn't do attachments. That was his mess to wade through, not mine.

But then he broke the silence, his voice a quiet murmur that drew me back in. "I know you think I'm reckless, maybe even crazy. But there's more at stake here than just finding him. It's about...I don't know...finding myself, maybe. Or maybe just proving to myself that I'm not the selfish bastard everyone thinks I am."

"Everyone, huh?" I arched an eyebrow, refusing to let him off the hook entirely. "You mean, everyone who's ever met you?"

His lips curved into a reluctant grin. "Guilty as charged. But you know what? Maybe this journey, this whole mess—it's the closest thing I'll ever get to redemption."

I crossed my arms, sizing him up, suddenly aware of how close he was, how every inch of his expression seemed laid bare. There was something reckless about him, something that should have made me run for the hills, but instead kept pulling me in. He was like a fire that you couldn't help but touch, even knowing you'd come away scorched.

"So, what's the plan?" I asked finally, hoping the question would bring us back to reality. "Once you have the relic, I mean. Assuming you find it."

He blinked, almost surprised, as if he hadn't expected me to ask. "I...don't actually know. I'm making this up as I go, same as you."

"You mean you don't have some grand master scheme? Some elaborate ten-step plan?" I feigned mock disbelief, and he rolled his eyes, though a small smile tugged at his lips.

"Believe it or not, I'm not quite that organized," he said dryly. "I've got ideas. But none of them mean much without the relic. Once we find it..." He shrugged. "Then I guess I just...hope."

There it was again—that damnable word, slipping out of his mouth like it had any right to be there. Hope was a luxury, a myth for people who hadn't seen the things we had, hadn't lost what we'd lost. And yet here he was, clinging to it like it was a lifeline.

I let out a sigh, shaking my head. "Well, here's hoping it doesn't blow up in our faces, then."

He smirked, the corner of his mouth quirking up in that familiar way that made him look less like a tragic anti-hero and more like a roguish pain in the ass. "With you by my side? I'd say the odds are fifty-fifty."

"Generous of you," I muttered, but a reluctant smile tugged at my lips, despite myself. This was madness, pure and simple, and I had every reason to turn and walk away, to leave him to his dangerous quest and find something safer, something saner. But the truth was, I didn't want to. Not anymore.

Somewhere along the line, I'd started to care about him—care about this reckless, flawed, impossible man with his ghosts and his fire, his bruised heart and his stubborn hope. And maybe that was the real danger. Not the relic, not the chase, but the way he made me feel like I was part of something bigger than myself, something worth fighting for.

We sat there, side by side in that dingy motel room, the world pressing in around us, both knowing that everything could come crashing down at any moment. But for now, we had this. And maybe, for the first time, that was enough.

The sun was barely a thought in the sky when we hit the road again, a sliver of gold smudged against the horizon as if painted by a halfhearted artist. The air was thick with early morning mist, clinging to the road and swallowing the trees in a hazy cloak. We drove in silence, the engine humming beneath us like a reluctant ally, as if even it doubted our chances of making it out of this mess unscathed. But he had that look in his eye, that stubborn glint that told me he'd go through hell if it meant finding the relic, and maybe even himself in the process. And against my better judgment, I'd somehow signed on to be there with him.

I watched him from the corner of my eye as he gripped the wheel, his knuckles pale against the leather. He was focused, lips pressed into a thin line, the faintest shadow of stubble along his jaw catching the early light. It was unsettling, the way I could see every detail, every flaw, as if he were drawn in charcoal, smudged around the edges in a way that felt both real and unreal. And yet, I couldn't look away.

"What?" he asked without looking over, a smirk teasing at the edge of his mouth. "You're staring."

I rolled my eyes, feigning boredom. "I'm just trying to gauge how long it'll take you to get us lost. You've been staring at that map like it's written in hieroglyphics."

"Patience, sweetheart," he drawled, throwing me a sidelong glance. "Navigation's an art. And art takes time."

"Tell that to every pothole you've nearly sent us into," I shot back, folding my arms and leaning back, watching the world blur by through the window.

The smirk didn't fade, but he went quiet, and for a moment, I let myself just listen to the rhythm of the road, the steady thrum of the tires against the asphalt, the way the wind whispered against the glass. It was almost peaceful, in a way that felt like an illusion, a lull before the storm. But then, that was us, wasn't it? Always riding the edge, somewhere between calm and chaos, never quite safe, never quite steady.

I felt his gaze flicker toward me, and I glanced over to find him studying me, an unreadable expression shadowed across his face. It wasn't the cocky grin or the exasperated sigh I'd grown used to; it was something deeper, something that seemed to weigh him down, and for a second, I could see the cracks beneath the mask. Whatever he was carrying, it went deeper than the relic, deeper than his brother's absence. It was like he was wrestling with himself, with something dark and twisting, and losing.

"What if we don't find it?" I asked, the words slipping out before I could stop them. "What if this whole thing is just...empty?"

His fingers tightened on the wheel, and he looked away, jaw clenching. "I don't let myself think about that."

"Maybe you should," I said quietly. "Hope's great and all, but it doesn't pay the bills. And it sure as hell doesn't fill an empty grave."

He shot me a glare, one that felt more defensive than angry, and I realized I'd hit a nerve. "What, you think I don't know that?" His voice was low, sharp, like a blade pressed against skin. "I know what it's like to lose everything, to want something so badly you'd tear yourself apart for it. But if you're so cynical, why are you here?"

It was a good question, one I hadn't let myself think about too deeply. Why was I here? Was it loyalty, stubbornness, some misguided sense of purpose? Or was it something simpler, something I didn't want to admit? I could feel his eyes on me, waiting, demanding an answer, but I didn't give him one. Instead, I just turned back to the window, watching the trees blur by, as if the answer might be hidden somewhere in the shifting landscape.

Eventually, the tension between us settled into something quieter, more resigned, like an old wound that had finally stopped throbbing. We drove in silence for a while, the road stretching out ahead of us like a path we couldn't turn back from, whether we wanted to or not.

Finally, after what felt like hours, we pulled up to a weather-beaten gas station on the outskirts of nowhere. The kind of place that looked like it had seen better days, back when gasoline was a nickel and strangers weren't a cause for suspicion. He killed the engine and climbed out, stretching as he looked around with that cautious, watchful gaze I'd come to recognize. I followed, glancing over at the flickering neon sign that hung above the door, half the letters burned out so it read something unintelligible.

"You think they've got coffee?" I asked, more to break the silence than anything.

"If they don't, I'll be filing a formal complaint with management," he replied dryly, shoving his hands into his pockets as he walked toward the entrance.

Inside, it was exactly as I'd expected—dim, cramped, with shelves cluttered with mismatched cans and bags of snacks that looked like they'd been there since the dawn of time. A lone clerk sat behind the counter, eyeing us with a disinterest that bordered on comical. But there, in the corner, was a battered coffee machine, the glass pot half-full with something dark and suspiciously thick.

I poured myself a cup, ignoring the strange smell, and took a tentative sip, trying not to grimace. "Not the worst I've had," I muttered, though it tasted more like burnt tar than anything remotely drinkable.

He snorted, grabbing a bottle of water instead. "Suit yourself. I'm not risking it."

We paid, the clerk barely looking up as he muttered something that might have been a "thanks" or a warning. As we stepped outside, I felt an odd sense of unease prickling at the back of my neck, as if something was watching us, something hidden just beyond the line of trees that circled the station like silent sentinels. I glanced over at him, but he seemed oblivious, fiddling with the map again as he leaned against the hood of the car.

Then, out of the corner of my eye, I saw it—a glint of metal, a flash of movement in the shadows near the edge of the parking lot. My stomach dropped, and I froze, the cup slipping from my fingers and shattering against the concrete, the sound like a gunshot in the quiet.

He looked up, eyes narrowing as he followed my gaze. "What is it?"

Before I could answer, a figure stepped out of the shadows, cloaked in darkness but unmistakable, the lines of his face familiar yet strange, twisted with something that looked like anger, or maybe grief. My breath caught in my throat, and I felt the ground shift beneath me, like the world itself was tilting.

It was him. The one he'd been searching for, the one he'd torn himself apart over. But he wasn't alone—and the look in his eyes was anything but friendly.

I barely had time to react before he raised his hand, something dark and sharp glinting in his grip, and then everything was chaos.

Chapter 8: The Relic's Curse

The relic lay in front of us, nestled in a shallow pit beneath the cracked, sagging floorboards of an abandoned church. We'd spent months tracking it down, following rumors and fragmented whispers passed between forgotten alleyways and dimly lit taverns. Each step brought us closer to it, yet no amount of anticipation could have prepared me for the strange thrumming energy it exuded. In the dim glow filtering through the shattered stained-glass windows, it glinted—a small, intricate object covered in strange symbols that looked almost alive. It felt as if it were watching us, a knowing sentience embedded in its ancient, twisted metal.

For a moment, I didn't move, my eyes glued to the relic. My heartbeat matched its pulse, an unearthly rhythm that made my head spin. It was cold, so cold my breath came out in wisps despite the heavy summer night outside. I could feel that chill creeping up my spine, settling into my bones like a stubborn shadow refusing to let go.

He cleared his throat, shattering the silence. "This is it, then." His voice was tight, a mixture of awe and unease. The usual cocky swagger he wore like a second skin had vanished, replaced by something quieter, almost reverent. I glanced over, surprised to see his face taut with concern, his normally bright eyes dark and cautious.

"Yeah," I whispered back, though my voice sounded foreign, far away. I took a slow, measured breath, trying to steady myself, but it was useless. The relic was drawing me in, the air around it humming with power so raw it felt like it might break apart at any second. I reached out, my fingers trembling, just to graze it—just a touch. How bad could one touch be?

The answer was immediate and unforgiving. A shock seared through my hand, a pain so intense it was almost blinding. My whole body jerked back, but the force held me for a breath too long, the relic clinging to me like a desperate, cold hand pulling me under. The symbols lit up in a sickly green glow, casting eerie shadows across my face, illuminating the sharp edges of the room in surreal clarity.

He lunged forward, gripping my wrist and yanking me away with a force that sent me stumbling back into his arms. I felt his heartbeat pounding against my back, fast and erratic, a mirror of my own. For a long, tense moment, we stood like that, frozen, too afraid to move, too afraid to look at each other. His fingers tightened around my wrist, grounding me, his touch a welcome warmth against the icy burn still lingering on my skin.

"You felt that, didn't you?" he murmured, his voice barely above a whisper. He didn't need to ask. The answer was written in the way my hands still shook, in the shallow breaths that were the only sounds breaking the heavy silence between us.

"Yeah," I managed to choke out, my voice raw, like I'd swallowed broken glass. "It's... alive. It's like it knows us."

His eyes narrowed, flicking back to the relic that lay innocently enough, but we both knew better. There was nothing innocent about it. That thing had a darkness to it, a weight that pressed down on my chest and made it hard to breathe. He stared at it, his jaw tight, and I could tell he was thinking the same thing. We'd stumbled onto something far more dangerous than we'd anticipated, and it was too late to turn back now.

"Come on," he said, his tone brisk, but I could hear the thread of fear weaving through it. "We have to get out of here. Now."

I didn't argue. With one last glance at the relic, I let him pull me out of the church, my feet heavy and reluctant, as though the artifact were calling me back, beckoning me with promises I couldn't understand but desperately wanted to. Once we were outside, I gulped in the night air, the warmth a stark contrast to the numbing chill that still clung to my skin.

We didn't speak as we walked, the silence stretching between us, filled with questions neither of us wanted to ask. I wanted to tell him about the strange images that had flickered through my mind when I touched it, fleeting impressions of shadows and voices that felt like they belonged to a time long past. But something held me back. Maybe it was the fear that saying it aloud would make it real. Or maybe it was the way he kept glancing over at me, worry etched into the lines of his face. Whatever the reason, I kept my mouth shut, swallowing the words that burned on the tip of my tongue.

Finally, he stopped, turning to face me, his gaze intense. "That relic," he began, his voice low, "it's not just an artifact. It's... something else, something powerful. And dangerous."

I laughed, a brittle sound that echoed harshly in the empty street. "You think I didn't notice that?"

He ran a hand through his hair, exasperation and something close to fear mingling in his expression. "I mean it, really mean it. This isn't like the other relics. Whatever curse is bound to this one... it's not something we can just walk away from."

The implication hung between us, unspoken but loud, like a thunderclap in the silence. This was more than just another job, another artifact to add to our collection. We'd opened a door we couldn't close, and the relic would haunt us until we saw it through.

I swallowed, the taste of fear bitter on my tongue. I wanted to argue, to laugh it off and pretend I wasn't rattled, but the truth settled over me like a heavy cloak, pressing down until I could barely breathe. We were in over our heads, and there was no one else to turn to, no easy way out.

"Well, then," I said, my voice steadier than I felt, "I guess we'd better figure out what it wants. Because I have a feeling it's not done with us yet."

He looked at me, surprise flashing across his face, then something else—admiration, maybe, or a begrudging respect.

Whatever it was, it warmed me, if only a little, like a candle flickering in the darkness. I squared my shoulders, meeting his gaze head-on.

The silence stretched between us as we moved further away from the church, our footsteps echoing on the cobblestone path. I glanced over, catching his gaze for a moment, sharp and thoughtful, but then he looked away, lips pressed into a thin line. There was no bravado left, no sardonic quip ready on his tongue. He looked as shaken as I felt, the weight of what we'd touched resting heavily in the spaces between us.

"So," I said, my voice breaking the stillness, "I think it's safe to say we have a bit of a situation."

He snorted, a dry sound that held no humor. "A 'bit' of a situation?" His eyebrows arched, an incredulous expression crossing his face. "If that's your idea of a bit, I'd hate to see your idea of a disaster."

"Just keeping things optimistic," I replied with a shrug, attempting to inject some levity. But it fell flat, dissipating in the cold air that still clung to me from the relic's touch.

We reached the edge of the city where the narrow cobblestone gave way to open roads, stretching out into the unknown. The moon hung low, casting a soft light that did little to dispel the tension hanging between us. I stopped, crossing my arms as I turned to face him fully. "We can't run forever, you know."

He sighed, shoulders sagging. "Who said anything about running?" He looked at me, his expression half-resigned, half-wary. "I just thought it might be wise to... consider our options before diving headfirst into whatever curse that thing has wrapped around it."

A small laugh escaped me before I could stop it, and I saw his eyes narrow. "Consider our options?" I echoed, raising an eyebrow. "I think it's a bit late for that. We're in this, whether we like it or not."

He rubbed a hand over his face, exasperated. "And I'm guessing you have some brilliant idea, then?"

I tilted my head, feigning thoughtfulness. "Oh, I don't know. I was thinking we could just ask it nicely to leave us alone. Maybe bring it a peace offering—a bouquet, chocolates?"

"Very funny," he muttered, but I could see the hint of a smile tugging at the corner of his mouth. It was fleeting, there and gone in a heartbeat, but it was enough to ease the tightness in my chest, if only a little.

"Look," I said, growing serious, "I don't think we can afford to waste time on doubts. Whatever curse is on that relic... it felt like it was inside me, clawing its way in. I don't think it's the kind of thing that's going to wait around while we weigh our options."

He was silent, eyes fixed on the ground as he mulled over my words. When he finally spoke, his voice was softer, almost resigned. "You're right. I just... I didn't think it would be like this."

"Neither did I." I felt a pang of sympathy, unexpected but real. He'd always been the one with the plans, the schemes. This must have felt like unfamiliar territory for him, a place where his charm and quick wit couldn't protect him.

We started walking again, slower this time, neither of us in a rush to get anywhere in particular. The city was asleep, quiet and peaceful, an odd juxtaposition to the chaos swirling in my mind. I could feel the relic's presence lingering, like a shadow draped over my shoulders. I shivered, and without thinking, wrapped my arms around myself.

He noticed, of course. "You alright?"

"Fine," I said, a bit too quickly. But then, softer, I added, "It just... it doesn't feel like it's gone. Like it's still... there, somehow."

His gaze sharpened, a flicker of concern crossing his face. "You think it's still connected to you?"

I shrugged, unwilling to put my fear into words. "I don't know. Maybe. Or maybe it's just in my head." But I didn't believe that, and neither did he. We both knew better than to dismiss the unexplainable so easily.

We walked in silence for a while, each of us lost in our own thoughts, until finally, he spoke again, his tone hesitant. "If it's really a curse... then there has to be a way to break it, right?"

I frowned, considering. "Maybe. But curses don't usually come with instruction manuals, do they?"

He let out a huff of laughter, one that held more nerves than humor. "No, I suppose not. Though that would be helpful."

The thought was absurd, but it was enough to pull a genuine smile from me. "Imagine it—'Curses for Dummies.' I'd buy it."

He laughed, the sound warm and genuine, and for a moment, the darkness felt a little less suffocating. I could see the tension in his shoulders easing, and I felt it in myself, too, like we'd both been holding our breath without realizing it.

Then, in a low, contemplative voice, he murmured, "We're going to have to go back, aren't we?"

I tensed, every instinct screaming against the idea. But he was right. If we were going to break the curse, we couldn't just run from it. We had to face it, whatever that meant. And as much as I hated the idea, I couldn't deny the logic.

"Yeah," I admitted reluctantly. "We're going to have to go back."

He gave a grim nod. "Then we'll go together."

The simplicity of his statement surprised me. No bravado, no grand declarations. Just quiet resolve. It grounded me in a way I hadn't expected, reminded me that I wasn't alone in this, no matter how terrifying it felt.

And somehow, knowing that made it a little easier to turn back toward the city, toward the ominous shadow of the church that loomed in the distance, waiting. The chill returned as we approached, a creeping, insidious cold that prickled along my skin, but I forced myself to keep walking, each step heavier than the last.

By the time we reached the doors, my stomach was twisted into knots. The silence inside was suffocating, pressing down like a weight on my chest. But then I felt his hand on my shoulder, steadying me, and I took a deep breath, centering myself.

"You ready?" he asked, his voice low but steady.

"No," I replied honestly, my heart pounding in my chest. "But let's do this anyway."

We stepped into the darkness together, side by side, the relic waiting somewhere inside. And as I crossed the threshold, I couldn't shake the feeling that the real danger had only just begun.

Inside, the church was darker than I remembered, shadows swallowing the faint traces of moonlight that dared to peek through the stained glass. The relic lay on the floor where we'd left it, as if waiting for us. That eerie, pulsing glow was gone, but I knew better than to trust it. Whatever lay dormant now could wake at any moment, and I had no intention of being caught off guard again.

He stepped forward, his movements slow and deliberate, scanning the room like he expected something to jump out at us. And honestly, I couldn't blame him. The air felt thicker, weighted with a presence I couldn't quite put a name to. It was as if the walls themselves were watching us, silently willing us to turn back. But we couldn't. Not now.

"I think it knows we're here," he murmured, his voice barely above a whisper. "It feels... different."

I nodded, feeling the same prickling sensation skitter across my skin. "Yeah. Like it's waiting for something."

He glanced at me, a hint of concern flashing in his eyes. "Maybe we should—"

"No," I cut him off, surprising even myself with the firmness in my voice. "We didn't come all this way to chicken out now. I want answers. And if that relic is the only way to get them, then I'm going to make it talk."

He raised an eyebrow, a reluctant grin tugging at the corner of his mouth. "Since when did you become the brave one?"

"Since you decided to get all cautious on me," I shot back, though the truth was I felt anything but brave. My heart was pounding so hard I was sure he could hear it, but I squared my shoulders, refusing to show it.

He let out a sigh, his expression a mixture of amusement and exasperation. "Fine. But if it tries to kill you again, I'm pulling you out of here. No arguments."

"Deal," I replied, ignoring the nagging voice in the back of my head that told me this was a terrible idea. I took a deep breath, steeling myself, and stepped closer to the relic, feeling that familiar chill seep back into my bones. My hand twitched involuntarily, but I clenched my fists, refusing to back down.

"Alright," I whispered, not entirely sure who I was talking to. "What do you want?"

The words barely left my lips when the temperature dropped sharply, and the relic began to pulse again, faint but insistent, like a heartbeat under layers of ice. I swallowed, fighting the urge to step back, and forced myself to stand still, watching as the green light grew brighter, casting ghostly shadows on the walls.

And then, out of nowhere, a voice—soft, hollow, and chilling—filled the room.

Free me.

The sound reverberated through me, cold and raw, leaving a strange ache in my chest. I shot him a look, but he seemed just as startled, his wide eyes darting around the room. He opened his mouth, but no words came out.

Taking a shaky breath, I forced myself to respond. "Free you? From what?"

Silence, thick and unnerving, followed. I felt a sudden pressure in my chest, as though something heavy had settled there, making it hard to breathe. I wanted to run, to turn and bolt out of the church and never look back, but I couldn't move. The relic held me there, its silent demand twisting in my mind.

Then, the voice returned, colder and sharper this time, each word like a knife scraping against stone. Bound. Cursed. Break the chains.

"Break the chains?" I echoed, trying to ignore the tremor in my voice. "How? What does that even mean?"

A surge of energy shot through the relic, and for a moment, the green light flared so brightly I had to shield my eyes. When I looked again, I saw faint tendrils of light—almost like chains—wrapping around the relic, binding it in place.

He stepped forward, his jaw set in determination. "If it's cursed, maybe there's a way to break it. We just need to figure out how."

I gave him a dubious look. "Right, because ancient curses are usually pretty straightforward."

He shot me a glare. "I'm just saying, it's worth a shot. What's the alternative? Leave it here and hope it doesn't come after us again?"

I hated that he was right. The relic had already proven it wasn't content to stay quiet. If we left it here, who knew what kind of damage it might do—or worse, what kind of hold it might keep on me.

"Fine," I said, though the word tasted like ash. "But if you've got any brilliant ideas, now would be the time."

He stared at the relic, his brow furrowed in concentration. "Maybe there's some kind of... ritual? Something to sever the curse from it. We could try—"

Before he could finish, the green light flared again, and the relic jerked violently, as if struggling against the chains that bound it. I stumbled back, heart hammering as the voice returned, louder this time, laced with a desperate fury.

Break the chains! Or suffer as I have!

The words sent a chill through me, and for the first time, I felt a flicker of something like sympathy. Whatever was trapped in that relic wasn't just angry—it was tormented, bound to this place in a way that defied reason.

He glanced at me, his face pale but resolute. "If we're going to do this, we need to be careful. Whatever's in there, it doesn't sound exactly... stable."

"That makes two of us," I muttered, but my pulse quickened as I took a tentative step toward the relic, keeping my movements slow and deliberate. "Alright," I said, my voice trembling just enough to betray my nerves. "We'll try to help you. But you have to tell us how."

Silence stretched once more, thick and stifling, until the voice responded, softer this time, almost pleading. Find the source. Break the chains. Free me.

I glanced over at him, meeting his gaze. He nodded, a small, steadying motion that was almost enough to calm the wild fear coiling in my stomach. Without another word, we moved in unison, closer to the relic, the strange tendrils of light casting an otherworldly glow across our faces.

But just as I reached out, something shifted—a sudden, sharp crack echoing through the church as the chains began to writhe, tightening around the relic like serpents. The green light pulsed, growing more intense, and the air filled with a low, ominous hum that made my teeth ache.

"Wait," he said, his voice tense. "Something's wrong."

Before I could respond, the ground beneath us shook, a violent tremor that sent me stumbling. I reached out, grabbing onto his arm for balance, and he held me steady, his grip reassuring despite the chaos erupting around us.

And then, with a shattering crash, the relic broke free, sending a surge of energy rippling through the air. The green light exploded outward, filling the room with a blinding brilliance that forced us both to shield our eyes.

When the light faded, I lowered my hand, blinking against the afterimage seared into my vision. My heart stopped as I took in the sight before me.

The relic was gone. In its place stood a figure, tall and shadowed, bound in chains that glowed with the same eerie green light. It lifted its head, and as its gaze locked onto mine, a slow, twisted smile spread across its face.

"Thank you," it murmured, its voice dripping with dark satisfaction. "I've been waiting for someone foolish enough to set me free."

Chapter 9: Fractured Trust

The tension in the room could have cut glass, and I was at the center, sharpening every edge with my anger. He stood opposite me, one arm propped against the wall, the other hand stuffed in his pocket as though he could pocket his own secrets if he pressed hard enough. I studied his face, every flicker of his eyes that looked anywhere but directly at me, and I knew—he was hiding something, something bigger than I'd been able to piece together so far. I could feel it in the way he avoided my gaze, how his body tensed with every step I took toward him. He was barricading himself in, and I was determined to break down every wall.

"Just tell me the truth," I said, keeping my voice low, steady, in a way that surprised even me. Maybe because a part of me feared that if I raised my voice, the truth might shatter everything irreparably. "After all this, I deserve to know."

He let out a breath, a rough, almost bitter sound, and for a moment, I thought he would actually answer me. But instead, he let his gaze drift out the window, his jaw tightening as if he were physically swallowing the words he wanted to say. Or maybe the words he didn't want me to hear.

"You think I'm hiding something?" he asked, his voice soft but laced with a challenge that sparked something deep in my chest. "What about you? You think you've been completely open with me?"

It was a deflection, a clear and obvious one, but it worked. I stumbled, not quite expecting the accusation to be hurled back at me, and I hated that he could still do this—turn my questions into mirrors I wasn't ready to look into. Still, I held my ground, lifted my chin, and refused to back down. He wasn't getting off that easily.

"This isn't about me," I said, my voice colder now, biting. "I'm not the one disappearing in the middle of the night or refusing to explain why I keep finding bruises and cuts on you that you won't talk about."

For a moment, a crack appeared in his expression, something raw and haunted flashing in his eyes. But just as quickly as it appeared, he shut it down, replacing it with that infuriating calm that only fueled my frustration.

"What if it is about you?" he shot back, his words sharp as broken glass. "What if the reason I don't tell you things is because I can't trust that you won't just—"

"Won't just what?" I interrupted, my voice laced with a dangerous edge. "Walk away? Betray you? Because newsflash—I've been here. Through everything."

He didn't respond, just clenched his jaw harder, the muscles working as he swallowed back whatever he wanted to say. And that silence, that refusal to give me anything, was worse than any confession. It was like watching someone pull back, closing a door in my face, and with every second that ticked by, I felt my patience unravel, felt something inside me snap.

"I can't keep doing this if you're going to keep me in the dark," I said, softer now, almost pleading. I hated the vulnerability in my voice, the way it shook just enough to betray me. "You think I don't know when you're hiding something? I've known since the beginning. But I thought... I thought maybe you'd trust me by now."

There was a beat of silence, a heavy, suffocating moment where the air seemed to thicken around us, and for a moment, I thought he might actually give in, let me in, even if just a little. But then he looked away, his eyes hardening, and just like that, the moment was gone.

"I don't need you to fix everything for me," he said, his voice flat, a finality that sliced through me. "Some things... some things are just mine to deal with."

I felt the weight of his words settle over me like a cold blanket, suffocating, stifling, and I took a step back, instinctively wrapping my arms around myself as if I could shield against the ache spreading through my chest. He was drawing lines, putting up walls, and no matter how much I wanted to break them down, I couldn't force my way past them.

"Fine," I said, forcing the word out past the lump in my throat. "If that's what you want, then fine. But don't expect me to keep standing here, waiting, while you decide when I'm worth trusting."

He flinched, just barely, but it was enough to spark a brief satisfaction in me, a flicker of triumph amidst the wreckage of the conversation. I turned on my heel, my footsteps echoing in the silence, a silence that stretched like a wound between us. But before I could reach the door, his voice stopped me, quiet, hesitant, as though the words were dragged from some place deep and dark he hadn't wanted me to see.

"It's not about you, you know," he said, so softly I almost didn't hear. "It's... it's me. I don't know how to let anyone in, not really."

I paused, my hand on the doorknob, torn between the urge to leave and the urge to stay, to find some way to bridge the chasm he'd dug between us. Because that vulnerability, that sliver of honesty, was something he rarely showed. And in that moment, I saw it—just a glimpse, but enough. Beneath the layers of secrecy and mistrust, he was just as afraid as I was, just as lost.

I turned to look at him, really look, and for the first time, I saw the weariness in his eyes, the haunted shadows that no amount of walls or distance could fully hide. And I realized, maybe for the first time, that I wasn't the only one afraid of losing something precious.

But just as quickly as he'd let me see that side of him, he shut it down again, his gaze hardening, his expression shifting back into that carefully controlled mask. And I knew then that whatever battle he was fighting, he wasn't ready to share it. Not yet.

So I left, closing the door quietly behind me, leaving him with his secrets and my fractured trust splintering into a million pieces on the other side. And as I walked away, I couldn't shake the feeling that something between us had broken, something that wouldn't be easy to mend.

The night outside had turned thick and black, with only a sliver of moonlight slicing through the clouds and casting a dim glow on the room's edges. The tension still hung between us like a live wire, crackling with the things neither of us dared to say aloud. I'd left him standing there in the half-light, shadows clinging to him like armor, but even from the hallway, I felt his presence as if it were a tangible force, pulling me back with a subtle gravity I wanted desperately to resist. And yet, the anger in my chest had shifted, cooling into something sharper, something that cut but didn't bleed. A dangerous kind of calm.

He didn't come after me, and I hadn't really expected him to, though a part of me—a small, defiant part—had hoped he would. It was pride, probably, some stubborn need for proof that I mattered enough to chase. But he stayed rooted there, stubbornly, resolutely silent, holding on to whatever it was that he thought was worth more than my trust.

I made it to the kitchen, my hands trembling just enough to make me curse under my breath as I flicked on the overhead light. The brightness startled me, almost as if I'd been jolted awake, and I squinted against it, feeling a sudden wave of exhaustion settle over me. The whole night felt like a fever dream now, edges blurred and slippery, as if any moment I might wake up and realize I'd imagined it all.

But I hadn't imagined his face, the guarded, haunted look he wore like a second skin, and I hadn't imagined the way he'd thrown my own secrets back at me, the way he'd managed to slice through me with just a few choice words. I hated him for it, in that moment.

And I hated myself for caring, for letting him get under my skin the way he had, for giving him even a sliver of power over me.

I reached for a glass, my fingers still unsteady, and filled it with water from the tap, the steady rush of it oddly comforting in the silence. I took a long sip, letting the coolness settle my nerves, and tried to think, tried to make sense of what I felt and why. It was like piecing together fragments of a broken mirror, each one reflecting something different, something confusing and contradictory.

The sound of footsteps behind me broke the silence, and I didn't have to turn around to know it was him. The air shifted, electric, and I felt him stop in the doorway, lingering there as if he were waiting for me to make the first move. I set my glass down with more force than I meant to, the sharp clink echoing in the stillness, and turned to face him, crossing my arms in a way that I hoped made me look less vulnerable, less affected.

"You came all the way here to say nothing?" I said, my voice flat, devoid of the warmth I usually reserved for him. It felt strange, wearing this armor around him, but it was necessary now. Self-preservation.

He leaned against the doorframe, arms crossed to mirror mine, his face unreadable. "What do you want me to say?"

I let out a short, humorless laugh. "Oh, I don't know. Maybe the truth, for a change? Maybe something real?"

His jaw tightened, and for a moment, I thought he'd fire back with another deflection, another attempt to twist this back on me. But instead, he stayed silent, his eyes holding mine in a way that felt almost like an apology. Almost. But not quite.

"I don't think you'd want to hear it," he said, his voice barely above a whisper. "The truth, I mean. It's... it's not pretty. It's not something you'd understand."

"Try me," I shot back, hating the note of desperation in my voice but unable to keep it from slipping out. "Because right now, I'm feeling like I don't understand anything."

He sighed, rubbing a hand over his face, and for the first time, he looked tired, vulnerable, as if the weight of his own secrets was pressing down on him. I almost felt a pang of sympathy, almost reached out to close the distance between us, but I held back, kept my arms crossed and my expression carefully neutral.

"Fine," he said, finally. "You want to know? It's not about you. It's... it's everything else. All of it. Things I can't explain, things I don't even know how to make sense of myself."

I waited, biting down on the urge to press him, to demand more. But I sensed that whatever he was about to say was fragile, like a thread stretched too thin, ready to snap at the slightest pressure.

"You think you know me," he continued, his voice soft, almost pained. "But there are parts of me I can't even let myself see. Parts that... that I don't want to drag you into because once you're in, there's no way out."

I swallowed, hard, the weight of his words settling over me like a shroud. I felt a chill run down my spine, a coldness that seeped into my bones, and for the first time, I wondered if maybe he was right. Maybe there was something in him that was too dark, too fractured to be healed. But a part of me—a stubborn, reckless part—refused to believe it, refused to let him scare me away.

"So what?" I asked, my voice softer now, almost a whisper. "You think you're protecting me by keeping me at arm's length? By shutting me out?"

"Yes," he said, without hesitation, and the raw conviction in his voice took me aback, left me reeling. "Yes, that's exactly what I'm doing. Because you... you don't know what you're asking for. You don't know what it would mean to trust me completely. To see the things I've done, the choices I've made."

I stepped forward, closing the distance between us in a single, determined stride. "Then show me," I said, the challenge clear in my voice. "Show me, and let me decide if I can handle it."

For a moment, he looked at me as if I were something he couldn't quite believe, something impossible and dangerous all at once. And then, just as quickly, the walls went up again, his expression hardening, closing off. But I'd seen it—the brief flicker of doubt, the crack in his resolve.

"You think it's that simple," he said, a wry smile tugging at the corner of his mouth, though there was no real amusement in it. "You think you can just walk into my life and make everything better with a few choice words?"

"No," I replied, meeting his gaze with a steady calm I hadn't realized I possessed. "But I think I deserve a chance to try."

He let out a breath, shaking his head as if in disbelief, and for a moment, I thought he might actually relent, might actually give in and let me in. But instead, he just looked away, his shoulders slumping, and I felt my heart sink with the realization that whatever battle he was fighting, he wasn't ready to let me join it. Not yet.

And in that silence, that heavy, unspoken tension, I felt the distance between us stretch even wider, like a chasm that no amount of words could bridge.

I couldn't sleep. Every time I closed my eyes, the last image of him, with that hardened look on his face, hovered behind my eyelids. And even in the quiet of the bedroom, where I'd tried to retreat and escape, his words echoed. Words that implied I didn't know him, not really. That he was hiding something so dark, so irreversible, it would turn my affection into ashes if I dared get close enough. Maybe that's what he wanted me to believe—to keep me at a safe distance. But I'd already fallen too far into his orbit, my curiosity and my heart tangled up in a knot I couldn't untangle even if I tried.

So there I was, lying in bed, staring at the ceiling and thinking of all the things he might be keeping from me, the questions I hadn't thought to ask yet. The house was quiet, too quiet, and it made me uneasy, like I was waiting for something to snap, for the silence to give way to the truth he was hiding. It was ridiculous, the way I was letting him consume me. But the more he tried to push me away, the more determined I was to close the distance between us, to bridge that impossible gap he insisted on leaving.

Unable to bear the silence any longer, I got up and slipped into the hallway, the dim light from the kitchen casting shadows that seemed to dance across the walls. I moved quietly, past the closed door to his room, past the reminders of the things we'd shared and the secrets that lingered like ghosts. I thought about knocking on his door, about demanding he finally tell me everything, but I knew it would be futile. He'd find some way to deflect, to twist my questions until I was the one left questioning myself.

Instead, I made my way to the study, where the faint smell of old leather and ink greeted me as I pushed the door open. The room was cluttered with stacks of books, papers scattered across the desk in a chaotic order that only he would understand. I'd always loved this room, loved the way it felt like a place caught between two worlds—his world and the world he let me glimpse. But tonight, it felt different. Charged. Like a minefield, one wrong step away from a discovery I wasn't sure I was ready for.

I hesitated, my fingers hovering over a pile of books on his desk. My heart pounded with the forbidden thrill of it, the audacity of rifling through his things, of finding out what he'd so carefully kept hidden. I knew I shouldn't, knew it was a line I shouldn't cross, but there was something about his evasions, his half-truths, that gnawed at me, an itch I couldn't scratch. And if he wouldn't tell me what he was hiding, then I'd find out myself.

Slowly, I began to sift through the papers, my hands moving with a deliberate caution. Most of it was innocuous—notes scribbled in his messy handwriting, lists of places and dates that didn't mean much to me. But then, tucked between two faded envelopes, I found something that stopped me cold. A photograph, worn at the edges, as though it had been held too many times, or maybe hidden away for too long.

In the photo, a younger version of him stood in front of an old, crumbling building, his arm slung around a woman with a wide smile and eyes that sparkled with a life I hadn't seen in his. They looked happy, carefree, their faces bright with a kind of joy that felt foreign to the man I knew. I traced my fingers over the image, over the way his hand rested on her shoulder with a familiarity, an ease, that I'd never seen in him with anyone. Not even me.

And there, scrawled on the back in his handwriting, was a date—a date that sent a chill down my spine. A date that didn't match up with anything he'd ever told me, a date that raised more questions than it answered.

"What are you doing?"

I spun around, the photo slipping from my fingers, fluttering to the floor like a fallen leaf. He stood in the doorway, his expression hard, his eyes dark and unreadable. There was a tension in his stance, a fury barely contained, and I realized too late that I'd crossed a line, a line he'd drawn without ever saying a word.

"I... I was just..." I stammered, my words faltering under his stare. But there was no excuse, no explanation that would make this better. I'd gone looking for answers, and now I was caught in the act.

"Didn't I make it clear?" he said, his voice cold, every word dripping with an anger I'd never heard from him before. "Didn't I tell you there are things you're better off not knowing?"

I felt a surge of indignation rise up in me, anger sparking beneath the guilt and fear. "Maybe if you'd just tell me the truth, I wouldn't have to go looking for it myself," I shot back, my voice stronger than I felt.

He shook his head, a bitter laugh escaping his lips. "You think you want the truth? You think knowing will somehow make everything better? You have no idea what you're asking for."

"Then tell me," I challenged, stepping forward, closing the distance between us. "If it's so terrible, so life-altering, then tell me. Stop hiding."

For a moment, he looked at me with a flicker of something that might have been regret, a hesitation that made my heart ache. But then, just as quickly, he steeled himself, his expression hardening into something cold, something unyielding.

"You won't understand," he said, his voice barely a whisper, but laced with a finality that cut deep. "Even if I told you, even if I laid out every terrible thing I've done, it wouldn't change anything. You'd only hate me."

"I'm not afraid of you," I replied, my voice steady, though my heart was pounding so hard I was sure he could hear it. "I'm not afraid of what you've done. I just want to know who you are. The real you."

He looked at me then, a long, searching gaze that felt like it peeled back every layer, every carefully constructed defense I'd put up. And for a split second, I thought he might relent, might finally let me in. But instead, he turned away, retreating into the shadows that clung to him like armor.

"Stay out of it," he said, his voice colder than I'd ever heard it. "This is a road you don't want to go down. Trust me."

With that, he was gone, disappearing into the darkness beyond the doorway, leaving me alone with the photograph and the suffocating weight of his secrets. I stood there, frozen, my mind racing, questions tumbling over themselves as I struggled to make sense of it all. But one thing was clear—I couldn't leave it alone. Not now. Not after seeing that glimpse of a past he'd kept buried, of a woman he'd once loved.

Without thinking, I picked up the photograph, tucked it carefully into my pocket, and followed him into the shadows, a fierce determination burning in my chest. Whatever he was hiding, whatever he was so afraid to reveal, I was going to find out.

Chapter 10: Secrets in the Dark

His fingers brushed mine as we crouched by a hidden door, cloaked by the shadows of a rundown tavern. I felt the charge snap through me, and I forced myself to focus on the task at hand. "It's locked," he whispered, his voice just a hair's breadth from my ear. I could feel his breath, warm against the chill that settled over us, mingling with the scent of cedar and earth that clung to him. In the low light, his profile was sharp, stoic, but his eyes held that familiar glint—mischief mixed with something darker, something he'd let slip just enough to keep me guessing.

"Let me guess," I murmured, fishing out the thin metal pick from my boot. "You have a hidden talent for breaking and entering?"

He tilted his head, a smirk ghosting his lips as he shrugged. "A man has to be versatile."

"Oh, is that what they're calling it now?" I muttered under my breath, focusing on the lock. A couple of twists, a soft click, and the door eased open, spilling us into a dim corridor lined with ancient tapestries. I was just about to step forward when he grabbed my wrist, pulling me back with a force that stole my breath.

"Look," he said, nodding toward the floor. Shadows from the dying sconces flickered over thin tripwires stretched across the hall, almost invisible unless you knew where to look. His grip lingered, his thumb tracing a light pattern on my pulse before he let go, and I hated how much I missed the contact as soon as it was gone.

I sighed, more to myself than to him. "This isn't exactly helping my trust issues, you know."

He gave a low chuckle, the sound surprisingly soft and real, as if it had escaped before he could stop it. "Oh, if this is what it takes to get under your guard, I must be slipping."

Rolling my eyes, I stepped carefully over the wire, navigating the traps laid like some twisted art gallery of paranoia. Each step was a calculated risk, a decision that could tip the scales from safety to disaster in the blink of an eye. As we edged farther into the maze, silence enveloped us, thick and weighted, and I could feel my heartbeat syncing to the ominous rhythm of our steps.

Finally, the corridor opened into a vast, vaulted chamber, the ceiling arched and painted with intricate designs that were half-eroded from years of neglect. At the center stood a massive pedestal draped in rich, dark velvet, and on top lay the relic—the object of every nightmare I'd had for the past month, glowing faintly as if taunting us to dare take it.

His gaze locked onto mine. "Are you ready for this?"

I swallowed hard, my throat suddenly dry. I could see the determination in his eyes, but also that flicker of doubt he tried to bury. "If you're looking for a reassuring pep talk, you've come to the wrong person."

"No, I think I came to exactly the right one," he replied, his tone edged with something raw and unguarded that took me off-balance.

Before I could respond, the sound of footsteps echoed from the corridor behind us. The hairs on the back of my neck stood up, a sharp jolt of adrenaline spiking through me. Without thinking, I grabbed his arm and pulled him toward a concealed alcove at the edge of the chamber. We flattened ourselves against the cold stone, barely breathing as the footsteps grew louder. Whoever it was, they weren't trying to be quiet. They wanted us to hear them, to feel the dread creeping in like the slow, icy bite of winter.

He leaned close, his voice a low whisper that sent a shiver down my spine. "Do you trust me?"

I wanted to scoff, to throw out a sarcastic retort, but something in his gaze, steady and unflinching, made me pause. "No," I admitted quietly. "But I trust myself when I'm with you, and that's enough."

He didn't reply, but his hand found mine, gripping it with a silent promise as the footsteps stopped just beyond our hiding place.

We held still, the tension between us stretched taut as a bowstring, waiting for that inevitable release. When the figure turned the corner, they lingered, scanning the room, their face obscured by a dark hood.

Seconds stretched into what felt like hours, my muscles screaming from the stillness, but I didn't dare move. My mind ran through a dozen escape scenarios, each more implausible than the last, and as I glanced sideways at him, I saw his jaw clenched, his eyes narrowed in concentration. Whoever this was, they weren't just a guard or some common thug; they were hunting, and their quarry was us.

The figure finally moved on, their footsteps receding back down the hall, leaving us in the thick silence of the empty chamber. I released a shaky breath, my hand still clasped in his, though neither of us acknowledged it.

"Well, that was fun," I muttered, and he shot me a dry look, one eyebrow raised.

"Your definition of fun is a little questionable."

I smirked, though the adrenaline was still singing through my veins, making it hard to feel anything but hyper-aware of his presence beside me. "Says the guy who thought breaking into a cursed chamber was a good idea."

"Touché." He loosened his grip but didn't let go entirely. "Shall we?"

The relic lay just a few paces away, almost innocuous in its simplicity. But as we moved toward it, I felt an oppressive weight settle over me, as if the very air thickened with each step. My pulse hammered as I reached out, fingers brushing the smooth surface of the object, cool and strange under my touch. For a brief, electric moment, it felt as though the world shifted, tilting us into some unseen realm.

Then his voice broke the spell. "If you're going to make a dramatic speech, now's the time."

I shot him a glare, half-amused despite myself. "If I die, I'm haunting you."

"Duly noted," he replied, the corners of his mouth twitching in that infuriating, roguish smile. "Though I imagine you'd make an insufferable ghost."

"Only for you," I retorted, feeling the tension dissolve just slightly, the laughter easing its grip on the fear that had been clawing at me. Whatever came next, we would face it, and even if trust was a distant fantasy, for now, we were bound by something deeper.

We moved through the streets under the cover of darkness, keeping our heads low and our steps light. The city, once familiar and mundane, had taken on a sinister, almost mystical quality under the weight of the secrets we carried. Every corner seemed to hide a potential trap, every shadow a lurking adversary. I could feel him beside me, his movements quick and sure, yet there was a tension in his jaw that I'd come to recognize as barely concealed worry. It was strange, really—to know him well enough to spot the small tells, to see beyond the practiced smirk and self-assured arrogance that had initially defined him in my mind.

We slipped into a narrow alley that twisted and turned, leading us farther from the main streets. The silence settled heavily around us, broken only by the occasional drip of water from an overhead pipe or the distant call of a stray cat. It was here, in these quiet spaces between the noise of the city, that I felt both the freedom and weight of my choices pressing down on me, nudging me toward a truth I wasn't ready to face.

At the end of the alley, he stopped suddenly, one hand raised to signal silence. I froze, instinctively holding my breath as he pressed himself against the wall, peering around the corner with practiced ease. After a moment, he beckoned me forward, his face shadowed and unreadable. We pressed ourselves against the cold brick, and he leaned in, his lips close enough to my ear that I could feel the faint warmth of his breath.

"There's someone following us," he whispered, his voice barely audible.

I felt a chill run down my spine, but I forced myself to stay calm, to keep my face as impassive as his. "How many?"

"Just one," he replied, a hint of satisfaction curling at the edges of his words. "Sloppy, too. They think they're invisible, but they're just loud enough to give themselves away." He paused, casting a glance over his shoulder, his gaze meeting mine with a flicker of something I couldn't quite name. "You up for a little game of cat and mouse?"

The challenge in his tone was unmistakable, and despite the dread coiling in my stomach, I found myself nodding, a faint smile tugging at my lips. "Let's see if they can keep up."

With a sudden burst of energy, we darted out from the alley, slipping into the crowd of the bustling night market just as the clock tower struck eleven. The market was a swirl of color and sound, vendors calling out their wares, the smell of exotic spices and freshly baked bread mingling in the air. I felt the prickle of our pursuer's gaze, the shadow lurking just on the edge of my vision, and I let the thrill of the chase ignite something reckless in me.

I grabbed his hand, pulling him through the throng, weaving between stalls and slipping into narrow passageways, each turn calculated to lose our tail. For a moment, it felt like we were just two ordinary people, running through the city for the sheer joy of it. But the weight of the relic in my pocket and the silent promise we'd made to each other reminded me that this was no ordinary chase.

Finally, we ducked into a quiet courtyard tucked away from the noise of the market, hidden by ivy-covered walls and the soft glow of lanterns. The faint sound of footsteps faded, and I exhaled, leaning against the cool stone wall as I tried to catch my breath. He stood across from me, his face flushed, a wild glint in his eyes that mirrored my own. We'd lost them, at least for now, and the rush of victory hummed between us like an unspoken promise.

"Well," I said, letting out a soft laugh as I brushed a stray lock of hair from my face. "If you were looking for excitement, I think we've found it."

His gaze softened, and for a moment, the mask slipped, revealing something raw and unguarded. "With you, excitement seems to follow," he replied, his voice low and full of something I didn't dare name. He took a step closer, the space between us shrinking, the air thick with the tension that had been simmering between us since this all began. I felt my heart stutter, the words caught in my throat as I met his gaze, unsure if I wanted to break the silence or let it stretch, letting the weight of everything unsaid hang between us.

But then, as if the universe couldn't bear to let us have even one moment of peace, the sharp crack of a twig snapped through the stillness, breaking the spell. Instinct kicked in, and we both moved, pressing ourselves against the wall as we scanned the courtyard, our senses on high alert. There, just beyond the archway, a figure emerged, cloaked in shadow, their face obscured.

He stepped in front of me, his posture tense, protective in a way that both comforted and unnerved me. Whoever this was, they hadn't just stumbled upon us by chance; they were here for a reason, and that reason was most likely resting in my pocket.

The figure's voice was low, almost a hiss. "You've taken something that doesn't belong to you."

I felt the weight of the relic shift, as if it, too, sensed the danger in the air. My hand tightened around the cool metal, the jagged edges digging into my palm, grounding me in the reality of the situation.

He shifted, positioning himself just enough to shield me from the stranger's gaze, his tone cold and cutting. "If you think you can just waltz in and take it, you're sorely mistaken."

The figure chuckled, the sound chilling in its quiet confidence. "Oh, I don't intend to take anything. I simply wanted to remind you both that the relic has its price, and no one escapes it."

With that, the stranger turned and disappeared into the shadows, leaving us standing there, the weight of his words pressing down like a dark cloud. I felt a shiver run through me, the reality of what we'd done settling like a stone in my chest.

He looked at me, his face unreadable, but I could see the flicker of fear in his eyes, a reflection of my own. "We've set something in motion," he murmured, almost to himself, as if saying it aloud would make it real.

For the first time, I felt the weight of doubt press down on me, creeping into the corners of my mind. But as I looked at him, standing there with a fierce determination in his eyes, I knew that whatever happened, I couldn't turn back now. We were bound together, by fate or by choice, and the path we'd started down would demand everything we had.

I swallowed, forcing a steady breath as I met his gaze, letting my own resolve harden. "Then let's make sure we're ready for whatever comes next."

We left the quiet courtyard with the stranger's words still echoing in my mind, each step taking us deeper into a web I wasn't sure we could escape. The city, sprawling and restless around us, felt like a living thing, holding secrets in its crooked streets and crumbling buildings, each whisper of the wind a reminder of the risks we'd taken. There was no more room for second-guessing. But there was also no room for mistakes. As we crossed the stone bridge that arched over the river, he walked beside me in silence, his shoulders tense, his gaze fixed ahead. I wanted to ask what he was thinking but sensed the answer was buried beneath layers I might never uncover.

A chill wind lifted off the water, cutting through my coat, and I tucked my hands into my pockets, my fingers brushing against the relic's cold, hard surface. Its weight was a constant reminder of the choices we'd made. Choices that, for better or worse, had bound us together in ways neither of us could fully understand. And there was something terrifyingly comforting in that bond, in knowing he was there beside me, equally trapped yet equally resolute.

"So," I said after a while, my voice breaking the silence between us. "Where do we go from here?"

He glanced at me, the faintest hint of a smile playing on his lips, though it didn't reach his eyes. "You say that like we have a choice."

"Humor me," I replied, arching a brow. "Pretend, just for a moment, that we're not running headfirst into disaster."

He sighed, his gaze softening as he looked out over the river, its dark surface reflecting the city lights in shimmering waves. "If I could choose..." he began, his voice quiet, almost lost to the wind. But then he stopped, his expression shifting as if he'd just remembered something, or perhaps someone, he'd tried hard to forget. "Never mind. Choices aren't exactly in our favor right now."

I nodded, understanding more than I let on. Whatever ghosts he carried, they weighed on him as heavily as the relic weighed on me, and I wasn't about to ask him to share them. Not yet, anyway. But I couldn't shake the feeling that the closer we got to unraveling this mystery, the more those secrets would bleed through, surfacing in ways neither of us could control.

We turned down a narrow street lined with old lanterns that cast long, flickering shadows over the cobblestones. The air felt thick, almost oppressive, and I sensed we were close to something—whether it was the truth or another trap, I couldn't say. Just then, he stopped, his hand reaching out to grab my arm, his eyes narrowed in the direction of a weathered building with darkened windows and a faded sign that hung crookedly above the door.

"There," he whispered, his gaze intent. "That's where the trail leads."

I looked at him skeptically, my heart pounding in a strange rhythm. "How do you know?"

He tilted his head, his expression unreadable. "Call it intuition. Or maybe it's the fact that every instinct I have is screaming at me to stay as far away from that place as possible."

I rolled my eyes, though his words sent a shiver down my spine. "Well, you do have an impressive track record of ignoring your instincts."

He shot me a glare, but there was a flicker of amusement in his eyes, as if he couldn't help himself. "Maybe I just have a thing for bad ideas."

"Clearly," I muttered, stepping past him toward the door, half expecting him to grab my arm again, to tell me to turn back. But he didn't stop me, just followed close behind, his presence a steady, grounding force in the unsettling quiet that had settled over the street.

Inside, the air was stale, thick with the scent of mildew and dust, as if no one had entered in years. The only light came from a single window where the moon cast a pale glow across the room, illuminating the broken furniture scattered like relics of a past no one wanted to remember. I took a tentative step forward, my eyes adjusting to the dim light, and I felt him move close beside me, his gaze scanning the room with the same careful intensity that had kept us alive thus far.

And then I saw it—a faint glint on the far wall, half-hidden behind a tattered curtain. I approached slowly, the floor creaking beneath my feet, and reached out to pull the curtain aside, revealing a small, intricately carved box, its surface covered in symbols that matched those on the relic. I glanced back at him, my heart hammering as I took in the significance of what we'd found.

"Looks like we're not the only ones with secrets," I murmured, running a finger along the edge of the box, feeling the cold bite of the metal.

He moved closer, his hand reaching out to touch the box as well, and for a brief, electrifying moment, our fingers brushed. I felt a jolt run through me, but I forced myself to focus, to ignore the thrill that his touch sparked. This wasn't the time to get distracted—not when we were so close to answers.

"What do you think it holds?" he asked, his voice barely above a whisper.

I swallowed, my gaze locked on the box. "Only one way to find out."

But before I could open it, a sudden noise broke the silence—a scraping sound from somewhere behind us, like metal against stone. We both turned, every nerve on high alert, and I felt the relic grow heavy in my pocket, as if it, too, sensed the danger closing in around us.

He moved in front of me, his body tense, his hand reaching for the knife he kept tucked at his side. The shadows shifted, and I could just make out the outline of a figure standing in the doorway, their face obscured but their presence unmistakable.

"Well, well," the stranger drawled, his voice a low rasp that sent a chill through me. "I knew you two would come sniffing around eventually. You've made quite the mess, haven't you?"

I swallowed, the weight of his words pressing down like a vice. But I forced myself to meet his gaze, refusing to let him see the fear I knew was written across my face. "Who are you?" I demanded, my voice steadier than I felt.

The stranger chuckled, a dark, humorless sound that grated against my nerves. "Oh, I'm just someone with a vested interest in keeping that little trinket out of the wrong hands. And, believe me, yours are just about as wrong as they come."

He stepped closer, his figure becoming clearer in the moonlight, and I felt a shock of recognition that I couldn't quite place. I glanced at him, my mind racing, trying to piece together the fragments of memory, of half-heard whispers and rumors, until suddenly it hit me, the realization so sharp it stole my breath.

"No," I whispered, taking a step back, my heart pounding as the truth settled over me. "It can't be."

The stranger's smile was slow, deliberate, as he took another step forward, his eyes glittering with dark amusement. "Oh, but it is," he murmured, his voice laced with a satisfaction that made my blood run cold. "And now, my dear, it's time you learned exactly what happens when you meddle in things you don't understand."

Chapter 11: The Betrayal

The candlelight flickered between us, casting his face into shadowed relief. The way his jaw clenched, the slight pull of his brows — I'd seen that look before, in every guarded word and half-smile he'd given me since we met. I'd spent months watching him, learning him. How could I have been so blind?

"You knew this whole time," I whispered, my voice barely scraping the space between us, heavy with betrayal.

He shifted, pressing his fingers against the edge of the table as if to ground himself. "I wanted to tell you," he said, each word measured, as if he feared they might explode in his mouth. "But I couldn't."

"That's a lie," I shot back. My hand was trembling. I'd been around betrayal long enough to know when someone was weaving it into a sweetly poisoned narrative. "You had every opportunity. You let me trust you. You let me..." I bit back the words, my pride stinging. He didn't deserve to know how deeply I'd felt.

His eyes caught mine, an infuriating shade of sorrow etched into their depths. "I had my reasons."

"Don't you dare give me that." The anger roared to life again, hotter this time. "Reasons? What, like how you're secretly working for another power? Or that every word out of your mouth since we met has been a well-crafted lie? I trusted you." The weight of my own admission sank like a stone in my gut. Admitting that felt like handing him a weapon.

He exhaled sharply, dragging his hand through his hair, making it messier than it already was. It was unfair, how he could stand there looking so contrite, like the hero who just made a mistake. This wasn't a mistake. This was deliberate.

"I'm not going to make excuses," he said finally, voice rough, as if he'd been rehearsing this in his head and knew it would never come out right. "But I swear to you, not all of it was a lie."

"Funny," I said, letting a bitter laugh slip out, "because I'm struggling to find the parts that weren't."

He took a step toward me, eyes locked onto mine, the desperation so stark in his face I could almost touch it. "You have to believe me—"

"Believe you?" My voice was a venomous whisper. "Don't ask that of me now."

I turned on my heel, too angry to look at him any longer. It was either that or let my fist meet his jaw — and I wasn't ready to let him see just how much power he had to hurt me. I could feel the weight of his gaze on my back, his tension radiating toward me like a bitter gust. He wanted me to stay, to listen to him stumble over apologies I didn't want to hear.

Outside, the night air was crisp and biting, the stars glaring down on me as if they, too, knew the secrets that had unraveled in that room. I could barely stand the sight of them, the way they seemed so mocking in their eternal calmness. Every breath I took felt too big, too jagged, as if my lungs were trying to force the fury out.

I'd always trusted my instincts, and for good reason. They'd kept me alive more times than I could count, steering me through murky alliances and dangerous deals. But this? This wasn't just a breach of trust — it was a blade to the gut, twisting with every minute detail of our conversations that now rang hollow in my memory.

Footsteps crunched behind me, deliberate, cautious. I didn't need to look back to know it was him. He stopped a few paces away, his silence a question I refused to answer.

"What do you want?" I asked finally, the words icy enough to cut through the warmth of his gaze, which I could feel prickling at the back of my head. The silence stretched, and I could almost imagine him retreating. Almost. But he stayed there, the weight of his presence pressing down on my shoulders.

"I want to make it right," he said quietly, his tone almost pleading. "I owe you that much."

The laugh that escaped me was bitter, hollow. "Make it right? There's no making it right. You can't just sweep this under the rug and expect me to forget." I paused, struggling to keep my voice steady. "You were my friend. You were supposed to be on my side."

"I was," he said, and his voice was raw enough that for a split second, I almost believed him. Almost.

"No," I said, my words flat, final. "You weren't. Not when it mattered." I could feel the ache under my skin, that hollow space where trust had once nestled comfortably, now ripped open, raw and unhealed. And he was the one who'd ripped it out.

He flinched as if I'd struck him. Good, I thought, savoring the rare moment of seeing him falter. Maybe now he'd understand the depth of what he'd taken from me. I didn't want apologies. I didn't want excuses. I wanted to see him pay for it, to carry the weight of it like I now did.

His shoulders dropped, and he looked at me, his face a mask of resignation. "I know you'll never forgive me. I don't deserve it."

A pang of something sharp twisted in my chest. Anger? Regret? I wasn't sure anymore. I'd spent so long guarding my heart, building my walls higher and higher until he came along and somehow slipped through them. I'd let him in. And now, he stood there, the reason for every ruined trust I'd ever had.

"You're right about that." My voice was barely a whisper, but it carried more weight than I'd ever thought possible. "You don't."

He nodded, a faint, sad smile curling at the corner of his mouth. And then, as if some unseen thread snapped, he turned and walked away. The darkness swallowed him up, leaving me standing there, staring into the emptiness where he'd been.

My fists clenched, nails digging into my palms as I forced myself to stand there, unmoving, until he was well and truly gone. This wasn't just a betrayal. This was a scar I'd carry for a lifetime, and I'd be damned if I'd let anyone else see how deep it cut.

The night felt colder than before, an icy tension filling the air, but there was no wind, no rustling leaves — just silence, the kind that settles after something irrevocable has shattered. I stood there, forcing my feet to stay grounded, while my mind threatened to spiral into the hundred things I should have noticed. But self-recrimination wasn't helping. Not now, not with the weight of his betrayal pressing against my ribs like a dull ache I couldn't rub away.

I should have left him in the darkness, turned my back and never looked again. But something about his quiet, steady retreat tugged at the corners of my stubborn heart. Staring at his disappearing form felt too final, too empty. Against all rational sense, I called out, each word tinged with an edge I couldn't soften if I tried.

"So, is that it?" I said, the bitterness in my voice carrying farther than I expected in the stillness. "You're just going to walk away, leaving me to pick up the pieces of whatever this was?"

He froze, his silhouette framed by the faintest glimmer of starlight. For a long second, he just stood there, shoulders rising and falling with a heavy sigh, before he turned, his face shadowed yet somehow so unbearably familiar. I hated that familiarity, the intimacy I'd unwittingly memorized: the curve of his jaw, the hint of regret he tried to hide behind a stoic gaze.

"You think I want to leave things like this?" he replied, voice quiet, yet laced with enough frustration to cut through the space between us. "Believe me, this isn't exactly how I pictured it, either."

I scoffed, crossing my arms tight against my chest. "No, I imagine you pictured me blissfully ignorant, still trusting you, blindly following every charming word you threw my way."

His eyes flashed, a flicker of anger sparking beneath the surface. "That's not fair."

"Oh, but lying to me is fair?"

"That's not what I meant," he said, his voice taut, barely reined in. "I didn't... this wasn't supposed to happen." He clenched his fists, his whole frame tight with a barely concealed frustration that almost mirrored my own. "It was supposed to be simple. In, out, no one gets hurt."

"'No one gets hurt'? Are you hearing yourself?" My laugh was sharp and humorless. "How convenient for you. Go in, play the part, take what you need, leave me in the dark. And you thought what, I'd just never find out?"

He looked away, his gaze lost somewhere in the night. The silence stretched long enough for regret to settle in his expression, deepening the shadows under his eyes. "I thought... I thought I could make it right before you ever had to know."

The words hung there, raw and exposed, and I realized I was staring, unable to look away from the way his face had softened, as if the facade he'd been holding onto was finally crumbling. And there it was, the glimmer of sincerity, of something I wanted to believe despite myself. But I'd learned better than to trust glimmers.

"Make it right?" I repeated, each word deliberate. "You mean, make it easy for yourself. Keep me just enough in the dark so I'd never question, never wonder, while you were off following someone else's orders."

He didn't deny it, and somehow, that was worse. I could feel the anger ebbing, replaced by something cold and hollow. I wanted him to argue, to fight back, to give me a reason to hold onto my fury. But he just stood there, hands clenched at his sides, his gaze unreadable, and I hated him all the more for it.

"I don't expect you to understand," he said finally, the words low, barely audible. "I never wanted you to get pulled into this."

"Oh, well, that makes it all better," I replied, my voice dripping with sarcasm. "As long as your intentions were noble."

The regret in his eyes deepened, but he didn't answer. I wanted him to answer. I wanted him to explain himself, to give me something, anything, that could make this make sense. But he just stood there, silent, and somehow that made it worse.

"Well, congratulations," I said, my voice trembling despite my best efforts. "You got what you wanted. I'm out. You're free to do whatever it is you came here to do without worrying about me getting in your way."

He took a step forward, his expression shifting into something like panic. "That's not what I wanted."

I held up a hand, stopping him in his tracks. "Don't. Just... don't." I swallowed, forcing down the lump in my throat. "You don't get to stand there and pretend this wasn't your choice. You don't get to act like you didn't know exactly what you were doing."

The words echoed between us, sharp and unyielding, and for the first time, I saw something break in his expression, a flash of something I couldn't quite identify. But it was too little, too late. Whatever sympathy I might have had for him was buried beneath layers of anger and hurt, and I wasn't about to let him see it.

He opened his mouth as if to say something, but then he stopped, his gaze falling to the ground. And then, just as quickly, he turned and walked away, his figure disappearing into the darkness. I stood there, watching until he was nothing more than a faint shadow against the horizon, until even that had faded into the night.

The silence settled around me, thick and suffocating, and I could feel the weight of it pressing down on my chest. For a moment, I felt like I couldn't breathe, the emptiness where he had been leaving a hollow ache that I didn't know how to fill.

I wanted to scream, to shout, to rail against the unfairness of it all. But instead, I just stood there, the cold night air wrapping around me like a shroud, and tried to remind myself that I was better off this way. I was stronger, smarter, more resilient. I didn't need him.

But even as I repeated the words in my mind, trying to convince myself that they were true, I could feel a part of me crumbling, breaking apart under the weight of everything I'd lost.

And as I turned and walked away, the ache in my chest only grew, a reminder of the price I'd paid for trusting him, and the scars I would carry long after he was gone.

By morning, the ache had hardened into something darker, like a stone lodged beneath my ribs. I'd spent half the night lying awake, every word he'd said gnawing away at the edges of my anger. I kept replaying the look in his eyes, that flicker of something resembling guilt — or was it regret? I wasn't sure anymore. The world felt like a maze I'd been dropped into blindfolded, left to stumble over the truth with only fragments of trust to light the way.

I pushed open the heavy door of the inn's common room, the chill from the night still lingering in the air. The scent of strong coffee and yesterday's burnt stew hit me as I entered, and I kept my gaze down, hoping to avoid any early risers. I wasn't in the mood for questions, for well-meaning smiles. I wanted to sit alone, to bury myself in a mug of something hot and bitter, to shake off the feeling that every eye in the room was a mirror, showing me all the ways I'd been a fool.

I slid into the farthest corner of the room, half-hidden by the shadows, and waved down the innkeeper, an older woman with a face like a crumpled map and a walk that said she'd seen it all. She set down a cup of coffee with a knowing look, and for once, I was grateful for the silence between us. Maybe she understood; maybe she didn't care. Either way, she left me in peace, and I sipped the dark brew, letting it scald my throat. The bitterness felt good, anchoring.

I was halfway through the mug, eyes lost somewhere in the patterns of the worn wooden table, when I felt it — a shift in the air, like the quiet anticipation before a storm. I glanced up, half-expecting him to be there, his shadow cutting across the morning light. But it wasn't him. It was a stranger, tall and wiry, with the look of someone who knew exactly where he was going and didn't care who got in his way.

His gaze settled on me, sharp and assessing, and he moved through the room with a confidence that put me on edge. When he reached my table, he didn't ask; he simply took the seat across from me, folding his hands together as if we were old acquaintances.

"Morning," he said, his voice a deep rumble that carried more authority than a shout ever could.

I raised an eyebrow, masking my surprise with a cool indifference I barely felt. "Do I know you?"

"Not yet." He smiled, but it didn't reach his eyes. They were cold, calculating, the kind that saw right through people. "But I've heard a lot about you."

"Is that so?" I leaned back, crossing my arms. "Well, you'll have to forgive me if I don't return the sentiment."

The smile widened, as if my response was exactly what he'd expected. "I hear you're missing something." He let the words hang in the air, a lure dangled in front of me, and every instinct screamed to ignore him, to brush him off and finish my coffee in peace. But the hook was set.

"And what exactly do you think I'm missing?" I asked, my tone sharper than I'd intended.

"A relic," he said, the single word falling like a stone into still water. "One that's... more powerful than you might realize."

I forced myself to keep my expression blank, even as my mind spun. "Interesting theory," I said lightly, glancing at the door as if I had somewhere better to be. "But I think you're mistaken. I'm not missing anything."

He chuckled, a dry, humorless sound that set my nerves on edge. "Oh, I think you are. And I think you'll find that your friend — or should I say, former friend — hasn't told you the full story."

The room seemed to close in around me, the walls narrowing until it was just the two of us, locked in a silent battle of wills. I kept my gaze steady, refusing to give him the satisfaction of a reaction, but my pulse thrummed with a new, uneasy rhythm. If he knew about the relic, if he knew about the lie...

"What do you want?" I asked, keeping my voice cool and steady, even as the question clawed at my insides.

"What I want is simple." He leaned forward, his eyes glittering with a strange intensity. "I want you to deliver a message to your friend. Tell him he has one chance to make things right, or he won't be the only one paying the price."

I kept my face impassive, every muscle taut as a bowstring. "And what makes you think I'll do anything for you?"

His smile vanished, and in that moment, I felt the weight of his threat settle over me like a shroud. "Because you want the truth as much as I do. And right now, I'm your only chance of getting it."

He stood, pushing the chair back with a scrape that cut through the tense silence. "I'll be around," he said, his tone casual, as if we were merely acquaintances discussing the weather. "When you're ready to know everything, you'll know where to find me."

And with that, he walked away, leaving me sitting there, the faint taste of coffee bitter in my mouth. I watched him go, the chill settling deeper into my bones, as if some unseen door had just opened, revealing a path I hadn't known existed.

I finished my coffee, forcing each sip down as I tried to gather my thoughts. This stranger was trouble; every instinct screamed it. But he'd planted a seed of doubt that was already taking root, twisting through the tangled web of my feelings and muddying everything I thought I knew.

As I rose from the table, I felt a strange heaviness, a quiet dread gnawing at the edge of my resolve. I wasn't ready to face him, to let him drag me back into the lies and half-truths I'd barely begun to escape. But the weight of his betrayal was no longer mine alone; it was a burden he would have to share, whether he wanted to or not.

The stranger's words echoed in my mind as I stepped outside, the daylight too bright, too sharp against the night's lingering shadows. I felt as if I'd stepped into a world where nothing was as it seemed, where alliances were as thin as mist and trust was a currency that held no value.

I'd make him tell me the truth. And if he wouldn't — well, there were other ways to get what I wanted. I'd learned enough from him to know that loyalty was just another mask, one that could be discarded as easily as a whispered promise.

I took a deep breath, steadying myself, and set off down the road, a path that led not just to answers but to the one place I swore I'd never go again. Each step carried the weight of all the betrayals that had led me here, and somewhere in the back of my mind, a dark certainty took root.

I wasn't just seeking the truth. I was going to make sure he paid for every lie, every secret, every shattered trust.

And he wouldn't see it coming.

Chapter 12: The Edge of Destruction

The night was cold and sharp as glass, each breath carving an edge into my lungs, reminding me why I shouldn't have come out here alone. I had no business wandering through the alleys on this side of town, especially not in the dead of night, but I had to make a point. Storming off dramatically had seemed like a fantastic idea at the time, leaving him there with that maddeningly calm expression that somehow still managed to be more infuriating than any actual retort.

Now, though, with shadows pooling under my feet and not a single soul in sight, the idea felt less than brilliant. I gritted my teeth, trying to shake off the gnawing sense that something was watching. My pride was a solid enough shield, but pride doesn't help when things go bump in the night—and this night felt bristling with those unseens that everyone pretends not to notice. I wasn't scared, exactly; fear would imply some respect for whatever waited in the dark. No, I was stubborn, and that kept me walking, step by resentful step, further into the tangled maze of backstreets I barely knew.

The alley narrowed until the walls pressed in, damp and stinking like mold that had grown arrogant in its old age. I kept my gaze forward, ignoring the rustles that prickled along the periphery. Out here, it wasn't unheard of for someone to vanish, swallowed up by the city's underbelly and never seen again, but I had no plans of becoming one of those whispered-about mysteries. No, I'd survive this if only out of sheer spite.

Then came the footsteps.

Slow and methodical, they echoed off the walls, closing in behind me in a rhythm that sent my heart into double time. The back of my neck prickled, every instinct screaming at me to move, to run. But I wasn't about to give whoever it was that satisfaction.

Swallowing the tremor that ran through me, I turned, fists clenched and defiance burning hotter than any hint of fear.

Three figures, shadowed and masked, loomed at the other end of the alley, blocking my exit. Another two flanked my sides, emerging from the murky shadows as if they'd been born there. I swallowed hard. I was completely surrounded, and from the measured way they advanced, these weren't random thugs. No, they knew exactly who I was, or at least who they thought I was, and the confidence in their strides told me they expected this to be an easy job.

"I don't suppose we could skip the whole intimidation routine and just get to it?" I quipped, forcing my voice steady. Maybe if I kept my nerve, they'd hesitate long enough for me to figure out a way out of this.

The leader of the group—a tall figure with eyes that gleamed coldly from behind the mask—stepped forward, his silence cutting sharper than any retort could. Something about him struck me as unsettlingly familiar, but I didn't have time to linger on that detail. He raised a hand, and as if choreographed, the rest of his companions closed in.

I dropped low, darting toward a narrow gap between two of them. My elbow caught one in the ribs, and I heard the satisfying oof of air leaving his lungs, but it wasn't enough. Before I could gain any ground, one of the others yanked me back by my collar, tossing me to the ground with a force that left my head spinning. I tried to scramble to my feet, but a boot pinned me down, pressing against my back as another hand yanked my head up, forcing me to look at the ring of masks that now surrounded me.

And then, just as the fear was sinking claws deep into my bones, there he was. His silhouette against the dim streetlight was a sight I hadn't expected—nor entirely welcomed in that moment, if I were being honest. The fact that he was here, that he'd followed me, was equal parts infuriating and, I had to admit, a little bit of a relief.

"Really? Now?" I managed through gritted teeth, throwing him a glare that I hoped communicated just how annoyed I was. But he didn't respond, his gaze locked on the figures surrounding me, calculating.

Without a word, he launched himself forward, moving with the practiced efficiency of someone who had seen his fair share of alleyway ambushes. In seconds, he'd drawn their attention, creating the distraction I needed to scramble to my feet. Despite myself, I found myself following his lead, moving in sync as if we'd been fighting together all our lives.

The masked figures were relentless, but we held our ground, striking out with everything we had. My knuckles stung, and my breath came in short gasps, but I matched him blow for blow, a strange exhilaration sparking between us as we fought side by side. It was like a dance, one step forward, one step back, weaving through fists and dodging kicks. Each time I stumbled, he was there, a steadying hand or a quick glance to ensure I was still standing.

Finally, the last of our attackers staggered back, clutching his side before disappearing into the shadows. As silence fell, broken only by our ragged breathing, I found myself facing him, the weight of unspoken words hanging between us.

"I didn't ask for your help," I muttered, brushing dirt off my scraped hands, trying to ignore the flicker of gratitude tugging at the edges of my anger.

He raised an eyebrow, crossing his arms in that infuriating way of his. "Clearly. Or you would've gone about this whole stunt a bit smarter."

"Oh, I'm sorry, were you planning on giving me a lesson in subtlety now?" I shot back, hands on my hips, despite the throbbing ache in my ribs. "Funny, coming from someone who makes an entrance like a wrecking ball."

A smirk played at the corner of his lips, and I had to fight the urge to knock it off. He tilted his head, his voice low and maddeningly calm. "You can be as mad as you want. Doesn't change the fact that you needed me."

His words, infuriating as they were, hung between us, and for a brief moment, neither of us spoke. It was as if the fight had stripped away all the barriers we'd built up between us, leaving nothing but the truth hanging in the cold night air. I opened my mouth to respond, to say something that would wipe that smug look off his face, but the words didn't come.

Instead, I found myself staring at him, heart pounding as the realization settled in.

The silence that stretched between us was as tense as it was unexpected, leaving me stranded in a moment I wasn't entirely sure how to navigate. A streetlamp flickered overhead, casting harsh light on his face, on the scrape across his cheek and the fresh bruise darkening along his jaw. Somehow, seeing him like that—still steady, still maddeningly unshaken—brought a strange calm to my own frantic pulse.

"You look terrible," I said, gesturing at his jawline with an unsteady hand. "Does it hurt? Or is that just how your face looks normally?"

The corner of his mouth quirked up, and that familiar, irritating smirk surfaced. "Pretty rich coming from someone with half an alley's worth of grime on her."

I pressed a hand to my forehead, wincing as I touched what felt like the beginning of a bruise. "Okay, fair. But if you want to get particular, I wouldn't be filthy if you'd just let me handle this myself."

"Handle it?" His voice was as cool and steady as ever, but I caught the faintest edge of disbelief cutting through. "In case you forgot, you were pinned to the ground by the time I showed up. I'm curious what your plan was from there."

My mouth opened in protest, but I shut it just as fast, heat rising to my cheeks. He wasn't wrong, as much as I hated to admit it. Still, the last thing I wanted to do was give him the satisfaction of saying so. I crossed my arms, trying to muster some semblance of dignity despite the ache in my side and the lingering adrenaline that still buzzed under my skin.

"Maybe my plan was to see if you'd finally show up in time," I said, tossing the words his way like I had any control over them.

There was a pause, his gaze sharpening as he took in my expression. "So, I'm a backup plan now?"

I shrugged, affecting an air of nonchalance that felt increasingly flimsy with each passing second. "If you want to think of it that way. Or you could just admit you showed up because you couldn't stand the thought of me getting out of this mess alone."

"Believe whatever you need to." He was close now, his tone softer than before, and I couldn't shake the feeling that he was studying me with a seriousness he usually kept hidden behind that calm façade. "But this? This was a risk you shouldn't have taken. You don't have to go it alone just to prove a point."

It was such an absurd statement, and yet, something in his words hit home. I swallowed, pushing away whatever strange flicker of vulnerability that tried to creep up on me.

"Oh, please," I shot back, looking away in an attempt to break the intensity of his gaze. "As if you wouldn't have done the same."

He didn't respond immediately, and when he finally spoke, his voice was low, edged with something I couldn't quite decipher. "Maybe I would have. But not when someone else was counting on me to make it back."

That single sentence hung between us, an unspoken reminder of the things we hadn't said, the barriers we'd carefully constructed over time. For a moment, we simply stood there, locked in a strange, fragile truce. Part of me wanted to challenge him again, to push back on whatever he thought he was implying. But another part of me, the part that was still rattled from the fight, wanted to cling to that fleeting connection we'd felt back there, when every punch and dodge had fallen in perfect rhythm between us.

The scrape of a shoe against pavement jolted me from my thoughts, and I glanced over my shoulder to find a straggler from the fight—a thin, wiry man, barely able to keep himself upright but determined enough to try. His hand reached for something in his coat, and without thinking, I stepped forward, adrenaline surging again. But before I could make another move, my companion lunged past me, swift and precise, disarming the man and pinning him against the wall with one swift motion.

"Not tonight," he muttered, the words soft yet carrying a weight that even I felt.

The man struggled briefly, but he was no match in his weakened state. With a resigned huff, he sagged against the wall, finally giving up. My companion released him, taking a step back, and I noticed a flash of pity in his gaze before he turned back to me. In another life, maybe this man would have had a chance. In this one, he was just another pawn in a twisted game neither of us fully understood.

"Still think you could've handled that yourself?" he asked, his tone a little lighter, though his gaze hadn't quite softened.

I crossed my arms, not entirely willing to admit defeat. "Maybe I would've had a better chance if you hadn't insisted on giving me the lecture."

"Right, because you're such a great listener."

I huffed, resisting the urge to roll my eyes. But instead of biting back, I found myself smiling, the tension in my chest loosening just a fraction. Maybe he was right; maybe I had been reckless. But right now, with him by my side, I felt a strange sense of comfort, one that I was almost tempted to trust.

"Fine," I conceded, the word barely more than a whisper, but he heard it, his gaze softening just enough to catch my attention. "Maybe... maybe you being here wasn't the worst thing."

For the first time since he'd appeared, his expression shifted, and something that almost looked like relief flickered in his eyes. He opened his mouth to respond, but before he could say anything, a sudden, sharp noise echoed from somewhere down the street. We both froze, instincts kicking back into high gear.

"That can't be good," he murmured, eyes narrowing as he scanned the shadows around us.

"I think I've had enough of dark alleys for one night," I said, already backing away, my pulse spiking again. But even as I tried to regain my composure, I couldn't shake the feeling that we were being drawn deeper into something neither of us fully understood.

"Agreed," he replied, moving to stand beside me, his hand brushing against mine just briefly before he pulled away, his focus shifting back to the growing shadows at the end of the alley.

I glanced at him, a question forming on my lips, but something in his expression stopped me. His jaw was set, his gaze steely, but beneath that, I caught a glimpse of something else—an uncertainty I hadn't seen before. It was as if he, too, was beginning to realize that this wasn't just a one-time fight, that maybe we were caught in something that went beyond either of our control.

In that instant, our bickering and rivalry felt distant, replaced by an unspoken understanding that we couldn't turn back now. We were both in this, for better or worse, drawn together by the strange, invisible threads that had bound our fates long before we'd even realized it. And no matter how much we might have wanted to fight it, some things were inevitable.

For the first time that night, I felt a twinge of something like hope—not because I thought we'd win, but because, for the first time in a long while, I knew I wasn't facing this alone.

His hand brushed mine, lingering for just a moment longer than necessary as we exchanged a look. It was a silent understanding, one I couldn't quite define but that made me want to reach for him, hold on for just a second longer than I dared. The night stretched thick and tense around us, the stillness pressing down as if holding its breath.

"Stay close," he said, his voice a whisper, almost swallowed by the alley's shadows.

I raised an eyebrow, trying to keep my tone light despite the way my pulse skittered. "Since when do you give the orders?"

He didn't answer, just threw me a glance that was equal parts exasperation and something else, something I couldn't quite put my finger on. Whatever it was, it softened his gaze, his usual steely edge tempered by something dangerously close to concern. It made my stomach flip, which, if I was being honest with myself, was almost more unsettling than anything else we'd faced that night.

We moved together, slipping through the narrow, winding alleyways with footsteps soft enough to be swallowed by the dark. I kept my senses alert, listening for the telltale shuffle of feet, the faint whispers that might give away anyone following us. The city around us had settled into an uneasy silence, the kind that felt like it was holding back, waiting for something—or someone—to make the first move.

"Do you know where we're going?" I asked after a while, more to break the silence than anything. The question came out sharper than I'd intended, and I saw him bristle, the slightest frown creasing his forehead.

"Trust me," he said, his voice calm but threaded with an edge I couldn't quite place.

"Funny," I muttered under my breath, "that's exactly what the last person to betray me said."

He let out a soft huff that might've been a laugh if it weren't so bitter. "I guess that makes two of us."

There it was again, that vulnerability slipping through his armor, quick as a spark and just as fleeting. I didn't press, even though I wanted to. I had a feeling that whatever he'd been through before we met had scarred him deeper than I realized. And as much as I hated to admit it, I could relate more than I liked.

The street opened up into a wider space, a long, deserted stretch of cobblestones that glistened under the pale light of the street lamps. For a moment, I relaxed, my gaze drifting up to the rooftops, where the moon hung low and watchful, a silent witness to our plight. The momentary calm was almost enough to make me forget why we were out here in the first place.

And then I felt it.

A chill ran down my spine, the hairs on the back of my neck prickling as a shadow moved in the corner of my eye. I tensed, the realization settling like a stone in my stomach.

"We're not alone," I whispered, barely moving my lips as I glanced around, trying to pinpoint the source of the movement.

He nodded, his body shifting almost imperceptibly, the predator-like stillness returning to him in a way that was both reassuring and slightly terrifying. He moved closer to me, his gaze scanning the edges of the square with a focus that made my own instincts sharpen in response.

"Whoever it is," he murmured, "they're watching, waiting for the right moment. Keep your guard up."

I swallowed, resisting the urge to reach out and take his hand, even though the contact might have calmed the frantic beat of my heart. Instead, I settled for matching his stance, feet planted and ready, every sense on high alert as we waited in tense silence.

A rustle to my left. I turned, but there was nothing there, only the empty, flickering light of a lone streetlamp.

To my right, I caught the faintest glimpse of a figure—a flash of movement so quick that if I'd blinked, I would've missed it. I grabbed his arm, squeezing tight enough that he shot me a look, but he didn't say anything, just nodded, his eyes narrowing as he followed my gaze.

There was another flicker of movement, and this time I saw them: a group, blending seamlessly into the shadows, barely distinguishable from the inky black that enveloped them. But their eyes glinted, feral and hungry, and I felt a jolt of recognition.

"Those are the same people from the alley," I muttered, my voice low but laced with urgency.

He swore under his breath, a word that sliced through the stillness, and I could feel his tension like a wire pulled taut. "Looks like we have unfinished business."

I couldn't help but shoot him a wry smile, the adrenaline making me feel strangely fearless despite the odds stacked against us. "Guess they didn't get the memo the first time."

He didn't respond, but his hand brushed mine again, a fleeting touch that steadied me just enough to hold my ground as the figures began to close in.

The leader of the group—a tall figure with a long coat that billowed like a shadow of its own—stepped forward, his face obscured by the hood pulled low over his brow. His voice was a rasp, as if he'd spent years breathing in dust and smoke.

"You thought you could escape us," he said, his tone smooth but edged with malice. "But you don't understand. This isn't a fight you can win."

I glanced over at my companion, catching the glint in his eyes that told me he was ready for whatever came next. If anything, the challenge seemed to invigorate him, his stance shifting as he prepared for what I could only assume would be an ugly battle.

"Well, I've got bad news for you," I called back, unable to resist the dig. "We're not exactly the 'back down' types."

The leader's lips curved into a humorless smile. "Then this will be over quickly."

With that, he raised a hand, and his followers surged forward, moving with a coordination that was as terrifying as it was impressive. They seemed to melt from the shadows, slipping around us in a blur of movement and menace, a wave of darkness that closed in faster than I could process.

"Stay close," he whispered, his voice barely audible as he shifted to cover my back, his body braced for impact.

I barely had time to nod before the first attacker was on me, lunging forward with a precision that left me breathless. I dodged, ducking low and driving my elbow up into their ribs with a satisfying crack, but another was already there, grabbing my arm and twisting until pain shot up my shoulder.

But he was there, quick as a flash, his fist connecting with the attacker's jaw, sending them sprawling before he pulled me close, his grip strong and reassuring.

"You're not getting rid of me that easily," he murmured, a hint of a grin flickering across his face despite the chaos around us.

I managed a breathless laugh, adrenaline and something else—something dangerous—thrumming through me as we turned, ready to face the next wave together.

The figures closed in tighter, their numbers seeming to double, and I felt a sharp pang of doubt pierce through the adrenaline-fueled haze. There were too many, and they moved with a purpose that spoke of experience, of battles won and lives taken. For the first time, I wondered if we were in over our heads.

Just as I opened my mouth to say something—anything to break the suffocating silence—a deafening noise ripped through the air, sharp and piercing, followed by the echo of footsteps rushing from the shadows. The attackers paused, their attention drawn to the source of the noise, and I felt a glimmer of hope.

But before I could react, something cold and sharp pressed against my throat, a grip iron-clad and merciless.

"Game over," a voice hissed in my ear, and my heart stilled, caught between fear and the desperate, foolish hope that somehow, some way, we'd find a way out of this yet.

Chapter 13: A Confession of Fears

The city had been transformed overnight. Streets that once hummed with life now lay quiet as tombstones. Shadows stretched long and deep over the cobblestones, like the city itself was hiding, cowering from the violence it had witnessed. We moved through it in silence, a pair of ghosts trying to blend into the cracks and crevices of a place that used to belong to us. But tonight, even the air seemed to resist us, thick and damp, pressing close around our faces as if it didn't want us here. I almost didn't recognize the world around me—it was as if every familiar landmark had turned its back on us in a silent accusation.

We slipped through a narrow alley, ducking under a wooden sign hanging askew. Rain dripped off the edge of it, tapping my shoulder as if to remind me I was still here, still painfully alive. My clothes clung to me, soaked through from a shower that had come and gone, leaving the smell of wet stone and iron hanging in the air. He led the way, his eyes flickering over every darkened window, every corner where something might lurk.

Finally, we ducked into the hollowed-out shell of what had once been a bakery. I remembered it, vaguely—the smell of fresh bread and cinnamon rolls had often drifted from its doors, a promise of warmth and normalcy. But now, it was gutted, empty shelves leaning at odd angles, as if they'd lost the will to stand upright. Broken glass glittered across the floor like diamonds, catching the moonlight that slipped in through a crack in the roof. The silence was deafening, punctuated only by the quiet drip of water pooling in a corner.

He pulled his hood back, running a hand through his damp, unruly hair. His face was tight, jaw set, but there was something different in his eyes. Gone was the usual hard edge, replaced by a weariness I hadn't seen before. I'd learned not to expect softness from him; he wore his cynicism like armor, and even when he'd taken me into his world, it had been with a wary distance, as if letting me too close might burn him. But tonight, he looked exposed, stripped bare by something deeper than fatigue.

"I guess this is where you tell me to go to hell," he said, voice rough, a bitter edge cutting through his words. He looked at me sideways, one eyebrow arched, as if daring me to walk away. I'd seen him like this before—holding out the blade for me to strike, almost hoping I would. It was his way of keeping people at arm's length, throwing up walls of sarcasm and sharp edges. But this time, I didn't bite. I was too tired for that game, too worn out from the night's violence.

"You're the one who dragged me here," I replied, crossing my arms and leaning against a splintered table. I held his gaze, challenging him to break this strange, heavy silence. For once, he didn't look away, didn't toss back a cutting remark. He just watched me, his expression unreadable, and for a moment, I wondered if he would actually let me in.

Finally, he sighed, a deep, weary sound that seemed to pull the last of his defenses down with it. "I've... lied to you," he began, each word slow, as if it took effort to pull them out. "About a lot of things." His eyes dropped to the ground, shoulders slumping slightly. It was a posture I didn't recognize, a hint of vulnerability that felt almost out of place on him.

I wanted to be angry. I wanted to lash out, to demand answers, to hurl accusations at him until he broke. But as I looked at him, something in his expression softened the sharp edges of my anger. It was an unfamiliar feeling, unsettling and almost unwelcome, but it crept in anyway, like a quiet voice telling me to listen, to let him speak.

"I thought I could protect you by keeping you in the dark," he continued, voice barely above a whisper. "But the truth is, I'm just... scared." The word hung in the air, raw and jagged. I could see him swallow, a small, almost imperceptible movement, as if saying it out loud had cost him something. "I've spent so long being afraid, hiding behind half-truths and secrets, that I forgot how to be anything else."

It was strange, hearing him admit to fear. He'd always seemed untouchable, a man who could laugh in the face of danger, shrug off threats as if they were nothing more than annoyances. But now, as he stood there, I realized just how much of his bravado had been a mask. I'd always suspected, in some distant, unacknowledged part of my mind, but hearing it from his own lips felt like a revelation.

He looked up, meeting my gaze, his eyes dark and searching. "I don't know how to fix this," he said, voice cracking on the last word. There was a tremor there, a hint of something fragile and human beneath the layers of his usual arrogance. And for the first time, I felt something other than anger for him. Something that surprised me. Empathy.

"We're both scared," I replied, my voice softer than I'd meant it to be. I felt the weight of my own words as I spoke them, an admission I hadn't planned to make. "And I don't think either of us knows what we're doing anymore."

He let out a short, humorless laugh, a sound that was half amusement, half despair. "You might be right about that." He shifted, rubbing the back of his neck, and for a moment, he looked almost sheepish, as if realizing the absurdity of the situation. Here we were, two broken people hiding in the ruins of a bakery, clinging to fragments of truth like lifelines in the middle of a storm.

I didn't know what tomorrow would bring, or if we'd even survive to see it. But as I looked at him, the hard lines of his face softened by an honesty that felt as rare as it was fragile, I felt the strangest sense of hope. It wasn't the kind of hope that promised happy endings or easy solutions. It was smaller, quieter—a flicker of understanding in the darkness, a silent acknowledgment that maybe, just maybe, we didn't have to face this alone.

And for the first time since this all began, I felt my anger slip away, leaving something raw and tender in its place. We were both broken, both scarred, and in that fragile moment, I knew one thing for certain: whatever happened next, we were in this together.

A silence settled between us, thick and uneasy, hanging in the air like a question neither of us dared to voice. Somewhere outside, a stray cat yowled, its cry echoing through the narrow streets. It was the kind of sound that would have made me jump before tonight, but now it seemed distant, another layer to the strange symphony of this forgotten corner of the city. I glanced at him, wondering if he felt it too—the weight of a hundred things left unsaid, pressing down on us like the gray clouds gathering overhead.

He shifted, looking down at his hands, fingers tracing an absent pattern over the grime-covered tabletop. I could tell he wanted to say something, but words seemed to evade him, slipping through his grasp like sand. For a man who could usually charm or provoke with a single glance, this reticence felt foreign, awkward, as if he was a stranger to himself. I waited, letting the silence stretch, daring him to fill it.

Finally, he spoke, his voice low, almost a murmur. "It wasn't supposed to be like this. I thought… I thought I'd have it all under control. Keep you safe. Keep myself safe. But nothing has gone the way I planned." A bitter laugh escaped him, short and sharp, like the crack of a matchstick breaking. "Turns out, I'm no better at this than anyone else."

His words struck me harder than I'd expected. There was a rawness in his tone, an edge of disappointment I hadn't heard before. He'd always seemed invincible to me, someone who moved through life with a kind of reckless certainty, as if he knew every outcome before the dice were even cast. But now, that certainty was gone, replaced by something darker and infinitely more fragile.

"So, what was your plan, exactly?" I asked, the question tumbling out before I could stop myself. There was a challenge in my voice, but it felt hollow, more out of habit than genuine frustration. I didn't want to hurt him, not really. I just wanted to understand, to find something solid in the mess we'd stumbled into.

He glanced up at me, a faint smile tugging at the corner of his mouth. "You wouldn't believe me if I told you," he said, shaking his head. "I barely believe it myself." He ran a hand through his hair, the movement quick and frustrated, like he was trying to shake off whatever thoughts were clouding his mind. "I thought I could fix things. That I could... I don't know, rewrite the rules somehow. But the more I tried to control it, the worse things got."

I leaned back, crossing my arms over my chest. "Well, that's the thing about control, isn't it? The tighter you grip, the more things slip through your fingers." My voice was softer now, the edge gone, replaced by something I hadn't meant to let show—empathy, maybe. I'd always been so quick to judge him, to assume I knew exactly who he was and what he wanted. But now, seeing him like this, I realized how little I actually knew.

He looked at me, surprise flickering in his eyes. For a moment, I thought he might laugh, brush off my words with one of his usual sardonic remarks. But instead, he nodded, a strange, thoughtful expression crossing his face. "You're right," he said quietly. "I've been clinging to control like it was some kind of lifeline. But all it's done is pull me under." He paused, his gaze shifting to the broken window, where a sliver of moonlight cut through the darkness. "I thought if I could just... keep everything in its place, I could keep you safe. But maybe I was just fooling myself."

There was a vulnerability in his voice that made my heart ache, a kind of wounded honesty that felt out of place in the hard lines of his face. I wanted to reach out, to touch his hand, to tell him that it was okay, that we'd figure it out somehow. But the words felt inadequate, too simple for the tangled mess of emotions swirling between us. So instead, I stayed quiet, letting the silence speak for itself.

After a moment, he sighed, the sound heavy with resignation. "I don't expect you to understand. Hell, I barely understand it myself." He looked at me, his eyes dark and searching, as if he was trying to find something in my gaze that would make sense of everything. "But I'm tired of pretending. I'm tired of trying to be something I'm not."

His words hung in the air, raw and unfiltered. It was strange, seeing him like this, stripped of the bravado and charm that usually defined him. I'd always thought of him as a man of action, someone who lived by his own rules, who faced danger with a smirk and a shrug. But now, that image felt hollow, a mask he'd worn so well that even I had believed it.

"I don't need you to be perfect," I said, my voice barely more than a whisper. "I just need you to be real." The words slipped out before I could stop them, a quiet plea that surprised even me. I hadn't realized how much I'd wanted this—this moment of honesty, of raw, unfiltered truth.

He looked at me, his gaze softening, and for a moment, I thought he might say something, that he might let down the last of his walls and let me in completely. But instead, he just nodded, a faint, almost wistful smile playing at his lips. "I don't know if I can be that person for you," he admitted, his voice tinged with a sadness I hadn't expected. "I've spent so long hiding, lying, pretending... I'm not sure I know who I am anymore."

The honesty of his words caught me off guard, stirring something deep within me. I wanted to reach out, to tell him that it didn't matter, that we'd figure it out together. But I knew it wasn't that simple. This was his journey, his struggle, and no amount of comforting words or empty promises would change that. All I could do was stand by his side and hope that, someday, he'd find his way back to himself.

For a long moment, we just looked at each other, the weight of our shared past hanging heavy in the air. There were so many things I wanted to say, questions I wanted to ask, but the words seemed inadequate, too fragile for the intensity of the moment. So I stayed silent, letting my presence speak for me, hoping that it would be enough.

Finally, he turned away, his gaze shifting back to the broken window, where the first faint hints of dawn were beginning to lighten the sky. "I don't know what tomorrow will bring," he said softly, his voice barely more than a whisper. "But I do know one thing—I'm done hiding. From you. From myself. From everything."

His words echoed through the empty room, a quiet promise that felt as fragile as it was profound. And as I looked at him, standing there in the faint light of dawn, I felt a strange sense of hope flicker within me, a tiny spark of something that felt like the beginning of a new chapter.

The faint glow of dawn filtered through the cracked window, casting a pale light across his face. There was something haunting about it, how the soft colors of morning highlighted every line and shadow, revealing a quiet vulnerability he usually kept buried. His confession, raw and unexpected, had changed something between us. The anger I'd clung to was gone, replaced by a fragile, tentative connection that made me feel both exposed and strangely alive.

For a while, neither of us spoke. I could hear the steady rhythm of his breathing, each rise and fall a reminder of how close we'd come to losing everything tonight. I traced my finger over a deep scratch in the table's surface, wondering how many lives had been lived in this room, how many secrets had been whispered under the shelter of its broken walls. When I finally looked up, I found him watching me, a faint curiosity in his eyes, as if he, too, was wondering what came next.

"So," I said, breaking the silence with a feigned casualness I didn't feel. "What's the plan now? Or is this where we both wander off into the sunrise and pretend none of this ever happened?"

A smirk tugged at the corner of his mouth, his usual humor flickering back to life. "As tempting as that sounds, I'm afraid we're well past the point of pretending." His gaze held mine, steady and unflinching, and I felt a spark of defiance flare up inside me. He was right, of course; there was no going back. Not after everything that had happened. But I wasn't about to make it easy for him.

"Alright, then," I replied, my voice steady, even though my heart was pounding. "If you're done hiding, what exactly are you planning to do about it?"

He leaned back, crossing his arms over his chest, his expression thoughtful. "I have a few ideas," he said slowly, as if testing the words. "But none of them are particularly... safe."

The way he said it sent a shiver down my spine, a reminder of the dangerous world we'd stumbled into. But instead of fear, I felt a thrill of excitement, a reckless urge to throw caution to the wind. I'd spent too long letting other people dictate my choices, keeping my life contained within neat, predictable boundaries. And now, with him standing in front of me, his eyes filled with a determination I hadn't seen before, I realized that I wanted to be part of whatever came next, no matter the risk.

"I'm listening," I said, raising an eyebrow in challenge. His gaze softened for a moment, a flicker of warmth that was gone as quickly as it came.

"There's something I've been trying to find," he began, his voice low, each word deliberate. "A way out of this mess. A way to end it all, once and for all." He hesitated, glancing out the window as if the answer might be hidden somewhere in the pale morning light. "But it won't be easy. There are people—powerful people—who would do anything to keep us from finding it."

I nodded, feeling a strange sense of anticipation settle over me. "And you think we can take them on?"

A dark laugh escaped him, bitter and humorless. "I don't think. I know." His gaze locked onto mine, intense and unyielding. "But it'll mean leaving everything behind. No turning back. Once we start, there's no way out."

The weight of his words hung heavy between us, the enormity of what he was asking sinking in. And yet, a part of me had already made up my mind. I wasn't ready to let him go, not now, not after everything we'd been through. Whatever lay ahead, I knew I wanted to face it with him, to stand by his side, come what may.

"Alright," I said, my voice steady. "Let's do it."

His expression shifted, a spark of something fierce and triumphant flashing in his eyes. But just as quickly, it was replaced by a wary caution, as if he couldn't quite believe I was willing to go this far. He reached out, his hand brushing mine, and for a brief, electric moment, the world fell away, leaving just the two of us standing on the edge of an uncertain future.

But then, before either of us could say another word, a noise shattered the fragile peace—a harsh, metallic clang from somewhere outside. My heart leapt, the sense of security we'd built crumbling in an instant. He tensed, his gaze snapping to the door, every muscle in his body coiled like a spring.

"Stay here," he whispered, the sharpness of his tone cutting through the air. Without waiting for a response, he slipped toward the door, his movements quick and silent, like a shadow dissolving into the night. I wanted to call after him, to demand that he stay, that we face whatever danger was lurking together. But something stopped me—a gut instinct, a feeling that whatever was coming, he needed to confront it alone.

Seconds stretched into an eternity as I stood there, my pulse racing, every nerve on edge. The quiet settled over me, thick and oppressive, broken only by the distant drip of water somewhere in the corner. I strained to hear, every sound amplified, each creak of the floorboards making my skin prickle with dread.

And then, I heard it—a low murmur, the unmistakable cadence of voices, too faint to make out but enough to send a chill down my spine. Whoever they were, they weren't here by accident. I pressed myself against the wall, inching closer to the doorway, trying to catch a glimpse of what was happening outside.

I could just barely see him, standing in the alley, his back to me, shoulders squared. A figure loomed in front of him, shadowed and indistinct, their face hidden in the dim light. They spoke in hushed tones, the words lost in the wind, but the tension was unmistakable, a palpable energy that crackled through the air.

And then, without warning, the figure lunged forward, a glint of steel flashing in the early morning light. My breath caught, panic surging through me as I watched him step back, narrowly avoiding the blade. The stranger moved with deadly precision, each strike quick and calculated, a relentless assault that forced him onto the defensive.

He dodged, deflecting each blow with a desperate grace, his movements growing more frantic with every passing second. I could see the strain in his posture, the slight hesitation in his steps, a crack in his usual confidence that sent a jolt of fear through me.

I wanted to help, to do something, anything, but my feet felt rooted to the floor, paralyzed by the intensity of the scene unfolding before me. And then, just as I thought he'd gained the upper hand, the stranger shifted, a swift, brutal movement that caught him off guard. The blade sliced through the air, finding its mark with a sickening finality.

A strangled cry escaped my lips, barely audible over the pounding of my heart. I stumbled forward, instinct overriding fear, desperate to reach him, to stop the blood I could already see spreading across his shirt, dark and foreboding.

But as I moved, a shadow blocked my path, a figure stepping into the doorway, their silhouette framed by the faint glow of dawn. They stood there, silent and unmoving, a cruel smile curving their lips as they raised a hand, pointing directly at me.

"Looks like you're next," they said, their voice low and taunting, each word dripping with menace.

And in that moment, with his life slipping away and danger closing in from all sides, I realized that our fight had only just begun.

Chapter 14: Bound by the Curse

In the flickering torchlight, Riven's face looked both haunted and captivating, the high angles of his cheekbones casting shadows that only sharpened his quiet anger. He stood there, arms crossed over his chest, tension in every line of his body, his gaze locked onto the relic as though it held answers he couldn't stand to hear.

The relic itself sat innocently enough on the stone pedestal between us, a misshapen piece of dark metal, wound with age and crawling with cryptic etchings that had begun to pulse the moment we found it. But it wasn't until we both touched it that the true weight of it crashed into us—a searing ache that seemed to root itself in our bones, tying us together as tightly as two ends of a tangled rope.

"If you would stop scowling at it like that," I muttered, unable to resist needling him, "maybe it wouldn't seem so smugly pleased with itself."

Riven's scowl deepened, dark eyes narrowing to a near glare. "Smug? It's a cursed artifact, Selene, not some spoiled cat."

"Tell that to the headache it's giving me. And you, with that delightful expression." I knew I should keep my sarcasm in check, but in moments like these, words had a way of slipping free before I could catch them. "Besides, you look ready to explode. Just let go of your pride for a second and admit we're...you know, cursed together."

Riven tilted his head, his frown sharpening. "I can acknowledge we're bound by something beyond our control. That doesn't mean I'm thrilled about it."

Neither was I, really, but there was no denying the thrill of it, the edge of mystery weaving between us. Our fates were tangled now, and despite the looming dangers and everything that stood between us, the pull was undeniable. I felt it every time he looked at me with that same, bewildered annoyance, as though he was still grappling with the shock of finding me there, in his life, disrupting everything.

But there was more to the relic's curse than even we could grasp. Ever since that first jolt of pain, it had haunted us both, filling my dreams with fragments of a story that didn't belong to me. Snatches of scenes flickered through my mind like candlelight behind old, cracked glass—a woman standing alone on a cliff, wind tearing through her cloak as she gazed over stormy seas, her heart clenched in a fear as ancient as the rocks beneath her feet. Another scene, more vivid and urgent, showed a man and woman, hands entwined, running through an endless forest with shadows at their heels, the curse following them like a dark ghost they could never outrun.

At first, I'd thought they were just dreams, but they began to linger in my mind long after I woke, moments replaying over and over, almost as if they were...memories.

"You're quiet," Riven said, dragging me back to the dim stone chamber, the echoes of ancient whispers still humming through my mind.

"Just...thinking," I replied, a vague answer that he didn't seem to buy. His mouth pressed into a line, the frustration etched in his brow almost amusing in its predictability. For a man who wore his emotions like armor, he was surprisingly easy to read, and right now, he was wrestling with a familiar impatience that only flared whenever we tried to talk about what this curse meant.

"You don't believe me, do you?" I ventured, a wry edge to my voice, masking the unease clawing up my spine.

He gave a dry, humorless laugh. "Believe you? About what? That we're linked by some ancient curse determined to ruin both our lives? Oh, I believe that plenty. What I don't understand is why the relic chose us. Out of all the people in this miserable world, it's you and me."

The way he said it, so sharp and accusing, stung. "Well, excuse me for being the last person you'd want to be cursed with," I snapped, crossing my arms. "Believe me, the feeling's mutual."

Riven's expression shifted, softening almost imperceptibly. He opened his mouth, closed it, and then turned away, running a hand over his face. "I didn't mean it like that, Selene," he muttered finally. "I just meant...you're right. None of this makes sense."

It was strange, seeing him falter. Riven was always so put-together, so sure of himself, that watching him grapple with uncertainty was like seeing a crack in an otherwise flawless mirror. I couldn't say I enjoyed it, exactly, but a part of me couldn't help but find it endearing.

"Well, what do we do, then?" I asked, lowering my voice. "If we can't break the curse, and we can't ignore it..."

He took a step closer, and I felt the air grow tense, the curse buzzing faintly, like a low hum just beneath the skin. "We find out what it wants from us," he said, his voice barely above a whisper. "And we give it exactly that."

There was something in his tone that unsettled me—a determination that went beyond curiosity. I opened my mouth to protest, to remind him that meddling with curses usually only led to worse outcomes, but the intensity in his gaze silenced me. For all his brooding and walls, Riven had a side to him that was reckless, a thrill-seeker veiled behind his steady demeanor. It made me nervous, but I couldn't deny it fascinated me too.

A long, fraught silence stretched between us, broken only by the soft drip of water from somewhere deeper within the cave. I could feel Riven's presence as acutely as the stone beneath my feet, grounding yet somehow stirring, our breaths mingling in the chilled air.

"Fine," I said finally, exhaling. "We figure out what the relic wants. But if this goes south, I'm blaming you."

"Oh, believe me, that'll be nothing new." He smirked, his wit cutting through the tension like a blade. "But you'll thank me in the end."

"Don't hold your breath," I shot back, the hint of a grin sneaking its way onto my face despite myself.

As we turned to leave, the relic gave one last ominous pulse, a reminder that this was only the beginning. Whatever it wanted, it would get. And we, bound as we were, would have to pay the price—together.

The forest was a tangle of shadows and moonlight, branches clawing at the sky like skeletal fingers. Riven moved through it as if he belonged to the darkness itself, slipping between the trees with a quiet ease that made me feel all the more graceless by comparison. I was no stranger to the woods, but something about the oppressive weight of the relic's curse made every twig underfoot seem to snap a bit louder, every brush of my sleeve against a branch feel like a siren's call in the silence.

"Would you mind keeping it down?" he whispered, his voice low but edged with impatience. He didn't even look back, and I could tell he was rolling his eyes without needing to see it.

"Oh, I'm so sorry," I shot back, ducking to avoid a low-hanging branch. "Next time, I'll try not to step on the invisible traps left here by ancient curses."

He stopped abruptly, turning to face me with a half-amused, half-exasperated look. "I think the curse has already trapped us plenty. Don't flatter yourself; you're not that important."

"Thanks for the confidence boost," I muttered, brushing past him as he shook his head. "But if you're quite finished critiquing my survival skills, maybe we could focus on getting answers before we end up ghosts haunting this very spot."

I half-expected him to snap back with some biting retort, but he was quiet as he fell into step beside me. His silence was unsettling, more so than any of his sarcastic barbs could be. I stole a glance at him, noticing the way his brows drew together, his gaze distant, almost as if he were listening to something I couldn't hear.

"Have you... have you felt anything strange?" he asked finally, his voice so low it was almost lost in the rustling leaves.

"Strange like ancient curses binding us against our will? No, nothing out of the ordinary there," I quipped, trying to lighten the tension that had crept between us. But when he didn't respond, I softened my tone. "Yeah, I feel it. Like a... like a tug, almost. In here." I pressed a hand to my chest, where the relic's pulse seemed to beat in time with my own heart. "It's like something is trying to tell us something. Show us something."

He nodded, and I noticed his hand twitch slightly, as if resisting the urge to reach for the relic himself. "That's what I'm afraid of."

I laughed, though there was no real humor in it. "What, afraid of getting a little peek into your past lives?"

He stopped walking, and I nearly ran into him. His face was shadowed, unreadable in the pale light filtering through the trees. "This isn't about me," he said quietly. "It's about us, and whatever the relic wants. It's been dragging us into its memories, its twisted little visions, and if we don't figure it out soon... I don't know what it'll make us do."

The air felt colder, heavy with his words. There was a sincerity in his voice that I hadn't heard before, and it unsettled me more than any sharp exchange ever could. For once, I didn't have a snappy response.

We kept walking in silence, the forest seeming to close in tighter around us. Every rustle in the underbrush, every hoot of an owl sent my nerves on edge, as if the relic itself had cast a shroud of paranoia over us. I didn't know if it was real, or just the curse twisting my senses, but either way, it made the hairs on the back of my neck stand up.

Just as I was beginning to wonder if we were lost, Riven slowed, his gaze focused on something just beyond the trees. I followed his line of sight, and there, nestled among the roots of an ancient oak, was a stone altar, worn and crumbling, but unmistakably the same one I'd seen in my visions.

"We're here," I breathed, feeling the pull of the relic grow stronger, almost magnetic. It was as if it was leading us, guiding us toward... what, exactly? Answers? Doom? I wasn't sure.

Riven approached the altar cautiously, his movements slow, deliberate. "If this is where the curse started, maybe there's something here we can use to end it."

"Just be careful," I warned, feeling a pang of unease as he reached out to touch the cold stone.

He looked back at me, and for a brief moment, there was something vulnerable in his eyes, a flicker of hesitation. "I'll try not to set off any ancient traps, if that makes you feel better."

I managed a tight smile, though my stomach twisted with worry. I couldn't shake the feeling that the relic, the curse, wanted us here for a reason—one that had nothing to do with freeing us.

Riven's fingers brushed the surface of the altar, and the forest seemed to hold its breath. A low rumble echoed from beneath the ground, the earth trembling as if awakening from a long sleep. I stumbled back, nearly losing my balance, but Riven remained where he was, his hand still pressed to the stone.

"Riven!" I reached for him, but an invisible force held me back, as if a wall had sprung up between us. Panic surged through me, but when I met his eyes, he looked strangely calm, as though he were in a trance.

"I can see them," he murmured, his voice distant, hollow. "The woman on the cliff... the man in the forest. They're us, Selene."

"What?" I barely registered my own voice, the words slipping from my lips as fear gripped me. "What are you talking about?"

"They were cursed, just like us. Bound to this place, bound to each other." His gaze drifted, unfocused, as if watching something only he could see. "They tried to break it, tried to run... but it followed them, tore them apart. And now..." His voice trailed off, and his hand fell away from the altar.

"Riven," I said softly, stepping forward as whatever invisible barrier that had held me back dissipated. I reached for his arm, grounding him. "Hey, come back to me."

He blinked, and the dazed look faded, replaced by a simmering frustration. "This curse, it's... it's a cycle. They failed, and it brought us here, trapping us in their place. I think..." He hesitated, his jaw clenched. "I think it wants us to finish what they couldn't."

A shiver ran down my spine, and I swallowed hard. "And what if we fail, too?"

He met my gaze, his expression grim. "Then the cycle continues. Until someone finally breaks it."

The weight of his words settled over me like a shroud. I wanted to argue, to say that we'd find a way out, that we weren't doomed to the same fate as those who came before us. But in that moment, standing together in the ancient forest with the relic's curse pulsing between us, I couldn't bring myself to believe it.

The chill settled deeper, winding into my bones, though whether it was the night air or the creeping dread that came from Riven's revelation, I couldn't say. He stood beside me, his face half in shadow, jaw set as he stared down at the altar with a mix of fury and resignation. The curse had wormed its way into every fragment of us, binding us in ways I hadn't realized were possible. For all my bravado, the reality of it finally hit me—there was no undoing this.

"So, just to be clear," I began, keeping my voice steady even as my heart threatened to hammer out of my chest, "we're supposed to finish whatever this ancient couple started... or risk being cursed for eternity?"

Riven looked up, his dark eyes flashing in the moonlight. "Something like that. But I don't know what that means. 'Finish what they started'? The curse isn't exactly handing us a manual here."

I rubbed my hands over my arms, trying to banish the persistent chill, but it clung stubbornly. "Typical ancient curse, right? All high-stakes demands, zero clarity." I let out a humorless laugh, though the joke fell flat between us. "So... where do we start?"

Riven glanced at the forest around us, his gaze thoughtful. "There has to be a reason we were drawn here, to this altar. Maybe it's not just about breaking the curse. Maybe we're supposed to understand something about them—who they were and why they failed."

"You're saying we need to piece together the love life of two ghosts before we end up as tragic fodder ourselves?"

He shrugged, giving a crooked smile. "Not my first choice for an evening's entertainment, but it seems the relic had other plans."

It was strange, standing here in this isolated, ancient place, half-joking about our own impending doom. And yet, I couldn't deny that having Riven here, with his deadpan humor and unyielding determination, made it all feel a little less terrifying. For all his brooding, there was a steadiness to him, a sense of quiet strength that had kept me from spiraling. And for reasons I didn't quite understand, that realization settled something within me.

Riven turned his gaze back to the altar, his brows knitting together in thought. "Maybe... maybe we need to recreate their last moments. If this is where the curse was first cast, there's a chance it's also where we can finally end it."

"Recreate their last moments?" I repeated, my tone incredulous. "What, just... guess our way through the most significant parts of their lives until something sticks?"

"You've got a better plan?" he asked, arching a brow.

I opened my mouth to protest but stopped short, realizing I didn't have a better idea. In fact, the more I thought about it, the more I realized he was right. The curse had shown us glimpses of the past—a woman on a cliff, a man and woman running through a forest. If we were to understand them, maybe we had to experience what they did, retrace their steps.

"Fine," I muttered, crossing my arms. "So we re-enact a tragic romance and hope we don't end up with the same miserable fate. No pressure, right?"

He smirked. "Nothing you can't handle."

Before I could come up with a retort, a soft breeze swept through the clearing, carrying with it the faintest whisper. It was so quiet, so subtle, I thought I'd imagined it at first, but then I saw Riven's expression shift. He'd heard it too.

The whisper came again, this time clearer, like a ghostly sigh weaving through the trees, trailing goosebumps in its wake. "Together... bound... forever." The words were faint, almost fragile, as if they'd been waiting centuries just to reach our ears.

Riven's jaw tightened, and he glanced at me, his face serious. "Did you hear that?"

"Unfortunately, yes," I replied, my voice barely above a whisper. My stomach clenched with dread, but curiosity tugged me forward. The relic had brought us here, led us to this moment. And now, like it or not, we were listening.

The forest seemed to hold its breath as we stood there, straining to catch another sound, another whisper. But only silence followed, stretching into a tense, aching stillness. Just when I was about to speak, Riven took a step toward the altar, his gaze dark and resolute.

"What are you doing?" I asked, though I already had a sinking suspicion.

"If we're supposed to reenact their final moments, maybe this is part of it." He looked at me, and there was a softness in his eyes, a vulnerability that threw me. "Do you trust me?"

The question hung in the air, charged and potent. In another life, maybe it would have been easy to laugh it off, to deny it with some witty remark. But here, under the weight of the curse, with the relic binding us closer with each passing second, I found myself nodding.

"Yes," I said, the word surprising even me. "I do."

A flicker of something passed over his face—relief, maybe, or gratitude. He took my hand, his fingers warm and solid against the cool night air. Together, we approached the altar, our footsteps synchronized as if we were two halves of the same shadow, moving as one.

When we reached the stone, a strange warmth pulsed through my hand, spreading through my veins. The relic thrummed with energy, as though sensing our unity, and in that moment, the vision returned, sharper and clearer than ever.

I saw the cliff again, the woman standing there with her eyes closed, arms outstretched as if bracing herself against a storm. But this time, I saw her face, pale and determined, a fierce sorrow in her eyes that made my heart ache. And beside her, the man—his hand on her shoulder, his face turned toward her with a tenderness that spoke of a love neither time nor death could erase.

The scene shifted, and I felt the urgency of their last moments, the desperation in their footsteps as they fled through the woods, their breaths quick and shallow, their hands clasped tightly together as though that simple touch could save them. They were fighting something—a shadow, a darkness that seemed to stretch endlessly, reaching for them, hunting them down.

The vision faded, and I was back in the present, my heart racing, Riven's hand still in mine. He looked at me, his eyes dark and intense.

"Did you see it too?" he asked, his voice barely a whisper.

I nodded, words failing me. The curse wasn't just binding us to each other—it was binding us to their memories, their pain, their fear. We were caught in the same web they'd woven, and there was no telling if we'd make it out alive.

A gust of wind swept through the forest, stronger than before, tearing leaves from the branches and sending them spiraling around us. The relic pulsed, its energy flaring as if it were waking up, as if it had been waiting for this moment. And in the midst of it all, that same whisper returned, louder now, more insistent.

"Finish what we could not. Free us... or suffer as we have suffered."

The words hung in the air, chilling and final. I met Riven's gaze, my breath shallow, my heart pounding.

"We're not alone, are we?" I whispered, fear creeping into my voice.

He didn't answer, but his grip on my hand tightened, grounding me in the face of whatever horror was coming.

And then, without warning, the relic blazed with a blinding light, and the ground beneath us began to shake.

Chapter 15: The Rising Danger

Darkness wrapped around us as we prowled through the alleys of the lower city, the smell of rain and old stone clinging to the air. I could almost hear the city breathing, its pulse quickening with every footfall that echoed off wet cobblestones. Shadows stretched longer here, thicker somehow, hiding whispers and secrets as dark and deep as the water pooling at my feet. The relic pulsed against my chest, cold and heavy beneath my coat, a constant reminder that danger was as close as my next breath.

My partner insisted we lie low—his voice was like gravel smoothed by whiskey, hushed in that maddeningly calm way he had about him. "You're impossible, you know that?" he murmured as he watched me sidle against a cracked stone wall, eyes flickering down the alley like I was tracking prey.

"You're welcome to leave anytime," I shot back, my voice edged with irritation, yet soft enough not to carry. "Oh wait, you need me. Like it or not, you're stuck."

He sighed, but his lips curved in a reluctant smirk, a look I'd grown used to despite the incessant tick of tension between us. He was right about one thing, though; it would be far safer if we were hidden away, somewhere unremarkable and quiet, somewhere we could pretend the world wasn't pressing down on us. But that wasn't an option. The city had its hooks in us, and its streets were our only chance of survival, at least as long as that relic remained in our possession.

A flicker of movement caught my eye—a figure darting between pools of light spilling from flickering street lamps. Someone was watching us. Again.

"Third one tonight," I murmured, glancing back at him. "We're either popular or unlucky."

"Try cursed," he replied, his voice low. He placed a hand on my shoulder, steadying me as we rounded a corner. "Let's make this quick."

We ducked down another narrow passage, slipping between stacks of rotting crates and rusting metal that seemed to groan under their own weight. The world had narrowed to this winding maze, this underground world of grit and grime. I felt more alive here than I ever had in a ballroom, more attuned to the night's hum, my senses honed to the near-silence. The relic's pull sharpened with each step, drawing us somewhere I wasn't quite ready to go.

I could hear his breathing beside me, steady and measured, as if he weren't even the slightest bit phased by the trouble nipping at our heels. It was maddening, really, the way he could keep his cool, his voice a monotone even when things felt like they were on the brink of collapse. But there was something else in that calm, a steadiness that was grounding, a subtle warmth I'd never admit I appreciated.

The footsteps grew closer. Our shadows danced wildly as I pressed against the cold stone wall, watching the alley beyond. A pair of figures appeared, their faces obscured by hoods. I could just make out the glint of metal at their hips.

My hand went instinctively to the knife tucked into my boot, a move that didn't go unnoticed. "Think we could negotiate our way out of this?" I whispered, though I knew the answer.

"Not with these types." He shook his head, his hand brushing against mine as we moved back, slipping into an even darker alcove. For a second, we were close enough that I could smell the faint hint of pine and rain that clung to him, an odd scent for a man who claimed to have no roots, no place to call home.

The two figures lingered near the end of the alley, muttering to each other in hushed tones. I strained to catch their words, but all I caught was a fragment: "the relic... blood debt... no witnesses." My pulse quickened.

"They know what we have," I said under my breath, the weight of the relic pressing cold against my chest as if it, too, understood the gravity of our situation.

He nodded, his eyes narrowing. "We need to get off the streets. Now."

But as we moved, one of the figures turned, catching a glimpse of us just before we slipped out of sight. A sharp curse sliced through the air, and they sprang forward, footsteps slapping against the wet ground, echoing off the narrow walls around us.

"Run," he urged, grabbing my hand and pulling me into a sprint. We tore through the alley, the pounding of our footsteps swallowed by the night. I could feel the relic pulsing against my chest, faster, colder, as if reacting to our fear, to the danger closing in. It was like an extra heartbeat, one that reminded me just how little time we had.

We reached the end of the alley and darted left, down a winding staircase that led into the labyrinthine depths of the lower city. The shadows here were different, somehow thicker, almost alive, clinging to us as we moved. The noise behind us grew louder, closer, the sound of pursuit. My mind raced, calculating the few routes we had left.

We slid into an open doorway, the rusted door scraping against the ground as we shut it behind us. Inside was dark, the air thick with dust and disuse, an abandoned shop that smelled of mold and forgotten things. We stood there, barely breathing, listening as our pursuers' footsteps grew louder, then faded as they passed by. We waited until silence returned, the kind that sinks into your bones and settles, heavy and thick.

"Well," he whispered, a rueful smile tugging at the corner of his mouth, "that was exciting."

"Oh, thrilling," I replied, rolling my eyes. "Remind me to book a vacation after all this. Somewhere with less... impending doom."

The sarcasm was a shield, a way to ignore the knot of fear coiling in my stomach. I didn't want to admit how close we'd come or how much it rattled me. But his eyes lingered on me for a moment longer, seeing through the facade, and I hated how much he could do that.

We waited a few more minutes before stepping out of the shop. The night had quieted, and the city seemed to hold its breath as we made our way through its veins, wary, restless, and with a danger that felt as alive as the relic pulsing against my skin.

The streets were still wet from the night's rain, glistening under the dim, hazy glow of the street lamps. We moved through them like specters, silent and quick, yet every step felt laden with risk, with the sharp edge of being watched. It was an unnerving feeling, that constant sense of eyes prickling along my back, but I forced myself to breathe, to focus on the next turn, the next shadow we could slip into. Somewhere in the distance, a dog barked, the sound bouncing off the narrow walls around us, almost swallowed by the night itself.

"Are you sure you know where we're going?" I asked, casting him a sidelong glance as we darted around a corner. He was navigating with such confidence it was either reassuring or maddening, and I hadn't yet decided which.

He smirked, barely glancing back. "Trust me."

"That's a big ask," I muttered, though I matched his pace, refusing to let him see even a flicker of hesitation.

He slowed as we neared an old, wrought-iron gate that looked like it hadn't been touched in years. Vines crawled up its sides, rust and age giving it an almost eerie charm. Without hesitation, he lifted the latch and pushed it open, the gate groaning in protest before revealing a hidden courtyard. It was tucked between two towering buildings, quiet and dark, save for a faint trickle of water somewhere in the back. We stepped inside, and he closed the gate behind us, securing it with an old lock that looked like it had seen better days.

"You've been here before," I noted, crossing my arms as I surveyed the space, every nerve in me still humming with the energy of our escape.

He nodded, glancing around as if seeing the courtyard anew. "Once or twice. It's not exactly a five-star hideout, but it'll do."

I rolled my eyes. "Noted. Next time, I'll bring my own accommodations."

The sarcasm rolled off him; he only arched an eyebrow, looking mildly amused. But as he moved to inspect the courtyard, his focus sharpened, his hands brushing against the damp stone walls as if searching for something hidden there. The space was cramped and shadowed, with overgrown plants and ivy swallowing parts of the wall, and in the center, a small fountain, its water trickling softly in a rhythm that was almost calming. Almost.

I leaned against the wall, arms still crossed. "So, what now? Do we just wait here and hope the people out there get bored?"

His eyes flicked to mine, a glint of something unreadable in them. "Waiting isn't really my style," he said, voice low and dry. "But tonight, we're making an exception."

"Fantastic," I replied, my voice dripping with forced cheer. "Nothing like waiting for inevitable doom in a courtyard that smells like mold."

He stifled a laugh, though his eyes warmed just a fraction, and I hated how much that tiny shift felt like a win. "You could always sing a song," he offered, deadpan. "Pass the time."

I scoffed. "Last time I checked, I wasn't here to entertain you."

But even as I said it, I felt the tension ease slightly between us, a moment of levity like a sliver of light breaking through. In another life, under different circumstances, maybe there would be time for jokes, for getting under each other's skin in a way that didn't feel like we were skirting the edge of survival. But here, in the heart of a city that held secrets sharper than knives, the lightness was fleeting.

"Look," he said after a pause, his gaze shifting to the relic hanging against my chest, its faint hum still present, like a whisper I couldn't quite hear. "Whatever's in that thing, whatever curse or power... it's not just about us anymore."

I swallowed, the weight of his words pressing down with an uncomfortable heaviness. He was right. This relic wasn't just a trinket—it was something far more dangerous, something that could upend everything if it fell into the wrong hands. And I wasn't naive enough to think we could hide forever.

Before I could respond, a noise cracked through the stillness—a low creak of the gate. My blood ran cold. Whoever was on the other side wasn't making any effort to hide their approach. Footsteps echoed off the stones, slow and deliberate, each one closer than the last. We tensed, his hand moving to the hilt of his knife, mine to the relic, a silent acknowledgment that we'd either make a stand here or fall trying.

A figure appeared in the shadows just beyond the courtyard entrance, tall and cloaked, their face obscured but their posture screaming intent. I felt my heartbeat slam against my chest, the relic's cold hum intensifying as if it sensed the threat, as if it was coming alive, feeding off the energy swirling around us.

"Seems you missed the memo," I called out, forcing my voice to stay steady. "Private event. Invitation only."

The figure chuckled, a low, raspy sound that grated against my nerves. "Oh, I'm more than welcome here," they said, their voice smooth and sinister, like velvet with a hidden edge. "You're the ones trespassing."

My partner stepped forward, his stance relaxed but his eyes sharp, calculating. "If you've come for the relic, you're wasting your time," he said calmly, though the tension in his jaw betrayed the effort it took to keep his composure. "You're not getting it."

The figure tilted their head, considering us in a way that made my skin crawl. "Such bravery," they mused, though I could hear the disdain lacing their words. "But bravery only takes one so far."

They stepped forward, and as they did, I felt a strange tug within me, as though the relic itself was responding to their presence, drawing me toward them in a way I couldn't explain. I gritted my teeth, fighting against the pull, the sensation like ice threading through my veins.

"What do you want?" I demanded, trying to steady myself, to block out the relic's unnatural allure.

They paused, their gaze flicking to the relic resting against my chest, a faint smile curling their lips. "Power is a dangerous thing," they murmured, almost to themselves. "But in the right hands, it can shape the world."

My partner edged closer to me, his shoulder brushing mine in a subtle but grounding way. "You're not getting the relic," he repeated, his voice like steel.

The figure sighed, as if disappointed, and for a moment, I thought they might turn and leave. But then their hand flicked out, a swift, almost careless motion, and a blade flew through the air, barely missing me as I twisted to dodge. It struck the wall behind us with a dull thud, embedding itself deep into the stone.

Instinct kicked in, and before I knew it, I'd drawn my knife, holding it up defensively, though my hands trembled. Beside me, he was already moving, stepping in front of me with a protectiveness that was as infuriating as it was strangely reassuring.

The figure only laughed, the sound sending a chill through me. "This is just the beginning," they said, voice dripping with a confidence that made my stomach twist. "I'll see you again soon. Enjoy your little game... while you can."

With that, they turned and slipped into the shadows, vanishing as quickly as they'd appeared, leaving us standing in the courtyard, breathless, the danger closer than ever and yet slipping just beyond our reach.

The night had a pulse to it, an unspoken hum that vibrated in my bones as we left the safety of the courtyard. Or maybe "safety" was a lie we told ourselves—if that recent encounter taught me anything, it was that safety was as fleeting as the shadow of a passing bird. He moved beside me, his pace measured and careful, though his gaze kept darting over his shoulder, checking for the ghost that had vanished so quickly it felt like a fevered hallucination.

"You think they'll come back?" I asked, trying to keep my voice steady. But I wasn't fooling anyone; the tension threaded through my words like barbed wire.

He glanced sideways at me, his expression a mix of something grim and resigned. "Someone will. They always do."

A part of me wanted to snap back with a snarky retort, something sharp enough to remind him that I didn't need his constant prophesies of doom. But the words stuck in my throat, lodged there by the memory of that figure's voice, of the blade that had flown so close I could still feel its icy breath. The pulse of the relic against my chest hadn't softened; if anything, it had quickened, as if sensing we were being hunted. And maybe we were.

We walked in silence for a few moments longer, moving away from the courtyard and into an area where the buildings were tall and dense, leaning over us like silent watchers. Windows glowed in patches above, throwing ghostly light into the street, but not enough to chase away the shadows. I felt their weight pressing in on me, dark and thick, like something alive.

He slowed his steps as we neared a small, dimly lit bar wedged between two decaying brick buildings. Its sign was barely hanging on by a few rusty nails, and one of the windows was cracked. Not the sort of place I would normally be caught dead in, but tonight, maybe that was the point.

He stopped, turning to me with a raised eyebrow. "Trust me?"

I huffed, crossing my arms. "We've been over this. Asking for my trust when you've done absolutely nothing to earn it is a bit of a reach, don't you think?"

His mouth quirked in that way it did when he found me particularly entertaining. "I've kept you alive this long, haven't I?"

I narrowed my eyes, glancing at the bar. "Not sure I'd call that 'earning trust.' But fine. Let's get this over with."

The inside of the bar was just as shabby as its exterior—dim lights, peeling wallpaper, and the faint smell of something stale lingering in the air. A few patrons sat hunched over their drinks, their faces obscured in shadow, their postures broadcasting that they'd be left alone or they'd have a problem with it. I could respect that.

He led us to a corner booth, away from prying eyes, and I slid in across from him, the worn leather creaking under my weight. For a moment, we just sat there, the heavy silence settling between us, pressing down like the weight of everything unspoken.

"So what's your plan?" I asked finally, my voice barely above a whisper. "And please don't say we're just going to sit here all night and 'lie low.'"

He leaned back, folding his arms with that maddeningly calm expression of his. "You got a better idea?"

I let out a slow breath, my fingers toying with the edge of the table as I tried to ground myself. "I don't like waiting. Every second we're sitting here, they're getting closer."

His gaze sharpened, and for once, the easygoing mask slipped, revealing a hint of the weight he carried, a burden that looked strangely familiar. "You think I like this? You think I want to sit here, watching the walls close in?"

There was something in his voice, a raw edge that made my stomach twist. It hit me then, how much we were alike, how much this chase was starting to feel like our very lives were entwined, tangled in a way that went beyond the relic hanging against my chest.

"Why didn't you walk away?" I asked, barely thinking before the words spilled out. "You could've left me to handle this on my own. You didn't have to stay."

He let out a low laugh, though it was devoid of humor. "Walk away? You think it's that easy?"

I didn't respond. Maybe I didn't have to. Whatever kept him here, it was as much a mystery to me as my own reasons for staying. But before I could dig deeper, before I could press him for answers I wasn't even sure I wanted, a loud crash echoed through the bar, shattering the brittle peace.

We both tensed, hands instinctively reaching for weapons. A figure staggered through the doorway, eyes wide with panic, gasping as if he'd run all the way from the city's edge. His clothes were tattered, his face streaked with dirt and sweat. The patrons nearest him muttered under their breath, annoyed at the disturbance, but no one made a move to help.

"Please," he choked out, his voice hoarse. "They... they're coming. They're after anyone who's... who's touched it."

My blood turned to ice, the relic on my chest throbbing with a new urgency. I didn't need to ask what "it" was. I glanced at my partner, our eyes locking in a silent understanding that cut deeper than any words could.

Before we could react, a second figure appeared in the doorway, moving with a slow, predatory grace. This one was no panicked messenger. He was cloaked in shadows, his face obscured, but the power radiating from him was unmistakable—a dark, relentless energy that seemed to suck the air from the room. Silence fell as every gaze turned toward him, a stillness descending that felt almost tangible, thick and suffocating.

The man at the door dropped to his knees, his voice a whisper. "Please... don't..."

The shadowed figure ignored him, stepping forward with the deliberate slowness of someone who enjoyed the effect of his presence, who reveled in the way the room bent to his will. His gaze flicked toward us, his eyes gleaming like a predator's, a knowing look that told me he recognized the relic, that he could feel its pulse from across the room.

My partner's hand moved to mine under the table, a brief, grounding touch, before he pulled away, his face hardening, his body shifting into a stance that could turn defensive—or deadly—in a heartbeat.

"Didn't take them long to catch up," he muttered, his voice so low I barely caught it.

I swallowed, my mind racing, calculating our options. We couldn't stay here; the walls felt like they were closing in, the air thick with fear and anticipation. The shadowed figure took another step, his gaze never wavering, his expression that of a hunter closing in on his prey.

"Any brilliant ideas?" I whispered, fighting to keep my voice steady.

He tightened his grip on his knife, his jaw set. "Just one."

The door behind us swung open, slamming against the wall, and a second figure entered—someone we hadn't seen, someone whose face brought a flash of recognition, followed by a sinking dread that settled in my chest.

I barely had time to react before the shadowed figure lunged forward, his arm raised, his eyes locking onto me with a look that promised there would be no escape.

And then everything went black.

Chapter 16: Heartbeats in the Silence

The night held its breath, dense with shadows and a silence that somehow felt alive, humming between the trees and rolling across the darkened hills. We were sprawled on the uneven grass at the edge of the field, a blanket haphazardly tossed beneath us, but it felt like the world itself was our sanctuary. His hand rested close to mine, fingers brushing in that maddeningly accidental way that had plagued us for weeks now. I could feel the warmth of his skin, the rough callouses at the tips of his fingers—fingers that seemed to hover, to hesitate, as though they were just as unsure as I was about what would happen if they closed the last inch between us.

The stars were bright, scattered in careless patterns across the sky, while the moon hung low, watching over us like some silent, benevolent guardian. It wasn't that we had planned this, lying here together in the cold night air, but somehow it felt preordained, like every step we'd taken before this had been leading to this moment. His arm pressed a little more firmly against mine, and I thought I could hear his breath catch, as if he'd been waiting for this too. I found myself holding my breath, as if exhaling would shatter the delicate balance, would break the spell that had kept us here, teetering on the edge of something we could barely name.

"What are you thinking about?" His voice was soft, rough around the edges, and it sliced through the silence, startling me more than I wanted to admit.

I hesitated, words suddenly feeling sharp and treacherous, like they might slice right through the fragile night. I wanted to say something light, something easy, but his gaze was on me, dark and serious and so piercing that it made the night itself seem shallow in comparison. "Nothing," I finally managed, hoping he couldn't hear the lie wrapped around that single, thin word. But I knew he did; I could feel it in the way his fingers tightened briefly, not quite a squeeze, just a pressure, a silent reminder that he knew me far too well to let me get away with that.

"Liar." His smile was a brief, crooked thing, and it faded almost as soon as it appeared. "You've got that look on your face, like you're miles away."

I swallowed, trying to find my voice. It was hard to form words under the weight of his gaze, with that low, familiar rasp in his voice sending a shiver down my spine. "I'm not miles away," I said, barely above a whisper. "I'm right here."

It was true, I realized with a sudden clarity that was almost startling. For once, I wasn't thinking about all the ways this could go wrong, or the walls I'd built up over the years. I wasn't thinking about the future, or the past. Right here, with his hand a breath away from mine, with the stars hanging heavy in the sky, it felt like there was nowhere else I was supposed to be.

His thumb brushed against the back of my hand, tentative and gentle, like he was testing the waters. My pulse leaped, wild and unsteady, and I saw his lips part, just barely, as if he'd felt it too. The night was cold, but his touch was warm, a steady heat that seeped into my skin, anchoring me there, grounding me in the silence. It was terrifying, this closeness, this raw honesty that came without words, without pretenses. But it was also more real than anything I'd felt in a long time.

The silence stretched between us, thick and tense, charged with a thousand things unsaid. And then, slowly, he lifted my hand to his lips, his eyes never leaving mine. The kiss was soft, barely more than a whisper against my skin, but it sent a shiver down my spine, a thrill that lingered long after his lips had left my hand. I felt the weight of it, the unspoken promise that lay hidden beneath that simple touch. It was a vow, not in words, but in the silent language we'd built between us, in the heartbeat I felt echoing in his pulse, steady and sure against my skin.

"I don't know where this is going," he said softly, his voice barely more than a murmur. "But I know I don't want it to end."

I let out a shaky breath, feeling a rush of something that was equal parts terror and exhilaration. "Neither do I," I whispered, surprised by the honesty in my own voice.

And for a moment, it felt like the whole world had narrowed down to just us, to the quiet pulse of our heartbeats, to the gentle brush of his thumb against my skin. It was as if the night itself was holding its breath, waiting, watching as we hovered on the edge of something vast and unknown. And in that moment, I realized that maybe, just maybe, I was ready to take the leap, to let myself fall, to trust that he would be there to catch me.

The silence stretched on, comfortable and warm, and as his hand tightened around mine, I felt the last remnants of my fear begin to fade. The world was still, the stars shining bright above us, and in that quiet, hidden corner of the night, I felt something shift, something settle into place. It was as if, for the first time in a long time, I'd found exactly where I was meant to be.

And as I looked into his eyes, I knew that he felt it too.

A sudden breeze swept through the field, brushing cool fingers against my cheek, and I felt the shiver it brought ripple through both of us. His hand stayed in mine, firm, almost possessive, and I could feel his gaze resting on me, waiting, like he knew I had words tangled inside that I hadn't managed to let out. The night was so still that the world felt a thousand miles away; here, it was just the two of us, suspended in this strange, intoxicating pull, like we were hanging on to the last moment before something monumental.

"I know you're thinking something," he murmured, his voice barely more than a whisper, yet it cut through the quiet like a confession. "Or maybe you're just trying not to think it."

It was such a direct statement that I nearly flinched, feeling caught and yet oddly relieved. There was no denying it anymore; I wasn't even sure I wanted to. I opened my mouth to respond, but he shook his head, his thumb brushing gently against the back of my hand, a silent plea for honesty.

"What do you want me to say?" I asked, finally, my voice unsteady. "That I haven't thought about this? About... us?"

The word felt heavy, a dangerous, intoxicating thing. I didn't dare look directly at him, instead choosing the stars as my witness. They sparkled, cold and indifferent, but maybe that was just what I needed—something to balance the heat rising in me, the thrill and fear mixed together. He was quiet, his silence heavy, and for a moment, I feared he wouldn't answer at all. But then he exhaled slowly, like he'd been holding his breath for longer than he'd admit.

"I think I just wanted you to say it," he admitted softly, the vulnerability in his voice catching me off guard. "To know that I wasn't just... imagining it."

My heart twisted, torn between relief and something deeper, something raw that I wasn't ready to name. But his hand in mine, the way he looked at me, so serious, so intense—it was impossible not to feel it. He was like a live wire, something electric and wild, and yet he held onto me with such gentleness, as though I were the only thing that kept him grounded.

"Imagining it?" I repeated, arching an eyebrow, trying for levity, though my pulse was anything but calm. "So you've been picturing this? Here I thought you were the type to play it cool."

He let out a quiet laugh, shaking his head. "You give me far too much credit." His eyes were on me again, dark and serious. "I've spent too long trying to convince myself it's nothing, that you and I are just... whatever we are. But every time I look at you—" He broke off, running a hand through his hair, looking almost angry at himself. "It's not nothing, and it never has been."

A thrill shot through me, the words striking somewhere deep. I didn't want to look away from him, afraid that if I did, the moment would vanish, that this delicate truth we'd stumbled upon would slip through our fingers. But I felt exposed, raw in a way I hadn't expected. It was as though he'd seen past every wall I'd so carefully built, stripping away all the pretense, until there was nothing left but the simple, undeniable truth.

"So what do we do now?" I asked, the question hanging between us like a challenge. I could feel the pulse of it, an invitation, an offering, and I wasn't sure if I wanted him to take it or leave it. There was a part of me that was still terrified of what might happen if he stepped into that space, if he claimed the words we'd both danced around for so long.

He looked at me, his gaze steady, unwavering. "I think that's up to you," he said, his voice low, rough. "I'm here, and I'm not going anywhere. But if this—" He gestured between us, his hand brushing mine again, sending a spark through my skin. "If this is too much, I'll back off. I don't want to make this harder for you."

Something shifted in me then, a small but undeniable realization. He wasn't just offering me an easy answer, a perfect, romantic promise. He was giving me a choice, respecting the boundaries I'd drawn and the fears I hadn't voiced. It was terrifying, but it was also exactly what I needed. And in that moment, I felt the last of my hesitation begin to fade.

"Don't go anywhere," I whispered, barely trusting myself to speak. "I don't think I could handle it if you did."

He didn't say anything, just squeezed my hand, and it was enough. The tension between us softened, the weight of unspoken words lifting just a little. The night air was cool, but his warmth beside me was a constant, steady presence, anchoring me in a way I hadn't realized I'd been missing.

We stayed there, wordless, watching the stars in a silence that no longer felt heavy, but peaceful. And for once, it was enough just to be here, to exist in this strange, quiet space we'd carved out, without needing answers or promises. It was enough to just be, to feel his hand in mine, to know that somehow, against all odds, we'd found our way to this moment.

The sky stretched on above us, vast and endless, and as I closed my eyes, I let myself fall into the silence, trusting for the first time in a long time that someone would be there to catch me.

A strange calm settled over us, the kind that feels like the eye of a storm, deceptive in its quiet but loaded with the unspoken weight of what lay beneath. We lay there, wrapped in a silence that felt both safe and perilous, and I couldn't shake the feeling that one wrong move could unravel everything. Still, his hand remained in mine, our fingers laced as if daring the world to challenge this fragile peace. I was breathing carefully, the stillness thick and heady, amplifying each small movement, each heartbeat. I didn't want to think too hard about what this all meant; I just wanted to feel it.

I felt his gaze shift to me, and I couldn't stop myself from meeting his eyes. They were dark in the moonlight, searching, serious. And then, just like that, he broke the silence with a soft laugh—a quiet, unexpected sound that made me glance at him in surprise.

"What?" I asked, feeling my own lips curve, though I had no idea what was so funny.

He shook his head, looking a little sheepish, though there was a playful glint in his eyes. "It's just... us. Right here, right now. It's kind of... ridiculous, isn't it?"

I raised an eyebrow. "You think lying here, in the middle of a field, in the dead of night, holding hands with me is ridiculous?"

"Completely," he replied, his voice warm, soft. "But in the best way." His thumb traced a small circle against my hand, almost absent-mindedly, and I could feel the effect of that little touch reverberate through me. "It's just that, of all the people I could've found myself out here with, on a night like this, I wouldn't have picked you."

I let out a mock gasp, pulling my hand from his, and he laughed, catching my hand again before I could even pull it back all the way. "Excuse me?" I said, feigning offense, though my voice wavered, my smile impossible to hide. "That's a terrible thing to say to a girl who's been gracious enough to lie here and listen to you babble."

"Oh, come on," he teased, grinning now. "You know what I mean. It's not... you're not what I expected. In the best way," he added hastily, as if afraid I'd take real offense.

It was impossible not to smile at that. "Well," I said, meeting his gaze. "I could say the same thing. I didn't think we'd ever... end up like this."

For a moment, he was silent, and I could feel the shift between us, the lightheartedness slipping away as his expression softened, his eyes searching mine. "I don't think I've ever wanted something to work out this badly," he murmured, his voice almost too quiet to hear. "With anyone."

The words hung between us, unadorned and bare, and I felt a strange, wonderful ache settle in my chest. I opened my mouth to respond, but a sudden flash of headlights down the road caught our attention, slicing through the night like a blade. I stiffened, feeling the hairs on the back of my neck rise as the car slowed, its headlights sweeping across the field and illuminating the edges of our hidden corner.

He sat up, his body suddenly tense, his hand falling from mine as he turned to watch the car. "Do you know who that is?" he asked, his voice low, his eyes narrowing in suspicion.

I shook my head, a nervous flutter rising in my stomach. "No. Maybe they're lost?"

But even as I said it, I could feel an edge of doubt creeping into my mind. The car had stopped at the entrance to the field, its headlights fixed on us like twin, accusing eyes. My instincts prickled, every alarm bell in my mind starting to ring, and I sat up, brushing the loose strands of grass from my hands, my pulse thrumming faster with every passing second.

"Stay here," he said, his voice a tense whisper, but I shook my head, ignoring the protest in his eyes. There was no way I was letting him handle this alone. We weren't exactly in the middle of nowhere, but it was close enough to feel unnervingly isolated, and I wasn't about to sit back while he played hero.

"Not a chance," I whispered back, pushing myself to my feet. "Let's just... be cautious. It could be nothing."

We moved carefully, slipping down to the edge of the field, staying low as we watched the car, which hadn't moved an inch. I could feel my heartbeat pounding in my ears, the earlier intimacy replaced by a cold dread that settled like stone in my stomach.

The driver's door opened, and a figure stepped out, silhouetted against the headlights, shadowy and indistinct. They took a few steps forward, their movements slow, deliberate, as if savoring the tension, like they knew we were watching and were drawing out the moment. I felt his hand find mine again, squeezing it tightly, and I wasn't sure if he was steadying me or himself.

The figure moved closer, and I could just make out the outline of a man—tall, broad-shouldered, his stance too relaxed to be innocent. A stranger, certainly, and yet something about him felt familiar, as if he belonged to a memory I'd buried and long forgotten.

"Do you know him?" he whispered, his voice barely audible.

I shook my head, my skin crawling with the uncomfortable sense that I did, that some piece of me recognized this person, even if my mind was drawing blanks. But before I could answer, the man spoke, his voice cutting through the air with a smooth, unsettling confidence.

"Well, well," he drawled, his tone thick with an unsettling familiarity. "Fancy finding you two out here. Almost as if you were... hiding."

A shiver ran down my spine, my throat tightening as his words sank in. He knew us—knew us well enough to find us, to stand there in the dead of night and make it clear that this was no chance encounter. I glanced at him beside me, and in his eyes, I saw my own shock and fear mirrored back at me, mixed with a raw determination that was both reassuring and terrifying.

The man took another step forward, and I could feel the tension in the air sharpen, every instinct screaming at me to run, to pull him with me and disappear into the night. But my feet felt rooted to the ground, caught in the chill of that voice, in the shadow of whatever past I'd unwittingly carried into this moment.

"Why don't we talk?" he continued, his smile visible even in the dark, predatory and all too familiar. "I've got a few things I need to say. And I have a feeling you'll want to listen."

I felt his hand tighten in mine, grounding me even as the world tilted sideways, caught between flight and the terrifying certainty that whatever came next, we weren't walking away unscathed.

Chapter 17: A Storm of Feelings

The city's underground thrummed around us, a maze of hidden passages and shadowed alcoves veined with the low hum of energy. The relic in my pack pulsed against my back, a constant reminder of the very real, very dangerous curse clinging to it. And yet, his hand brushed against mine, steady and warm, grounding me in a way I hadn't expected. Every time I looked at him, I could see the weight of secrets he carried, hidden in the slight downward tug at the corners of his mouth, in the careful way he chose his words as if each one could be a key to the lock around his heart. I knew better than to trust anyone here, and yet... there was a tenderness in him, a quiet depth, that slipped under my guard when I least expected it.

A low rumble echoed through the stone walls, shaking dust from the ceiling, and we pressed ourselves against the damp, rough rock as the air filled with the scent of iron and mildew. His eyes met mine in the dark, a silent question lingering there—are you all right? I gave a quick nod, though my pulse raced, and not from fear. He turned, a faint smirk brushing his lips, and the edges of my defenses weakened even further.

"Think we'll make it out of here in one piece?" I asked, trying to sound nonchalant, but my voice betrayed the tremor of uncertainty.

"Depends," he said, his tone infuriatingly calm as he cast a glance at me, one brow raised in that devil-may-care way that made my heart skip. "Do you plan on sticking close, or do you think you'll bolt as soon as things get rough?"

I scoffed, shoving him playfully with my shoulder as we kept moving. "Please. I'm not the one who tried to run the last time the relic did... whatever it does. I'd say you're more likely to make a dash for it than me."

His laughter echoed softly, a rare sound in the oppressive silence of the tunnels. But before he could retort, a sudden, icy sensation prickled down my spine, and instinct took over. I grabbed his arm, pulling us both into a narrow crevice just as a dark figure stalked past, its footsteps echoing with an ominous click.

He tensed beside me, the warmth of his hand closing around mine in silent solidarity. We barely breathed as the figure paused, its shadow stretching long across the opposite wall. It stayed, motionless, for what felt like hours, and I could hear his heartbeat steady and strong beneath my hand, calming me even as fear coiled tight in my chest. Finally, the figure moved on, the echoes of its steps fading into the depths.

I let out a shaky breath, releasing his hand reluctantly. "Well," I said, trying to sound breezy even though my knees felt like jelly, "I guess that's what we get for loitering."

He chuckled softly, a low sound that stirred something in me I'd buried deep down. "Look at you, acting all brave. You're shaking like a leaf."

"It's cold down here, all right?" I shot back, rolling my eyes but feeling a smile tug at my lips. I couldn't let him see just how much his presence steadied me—he'd never let me live it down.

We emerged from the crevice and continued deeper into the labyrinth, the shadows thickening with every turn. The air grew colder, and the distant sound of water dripping somewhere echoed, making the silence all the more haunting. I could feel the curse pressing around us, an unseen force lurking, waiting, as if testing just how close we could get without unraveling.

The relic's pulse grew stronger, almost like it could sense the tension between us. My fingers brushed over it unconsciously, and a faint spark flickered beneath my touch, a reminder of the dangerous power we were toying with. I couldn't tell if it was real or if my mind was playing tricks on me. But one thing was certain—this wasn't a game anymore. I could feel it in the way he looked at me when he thought I wasn't paying attention, the silent, unspoken promise that bound us now.

"You ever think about what happens if we don't make it out of here?" he asked quietly, breaking the silence.

"Not really my style," I replied, my tone more defensive than I intended. "I'd rather focus on getting us out of here alive. Besides," I added, attempting a grin, "you know I'm not exactly thrilled at the thought of your ghost haunting me if this all goes sideways."

"Who said I'd haunt you? Maybe I'd find someone less stubborn," he shot back, his voice soft but laced with that teasing edge. But there was something deeper in his gaze, a flicker of vulnerability that felt like an invitation I was too afraid to accept.

And then he did something unexpected. He reached out, his fingers brushing my cheek as if testing the reality of it, as if he couldn't believe I was really there. My breath caught, and for a moment, I was certain he was about to kiss me. My heart thundered, a wild mix of hope and fear churning in my chest.

But before he could move any closer, the relic pulsed again, a fierce, burning heat that sent us both stumbling back. The force of it crackled in the air, a physical barrier that seemed to scream at us to stay apart. I clutched at the cold wall behind me, watching as he steadied himself, his face twisted in a mix of anger and frustration. It was as if the relic sensed our growing connection and was determined to punish us for it.

"So, that's how it's going to be, huh?" he muttered under his breath, glaring down at the relic. But his eyes shifted back to me, the challenge still there, defiant.

"What? Are you talking to the relic now?" I asked, attempting a laugh to ease the tension, though it came out more like a strangled gasp.

"Maybe I am. Seems to have a mind of its own," he said, his gaze intense as it lingered on me. "I don't like anyone telling me what I can and can't do."

A thrill shot through me, but I quickly masked it with a shrug, unwilling to give him the satisfaction of knowing how much he affected me. "Then maybe you should take it up with the curse. I'm sure it'll listen to you."

He chuckled, shaking his head, but that fierce light in his eyes hadn't faded. "Maybe I will. But in the meantime..." He paused, his expression softening as his gaze held mine, a silent promise lingering between us.

The walls seemed to close in tighter the further we went, pressing us together in more ways than one. Silence draped over us like the damp fog that seemed to seep from the walls themselves, swirling in cold tendrils around our ankles as we moved deeper, deeper into the unknown. The path narrowed, then opened into a dark cavern, the air thick with the scent of moss and something faintly metallic, like old blood or forgotten iron. I shivered, though I wasn't sure if it was from the chill or from the way his hand rested at the small of my back, steadying me with just a hint of possession.

He must have felt it too, because his fingers tightened, just slightly, as if he wanted to pull me closer but knew he shouldn't. His voice, usually carrying that playful, devil-may-care tone, softened into something almost reverent. "You feel it too, don't you?"

I managed a short, breathy laugh, even as my skin prickled with awareness. "Feel what? The fact that we're probably walking straight into another trap?"

"Maybe," he replied, that small smirk I knew so well playing at the corner of his mouth. "Or maybe it's the fact that every time we get closer to this... thing, whatever it is, it feels like something's holding its breath, waiting for us to make a mistake."

The admission caught me off guard. It was as close as he'd come to voicing the fear we both felt: that this wasn't just a curse lurking in the relic, but something alive, something watching, biding its time. For a moment, I thought of my life before all of this, back when my biggest worry was making rent on time and dealing with my sister's endless questions about when I'd "settle down." I never thought I'd be risking my life with a man who was equal parts frustrating and intoxicating, clutching a cursed relic that seemed to feed off the tension between us. And yet, here I was.

"What's the plan, then?" I asked, tilting my head up at him, trying to ignore the way his closeness made my thoughts feel too warm and too scattered. "Or are we just walking in circles and hoping for the best?"

"Funny you should ask," he said, his smirk fading into something more serious. He leaned in, his breath warm against my ear, and I could feel his words more than I heard them. "I thought you'd have a plan. But if you're out of ideas... well, maybe it's time we get creative."

He moved before I could respond, pulling me down behind a low stone ledge, hidden from view just as another figure appeared in the cavern's entrance. The stranger was cloaked, moving with an eerie, otherworldly grace, as if his feet barely touched the ground. My heartbeat quickened as I watched, clutching his arm tighter than I meant to. He didn't flinch, but I could feel the tension humming through him, matching my own. Whoever this stranger was, they were dangerous in a way that made the curse feel almost benign.

"Stay low," he murmured, his mouth so close to my ear that his words brushed against my skin, sending an unbidden thrill down my spine. "Whatever you do, don't let him see you."

I nodded, barely breathing as I watched the figure scan the room, his face obscured by the hood's shadow. He paused, and I felt my heart stop as he turned slightly, looking in our direction. For a split second, I thought he saw us; his gaze lingered, an eerie silence filling the air. Then he turned away, his footsteps echoing as he disappeared down a hidden corridor on the far side of the cavern.

The tension eased only slightly, but I felt his hand on mine, steady and reassuring. I hadn't realized how tightly I was gripping him until he gently pried my fingers free, holding them in his own with surprising gentleness.

"Seems like you might actually need me around after all," he said, a sly smile playing at his lips, though his voice was tinged with genuine relief. "What happened to being the fearless one?"

I pulled my hand back, though a traitorous part of me regretted the loss of his touch. "Fearless doesn't mean stupid. Besides, I don't remember you doing much in the way of heroics back there."

He chuckled, glancing over at the empty cavern before looking back at me. "I would have if you'd given me the chance. But somehow, I feel like you'd just find a way to take all the credit anyway."

I opened my mouth to respond, but something shifted in his gaze—a seriousness that made my heart skip a beat. He looked at me as if he were seeing me for the first time, his smile fading into something raw, unguarded. For a moment, it was just the two of us, standing in the shadows of a cursed labyrinth, with no one else to see or judge.

"What are we doing here?" he asked softly, his voice barely a whisper. "Not just here in this cave, but... here. You and me."

The question hung in the air between us, charged and vulnerable, and I had no answer. I wanted to brush it off, to make a joke, but the words caught in my throat. Because in that moment, I realized that all the quips, all the banter—it was just a mask. A thin, brittle mask that was starting to crack under the weight of whatever was building between us.

But just as I opened my mouth, a sound shattered the fragile moment—a faint, metallic scraping from the corridor where the cloaked figure had vanished. We both tensed, instinctively moving closer together as the sound grew louder, echoing off the cavern walls like a death knell.

Without thinking, he grabbed my hand, and we sprinted for the far side of the room, ducking behind another ledge just as the figure returned, this time dragging something that glinted in the dim light—a chain, heavy and thick, scraping along the floor as he moved. I felt him tense beside me, his grip on my hand tightening, and I knew he was thinking the same thing I was. Whatever this man was, he wasn't just an agent of the curse. He was something darker, something that didn't belong in any world I knew.

"We need to get out of here," he whispered, his voice barely audible over the scraping sound. "Now."

I didn't argue. We crept along the edge of the cavern, staying in the shadows, our footsteps barely making a sound. My heart pounded, adrenaline surging through me, every nerve on edge as we moved further from the relic's pull. I could feel its resentment, a seething presence in the air, but I didn't care. Not anymore. We had to get away.

Just as we reached the exit, I glanced back, one last look at the figure. But he had vanished, leaving only the chain glinting in the low light, coiled in the center of the room like a serpent waiting to strike. The sight sent a chill down my spine, but I forced myself to turn away, focusing on the path ahead.

As we slipped into the narrow passageway, I could feel him beside me, his presence solid and reassuring, a strange comfort in the midst of chaos. I didn't know what lay ahead, but I knew one thing—whatever happened, I wasn't facing it alone. And somehow, against all odds, that felt like enough.

We moved in a breathless silence, feet slipping on the slick stones as we navigated through the twisting tunnels that felt like they'd swallow us whole if we dared let down our guard. The air was thick, damp, tinged with the scent of mold and rust, and every drop of water from above seemed like a thunderclap in the narrow passageways. His hand was still on mine, fingers laced in a way that felt so natural I couldn't tell where his warmth ended and mine began. It was the only thing keeping me tethered as we moved deeper into the maze, away from the relic's insistent pull.

He squeezed my hand, the silent pressure asking if I was all right. I squeezed back, though I didn't dare look at him. Because somehow, in this moment, I was more afraid of what I'd see in his eyes than of the curse that stalked us.

Ahead, the tunnel widened again, revealing another cavern, but this one was different. Smooth stone pillars rose from the ground, arching up to the ceiling in strange, twisted shapes, casting shadows that seemed to writhe and shift. The air felt colder here, sharp enough to sting with every breath, as if something ancient and hungry waited in the dark.

"Is it just me, or does this feel like the part where something horrible happens?" I whispered, though my voice sounded too loud in the silence.

He shot me a sidelong glance, a half-smile playing on his lips. "When has anything we've done so far not felt like that?"

A laugh bubbled up before I could stop it, half-nervous, half-relieved. He was right—every step had felt like we were teetering on the edge of disaster. But somehow, laughing in the face of it made the fear a little more bearable, like the weight of it could be shared between us.

But before I could respond, a low growl echoed through the cavern, the kind that raises the hairs on the back of your neck and makes your instincts scream to run. His hand tightened on mine as we both froze, eyes scanning the dark for the source. And then, from the shadows between two of the twisted pillars, something massive moved—a dark shape that slinked forward, its eyes glinting like shards of broken glass in the dim light.

It was a beast, one that looked like it had been stitched together from nightmares, with fur that bristled like needles and claws that scraped against the stone, leaving deep, jagged grooves. Its gaze locked onto us, unblinking, predatory, as if it knew exactly what we were, exactly how fast we could run, and exactly how much it would enjoy chasing us.

I felt his hand slip from mine, and he stepped in front of me, his shoulders squared, his stance tense but unyielding. I wanted to protest, to tell him he didn't have to be the hero, but the words stuck in my throat. Because in that moment, with the creature's eyes fixed on us, I knew he'd made his decision. He'd protect me, even if it meant facing whatever horror lay in front of us alone.

But I wasn't about to let him. Not this time.

"So," I whispered, forcing my voice to sound steady, "how do you feel about the classic 'you go left, I go right' plan?"

He glanced back at me, a mixture of surprise and something else flickering in his gaze. "Oh, so now you want to get creative?"

"Hey, it's worked so far, hasn't it?"

He rolled his eyes, a grin breaking through the tension. "You and your brilliant ideas."

The creature let out another growl, its muscles tensing as if preparing to pounce. Without another word, we moved in opposite directions, each slipping behind one of the twisted pillars, trying to draw its attention in two places at once. The beast hesitated, a low snarl vibrating through the air, and for a heartbeat, I thought it would go after him. My chest tightened, fear clawing at me. But then, it turned, locking its cold, relentless gaze onto me.

The blood froze in my veins as the creature began to stalk toward me, its paws landing with deadly precision, silent and smooth. My mind raced, desperate for a plan, any plan, that didn't involve ending up as a midnight snack. But before I could act, he called out, his voice sharp, taunting.

"Hey! Ugly! You think she's your meal ticket? Think again!" He held up a glinting object, one I instantly recognized—the relic.

My breath caught as he brandished it, a reckless, dangerous glint in his eyes. The beast's attention snapped to him, drawn by the artifact's dark allure, its eyes narrowing as it seemed to recognize its own curse reflected in his hands.

"Get ready to move!" he called to me, his voice tight with urgency.

I barely had time to register his plan before he flung the relic with all his strength, sending it skittering across the ground, its glow pulsing like a heartbeat. The beast snarled, lunging after it with a single-minded ferocity, and in that moment, we bolted, darting past the pillars, through the shadows, and into another passage.

We ran side by side, our breaths ragged, our footsteps echoing in the narrow tunnel. The walls seemed to close in, and I could still feel the beast's presence behind us, its rage filling the air like a storm cloud. But we kept going, our steps in perfect sync, neither of us daring to look back.

"Nice throw," I managed to gasp, shooting him a quick grin.

"Don't get too comfortable," he replied, his face grim. "We're not out of this yet."

The passage twisted, curving downwards into a steep descent, and we skidded to a halt as the ground beneath us gave way to a gaping chasm, a dark void stretching endlessly below. I stared down, my stomach twisting, but he grabbed my arm, pulling me back before I could fall.

"Looks like we've reached the end of the line," he murmured, his gaze scanning the darkness, searching for a way across. But there was none—just the black abyss waiting below.

Behind us, I could hear the creature's growl growing louder, closer, and I realized with a sinking dread that it had followed us. There was nowhere left to run. He looked at me, his face shadowed, his expression fierce and unyielding.

"If you've got any more brilliant ideas," he said, his voice tight, "now's the time to share them."

I swallowed, my mind racing, grasping for something—anything—that might save us. But before I could speak, a low, rumbling vibration shook the ground beneath us, sending small rocks tumbling into the chasm. I grabbed his arm for balance as the tremor intensified, the walls seeming to buckle and shift around us.

Then, from the depths of the chasm, a faint glow appeared, a strange, ethereal light that seemed to rise, coiling upward like smoke. It pulsed, a silent beat that seemed to echo the relic's cursed rhythm, and I felt a pull, an inexplicable urge to reach out, to touch it, to let it guide us.

He must have felt it too, because his gaze met mine, wide and questioning. "What is that?" he asked, his voice barely audible over the rumbling.

"I don't know," I whispered, but something deep within me knew that whatever it was, it wasn't friendly. The light began to twist, taking shape, forming a dark silhouette that seemed to hover, waiting.

The creature's growl echoed behind us, a vicious snarl that reverberated through the tunnel, and I knew we only had seconds left. I turned to him, desperation clawing at my throat. But before I could speak, he grabbed my hand, his grip strong and certain.

"Trust me," he murmured, pulling me closer. And before I could argue, he leapt forward, pulling us both into the chasm, plunging into the darkness just as the cursed light surged toward us.

Chapter 18: The Dark Revelation

The day began like any other, though with a slight bite to the air that hinted at the turn of the season. Fall had crept in quietly, nudging leaves to a dusty orange and tinging the morning sky with a pink blush that whispered of colder days to come. I'd always been a summer girl myself, partial to the lazy heat and the languid days that felt like honey dripping off the spoon. But there was something enchanting about autumn in this place, how it settled over the town like a thick wool blanket, how the mountains seemed to grow taller and more foreboding as their tips grew dusted with frost.

But today, that serene beauty felt more like a trap, a reminder that something was coming, something big and irreversible. I could sense it in the air, an electric charge that set my teeth on edge and made my fingers tremble. And I knew, instinctively, that this unease was more than just seasonal jitters. It was the relic. The cursed, beautiful, maddening relic that had inserted itself into my life like a needle into soft skin, injecting a poison that I hadn't noticed until it was too late.

He was waiting for me at the edge of the clearing, silhouetted against the bruised sky, his face half-hidden by shadow. I could tell by his stance—the way he was shifting his weight, arms folded across his chest—that he was nervous, too. He looked up as I approached, his expression carefully blank, though his eyes held that familiar spark of intensity that had first drawn me to him. It was unsettling, that spark, because it felt like something more than attraction or curiosity. It felt like recognition, as if he saw something in me that I'd never known was there.

"What took you so long?" His voice was rough, tinged with impatience. The sound of it settled into me, a dark and comforting warmth.

"Traffic," I said dryly, glancing around the deserted woods. "It was brutal. You know how it gets out here."

He snorted, but there was a flicker of something in his expression that softened, a crack in the armor. "Always the comedian."

"Well, someone has to lighten the mood," I shot back, but the words felt hollow, as if my voice couldn't quite carry them. My gaze drifted to the object in his hands—a slender, obsidian fragment, jagged at one end like a shard of broken glass. It looked so innocent, so mundane, yet I knew that this piece, this small and unassuming relic, was anything but harmless.

I reached out without thinking, fingers itching to touch it, to feel its weight in my hand. But he pulled it back, his face tightening, his body coiling like a spring. It was a small gesture, but it cut deep. It was a reminder of the gap that had opened between us, a chasm carved by secrets and fears and that damned relic.

"Still don't trust me?" I asked, forcing a smile that felt more like a grimace.

"It's not about trust," he said, too quickly, too defensive. "It's... complicated."

"Of course," I replied, letting the sarcasm drip like honey. "Because nothing in our lives is ever simple, is it?"

He looked away, his jaw clenched, and for a moment, I thought I'd pushed him too far. But then he spoke, his voice barely a whisper, as if he were afraid of the words themselves. "This relic... it's not just a curse. It's... it's part of us. Part of you. Part of me. Like we're... tied to it. Bound."

A chill crept down my spine, settling in my bones like frost. "What are you talking about?"

He hesitated, glancing down at the shard in his hand. "It's in our blood. In our families, our histories. We weren't just... chosen for this. We were born to it."

The words hung in the air, heavy and terrible, a revelation that settled over me like a shroud. I wanted to laugh, to brush it off as nonsense, but I couldn't. Deep down, I'd always felt something strange, something pulling at me like an invisible thread. And now, hearing him say it out loud, I felt that thread tighten, binding us together in ways I hadn't understood until now.

"So... what does that mean?" I asked, my voice barely a whisper.

He looked at me, his eyes filled with a strange mixture of fear and determination. "It means we can't walk away from this. Not without losing... ourselves. Maybe even each other."

I felt a lump rise in my throat, my chest tightening with a dread that felt ancient and all-consuming. This wasn't just a choice, a mission we could take or leave. This was something deeper, something that had its claws in us from the beginning, and there was no way out. Not without a cost.

I took a step back, my hands clenching into fists as I tried to process what he was saying. "So, what? We're doomed? Destined to suffer because of some ancient family curse?"

He shrugged, his mouth twisting into a grim smile. "Sounds about right."

I wanted to hit him, to scream, to rail against the unfairness of it all. But I didn't. Because deep down, I knew he was right. This was bigger than us, bigger than anything I could have imagined. And no amount of anger or bitterness could change that.

For a moment, we stood there in silence, the weight of the truth settling over us like a storm cloud. Then he reached out, his hand brushing against mine, a hesitant, fragile gesture that spoke of a truce, of an understanding that went beyond words.

"We'll get through this," he said softly, his voice tinged with a gentleness I hadn't expected. "Together."

I looked at him, searching his face for any sign of doubt, of hesitation. But all I saw was resolve, a fierce determination that made my heart ache with a mixture of fear and hope.

"Together," I echoed, the word feeling strange and unfamiliar on my tongue, yet somehow... right.

In that moment, standing in the shadow of the curse that bound us, I realized that I was willing to face whatever horrors lay ahead, as long as he was by my side. Because, curse or no curse, he was part of me now, as much a part of me as the relic itself.

And there was no turning back.

My head was swimming with the weight of what he'd just told me. The idea that this curse, this relic, had somehow latched itself to our bloodlines felt absurd, like something out of a storybook. And yet, here we were, standing on the edge of the woods, with that strange and sinister shard glinting like a dagger between us. There was a chill in the air that had nothing to do with the season, an icy dread that seeped into my bones, anchoring me to the spot.

"Let me see it," I said, reaching for the shard again, but he kept his hand tightly wrapped around it, his knuckles white with tension.

He shook his head, giving me a look that was both pitying and protective, which only made me want to punch him. "It's not safe," he said softly.

"Not safe?" I echoed, crossing my arms. "You mean it's safer in your hands, right? Because you have some mystical expertise on ancient curses I don't know about?"

His mouth twitched, barely containing a smile, but there was a sadness behind it. "Believe me, I wish I didn't know as much as I do."

"Oh, how noble of you," I shot back, but the anger was thin, deflated by the worry that was clawing at my stomach. I couldn't shake the feeling that we were on the brink of something terrible, that this relic was more than just a cursed trinket we'd accidentally stumbled upon. If we were truly bound to it... if it was really tied to our blood... then what did that mean for us?

I took a step back, looking up at the trees, their branches stretching over us like skeletal fingers. The light was fading, casting long, thin shadows that made the world seem warped and distorted. For a moment, it felt as though we were the only two people left in existence, as if the rest of the world had slipped away, leaving us stranded in some twisted version of reality.

"Fine," I said finally, swallowing my pride. "Tell me what you know, then. No more half-truths, no more vague warnings. If we're bound to this thing, if it's somehow in our blood... I need to know what that means."

He hesitated, glancing down at the shard as if it might have the answers. His face was hard to read, but there was a flicker of something there—guilt, maybe, or fear. And that scared me more than anything else. If he was afraid, then maybe I should be, too.

"Alright," he said, his voice barely a whisper. "You want the truth? Here it is." He looked at me, his eyes dark and intense, and I felt a shiver run down my spine. "This relic... it wasn't just found. It was hidden. Hidden by our ancestors. They knew what it could do, what it was capable of. But they also knew that it was... part of us. Part of who we are."

The words made my skin crawl. I opened my mouth to protest, to argue that this was impossible, that curses and bloodlines and ancient relics were just fairy tales. But something in his expression stopped me. He was deadly serious, and for the first time, I realized just how much he believed it.

"You're saying... this thing is some sort of family heirloom?" I asked, trying to inject a note of disbelief into my voice. But it fell flat, and I knew he could tell I was just as scared as he was.

"In a way," he replied, nodding. "But it's not just an heirloom. It's a bond, a contract. Our ancestors bound themselves to it, tied their lives—and ours—to it. They thought it would protect them, give them power, keep them safe. But it came with a price."

"A price?" I echoed, my stomach sinking. "What kind of price?"

He looked away, his face shadowed, and for a moment, I thought he might not answer. But then he took a deep breath, the kind that seemed to pull all the air from the world around us, and spoke in a voice so quiet I had to strain to hear it.

"The kind that doesn't go away. The kind that follows you, generation after generation, until it's paid in full."

The words hit me like a punch to the gut, knocking the wind out of me. I felt as though I'd been plunged into icy water, my thoughts scattering like leaves in a storm. "Are you saying... we're trapped? That there's no way out?"

He didn't answer right away, and that silence told me everything I needed to know. My heart began to race, pounding so hard I could feel it in my throat. I had spent so long running from the idea of destiny, from the notion that my life could be anything but my own. And now, here I was, face to face with the realization that maybe, just maybe, I'd never had a choice at all.

"This is insane," I whispered, pressing a hand to my forehead. "You can't seriously believe that some ancient relic has control over us. That's... it's ridiculous."

"Maybe it is," he replied quietly. "But that doesn't change the fact that it's real. We're connected to it, whether we want to be or not."

I stared at him, my mind racing, trying to make sense of it all. Part of me wanted to turn and run, to get as far away from him—and that cursed shard—as possible. But another part of me, a part I barely understood, felt drawn to it, as if some invisible force was pulling me toward it.

"So what do we do?" I asked, my voice trembling despite my best efforts to keep it steady.

He looked at me, his expression fierce, determined. "We find a way to break the bond. To sever our ties to it. But it won't be easy. This curse... it's like a parasite. It feeds on us, on our fears, our desires. It won't let go without a fight."

The words sent a chill through me, and I realized that, deep down, I was terrified of what that fight might look like. But there was no turning back now. The moment I'd touched that shard, the moment I'd felt that strange, electric connection, I'd become part of something bigger than myself, something dark and dangerous.

"All right," I said finally, steeling myself. "Then let's fight it. Whatever it takes, whatever we have to do, let's end this."

A strange look crossed his face, a mixture of relief and sorrow, as if he'd been waiting for me to say those words but had hoped, somehow, that I never would. He reached out, his hand brushing against mine, and for a moment, I felt that same electric spark, that pull that bound us together.

"Together," he said softly, his voice barely a whisper.

"Together," I replied, my heart pounding as I looked into his eyes, seeing the shadows that lingered there, the ghosts of the past and the weight of the curse that bound us.

And as we stood there, in the gathering dusk, I realized that this was only the beginning.

The moon had risen above the trees, casting a pale, unsteady light that seemed to shift and twist, making shadows slither across the ground. I kept my arms crossed, partly to ward off the night chill and partly as a flimsy shield against the thoughts swirling in my head. I was standing next to a man I barely recognized now, and yet somehow knew better than anyone else, bound to a curse that felt older than time. And all of it—the secrets, the darkness, the weight of the past—had twisted together to form a knot I couldn't untangle.

I glanced sideways at him, studying the way his jaw tightened as he gazed into the distance. He was holding back; I could feel it in the tense line of his shoulders, in the way his hands curled into fists. "You're still not telling me everything, are you?" My voice was sharper than I intended, but I didn't care.

He turned to me slowly, his expression unreadable. "Would it change anything if I did?"

"It might," I shot back. "You dragged me into this mess. The least you can do is be honest about it."

He let out a sigh, the kind that seemed to carry the weight of years. "Fine. You want the truth? Here it is." He met my gaze, and there was something raw and unguarded in his eyes that made me want to look away, but I forced myself to hold his stare. "This curse isn't just about bloodlines or destiny. It's... it's fueled by emotion. By anger, by grief, by desire. Every time we give in to those things, we feed it. Make it stronger."

I blinked, taken aback. "You mean to tell me this thing is... alive?"

"Alive is a strong word," he said, his tone almost flippant, though his face was deadly serious. "It's more like... a parasite. It lives off us, drains us. And the stronger the emotion, the tighter it digs its claws in."

I tried to process this, my mind racing to make sense of it. A parasite feeding on our emotions? It sounded absurd, like something out of a bad horror movie. But as I thought back over the past few months—the strange outbursts, the sudden bouts of anger or sorrow that seemed to come out of nowhere—it started to make a horrible kind of sense.

"So, what are we supposed to do?" I asked, my voice quiet. "Just... stop feeling?"

He shrugged, looking away. "If only it were that easy."

The silence stretched between us, thick and suffocating. I looked down at my hands, feeling a sudden, overwhelming urge to laugh. Here I was, standing in the middle of the woods, talking about curses and parasites and bloodlines, as if any of this was remotely normal. As if any of this could be solved by logic or reason. But the more I thought about it, the more I realized that this was my reality now. I was in it, bound to it, whether I liked it or not.

"Okay," I said finally, forcing myself to take a deep breath. "So we're stuck with this thing, and it feeds on us. But there has to be a way to stop it. To starve it, or weaken it, or something."

He nodded slowly, though his expression was grim. "There is. But it's not exactly safe."

"Define 'not exactly safe.'"

He hesitated, his jaw clenching as he considered his words. "The only way to weaken it is to confront it. To bring it to the surface, make it show itself. And that... that requires tapping into the strongest emotions we have. The ones it feeds on the most."

My stomach dropped. "You're saying we have to... what? Invite it in?"

"Something like that." He met my gaze, his eyes dark and unflinching. "If we want to break this curse, we have to give it what it wants. We have to let it feed, just enough to lure it out."

The idea sent a shiver down my spine, a cold, creeping dread that settled in my chest like a stone. I knew, instinctively, that this was dangerous, that we were playing with fire. But at the same time, I felt a strange, reckless thrill at the thought of facing this thing head-on, of finally confronting the force that had haunted my life for so long.

"Fine," I said, squaring my shoulders. "Let's do it."

He looked at me, surprise flickering across his face, as if he hadn't expected me to agree so readily. But then his expression softened, a faint smile tugging at the corners of his mouth. "You're braver than I thought."

I snorted. "Or stupider. Time will tell."

We stood there for a moment, caught in a strange, tense silence, both of us acutely aware of what we were about to do. I could feel the weight of the night pressing down on us, the shadows deepening, as if the very air around us was holding its breath.

"So, what now?" I asked finally, my voice barely a whisper.

He looked away, his gaze distant. "Now... we go to the place where it all started. The place where our ancestors first bound themselves to this thing."

A chill ran down my spine. "You mean... the old ruins?"

He nodded, his expression dark. "It's the only way. If we're going to face this thing, we have to do it on its own ground."

The ruins were a place I'd avoided my whole life, a crumbling, moss-covered structure hidden deep in the woods, a place that was rumored to be haunted, cursed, filled with spirits of the past. The thought of going there, of facing whatever ancient darkness lay waiting, filled me with a sense of dread so intense I could barely breathe. But I knew, deep down, that I had no choice. If we were going to break this curse, we had to face it together.

"All right," I said, trying to keep my voice steady. "Let's go."

He glanced at me, a strange look in his eyes, as if he were seeing me for the first time. "Are you sure?"

I met his gaze, my heart pounding. "I'm sure."

Without another word, he turned and started walking, his movements swift and sure, as if he'd been preparing for this moment his entire life. I followed, my footsteps echoing in the silence, the weight of the relic heavy in my mind, a dark presence that seemed to pulse with every step we took.

As we made our way through the forest, the trees loomed above us like silent sentinels, their branches twisted and gnarled, reaching out like skeletal fingers. The air grew colder, thicker, and I felt a strange sense of foreboding, as if the very earth beneath my feet was warning me to turn back.

But I kept going, my heart pounding, my mind racing, every nerve in my body alive with anticipation and fear. I could feel the relic's presence growing stronger, a dark, insidious energy that seemed to seep into my very bones.

And then, just as we reached the edge of the clearing, he stopped abruptly, his hand shooting out to grab my arm. I stumbled to a halt, my heart leaping into my throat.

"What is it?" I whispered, my voice barely audible.

He didn't answer. He was staring straight ahead, his face pale, his eyes wide with a mixture of fear and disbelief. And as I followed his gaze, my breath caught in my throat.

There, standing in the center of the ruins, was a figure—a dark, shadowy silhouette that seemed to pulse with an otherworldly energy, its eyes glowing like embers in the darkness.

I felt a scream rising in my throat, but before I could make a sound, the figure moved, gliding toward us with an unnatural, predatory grace. And as it drew closer, I realized, with a sickening sense of dread, that it was looking directly at me.

Chapter 19: A Desperate Choice

The forest at night is a strange thing. Quiet, heavy, almost alive in the kind of way that presses against your skin and makes every inhale feel like it's not entirely your own. Standing there, bathed in shadows and the silvery splinter of moonlight, I felt the weight of it—the relic wrapped tight in cloth against my chest, a leaden promise that had turned my bones to steel and sand. I glanced over at Ezra. He looked exactly the way he always did—stoic, handsome in that annoyingly unruffled way—but his hand trembled as it closed around the hilt of his sword. I couldn't tell if it was fear or anger. Maybe both. It was a comforting thought, in a strange way, that I wasn't the only one terrified.

The plan was ridiculous, a last-minute, half-baked idea that relied far too heavily on luck and the unpredictable goodwill of whatever forces governed curses and ancient magic. Ezra had laid it out calmly enough, as if we were simply drawing up a schedule for a garden party instead of orchestrating the destruction of an artifact rumored to be so powerful it could—well, no one actually knew. I doubted it was anything pleasant, given what little we'd seen so far. But it didn't matter, did it? There was no going back. No carefully drawn plans or alternate paths. I swallowed, hard, feeling the rough edge of my breath catch in my throat.

Ezra's eyes caught mine, and for a moment, everything settled into a fragile quiet. His mouth quirked up on one side, the closest thing to a reassuring smile he ever seemed to manage. "Ready, then?" he asked, voice low enough to barely scrape the stillness around us.

"About as ready as one can be when attempting to destroy a relic that wants to kill us both," I replied, trying to keep the tremor out of my voice and failing miserably. He chuckled, the sound rich and almost foreign in the cold night air. I wished I could be as nonchalant as him, treating this like some unfortunate hiccup in an otherwise routine expedition. But Ezra wasn't carrying the thing against his chest, wasn't feeling the pulse of it beat out of sync with his own heart, a constant reminder of the power trapped within.

"Don't worry," he murmured, half to himself. "You're not getting rid of me that easily." He grinned, though there was something behind his eyes that suggested he didn't entirely believe his own words. I appreciated the effort, though. We were both tangled up in this mess, bound to it in a way neither of us had foreseen. And if I was being honest, I wasn't entirely sure if I wanted to let go of that tangled knot.

As we moved deeper into the forest, the air seemed to thicken, a sensation that felt like trying to wade through memories—half-formed, fleeting things that tugged at the edges of my mind. Branches clawed at my cloak, the ground squelched underfoot, and the shadows stretched long and lean, reaching out to brush against our skin like skeletal fingers. I shivered, pulling my cloak tighter around me, feeling the relic shift against my ribs with a weight that felt almost sentient. The knowledge that it could, theoretically, end everything—us, this forest, the sky—well, it made me wish I had a stronger stomach.

Ezra's hand found mine, rough fingers lacing through mine without a word, grounding me in the reality of it all. I stole a glance at him, and he gave me that small, almost imperceptible nod, the kind that told me he trusted me implicitly, even if the plan was barely one step above foolhardy. I hated that it made my heart skip. This was no time to be caught up in Ezra's steadying presence or the way his jawline looked absurdly appealing in the moonlight. But there was something unshakable about him, and I found myself holding onto it, letting it steady my steps as we pushed forward, inch by inch, breath by shallow breath.

And then we were there, standing at the mouth of the clearing that stretched wide and empty under the cold eye of the moon. In the center, a low altar of stone sat half-buried in the earth, etched with markings I couldn't decipher, though I felt them hum beneath my skin. Ancient words, older than language, older than anything I'd ever touched or known. I looked to Ezra, but his gaze was fixed on the altar, jaw clenched, eyes unreadable.

"This is it," he said, voice soft but hard-edged. "Once we start, there's no stopping until it's done."

The relic pulsed in response, as if it could hear him, and for a dizzying second, I thought I felt it hesitate. Ridiculous, of course. It was an object, a cursed one, yes, but just a thing. Still, the moment was enough to send a prickle of unease through me. What were we doing? I didn't know the answer, but the relic's hum grew louder, settling into a rhythm that matched my heartbeat, fast and uneven.

Taking a deep breath, I stepped forward, feeling the weight of Ezra's gaze on my back, and unwrapped the relic from its cloth. Cold metal glinted under the moonlight, sharp lines and brutal angles carved with care that seemed almost reverent, the kind of thing you could believe had been made for something far greater than anything we'd ever understand. As I held it out over the altar, my hands shook. I couldn't help it. For all my bravado, the knowledge that this thing could kill us, that it could do things I couldn't even imagine, was overwhelming.

Ezra's hand rested on my shoulder, grounding me, his voice low in my ear. "Whatever happens, I'm here."

It was a lie, we both knew that. The relic's power didn't allow for togetherness, for promises that stretched into the future. And yet, his words steadied me, gave me the push I needed to let the relic fall from my hands and onto the stone altar with a sharp clang that reverberated through the clearing like a death knell. The air stilled, every sound swallowed up, even the restless rustling of the trees gone silent. It was as if the world was holding its breath, waiting for the fallout.

A crack split the altar, thin at first, then widening with a slow, relentless certainty. I stumbled back, clutching Ezra's arm, but he didn't move, watching with a grim determination as if daring the relic to strike first. My heart hammered against my ribs, and the crack spread, jagged and terrible, light spilling out from beneath the altar like molten silver. It seared my eyes, but I couldn't look away, mesmerized by the way the relic seemed to fight, resisting the force pulling it apart, as if it had a mind of its own.

And then, with a final, thunderous snap, the light exploded outward, swallowing everything.

When the light died, it left behind a bruising silence, heavy and unnatural, as if the world had paused, holding its breath. My heart still hammered against my ribs, wild and out of rhythm, but I forced myself to look down. The altar lay in ruins, shards of stone scattered around us like the remnants of a broken mirror. And there, at the center of the rubble, lay the relic—intact, unscathed, and humming with a quiet, almost smug energy.

Ezra's voice was a low growl beside me. "Of course. Why would it be that easy?"

A laugh bubbled up in my throat, bitter and sharp. "I suppose we can't just ask it nicely to dissolve into dust, can we?" I ran a hand over my face, brushing away dirt and sweat, trying to ignore the prickling sensation crawling up my spine. Whatever magic held the relic together was more powerful than anything we'd ever encountered, and I felt as small as an ant beneath the weight of it. I turned to Ezra, forcing a smile that felt like a mask. "You don't happen to have a backup plan, do you?"

He didn't look at me, his eyes still fixed on the relic, his face unreadable. "Not unless you count running as fast as we can in the opposite direction."

"Tempting," I admitted. "But I have a feeling this thing doesn't exactly adhere to spatial limitations."

His lips twitched, and for a split second, I thought he might actually smile. Then he shook his head, giving the relic a look that was equal parts annoyance and resignation. "All right. So maybe we're stuck with the stubborn little menace for now. But there has to be a way."

"We don't have time," I muttered, pacing the edge of the clearing, my mind racing. "The curse... it's already spreading." I could feel it, an insidious chill creeping up from where the relic had pressed against my skin, a darkness that settled in the pit of my stomach like a coiled snake. There was no time for second guesses or waiting for an answer to reveal itself.

Ezra stepped forward, bending down to examine the relic more closely, his fingers grazing the edge of it as if testing its boundaries. "Maybe," he murmured, half to himself, "it's not about destroying it. Maybe it's about weakening it."

"Great," I muttered, throwing up my hands. "So we're looking for... what, an ancient dampening charm? A magic water gun?"

His eyes narrowed, but a hint of amusement flickered there, cutting through his usual stoic expression. "Not exactly what I had in mind, but sure. If you can conjure one of those, I'd be happy to try it."

I snorted, crossing my arms as I studied the relic with renewed scrutiny. We both knew that brute force wasn't going to work, not against something as old and intricate as this. The relic had survived centuries, maybe longer, guarded by curses and protected by layers of spells that were as ruthless as they were cunning. There was no easy solution, but maybe—just maybe—we could find a loophole.

A low rustling came from the shadows beyond the clearing, and my heart stilled. My instincts flared, every muscle tightening as I glanced at Ezra, who had gone completely still, his hand on the hilt of his sword. "Did you hear that?" I whispered, barely breathing the words.

He gave a slight nod, his gaze fixed on the shadows. "We're not alone."

My skin prickled as the silence stretched out, thick and oppressive, until the air seemed to hum with an electric tension. Whatever was out there, it was waiting. Watching. And it didn't feel friendly.

"On the count of three?" Ezra murmured, his voice barely a breath.

"One," I whispered, feeling the weight of my own heartbeat thud through my chest. "Two—"

A blur of motion lunged from the shadows, fast and silent, a flash of claws and gleaming eyes that were far too close. Ezra moved before I even had a chance to scream, his sword cutting through the air in a swift, controlled arc. The creature—a monstrous thing, all teeth and sinew—jerked back, letting out a guttural hiss that raised the hairs on the back of my neck. It was huge, with matted fur that gleamed in the moonlight, muscles rippling under its skin as it crouched, coiled, ready to strike again.

I grabbed the closest thing I could find—a broken piece of the altar—and held it out like a shield, my hand shaking. "Back off!" I snapped, though I wasn't sure if I was warning the creature or trying to convince myself that I had any control over the situation.

The beast's gaze flickered to me, and for a horrifying second, I saw intelligence there—an awareness that was far more terrifying than its sheer size. It let out a low growl, lips peeling back to reveal a set of sharp, yellowed teeth. My throat went dry.

Ezra didn't waste a second. With a swift, practiced movement, he lunged, his sword glinting in the faint light as he drove it toward the creature. The beast recoiled, but not fast enough. The blade sliced into its side, drawing a wet, dark stain across its fur. It let out a screech, stumbling back, eyes wild with pain and fury. It wasn't dead, but it was hurt, its movements slower, more cautious as it circled us.

"Any more brilliant ideas?" I hissed, keeping my eyes locked on the creature as it bared its teeth at us again, low and menacing.

"Just one." Ezra's voice was steady, but his gaze was fixed on the relic. "If we can't destroy it, maybe we can use it."

I stared at him, incredulous. "Use it? You mean... throw it at the monster and hope it explodes?"

A grin flashed across his face, reckless and far too confident. "Not quite. But if the relic is as powerful as they say, maybe we can harness it—turn its curse against itself."

"That sounds incredibly risky," I said, my heart racing as I tried to wrap my mind around the idea. "And slightly insane."

"Only slightly?" His grin widened, that familiar glint of mischief in his eyes that made me want to both slap him and kiss him at the same time. "Come on. It's us. Insanity is practically our brand."

I huffed, rolling my eyes, but a reluctant smile tugged at my lips. "Fine. But if this goes horribly wrong, I'm haunting you."

"Wouldn't have it any other way." He reached down, picking up the relic with a careful, almost reverent touch, the faint hum of its energy vibrating through the air. His face was taut with concentration, eyes narrowed as he held it out, focusing all his attention on the creature that crouched, watching us with a wary, predatory gleam.

The relic pulsed, a sharp, hot throb that sent a jolt of energy through my veins, and I could feel it—the power, dark and ancient, curling around us like a living thing. The creature froze, its gaze fixed on the relic, and for a moment, I almost thought I saw fear in its eyes.

Ezra took a step forward, the relic glowing brighter in his hand, and the creature let out a shuddering, almost plaintive sound, slinking back into the shadows, its gaze lingering on the relic before it finally vanished into the night.

I released a shaky breath, glancing at Ezra, who looked just as stunned as I felt. "Did... did we just scare off a monster with a cursed relic?"

He laughed, low and breathless, the sound raw and triumphant. "Looks like we did." His eyes met mine, and in that shared moment, amidst the ruins and the aftermath, I felt something shift between us, something fragile and electric, lingering in the space where fear had just been.

"Maybe," I said slowly, letting the words roll off my tongue, "we're not so bad at this after all."

The glow of the relic dimmed in Ezra's hand, settling back into a steady pulse, like the calm, indifferent beat of a heart that belonged to something far older, far colder, than either of us. The forest seemed to breathe again around us, the tense silence breaking into the familiar, rhythmic sounds of rustling leaves and distant night creatures. I could feel my heartbeat slowing, steadying as the adrenaline ebbed, but an uneasy itch remained beneath my skin, reminding me that this wasn't over. Whatever power we'd summoned, whatever had driven the beast back into the shadows, was only temporary.

Ezra exhaled, a wry smirk tugging at the corner of his mouth. "Well, I'd say that went better than expected."

I scoffed, glancing at the relic in his hands. "Better than expected? We still have a cursed relic with a mind of its own, a forest full of things with way too many teeth, and exactly zero actual plans for survival. You really know how to set the bar low, don't you?"

"Hey," he shrugged, still grinning, "if setting low bars gets us out of situations like this, I'm all for it." He held the relic up, examining it closely, his eyes narrowing with a flicker of something I couldn't quite place. Worry? Or maybe a grim sort of satisfaction, the kind that comes when you've barely survived a fall only to find the ground cracking beneath you.

I bit my lip, suddenly aware of the quiet, lingering weight of his gaze on me. There was something different in his expression, something raw and unguarded, like he was seeing me through the haze of danger for the first time. "What?" I asked, crossing my arms in a deflective, familiar motion, trying to ignore the warmth that crept into my cheeks.

He shook his head, a faint smile breaking through his seriousness. "Nothing. Just—this is not how I expected to spend my evening."

"Oh, and how did you plan on spending it?" I shot back, rolling my eyes. "Reading a nice book by the fire? Maybe enjoying a cup of tea?"

"Is that so hard to imagine?" he said, grinning, but there was a glimmer in his eyes, a flicker of something softer, something that caught my breath. For a second, the world seemed smaller, the weight of the relic and its dangers fading, leaving just us standing there, a heartbeat away from something terrifying in its own right. But then the relic flared, a sharp jolt of energy that sent a crackling pulse through the air, breaking the moment with all the grace of shattered glass.

We both froze, our eyes drawn to the relic as it glowed brighter, an angry, seething light that seemed to pulse in time with my own heartbeat. "Ezra," I whispered, my voice barely more than a breath. "What's it doing?"

He didn't answer, his gaze locked on the relic with a focus that was almost frightening. The air around us felt heavy, electric, like the seconds before a lightning storm. I took an instinctive step back, but Ezra's hand shot out, gripping my wrist with a force that made my pulse jump. "Stay close," he said, his voice tense. "Whatever happens... don't let go of me."

I wanted to ask what he meant, to demand answers, but the relic flared again, cutting off my words as a blinding light spilled out, filling the clearing with an intensity that made my vision blur. I squeezed my eyes shut, feeling the ground shift beneath us, as if reality itself had been thrown into a whirlpool.

And then, just as suddenly, the light was gone, replaced by a thick, impenetrable darkness. My breath caught, my hand finding Ezra's, clutching it tightly as we stood there in the blind, suffocating silence. "Ezra?" I whispered, my voice shaking.

"I'm here," he replied, his voice steady, a tether in the darkness. "Just... don't move. We're not alone."

A chill swept over me, as if a thousand invisible eyes were watching from all around us, observing with a quiet, predatory curiosity. I forced myself to stay calm, to focus on the solid warmth of Ezra's hand in mine, grounding myself in that small, fragile point of reality. But the air felt wrong, dense and thick, pressing against my skin like an invisible weight.

Then I heard it—a soft, murmuring whisper, curling through the darkness like smoke. It was a voice, hollow and broken, layered with echoes, as if spoken by a chorus of shadowed things. I couldn't understand the words, but the sound of it sent a sharp, icy shiver down my spine. My hand tightened around Ezra's, and I felt him respond with a reassuring squeeze, though I could sense his tension too, coiled and ready, like he was bracing for something I couldn't see.

The whisper grew louder, building into a chaotic murmur that filled my head, swirling and distorting until it became a cacophony of voices, each one more frantic, more desperate. I clapped my hands over my ears, my breath coming in sharp, shallow gasps as I fought to drown out the noise. But it was relentless, a relentless tide of voices crashing against my mind, each word clawing at my thoughts, fraying the edges of reality.

And then, through the madness, I heard it—a single, clear voice, cutting through the noise with a sharpness that felt like a blade against my skin. "Release me," it said, low and commanding, echoing in my mind with a force that left me reeling.

Ezra's hand tightened on mine, grounding me, pulling me back from the edge of panic. "Don't listen," he whispered, his voice fierce and urgent. "It's a trap. It wants you to give in."

I shook my head, trying to focus on his voice, to cling to that single thread of sanity. But the other voice was insistent, weaving its way through my thoughts with a persuasive, silken tone. "You hold the key, and you will surrender it. You are bound to it, as I am bound to you. Let go, and be free."

"No," I whispered, the word barely audible, but I held onto it, a single point of defiance in the sea of chaos. I clung to Ezra's hand, anchoring myself, feeling the warmth of his touch like a lifeline.

But the voice only laughed, a dark, bitter sound that echoed in my mind, filling me with a cold, gnawing dread. "You cannot resist forever. You are bound to me now, and the curse will consume you, as it has consumed all before you. You will give in."

I felt the words seep into my mind, the weight of them pressing down, curling around my thoughts like chains. I could feel it—the relic's curse, pulsing in time with the voice, an insidious darkness that seemed to coil around my heart, squeezing tighter with every beat.

"Ezra," I gasped, my voice strained, my vision blurring as the curse pressed down, overwhelming, suffocating. "I can't... I can't hold on..."

His grip tightened, his voice fierce. "Yes, you can. Fight it. I'm right here." His words cut through the darkness, a sharp, unwavering presence that broke through the curse's grip, pulling me back from the edge.

But the relic's power surged, a fierce, blinding wave that sent me stumbling, wrenching my hand from his grasp. For a terrifying moment, I was alone, caught in the thrall of the relic's power, the voice laughing as it pulled me deeper, farther away from everything I knew.

And then, just as I felt myself slipping away, a new light blazed through the darkness, bright and searing, a force that pushed back against the curse with a raw, fierce energy. I looked up, disoriented, blinking through the haze, and saw Ezra standing there, his face fierce and determined, his hand outstretched toward me.

But before I could reach for him, the darkness surged back, a wave of shadows that swallowed him whole, leaving me alone, stranded in the depths of the relic's power, with only the voice's mocking laughter echoing in my mind.

Chapter 20: Into the Abyss

Our footsteps echoed against the stone, a staccato rhythm that seemed to chase us deeper into the belly of the earth. I felt the texture of the path change beneath my boots, from smooth and worn, as if hundreds had walked this road before, to uneven and jagged, the work of some ancient upheaval. The air was cold, metallic. It tasted of rust and something older than dust—something that, if given a voice, might whisper secrets too dark for the living to understand. My heart was pounding, a steady reminder of my own pulse as I tightened my grip on his hand, not daring to let go for even a second.

He glanced over, his face a mask of concentration with a flicker of something else—concern, maybe? A hint of fear, quickly swallowed. It was one of the things I liked about him; he wore his bravery like an old coat, patched and worn but dependable. And even here, surrounded by an ancient, lurking darkness that seemed to pulse around us, he made me feel that, somehow, we'd get through this.

The tunnel walls curved, narrowing as we pressed forward. Strange symbols etched into the rock glowed faintly, illuminating just enough for us to see, but not enough to banish the creeping shadows. Each symbol, twisted and looping, seemed to twist further into my mind, drawing forth memories I didn't know I had, or maybe fears I'd tried too hard to bury. They whispered promises of power, of safety, of doom. I shook my head to clear the fog of their seduction.

"Remind me again why we thought this was a good idea?" I whispered, trying to inject humor into my tone. It came out more like a shiver.

He didn't respond at first, just gave my hand a gentle squeeze. His silence felt heavy, as if he were choosing his words carefully, a trait I was coming to recognize. "Because," he said finally, voice low, "we're either brave or incredibly foolish. And if we're going to find out which, we may as well do it together." He threw me a sideways smile, crooked and entirely too charming, a sliver of brightness in the oppressive dark.

Despite myself, I grinned back, a laugh slipping out before I could stop it. The sound bounced around us, startling in its clarity, a fleeting note of life in a place that felt long dead. I could almost feel the walls shudder with disapproval, as if our laughter was a foreign, unwelcome thing here.

As we walked, I kept one hand on the rough stone beside me, the other clasped in his. The walls were damp, and every now and then, my fingers would brush over a small indentation, like teeth marks in the rock. My mind played tricks on me, conjuring images of what might have made those marks—claws, fangs, creatures too terrible to imagine. I pulled my hand back, wiping it on my coat as a shiver ran down my spine.

Ahead, the tunnel began to widen into a cavernous space, barely lit by the symbols crawling across the stone. The air was colder here, sharp and brittle, with an undertone of something rotten that made my stomach twist. I could see the outline of something massive in the center of the room—a dark, looming shape, almost invisible against the shadows. The relic. It stood on a pedestal carved with more of the symbols, its form cloaked in layers of dust and mystery.

We moved closer, the silence pressing in around us. I could feel every nerve in my body alight, senses stretched to the breaking point as I gazed at the relic. It was both beautiful and terrible, a dark jewel that seemed to pulse with a faint, otherworldly glow. There was a crack down its middle, a fault line that split it like a wound, and for a moment, I felt a strange urge to reach out and touch it, to feel the power that hummed beneath its surface.

He caught my gaze, eyes sharp. "Don't," he said, his voice more warning than command. "Not unless you want it to claim you."

I nodded, swallowing the impulse, my fingers curling tightly at my side. The relic was a lure, a trap set long ago, and I could almost feel it tugging at the edges of my mind, promising things I didn't want to admit I desired. But there was something else here, something beyond the relic's seductive pull. I could sense it in the shadows, lurking just beyond our sight, watching us with a patience that felt ancient and hungry.

Then, the silence shattered.

A low growl echoed through the cavern, vibrating through the floor and into my bones. I froze, my heart seizing as I scanned the darkness, eyes straining to find the source of the sound. He pulled me close, positioning himself between me and whatever lay in the shadows. My breath hitched as a shape began to emerge, a hulking figure that seemed to blend with the darkness itself, its eyes glowing with a cold, predatory intelligence.

"Well," I whispered, forcing my voice to steady, "I suppose it was too much to hope that we'd just be able to grab it and leave."

His lips quirked in a grim smile. "Wouldn't be much of an adventure if it were that easy, now would it?"

I felt a wild laugh bubbling up, a defiant surge of adrenaline that banished the fear, if only for a moment. We were in the heart of danger, facing a creature straight out of a nightmare, and yet I felt alive, more than I had in years.

The creature took a step forward, its movements slow, deliberate. It was testing us, sizing us up, and I could see the calculation in its eyes, a predator assessing its prey. I took a deep breath, forcing myself to remain still, to hold my ground. This was it, the moment we'd been building towards, the point of no return.

And as I looked into those cold, unblinking eyes, I realized something unexpected: I wasn't just afraid. I was ready.

The creature prowled closer, its massive form almost blending into the darkness until it was barely more than a set of gleaming, hungry eyes. I could see the ripple of muscles beneath its blackened fur, a predator coiled and ready, and the air seemed to crackle with its cold intent. A strangled part of me wanted to turn and run, but the thought was laughable—we were far too deep for any retreat. I swallowed, tasting the metallic tang of fear in the back of my throat. Beside me, he was still, poised, the slightest shift of his weight indicating he was ready to face whatever might come.

But, instead of attacking, the creature stilled. Its head tilted, watching us with a bemused, almost curious expression, as if we were some novelty in its otherwise predictable world. I glanced at him, raising an eyebrow. "So, what's the protocol here? Do we introduce ourselves or just hope it has a busy schedule?"

His lip twitched, though his eyes remained fixed on the beast. "Let's try not to insult it. I get the feeling it doesn't appreciate sarcasm."

The creature's low growl hummed like a drumbeat, vibrating through the cavern. It was close enough now that I could make out the deep ridges on its skin, the scars that marred its flank like battle-worn armor. Every inch of it screamed danger, a creature shaped by survival, and as its gaze lingered on us, I felt a twinge of doubt for the first time.

But that's when it happened—a flicker in the shadows behind the creature. A shape darted from the darkness, fast and nearly silent, but enough to make the creature turn with a snarl. It lunged at the new arrival, and I saw a glint of steel, a blade flashing out, aimed with deadly precision. I held my breath as the newcomer dodged, the cloak they wore flaring out like a shadowed wing, obscuring their face. Whoever they were, they moved with a grace that seemed almost otherworldly, a dance of evasion and attack.

The creature lunged again, but the figure stepped aside, quick as a shadow, and the beast's claws scraped against the stone with a piercing screech. It was distracted, momentarily thrown off-balance, and I felt his hand on my arm, pulling me back. He was already moving, using the distraction to edge us away from the danger, but I could barely tear my gaze from the battle unfolding before us.

The stranger ducked beneath a swipe of claws, close enough now that I caught a glimpse of their face—a mask, dark and expressionless, with eyes that glinted in the faint light. Another blade shot out from their sleeve, and in a flash, they drove it deep into the creature's flank. The beast roared, a sound that shook the walls and seemed to warp the very air around us. I felt the pulse of its rage ripple out, a shockwave that made me stagger back.

The creature spun, its claws slicing through the air, but the masked figure moved like smoke, slipping past each swipe and landing another blow. I could see the creature weakening, its steps slowing, blood darkening the ground beneath it. For a moment, it seemed as if the masked figure would win, and I dared to hope. But then the creature reared back, a surge of fury fueling its last attack, and its jaws snapped around the figure's shoulder, sending them crashing to the ground.

"No!" I hadn't even realized I'd shouted until my voice echoed in the cavern.

His grip on my hand tightened, a silent plea to stay back, but something inside me surged forward, reckless and stubborn, refusing to let this stranger—whoever they were—fight alone. I fumbled for my dagger, the one weapon I'd brought, its hilt familiar in my hand but suddenly feeling much too small, much too inadequate.

Before I could move, though, the stranger was up again, staggering but defiant. They held their ground, blade raised, their voice echoing in a low, steady command. "Leave, beast. Go back to the dark from which you came."

The creature paused, its gaze flickering, a hint of confusion crossing its bloodied face. The stranger's words resonated, not just a plea but a binding command, and I could feel the power woven through them, ancient and unyielding. The creature let out a snarl, but it backed away, its head lowering, its form retreating into the shadows with a grudging obedience.

The stranger turned to us, their mask still in place, and I could feel their gaze piercing through the darkness. They lifted their chin slightly, a silent question in the tilt of their head. "And you two," they said, their voice muffled but sharp, "what foolish business brings you to this forsaken place?"

I glanced at him, but he was already stepping forward, offering a slight bow, his tone wry. "Let's call it an unfortunate hobby. We're after the relic."

The stranger was silent for a long moment, the mask expressionless, though I sensed a flicker of amusement behind it. "You're either very brave or very foolish," they said finally. "Most would be wise enough to leave these dark things to their slumber."

"Oh, we're definitely both," I replied, crossing my arms. "But we've come this far, so we might as well see it through."

The stranger tilted their head again, studying me, and though I couldn't see their expression, I felt the weight of their gaze, an appraisal that left me feeling raw and exposed. After a long pause, they sheathed their blades, a resigned sigh escaping them. "Very well. But if you're set on this path, I'll see you don't get yourselves killed."

The relief was palpable, though I tried not to show it. I offered a tentative smile, glancing up at the looming shadows. "Much appreciated. Seems the locals aren't too fond of visitors."

The stranger chuckled, a low sound that reverberated in the cavern, surprising in its warmth. "No, they're not. But they'll respect strength, and you two"—they paused, glancing between us—"have a peculiar resilience."

He raised an eyebrow, grinning. "Peculiar? I'll take that as a compliment."

They gave him a slight nod, their mask concealing any hint of expression. "Consider it what you will. Just know that the relic is not just a prize to be won. It's a weight, a darkness that will claim anyone not strong enough to wield it."

The stranger's words hung in the air, a caution that settled heavy between us. I felt the pull of the relic even more intensely now, a dark allure that thrummed through the ground and into my bones, whispering promises I didn't dare listen to.

With one last nod, the stranger turned, gesturing for us to follow. As we moved deeper into the cavern, I felt a spark of something unfamiliar, something akin to hope, tempered by the thrill of facing the unknown. And though fear gripped me, there was something undeniable in my heart—a fierce, reckless determination that would not be silenced.

The stranger led us deeper into the winding stone passages, their cloak blending seamlessly with the shadows. I found myself straining to catch a glimpse of their face behind the mask, to glean anything that might reveal a hint of identity or motive. But there was nothing—just those eyes, sharp as daggers, glancing back occasionally to check if we were keeping up. I could feel his fingers tighten around mine, and I dared to squeeze back, grateful for his warmth in this tomb of stone and secrets.

"So," I murmured, letting my voice cut through the tense silence. "Does our new friend have a name, or do we just call you 'Masked Mystery'?"

The stranger glanced over their shoulder, a glint of amusement flashing in their eyes. "You may call me whatever you wish, but names are a burden in places like these."

"Right," I whispered, my mouth twisting into a grin I hoped looked braver than I felt. "I was really hoping for something simple. Bob, perhaps?"

His laugh was low, a soft rumble in the silence, and I felt him shift closer, a steadying presence in the uncertain dark. The stranger didn't dignify my suggestion with a response, which felt both disappointing and entirely in character. Still, the silence around us took on a different quality, warmer somehow, like the crackle of a shared secret.

The walls around us began to change, shifting from rough-hewn stone to something smoother, something disturbingly polished. Strange glyphs began to appear more frequently, spiraling and twisting in patterns I couldn't begin to understand, each one seeming to pulse as we passed. They looked almost alive, their symbols writhing, as if straining to break free of the stone. I shivered and pressed closer to him, fighting the urge to look away.

Our guide's voice cut through the silence, echoing against the walls with an unsettling clarity. "You should both know that what lies ahead is not merely a relic. It is something older, something that has seen and survived the collapse of entire empires."

"Cheery," he muttered, glancing sideways at me with a smirk. "Anyone else starting to think this is less of a rescue mission and more of a suicide pact?"

I bit back a laugh, feeling the flicker of nerves twist into something lighter, more bearable. "You know I'd follow you into a volcano if it came down to it, right?"

He chuckled, the sound rolling warmly between us, and for a moment, it was just us again, a small oasis of familiarity in a sea of strange and foreboding shadows. But as we turned a corner, the light began to change, casting an eerie glow across the smooth, gleaming walls. The air grew colder, thick with a tension that prickled at my skin, and I knew, with a chill settling in my bones, that we were close.

The chamber opened before us, vast and cavernous, with a ceiling that stretched far beyond the reach of our lanterns' light. Pillars, carved with intricate scenes of battles and rituals, rose around us, reaching up into the gloom, and at the center of it all, on a stone pedestal, sat the relic. It looked almost ordinary, like something forgotten and harmless, but the air around it shimmered, thick with a power that felt alive and malevolent.

I took a cautious step forward, barely breathing, as my eyes locked onto the relic's form. It was smaller than I'd expected, no larger than a fist, its dark surface marred by a single crack down the middle. Despite its size, it seemed to pulse with a gravity all its own, as if the very stone beneath it bowed under its weight.

His hand fell away from mine, and I watched as he stepped forward, his face set in grim determination. I wanted to reach out, to pull him back, but the words died in my throat as he drew closer to the relic. The stranger watched in silence, their expression hidden, though something in their posture seemed wary, almost as if they too feared the power that lay coiled within that small, unassuming object.

As he reached out, a low rumble shook the chamber, a vibration that seemed to come from the depths of the earth itself. Dust rained down from the ceiling, and I felt a swell of panic as the ground trembled beneath us. He froze, his hand hovering just inches from the relic, as if some unseen force held him back.

"Wait," the stranger's voice was sharp, cutting through the growing noise. "Touch it, and you may wake something that should never see the light of day."

He turned to them, brow furrowing. "We didn't come all this way to leave empty-handed."

The stranger's hand shot out, gripping his shoulder with surprising strength. "Then you should know that this relic does not belong to the living. It is bound to something ancient, something that feeds on the souls of those who attempt to wield it."

I watched his jaw tighten, frustration flickering across his face as he looked between us. "So, what then? We just leave it here? Turn around and walk away after everything?"

I felt the weight of his words settle over me, a heavy, aching truth I didn't want to face. Every step we'd taken had been toward this moment, this single object that could save—or destroy—everything we cared about. And now, standing on the precipice of everything we'd fought for, the reality of what lay before us felt crushing.

The stranger's gaze shifted to me, and though I couldn't see their expression, I felt the intensity of their stare. "There is another way," they said quietly. "But it requires a sacrifice."

The words hung between us, stark and unyielding. He looked back at me, and in his eyes, I saw a flicker of fear, something raw and unguarded. He knew what they meant, as did I. The relic demanded more than courage; it demanded something that could not be given lightly, something that could only be taken.

"What kind of sacrifice?" I asked, my voice barely a whisper, though I dreaded the answer.

The stranger tilted their head, their voice softened, almost gentle. "A piece of your soul. A bond, willingly forged and willingly broken, but one that will forever change whoever undertakes it."

He drew a breath, steadying himself, but I could see the resolution hardening in his gaze. He took my hand, the warmth of his skin grounding me in the midst of all this darkness. "If this is what it takes, then so be it."

My heart pounded, torn between fear and resolve. I held his gaze, knowing that whatever lay ahead, we would face it together. But even as I nodded, a shiver ran through me, the realization sinking in that this was more than we'd bargained for.

With one last glance at the stranger, we stepped forward, hands clasped, and reached for the relic. As our fingers brushed its surface, the chamber seemed to inhale, a sharp, searing breath that stole the air from my lungs. I felt the burn in my chest, a pull so fierce it seemed to tear through my very core, binding us to the relic and each other in a way I couldn't explain, couldn't resist.

And then, with a shudder that shook me to my bones, the chamber plunged into darkness, and I felt the cold grasp of something ancient and unyielding pulling us down, deeper into the abyss.

Chapter 21: The Guardian's Warning

The chamber was vast, echoing with the cold silence of ancient secrets. Stalactites hung from the ceiling like the teeth of some beast waiting to snap shut, while faint streams of water trickled down the walls, their paths glistening like veins. The air was thick with something—an invisible weight that pressed against my lungs, made me struggle to breathe without letting on how much it affected me. I felt the pulse of energy in my bones, some thrumming, rhythmic force that seemed to come from deep below, deeper than the roots of the mountains themselves. It was as though the earth itself was alive, watching us as we inched forward. I glanced sideways, caught my companion's eye, and read the same mix of anticipation and dread in his face.

Just when I thought we might traverse the entire length of the chamber in tense silence, the shadows coalesced into a figure—there, standing before us, one moment nothing, the next a presence so palpable I took a stumbling step backward. I felt my hand tighten instinctively around the hilt of the dagger at my side, a comfort I didn't really believe in, not against something like this. The figure was cloaked, a dark mass of swirling fabric that seemed less sewn than conjured. Shadows played over him as though they found him more substantial than light. When he spoke, his voice was low, yet each syllable rolled through the cavern like thunder far off in the distance.

"You come seeking destruction," he said, his voice unsettlingly calm. It wasn't a question; it was a statement, as though he had known we were coming for longer than we'd known ourselves. I felt a cold bead of sweat trickle down my back, a sensation as unnerving as the voice itself.

"We come to end this," I managed to say, though my voice sounded hollow against the walls. My companion shot me a wary glance, and I saw the warning in his eyes, but I couldn't hold back.

"It's cursed half a continent. It's left scars that'll last generations. We're here to put it down, for good."

The guardian tilted his head ever so slightly, a subtle movement that somehow made me want to shrink away, but I held my ground. The silence stretched, a tightrope I could almost feel beneath my feet. And then he spoke again, his words laced with something almost like sorrow.

"To sever what you hold is to sever a part of yourselves," he said, gesturing with a hand that flickered at the edges as though he were part shadow himself. "The bond you share with it is a tether that will not break without a cost."

I felt my heart sink, and I knew without looking that my companion felt it too. He exhaled sharply, the sound echoing like a whispered curse in the cavernous space. All at once, the weight of our journey, of every choice we'd made to get here, pressed down on me. My mind raced through memories I hadn't dared to revisit—moments of doubt, brief flickers of hesitation, nights spent staring into the dark with the nagging question, Is this worth it? Yet each time, the answer had been the same.

My companion turned to me, his face a mixture of fear and resolve. "If we walk away," he said quietly, almost as though afraid the guardian would hear, "it'll keep spreading. The curse. We'd be back where we started. Worse than before."

"We don't have a choice," I whispered, even as I felt the truth of the guardian's words sink in, deeper than I wanted to admit.

But the guardian seemed almost amused at our back-and-forth, a silent observer, patient as the stones around us. He took a step forward, and I felt an icy draft sweep over me, sending shivers prickling down my skin. He raised one hand, and in his palm, I saw something dark, a shape coiled tight and shimmering faintly in the dim light. It was a vision, or a memory maybe, or something between both, a flickering glimpse of what could be if we took this step.

I saw fields burning, homes reduced to ash. I saw faces I recognized twisted in agony, shadows overtaking them one by one. And there, amidst the destruction, was the relic, pulsing with a malevolent life of its own, feeding off the chaos, growing stronger.

"Sever it," the guardian intoned, his voice low but relentless, "and it will not merely vanish. It will take root elsewhere, growing anew in darkness, its hunger unquenchable. To end it, truly end it, you must be prepared to lose everything."

His words settled over us like a shroud, the weight of them pressing against my resolve. I felt the grip of terror twist in my stomach, the cold certainty that what he spoke was true, that there was no simple end, no clean severance. I could feel the weight of the choice sinking into my bones. It was a warning, a choice that would demand more than I had prepared to give.

My companion met my gaze, his eyes reflecting the same determination I felt rising in my chest, defiance swelling like a shield. "We've come this far," he said, the words almost a whisper, meant for me alone. "I'd rather face whatever comes next than live with knowing we walked away."

And there it was, the decision slipping into place as though it had been inevitable all along. I reached out, took his hand in mine, the touch a promise that whatever came, we would face it together. I looked back at the guardian, felt the tremor of fear give way to something fiercer, something unbreakable.

"We're ready," I said, the words filling the silence, strong and steady.

The guardian's expression shifted, and for a fleeting moment, I thought I saw a flicker of something human beneath the shadows—respect, perhaps, or sorrow. It vanished before I could be sure, and he simply inclined his head in a solemn nod.

"Then may you be prepared," he murmured, "for what fate demands."

As he faded back into the shadows, his warning lingered, a bitter aftertaste that clung to the air long after his presence had vanished. And as we stood alone once more, my companion and I shared a silent vow: we would not leave this place until we had either vanquished the curse or let it consume us, and neither of us was ready to give up just yet.

The silence in the cavern became oppressive as the guardian's figure faded, leaving behind a suffocating weight. The shadows seemed to crawl closer, more alive than they'd been before, as if they, too, were invested in this choice. I could feel the chill seep through my bones, though I didn't dare let go of my companion's hand. He squeezed it, a silent reassurance—or perhaps a reminder that we were still here, still mortal in the face of something ancient and indifferent to our fate. The air tasted metallic, and I found myself holding my breath, afraid that even breathing too deeply might stir the wrong kind of attention.

"I'll give him this," I murmured, breaking the quiet, "he certainly knows how to make an exit."

My companion let out a snort, a faint smile ghosting over his face, though his grip on my hand stayed firm. "Nothing like ominous warnings from ageless, shadow-clad guardians to spice up a Tuesday."

I felt a laugh bubble up, absurdly, wildly inappropriate, and yet it eased some of the tension winding through me. "At least we know we're in over our heads. That's... something, right?"

"Oh, absolutely," he replied, deadpan, his tone so matter-of-fact that it nearly convinced me this was all perfectly reasonable. "We're absolutely doomed. But hey, think of the stories we'll tell if we make it out of here."

I rolled my eyes, though I couldn't hide the smirk tugging at my lips. "Stories for whom, exactly? You planning on starting a campfire for the next group of fools who stumble in here?"

"Maybe I'll stick to dramatic retellings," he said, casting a glance around the cavern, as if daring the shadows to disagree. "The ones where we emerge victorious, unscathed, and only mildly traumatized. Let's give future generations some hope, at least."

The banter calmed me more than it should have. I'd lost track of how many times he'd steadied me like this, one dry quip at a time. We'd shared countless dangerous moments, but somehow, this one felt different—heavier. I looked at him, his face set and serious beneath the sarcasm, and a flicker of something close to panic flared in my chest. Because if we went through with this, if we were as bound to the relic as the guardian had suggested, I wasn't sure I was ready for what that meant. Not for me, and certainly not for him.

He seemed to sense my hesitation, his gaze softening as he took a small step closer. "Hey," he said quietly, dropping the bravado. "We've come too far to turn back now. No matter what he said, we're not alone in this. We face it together, remember?"

I swallowed, nodding, trying to cling to his words like a lifeline. But there was an undercurrent of inevitability now, a sense that whatever lay ahead was something neither of us fully understood. The guardian's warning had burrowed deep, gnawing at my certainty, and I felt it settling like a lead weight in the pit of my stomach.

"Then let's finish this," I said, a final surge of determination carrying my voice. "If fate wants to meddle, it can at least do it on our terms."

We pushed forward, and each step seemed heavier than the last, the relic's pull growing stronger. I could feel its energy throbbing through the walls, a pulse like some sinister heartbeat guiding us deeper into the cavern. The path narrowed, forcing us to walk single file, my companion leading, though he kept a hand outstretched for me to hold, a silent reassurance as the darkness thickened. I clung to his fingers as we moved, the silence only broken by the steady drip of water echoing through the cavern.

Finally, we reached an open chamber, and there, resting on a pedestal carved from some dark, glistening stone, was the relic. It was smaller than I'd expected, unassuming in its simplicity—a sphere of polished obsidian, no larger than an apple, yet emanating a power so intense that I felt my knees weaken. Every instinct screamed at me to turn, to run, but I forced myself to stare, to confront it. The relic seemed to shimmer, pulsing with an unnatural life, and I had the unnerving sense that it was watching us, waiting.

My companion's face had gone pale, his jaw set tight, but he didn't waver. He took a step forward, and I followed, the air growing thick, as if it were struggling to contain the relic's energy.

"Are you ready?" he asked, his voice barely more than a whisper.

"No," I admitted, my voice steadier than I felt. "But I don't think that matters anymore."

We approached the pedestal, our movements cautious, as though the relic might spring to life at any moment. The energy around it was almost tangible now, crackling like static in the air. I felt its power tugging at me, not with the hostility I'd anticipated, but with a dark, insidious allure. The guardian's words echoed in my mind: To sever what you hold is to sever a part of yourselves.

For a brief, dizzying moment, I wondered if he'd been right—if perhaps, in some twisted way, the relic was as much a part of us as we were of each other. But I couldn't let that thought take root. I had made my choice, and I would see it through.

With a shaky breath, I reached out, my fingers grazing the surface of the obsidian sphere. A shock ran through me, a pulse of energy so intense that I nearly pulled back. But my companion was beside me, his hand covering mine, grounding me in place. Together, we pressed down, and a surge of heat shot through my veins, raw and scorching, as though the relic were fighting us, resisting.

The chamber shook, dust and loose rocks cascading from the ceiling as the relic pulsed beneath our grip, its dark power spilling over, flooding through me. My vision blurred, and I could feel it reaching into my mind, pulling at memories, emotions, twisting them until they were almost unrecognizable. I felt a thousand different fears, a lifetime of doubts, all rushing through me at once.

But then I felt his hand, warm and steady, his presence anchoring me, reminding me of who I was. I clung to that feeling, to him, and somehow, through the haze of pain and confusion, I felt a shift. The relic's power began to wane, its hold loosening as we poured our will into it, breaking its bond.

And just when I thought we'd succeeded, just as the relic's energy was fading, I felt a sharp, searing pain—a price exacted. The guardian's words echoed once more, a haunting reminder of the cost we'd chosen to ignore. The bond was breaking, but it was taking something from us, something I couldn't name but felt slipping away, piece by piece.

When the relic finally went still, a lifeless hunk of stone in our hands, we both collapsed, the weight of what we'd lost settling over us. I looked at him, my vision still blurred, but I could see the same exhaustion, the same unspoken grief mirrored in his eyes. The price had been steep, and though we'd won, I wondered if we would ever be the same.

He managed a weak smile, his hand still wrapped around mine. "Worth it?"

I forced a smile in return, though my heart felt heavy, aching in a way I couldn't explain. "I think so," I whispered, hoping that one day I would believe it.

The silence lingered as we sat on the cavern floor, each of us lost in the quiet aftermath of what we'd just unleashed. The relic lay lifeless between us, a harmless stone now, nothing more than a relic in the truest sense. Yet its final act felt anything but harmless. I could still feel the ache radiating from some deep part of myself that had been wrenched away, the remnants of whatever connection it had leeched from us in those final moments.

My companion let out a shaky breath, his fingers tracing circles on the back of my hand as if reassuring himself of my presence. I caught his eye and saw the same exhaustion weighing him down, pulling him toward some place I couldn't quite follow. For once, there were no words between us, no witty retort or sarcastic quip that could shake off the weight of what we'd lost. It felt strange, foreign, like stepping onto uneven ground and trying to regain my balance without knowing what had thrown me off in the first place.

"Do you feel it, too?" I whispered, barely trusting my voice. The words sounded too loud, echoing off the cavern walls and breaking the fragile silence that had cocooned us.

He nodded slowly, his gaze distant, focused somewhere past the dim, fading light of our lantern. "Yeah," he murmured. "Like something was... I don't know. Stolen, maybe. Taken before we even knew it was ours to lose."

I wanted to tell him he was wrong, that we were fine, that whatever had happened, we'd survived it—and wasn't that enough? But the hollow ache in my chest refused to be ignored, growing sharper with each breath, each heartbeat. It was as though the guardian's warning had taken root, some poisonous seed planted deep within us, and I could almost feel it spreading, tendrils winding through every part of me, curling around memories I hadn't realized were fragile until now.

"Well," I said, forcing a hollow smile, "at least we're not dead. I think that counts as a win, considering."

His laugh was quiet, bitter at the edges. "High standards you're setting there. Surviving's a bit overrated, don't you think?"

I nudged him lightly, though even the movement felt strained, forced. "Not when the alternative is death. I'm rather partial to staying alive, actually."

"Can't argue with that," he admitted, though his voice was far from its usual levity. He let his gaze wander, tracing the dark walls of the cavern as if seeing something I couldn't. When he spoke again, his words came out soft, almost hesitant. "Do you ever wonder if maybe... maybe we weren't meant to destroy it?"

The question hit me like a punch to the gut, a thought I'd kept buried surfacing despite my efforts to keep it down. "I can't believe you'd say that. Not after everything it's done."

"I don't know," he said, rubbing his temple as though trying to scrub away his own doubts. "It's just—what if we weren't supposed to take this path? What if there was another way, one that didn't demand so much?"

A fierce anger flared up inside me, burning away some of the numbness. "No. Don't do that. Don't second-guess this now." I knew my voice was sharp, harsher than I'd meant it to be, but I couldn't help myself. "We came here to end this curse, to stop it from consuming anyone else. We did what we had to."

"But at what cost?" He met my gaze, his eyes dark, filled with a pain I recognized because it mirrored my own. "What if it wasn't just a relic bound to us? What if it's us who can't let it go?"

The question hung between us, a specter in the dim light. Part of me wanted to deny it outright, to tell him he was wrong, that we were done with this, free at last. But deep down, I felt it too—the tug, the unyielding connection that hadn't dissipated even when the relic had gone still. It was as if the curse had left a mark, some indelible stain that couldn't be washed away, no matter how much distance we put between ourselves and this place.

I tried to shake it off, brushing dirt from my hands as I rose to my feet, unwilling to linger any longer in the gloom. "Let's get out of here. We'll feel better with some fresh air."

He looked up at me, skepticism clear in his expression, but he pushed himself to his feet, his fingers brushing against mine as though seeking some assurance. I gripped his hand tightly, more out of habit than necessity, and we began our slow trek back, weaving through the narrow passageways, our footsteps echoing like ghostly whispers.

As we neared the entrance, a faint glimmer of light reached out to us, soft and welcoming. I could almost taste the freedom, feel the tension start to unravel as the cavern walls opened up to the outside world. But just as we reached the threshold, a sudden, chilling wind swept through the passage, freezing us in our tracks.

I shivered, instinctively moving closer to him, but he was just as still, his face pale as his gaze fixed on something behind us. I followed his line of sight, my stomach twisting at the sight that awaited us.

There, blocking our path, was the shadowy figure of the guardian, materialized as if he'd been waiting all along. His expression was unreadable, a blend of regret and inevitability etched into the lines of his face, and I felt a flicker of dread creep up my spine.

"You believed it was over," he said, his voice carrying a note of quiet sorrow. "But you have only severed the first bond."

My heart pounded, my mouth going dry as I searched for words that wouldn't come. He held up one hand, and I saw something shimmer within his grasp—a fragment of the relic, the same dark stone, cracked but pulsing faintly, a heartbeat that echoed through the air.

I glanced at my companion, his face stricken, mirroring my own disbelief. We'd destroyed it, I was certain of it. But here it was, fractured yet alive, its presence as palpable as before.

"What do you want from us?" I demanded, anger masking the fear clawing its way up my throat. "We did what you asked. We ended it."

The guardian's gaze softened, his voice a gentle reprimand. "Ended? No. You merely began."

A cold realization washed over me, a dawning horror that sank its claws into my chest. Whatever we'd thought we'd accomplished, whatever we believed we'd severed, it had only been a piece, a fragment of something far greater, something that had taken root in ways we couldn't yet understand.

My companion gripped my hand tightly, his own fear mirroring mine. "What does that mean?"

The guardian's answer was no more comforting than his presence. "You carry a part of it now, within yourselves. The relic's curse has bound itself to your very souls, and it will not rest until its purpose is complete."

I staggered back, the weight of his words nearly knocking me off balance. The ground seemed to shift beneath us, the air thick with a sense of dread I hadn't felt even in the deepest part of the cavern.

"Then what—what do we do?" My voice was barely a whisper, a plea born of desperation.

The guardian's shadowed face twisted in something that might have been pity. "There is no choice," he said softly, his figure beginning to fade. "The bond must be fulfilled."

And with those final words, he vanished, leaving us standing alone, the dark fragment pulsing between us, a heartbeat we could no longer deny, a fate we could no longer escape.

Chapter 22: A Binding Promise

The relic's surface was cold against my fingertips, yet somehow, a heat spread through my veins like liquid fire, winding and curling its way to my chest. Its glow, faint and fickle, pulsed like a heartbeat. I watched as it cast fractured light across the stone floor, shifting between silver and shadow. I wanted to pull away from its magnetic grip, from the sense that it was somehow alive, aware. But I couldn't. The relic had a power that had crept under my skin, an itch too deep to scratch, leaving me both terrified and utterly captivated.

Beside me, Alec's fingers tightened around my wrist, his hold grounding and steadying. In the flickering light, his face was cast in sharp relief, brows drawn tight, jaw set with that usual intensity. But now, there was something else there too, a flicker of fear, perhaps, or awe. I couldn't quite tell. Alec was never one for emotions easily worn. Still, I felt him tremble slightly, a faint pulse that matched the relic's, as if even his iron will was bending to its demand. His thumb brushed over my pulse, perhaps unintentionally, but the slight gesture sent a shiver down my spine, tying me to the moment, to him, to the strange magic coiling between us.

I opened my mouth to say something, maybe to break the silence or to shatter the invisible tether forming between us, but the words died on my lips. Alec's gaze shifted to meet mine, sharp, probing, the kind of look that seemed to peel back the layers and expose every hidden part of me. It made me want to flinch, to turn away, but I couldn't. Not now. Not with the relic drawing us deeper into whatever binding promise it demanded. His expression softened, just for a breath, but in that instant, I knew he felt it too—the weight of the vow that was forming, one we didn't fully understand but were powerless to resist.

"Are you sure?" His voice was quiet, a murmur barely audible above the hum of energy, yet it was sharp enough to slice through the haze. Alec didn't ask questions often; he was more of a man of decisive action, but the uncertainty in his tone startled me.

Am I sure? The question echoed through me, clanging around like a bell in an empty church. There was no real certainty here. Only the sense that once we moved forward, once we completed this binding, there would be no going back. And yet, with my hand clasped in his, tethered by some ancient magic and an unspoken understanding, I found that I was sure. Because while I didn't trust the relic, I trusted Alec. And somehow, that was enough.

"Does it matter?" I shot back, trying to sound more nonchalant than I felt, trying to match his signature, unshakable confidence. But the waver in my voice betrayed me, and his lips quirked, one side lifting in that half-smirk that always managed to infuriate and amuse me in equal measure.

"Only if you're planning on backing out." His smirk turned into something sharper, a challenge, and I had to resist the urge to smack him right there. If the relic didn't kill us, I very well might.

"Hardly." I tossed my hair back, feigning an ease I didn't feel. "Besides, you're stuck with me now. Better get used to it."

His gaze softened, but only for a second before he masked it again, slipping back into that impenetrable armor he wore so well. "I guess I don't have a choice," he murmured, and there was something in his tone, an almost wistful undertone, that made my chest tighten, though I couldn't place why.

The relic pulsed again, this time brighter, its light casting eerie shadows along the walls, pulling our attention back. The sensation of it grew, seeping into every part of me, sinking into my bones, filling my lungs. It wasn't just a binding—it was a claiming, an insidious tether that stretched and clung, imprinting itself in ways I would never fully understand. I wanted to scream, to shake it off, but the sensation felt like it was rewriting something inside me, carving out spaces I hadn't even known existed. And in the midst of it all, Alec's hand was there, solid and warm against mine, an anchor I clung to even as the darkness closed in around us.

The relic demanded something more. I could feel it, a silent plea, a whisper in the deepest corners of my mind. It wasn't enough that we stood here together. It wanted words, promises, threads woven from our very souls. The vow it demanded was ancient, and even without speaking it aloud, I knew it was unbreakable.

"We have to say something," I whispered, my voice barely audible above the soft hum of the relic's pulse. "It's...waiting."

Alec's brows drew together, but he nodded, seemingly at a loss for words himself. For a man who always had a plan, who was never caught off guard, this was new territory, and that fact alone made me uneasy. But he met my gaze, a slight flicker of vulnerability crossing his features, and I felt the tension in me ease, if only a little.

"We promise," he began, his voice stronger than I'd expected, filling the space with a resonance that seemed to amplify against the walls. "To protect each other...no matter what."

The words sent a chill through me, not because of their simplicity but because of the certainty with which he said them. They were words we'd both taken lightly in the past, words we'd thrown around as if they were jokes. But now, standing in the relic's presence, they took on a weight I couldn't ignore.

I felt the relic respond, a surge of energy binding to his words, drawing them into itself, as if knitting our fates together. And before I knew what I was saying, the response slipped from my lips, an answer as old as the magic in the air.

"I promise," I whispered, my own voice surprisingly steady. "To keep you safe...even when you don't want me to."

His eyes widened, just slightly, and a flicker of something softer passed through his gaze, gone as quickly as it had come. The relic pulsed once more, brighter than before, bathing us in light, and I felt the binding settle between us, unbreakable and undeniable.

Our souls, I realized with a sickening clarity, were now inextricably tied, bound by a force older and more powerful than I could have imagined. And as the relic's light began to fade, casting the room back into shadow, I couldn't shake the feeling that we had both lost something of ourselves in that binding promise, something we would never get back.

The air felt thicker now, a tangible weight pressing down on us, as if the relic's energy had wrapped itself around the very fabric of the room. I could barely make out Alec's silhouette, cast in fragmented shadows by the dim light. He was close enough that I could feel his breath, warm against the coolness that emanated from the relic. The silence settled between us, a silence neither comfortable nor calm, filled instead with the unsaid and the unknown. My mind spun in a thousand directions, each thought tugging at the edges of reason, searching for some anchor in the madness of the moment.

"Are you regretting this already?" I asked, my voice softer than intended, almost swallowed by the heavy quiet. I didn't know why I asked—it wasn't like him to doubt, and I was hardly in a place to question him now. But something about the way he stood there, tense and unmoving, made me wonder if he felt it too: that quiet hum of dread slipping between us like poison.

He let out a low, humorless chuckle, his eyes glinting in the dim light as he looked at me. "I stopped regretting things years ago," he replied, though his voice held an edge I wasn't used to, something that hinted at more than the usual confidence he wielded so casually. "Besides, you've hardly left me with a choice. Bound for life, aren't we?"

"Bound for life," I echoed, and the words left a strange, hollow taste on my tongue. I hadn't intended for things to get this complicated. Well, that was a lie. Complications had practically been the one thing I could count on since meeting Alec, but this? Bound to him by some relic-born vow we barely understood, our souls tethered to a fate beyond our control? I couldn't have imagined this if I tried.

Alec reached out, his hand brushing a strand of hair from my face, and for a moment, his expression softened. His fingers lingered, a touch so brief I might have missed it if not for the way my skin prickled in its wake. It was impossible to say whether he was as affected by the binding as I was, whether he could feel the weight of it twisting into his veins, but for just a breath, it felt like he did.

And then he pulled away, his eyes returning to their usual guarded intensity, as if that small moment of vulnerability had been an accident he couldn't afford to repeat.

"We should go," he said, his tone brisk, all business now, and the slight softness I'd seen was gone. "Whatever this...promise entails, we're not going to figure it out standing here in the dark."

I bit back a retort, wanting to say that perhaps this wasn't something we could just walk away from, that perhaps we were tied here as much as we were tied to each other. But I kept quiet, knowing better than to argue with Alec when he was in one of his "solve it later" moods. Instead, I turned, forcing myself to take a step away from the relic's relentless pull, feeling a faint resistance as if some invisible chain tethered me to it, refusing to let go.

As we walked through the shadowed corridors, the silence between us grew heavier. Neither of us knew what we'd just promised or how deep the roots of the binding had gone, but the weight of it pressed on my chest, making it hard to breathe. Every footstep echoed, reminding me with each reverberation that something fundamental had changed. I could feel Alec's presence beside me, a warmth both comforting and unnerving, our steps in sync as if even our bodies recognized the bond that now tied us.

A flicker of torchlight appeared in the distance, a hint of something familiar in the otherwise unfamiliar halls, and I quickened my pace, eager to escape the oppressive darkness. But before I could take another step, Alec's hand shot out, grabbing my arm and pulling me to a stop. His expression was fierce, and in the dim light, I could see the strain etched across his face.

"Something's not right," he said, his voice a low murmur, barely more than a whisper. His eyes darted around the corridor, scanning every shadow, every flicker of light, as if expecting something to leap out at us. "Can you feel it?"

I stilled, focusing on the air around us, letting my senses stretch out. There it was—a low, insidious hum, almost imperceptible but unmistakable, a vibration that seemed to sink into the walls, threading through every stone, every crack. It felt...wrong, somehow, like a sour note in a familiar melody, throwing everything out of balance.

"A trap?" I asked, keeping my voice low, not wanting to disturb the silence any more than necessary.

Alec's jaw clenched. "Worse, I think." He released my arm, shifting so that he stood slightly in front of me, his usual position when he thought danger was near. I tried not to roll my eyes at the gesture—it wasn't that I couldn't handle myself. But Alec's protective instincts were practically hardwired, especially when it came to me, and I wasn't about to argue with him over it.

The hum grew louder, vibrating up through the floor, seeping into my bones. It wasn't a sound, not really, more like a pulse of energy, a warning that something was coming, something we couldn't outrun. I looked up at Alec, meeting his gaze, and for the first time since we'd touched the relic, I saw fear in his eyes.

"What now?" I whispered, hoping he had a plan, some way to deal with whatever ancient curse we'd managed to awaken. But his expression remained stony, unreadable, his mind clearly racing as he calculated our options.

Before he could respond, a sharp crack echoed down the corridor, a sound so loud it made my ears ring. A cold wind swept through, chilling me to the core, and I shivered, instinctively stepping closer to Alec. The relic's energy flared, and I could feel it now, wrapping around us, tightening like a noose.

"We have to go," Alec said, his voice urgent. His hand found mine, and though I wanted to pull away, to prove I didn't need his protection, I didn't. I let him lead, let him guide me through the darkness, our footsteps pounding against the stone floor as we fled whatever unseen force was chasing us.

We rounded a corner, the torchlight barely illuminating the path ahead, and I stumbled, my foot catching on a loose stone. Alec's grip tightened, steadying me, but in that split second, I felt the relic's energy surge, yanking me back, as if some invisible hand had latched onto my very soul. The world spun, and for a moment, I felt as if I were suspended in time, caught between one breath and the next.

And then it released me, just as abruptly, leaving me gasping for air, clutching Alec's hand as if it were the only thing keeping me grounded. I could feel the sweat on my skin, the hammering of my heart, and the faint echo of the relic's pulse, still thrumming within me, as if it were now a part of me, impossible to escape.

Alec looked back at me, his eyes wide with something like horror. "It's not going to let us go," he whispered, his voice barely audible over the pounding in my ears.

The realization settled over us like a lead weight, cold and unrelenting.

We kept moving, Alec's grip steady on my wrist, his hand a warm reassurance against the cold bite of the relic's magic that still hummed within me. The air was thick, tinged with an odd metallic scent that made my throat burn. My heart pounded, half from the fear still coiling in my gut and half from the feeling of Alec's hand anchoring me, solid and warm, as we navigated through the twisting, endless hallways. Shadows flitted in and out of our path, stretching out in strange, distorted shapes as our steps echoed against the stone, making it feel as though we were not alone.

At one point, Alec slowed, his gaze darting around as if he were seeing something I couldn't. I tugged on his hand, unwilling to stop, but he didn't budge. "Wait," he murmured, his voice low, laced with tension. "Listen."

I stilled, straining to hear whatever he did, and there it was—a faint, whispering sound, like the rustle of fabric in an empty room. I felt a shiver crawl up my spine, icy and insistent. It was close, too close, and I tightened my grip on Alec's hand, barely resisting the urge to bolt.

"Whatever it is, it's moving," he said, his jaw clenched as he listened, his whole body tense. "It's not just a spell or some...echo. It's real." His voice dropped even lower, and his eyes, when they met mine, were sharp with a mix of determination and fear that made my stomach twist.

I bit my lip, trying to steady my breathing, refusing to let the panic building in my chest take hold. Alec wasn't one to rattle easily, and seeing him on edge was unsettling, to say the least. "Well, we can't exactly introduce ourselves, can we?" I whispered, trying for a wry smile that probably looked more like a grimace. "So what's the plan, fearless leader?"

He almost smiled, a shadow of the familiar smirk that usually graced his lips, and I felt a strange surge of relief at the sight. Even now, facing gods knew what, Alec was still Alec—bold, infuriating, and, against all odds, strangely comforting.

"Plan?" he repeated, his brow quirking. "I thought we agreed I'd do the thinking, and you'd—"

"Blindly follow you to certain doom? Yes, I remember," I shot back, but the banter steadied me, grounding me in a way nothing else could. "Just tell me where to point the dagger if things go south."

He let out a low chuckle, shaking his head. "Don't worry, I've seen you fight. I'll just stand back and let you handle it." His tone was light, but I caught the gleam in his eyes, the unspoken promise that he wouldn't let anything happen to me. Not if he could help it.

We turned another corner, and suddenly, the air shifted. The faint whispering sound stopped, replaced by an eerie stillness, the kind that made my skin prickle, as if we'd stepped into another world entirely. The shadows deepened, thickened, their edges blurring, and I felt a strange pull in my chest, a weight that seemed to drag me forward, toward whatever lay in the darkness ahead.

Alec's grip on my wrist tightened, his fingers digging in just enough to ground me, pulling me back from the edge of whatever force was calling to me. "Stay with me," he murmured, his voice steady but tense. "Don't let it...don't let it in."

I nodded, swallowing hard, fighting the urge to give in to the pull, to let the strange energy wash over me. It felt like the relic's magic, that same ancient, insidious power that had bound us together, but stronger, darker. I could feel it creeping into my mind, whispering promises of knowledge, of power, tempting me to let go of Alec's hand, to step forward and let it claim me.

But then Alec's voice cut through the haze, sharp and unyielding. "Focus, Lena. Look at me."

I blinked, pulling my gaze from the shadows to meet his eyes, fierce and unyielding, and the fog in my mind began to clear. The weight in my chest lifted, just slightly, enough for me to catch my breath.

"Thanks," I managed, my voice shaky, barely more than a whisper.

"Don't mention it," he replied, his tone light but his expression deadly serious. "If you start talking to shadows, though, I might rethink this whole 'bound for life' thing."

A laugh slipped out before I could stop it, a shaky, breathless sound that felt oddly liberating. Even here, in the heart of whatever madness the relic had unleashed, Alec could still make me laugh. It was infuriating and comforting, all at once.

But before I could respond, a new sound cut through the silence—a low, rumbling growl that seemed to vibrate through the very walls. I felt Alec's hand tense around mine, his eyes narrowing as he turned toward the source of the sound.

The growling grew louder, more distinct, and as the shadows shifted, I saw it—an enormous, hulking shape emerging from the darkness, its eyes glinting with a cold, hungry light. It was like nothing I'd ever seen, a creature born from nightmares, its massive form rippling with muscle, its skin a mottled, dark gray that seemed to blend seamlessly with the shadows. Its teeth gleamed, sharp and wicked, and a low snarl escaped its throat, echoing through the hall like a warning.

Alec stepped forward, positioning himself between me and the creature, his stance tense but ready. "Lena," he said, his voice low and calm, "when I say run, you run. Got it?"

My heart hammered in my chest, but I forced myself to nod, gripping my dagger tightly, feeling its reassuring weight in my hand. "Don't do anything stupid," I whispered, barely able to keep the tremor out of my voice.

He flashed me a grin, reckless and infuriating. "Who, me? I'm insulted."

The creature snarled again, its massive form shifting, preparing to pounce, and I held my breath, every muscle in my body taut, ready to flee. But then Alec did something I hadn't expected—he took a step forward, raising his hand, palm out, as if he were going to…reason with it?

"Alec, are you out of your mind?" I hissed, my heart racing as I watched him face down the creature with nothing but sheer bravado.

"Trust me," he murmured, though he didn't look back, his gaze locked on the beast. "If I'm wrong, well, you'll know soon enough."

The creature growled, baring its teeth, but it didn't move, watching Alec with a strange, almost wary intensity. I held my breath, torn between the urge to run and the absurd hope that maybe, just maybe, Alec knew what he was doing.

For a tense, agonizing moment, nothing happened. And then, just as I began to think he'd pulled off some miraculous trick, the creature lunged, its massive jaws snapping inches from Alec's face. He dodged, barely, rolling to the side as the beast let out an enraged roar that shook the walls.

"Run!" Alec shouted, his voice hoarse, filled with a desperation I'd never heard from him before.

I didn't need to be told twice. I turned, sprinting down the corridor, the sound of the creature's snarls and Alec's shouts echoing behind me. But even as I ran, I couldn't shake the sinking feeling that I was leaving something—someone—behind. The relic's power still pulsed within me, a dark, binding promise that pulled at my soul, demanding that I turn back, that I fight, that I fulfill whatever twisted fate it had set for us.

But I kept running, my heart pounding, my mind racing, Alec's voice still ringing in my ears, urging me forward, even as the shadows closed in around me, leaving me with nothing but the certainty that this was far from over.

Chapter 23: The Attack

As soon as the cool night air hit my face, my heart began to drum out a warning. I barely had time to take a single step into the open square before they appeared, figures leaking out of the shadows, silent as death. I didn't know if they'd been waiting in those dark corners, or if they had some way of sensing the relic's energy from a distance, like sharks tasting blood in the water. Either way, they moved with a predatory grace, forming a tight circle around us, eyes flashing beneath their hoods. These weren't the usual mercenaries or bounty hunters we'd tangled with before; these were something worse.

Before the relic, maybe I would have felt the kind of fear that paralyzes you, that makes your stomach drop into your boots and your heart forget its rhythm. But as I gripped it tighter, something inside me steadied. There was a warmth that spread up my arm and down into my legs, centering me. We moved as one, like dancers in perfect step. I didn't have to look at Rowan to know what his next move would be; it was like the relic's power had fused our thoughts, our instincts.

They lunged. Steel flashed, blades angled to slice, but Rowan parried effortlessly, his sword moving so quickly it left trails of silver in the dark. I spun low, letting one of our attackers' swings pass harmlessly over my head, before kicking out and sending him stumbling backward. There was no time to think, no room to breathe—just movement and heat and the clash of metal.

Rowan's voice cut through the frenzy, calm but with an edge of urgency. "We need to break through. Get to higher ground."

I glanced around, searching for an escape, but our attackers closed in, pressing us back, herding us like wolves to a cliff. They knew how to handle fighters like us, and they knew how to block every exit with ruthless precision. I felt my pulse quicken again, but the relic pulsed too, its energy flooding through me, whispering that I didn't need to run.

There was something else, though—something strange, like an electric thrill in the air, a dangerous excitement I could almost taste. I didn't know if it was the relic's influence or something inside me finally embracing this fight, but it spurred me on. Each time one of them lunged, I spun with the fluidity I never remembered having before, a confidence I didn't quite recognize. Rowan was at my back, his movements sharp and controlled, and somehow, amid the chaos, we found a rhythm.

Yet even as we struck, cutting down each assailant who dared approach, I could feel the truth settling coldly in my bones. This was only the beginning. More would come. This relic, with all its strange power, had painted a target on our backs so large it might as well have been glowing. No matter how many we defeated tonight, there would always be another wave, and the relic's allure would only make them more desperate, more relentless.

A sharp cry from Rowan brought me back to the moment. One of them—a hulking figure with a jagged scar tracing his jaw—had landed a strike, slicing across Rowan's arm. His face twisted in pain, but he barely paused, meeting the attacker with a brutal counter that sent him sprawling to the ground. I moved closer, holding my ground as I fended off two more figures, my heart tight with worry even as I kept my expression hard.

"You okay?" I asked through gritted teeth, blocking a blow aimed at my shoulder.

"Nothing I can't handle," he replied, but I could see the way his arm trembled slightly, the wound already soaking his sleeve in dark crimson. He wouldn't last if we didn't end this soon. I didn't know how, but the relic did. I could feel it now, like a whisper at the edge of my thoughts, urging me to let go, to let it take over.

Instinct warred with common sense. The relic's power had come with no instruction manual, no guide, just a relentless hum that both protected and warned. But right now, there was no choice. I loosened my grip on the control I'd been holding onto and felt the relic surge in response, flooding me with a raw, potent energy.

Time seemed to slow. Every sound, every movement became sharper, clearer. I saw the precise moment each of our attackers shifted their weight, could anticipate where they would strike before they even moved. My body reacted as if it had known this power all along, gliding through the attacks, every step a calculated counter.

Rowan was watching me, surprise flickering across his face as I dropped our enemies one by one, moving through them like water through cracks in a stone. The relic's energy surged through me with a wildness that bordered on terrifying, a fire that almost felt like it could consume me if I didn't keep a tight grip on its reigns. But for now, it was enough.

In minutes, we'd carved a path out of the square, leaving behind bodies and the twisted remains of whatever trap had been set for us. Rowan stumbled slightly as we broke free, the fight finally catching up to him, and I caught him, keeping my grip steady as I guided him into a narrow alley. We couldn't rest yet; they might be right behind us.

The relic buzzed in my hands, its power slowly retreating as if it, too, was catching its breath. I met Rowan's gaze, and a wry smile crept across my lips despite the tension still knotting my chest. He chuckled softly, his eyes alight with an amused respect.

"Remind me not to get on your bad side."

I rolled my eyes, but the corner of my mouth quirked upward. "Too late for that, isn't it?"

We took a moment, just long enough for me to tie a piece of my shirt around his wound, trying to ignore how his skin felt beneath my fingers, warm and solid. The silence between us stretched, comfortable in a way that shouldn't have made sense with the relic humming between us and our enemies closing in. But it did.

"We need a plan," he finally said, his voice steady despite the exhaustion I could see in his face.

I glanced at the relic, feeling its energy like a steady heartbeat, and nodded. "Then let's find one."

The alley stretched before us, dark and silent, as if the city itself had conspired to give us a moment of reprieve. I leaned Rowan against the wall, careful not to let him see the worry tightening my face. His wound was deeper than I'd thought; even in the faint moonlight, I could see the blood soaking through the makeshift bandage I'd tied around his arm. But if there was one thing I'd learned about Rowan, it was that he'd never let on just how hurt he was.

He met my gaze, one eyebrow quirking upward in that familiar, maddeningly calm expression that told me he'd fight until he collapsed if he had to. "You don't look so relieved to have escaped," he said, his voice laced with a mix of humor and exhaustion.

"I wouldn't get too comfortable," I shot back, glancing over my shoulder. The relic hummed softly in my hands, its energy pulsing like a heartbeat. "They're probably regrouping as we speak. Whatever that thing's doing"—I nodded to the relic—"it's calling every dark soul in a mile radius straight to us."

Rowan winced as he tried to adjust his position, giving a low laugh that sounded more like a groan. "You're the one who said we needed it, remember?"

"Oh, I remember," I muttered, glancing down at the relic. Its strange symbols gleamed under the moonlight, twisting and shifting like they were alive. I couldn't deny the rush it had given me during the fight—the way it had heightened my senses, made me faster, stronger. But there was something else, a lurking power that I wasn't entirely sure I wanted to understand. I could still feel it humming beneath my skin, a constant reminder of the danger I'd chosen to carry.

Rowan's hand brushed mine, his fingers lingering for just a second longer than necessary. "Whatever happens, we're in this together. You know that, right?"

I nodded, swallowing against the sudden tightness in my throat. The words I wanted to say tangled inside me, words that felt too heavy, too vulnerable for the flickering silence of the alley. Instead, I forced a smile and gave his hand a quick squeeze before pulling away. "Let's just hope we're not in it together against an entire army."

But even as I said it, a shiver of foreboding ran through me. The power of the relic felt stronger now, as if it had been fed by the violence of the fight. I wondered, not for the first time, if I'd made a mistake in taking it. But there was no time to dwell on that. We had to keep moving.

Rowan nodded toward a narrow, twisting path that disappeared between the buildings. "There's a safe house a few blocks from here. If we're lucky, we can make it before they catch up."

I scoffed. "Luck doesn't exactly seem to be on our side tonight."

He gave me a wry grin. "Then I guess we'll have to make our own."

We moved as quickly as Rowan's injury allowed, the tension between us sharper with every step. The streets were empty, but I could feel eyes watching us from the windows above, shadows shifting behind curtains and cracked shutters. This part of the city was a maze of crumbling stone and forgotten corners, the kind of place where secrets hid in plain sight. I'd spent enough time here to know that every alley had its dangers, but tonight, it felt like the entire city had turned against us.

As we rounded a corner, I caught sight of a flicker of movement ahead. I stopped, pulling Rowan back against the wall, and he grimaced, clutching his injured arm. I held a finger to my lips, signaling him to stay silent. Slowly, I peered around the edge of the wall, heart pounding.

Three figures stood at the end of the street, their backs to us. They were dressed like the others—dark cloaks, faces hidden—but something about their stance made my stomach twist. They weren't moving, just standing there, waiting. As if they knew we were coming.

Rowan's breath was warm against my ear as he whispered, "Do you think they know?"

"I don't know," I replied, keeping my voice low. But I had a sinking feeling that they did. The relic's power was a beacon, and these weren't ordinary thugs. They were disciplined, patient. And they weren't going to leave without a fight.

Rowan's jaw tightened, and he gave me a determined nod. "We can take them. Like you said, we're stronger with the relic."

"Or they're stronger because of it," I muttered, but the words came out more uncertain than I'd intended. The relic pulsed again, as if in agreement, and I felt a surge of power ripple through me, hot and unyielding.

Rowan must have felt it too because his gaze sharpened, his mouth set in a hard line. "Ready?"

"Always," I replied, slipping the relic into my satchel where its weight pressed against my side, both comforting and ominous. With a quick nod, I braced myself, drawing a deep breath before stepping into the street, Rowan close at my side.

The moment they saw us, the figures moved with a swift, almost unnatural precision. They didn't waste time with threats or taunts—no, these were professionals, killers trained to move without hesitation. One of them lunged at Rowan, a blade flashing under the moonlight, and Rowan parried, gritting his teeth against the strain on his injured arm. I didn't have time to worry about him; two of them were coming at me, and their attacks were fast, brutal, as if they'd anticipated my every move.

But the relic was with me, its energy burning through my veins, pushing me beyond the limits I'd known. I moved through their strikes, ducking, dodging, my body almost moving on its own. One of them snarled in frustration as I slipped past his guard and drove my elbow into his ribs, sending him stumbling back.

Rowan was beside me in an instant, his movements sharp and controlled despite his injury. Together, we fought as if we were one mind, one body. I could feel his presence beside me, his rhythm syncing with mine, each of us covering the other's weaknesses without a second thought.

But even as we fought, I could feel the relic's power building, pushing against the edges of my control. It wanted more, urging me to unleash it fully, to let it take over. The thought sent a shiver down my spine, but there was no time to consider the consequences. Not with another wave of attackers closing in, their faces twisted with grim determination.

Just when I thought we'd gain the upper hand, I saw a flicker of movement behind Rowan—a figure raising a blade, poised to strike him down. I didn't think; I reacted. The relic's power surged through me in a violent, blazing wave, and before I even realized what I was doing, a burst of light shot from my hand, hitting the attacker square in the chest. He crumpled to the ground, eyes wide with shock as the light faded.

Rowan turned to look at me, eyes wide with something between awe and horror. I didn't know what to say. The power had taken over, and for a terrifying moment, I hadn't been sure if I'd controlled it or if it had controlled me.

Rowan's eyes burned into mine, searching for answers I wasn't sure I could give. The air between us was charged, thick with unsaid words and unasked questions. But we didn't have the luxury of lingering in the aftermath of what I'd just done. I forced my gaze from his, scanning our surroundings for any sign of reinforcements. The last of our attackers lay scattered on the cobblestones, some still groaning, others unmoving. Their dark cloaks blended with the shadows, turning the alley into a graveyard of indistinct shapes.

Rowan stepped closer, his voice low and edged with concern. "That...whatever that was—you've been holding back on me."

I kept my face neutral, even as my mind raced. What could I say? That I hadn't meant for the relic to unleash itself like that? That I wasn't sure if I'd controlled it, or if it had taken over me entirely? I bit back the truth, settling for a half-smile that I hoped looked more confident than I felt.

"I guess I was saving it for a special occasion," I replied lightly, trying to mask the tremor in my voice.

His eyebrow lifted, but he didn't press further. Instead, he wiped his blade on one of the fallen cloaks and looked down the alleyway, his expression hardening. "We don't have time for any more surprises. Can you keep it under control?"

There was a flicker of doubt in his gaze, and I hated that I'd put it there. But I nodded, clenching my hand around the relic as if I could press it into obedience. "As long as they stop throwing half the city at us, I think I'll manage."

He gave a short nod, and we started forward, weaving through the maze of alleys that twisted and coiled around each other like a snake. Each step brought us closer to the outskirts of the city, closer to escape—or so I hoped.

But even as we moved, a chill settled over me, raising the hairs on the back of my neck. It wasn't just the relic's unpredictable power that made me uneasy. There was something else, a feeling like a shadow creeping at the edges of my awareness. I glanced over at Rowan, wondering if he felt it too, but his face was set, focused.

Just when I thought we might make it out undetected, a flash of movement caught my eye. I froze, grabbing Rowan's arm to stop him. Ahead, a tall, narrow figure stood at the mouth of the alley, draped in a dark, flowing robe that moved like water in the faint light. I could barely make out their features, but the glint of steel in their hand was unmistakable.

"Another one?" I whispered, more to myself than to Rowan, who had already positioned himself between me and the figure.

Rowan's voice was tight, barely a murmur. "I don't think they're here to chat."

The figure took a step forward, and the strange, unsettling feeling intensified, like icy tendrils winding their way up my spine. They didn't move like the others had, with the sharp, calculated efficiency of an assassin. No, this person moved slowly, deliberately, as if they had all the time in the world.

I took a step back, feeling the relic's hum grow louder, more insistent. There was something wrong about this person—something that set them apart from the mercenaries we'd been fighting. Rowan must have sensed it too because his stance shifted, his grip on his sword tightening.

The figure stopped just a few feet away, close enough that I could see the faint glow of their eyes beneath the hood. A voice drifted out, soft and silken, laced with an accent I didn't recognize. "You have something that doesn't belong to you."

The relic burned hotter in my hand, and I fought the urge to fling it away. "And you think it belongs to you?" I shot back, hoping my voice didn't betray the fear tightening my throat.

The figure tilted their head, a ghost of a smile appearing on their shadowed face. "Belong is such a limiting word. Let's just say... it was meant for someone who understands its potential."

Rowan shifted beside me, his eyes narrowing. "And I'm guessing that someone is you."

A low laugh drifted out from beneath the hood. "I am but a messenger. I am here to retrieve what was lost, to return it to its rightful place. And if you wish to leave this city alive, I suggest you hand it over."

I tightened my grip on the relic, feeling its pulse thrumming against my skin, sharp and fierce, as if it were challenging the stranger's claim. There was a part of me that wanted to give it to them, to rid myself of the relentless power that felt more like a curse with every passing moment. But another part of me, deeper and stronger, rebelled against the idea. The relic had chosen me—or maybe I'd chosen it. Either way, I wasn't about to let it go without a fight.

"You'll have to take it from me," I said, my voice steadier than I felt.

The stranger's smile widened, and a ripple of dark energy shimmered around them, distorting the air. They raised a hand, and I felt a force slam into me, like a wave of ice-cold water. I stumbled back, barely managing to keep my footing as Rowan lunged forward, swinging his sword in a powerful arc. But the stranger moved with a fluid grace, sidestepping Rowan's attack as if it were nothing more than a gentle breeze.

I tried to focus, to summon the relic's power again, but it felt distant, elusive. My heart pounded, a frantic rhythm that drowned out everything else. The stranger was closing in, their eyes gleaming with a terrifying intensity that made my skin crawl.

Then, just as they were about to reach me, Rowan threw himself between us, blocking their path. "Run," he shouted, his voice raw with urgency. "Get out of here!"

I hesitated, torn between the impulse to stay and fight and the undeniable logic of Rowan's command. But the stranger's gaze snapped to mine, and I felt a pressure in my mind, a dark, insistent pull that made me stagger. They were reaching for the relic, not with their hands, but with something deeper, something I couldn't see or touch.

Desperation flared inside me, and I took a step back, clutching the relic to my chest. I couldn't let them take it. I didn't know what they wanted it for, but I could feel the wrongness radiating from them, like a sickness in the air.

Rowan's voice cut through my fear, fierce and commanding. "Go, now!"

And then, before I could argue, he lunged at the stranger again, his sword flashing in the dim light. This time, he caught them off guard, his blade slicing through the fabric of their cloak. But instead of blood, a strange, smoky shadow seeped from the wound, curling into the air like wisps of fog.

The stranger hissed, their face twisting in fury. They turned to me, their eyes blazing, and I felt a sudden, intense pull on the relic, as if invisible hands were trying to tear it from my grasp. I dug my heels into the ground, fighting against the force, but it was too strong, relentless.

My vision blurred, and I felt myself slipping, the relic's power swirling chaotically, slipping from my control. In a final act of defiance, I closed my eyes, bracing myself for whatever came next, refusing to let go.

But then, with a shock that jolted me back into full awareness, the relic's power surged, fiercer and brighter than ever, flooding me with a blinding light. When I opened my eyes, the stranger was gone, vanished as if they'd never been there. Rowan was staring at me, his face pale, his eyes wide with something that looked alarmingly like fear.

And that's when I felt it—the relic was no longer in my hand. It was inside me.

Chapter 24: The Revelation of Love

We sat in the quiet aftermath of the skirmish, breathing in the night air tinged with smoke and earth. Our makeshift camp was strewn with remnants of the battle: twisted branches, discarded weaponry, and the faint shimmer of broken glass catching the moonlight. I leaned against the cold, rough bark of a tree, feeling its age and permanence steady me in the face of everything so deeply unsettled. He sat a few feet away, close enough to reach out and touch if I dared. His face was half in shadow, and for a moment, I could pretend that we were just two travelers resting, not warriors or fugitives or whatever strange, unpredictable thing we'd become.

The silence between us grew, filling the air with a weight that was almost comfortable, like a heavy woolen blanket on a winter night. He was bandaging a cut on his arm, his movements careful but practiced, his eyes flickering up now and then to meet mine, as if he were checking for... what? Disapproval? Disappointment? Some unspoken accusation? I kept my face neutral, or at least tried to. After all, my heart had been doing its level best to betray me for weeks now, thumping out of rhythm every time he so much as breathed in my direction.

But tonight felt different. Maybe it was the adrenaline still buzzing in my veins or the strange, bittersweet relief of knowing we'd both survived yet another close call. Or maybe it was that thin veil of exhaustion that peeled back just enough of my defenses to make me want to reach for something real, even if it was temporary, even if it was impossible. My chest tightened, and I let out a slow breath, watching it curl into the cold night air. When he looked up this time, his eyes seemed to ask a question that neither of us had dared put into words.

"What?" His voice was low, rough-edged, as if he'd been surprised by the sound of it.

I hesitated, then shrugged, trying for nonchalance, as if he hadn't just shattered the quiet with a single syllable. "Nothing. Just... you're surprisingly bad at bandaging, for someone who supposedly lives for this stuff."

He raised an eyebrow, his lips twitching in the ghost of a smile. "Surprisingly bad? I'd call it utilitarian. Functional. Not every wound needs to be gift-wrapped."

I rolled my eyes, but he caught the hint of amusement I couldn't quite smother. "Sure. Because what would warriors be without their rugged, no-nonsense bandages?"

He shrugged, but I saw the flicker of something softer in his gaze. "You say it like it's a bad thing."

"Not bad, just... predictable." I leaned forward, tugging the edge of his makeshift bandage so it wouldn't unravel. "Besides, you're not fooling anyone. I've seen the way you check every single weapon before we leave camp. Methodical to a fault."

He chuckled, the sound rich and unexpected, like a warm drink on a cold night. "Caught me. What can I say? Old habits die hard." His gaze softened, lingering on me with an intensity that made the breath catch in my throat. "It's how I survive. How we survive."

For a moment, the silence returned, but it was different now, charged with a strange vulnerability that made me feel unsteady, as though the ground beneath me might shift at any moment. I could see the weariness in his eyes, the kind that went deeper than mere exhaustion, settling into his bones. This man, this infuriating, guarded, occasionally sarcastic man, had been my constant companion, my unexpected ally, the person I'd turned to in the darkest hours.

And without meaning to, without even realizing it, he had become something more. The realization settled over me with a quiet but undeniable weight. My pulse quickened, my heart pounding in a rhythm that felt reckless and unfamiliar. I barely noticed the chill of the night air or the ache in my own wounds, because all I could feel was this terrible, impossible truth.

"I—" My voice was barely a whisper, and I struggled to find the words, to name the feeling that had been building, unnoticed and unstoppable, like the tide.

He looked at me, a question in his eyes that dared me to continue, to step over the line we'd both drawn so carefully. The vulnerability in his expression was so raw, so unguarded, that it took my breath away. And then, before I could lose my nerve, I spoke, letting the words tumble out in a rush that felt both terrifying and inevitable.

"I think I've fallen in love with you." The confession hung between us, shimmering and fragile, like a snowflake suspended in the air.

For a heartbeat, there was only silence. And then, slowly, he reached out, his hand grazing mine, his touch feather-light and hesitant, as though he feared I might vanish at any moment. "You don't know what you're saying," he murmured, his voice a rough whisper, filled with a desperate caution that only made my heart ache more.

But I shook my head, refusing to let him turn away from the truth I could finally see so clearly. "I know exactly what I'm saying," I whispered back, my gaze unwavering. "I've been trying not to admit it, but... it's the only thing that makes sense. The only thing that's ever made sense."

He closed his eyes, exhaling a breath that sounded almost like a laugh, as though he couldn't believe what he was hearing. And then, as he opened his eyes again, something in his expression shifted, softening into an understanding that was both beautiful and bittersweet.

"You're insane," he murmured, a wry smile tugging at his lips. "Completely, hopelessly insane."

"Maybe," I replied, feeling a smile of my own creeping up despite the tension in my chest. "But you're the one who kept sticking around, aren't you? So what does that say about you?"

His laughter was low and rough, filled with a warmth that cut through the cold night air like a balm. He leaned closer, his face so near that I could see the faint stubble on his jaw, the small scar near his temple, the fine lines around his eyes that hinted at laughter and loss and a life lived far too intensely. And in that moment, I knew that whatever came next, whether it was the heartbreak I feared or something even stranger and more beautiful, I was willing to risk it all. Because this was real, in a way I'd never expected, and that was worth every danger, every uncertainty.

He pressed his forehead gently against mine, his breath warm on my skin, and in the darkness, I felt the weight of his unspoken answer, the silent acknowledgment of a truth we'd both tried to ignore for far too long. And in that shared silence, beneath the pale, watchful light of the moon, we found something that was neither promise nor goodbye but a fragile, precious beginning.

As his forehead lingered against mine, I could feel the steady beat of his breath, matching the pulse racing through me. He stayed there for a heartbeat longer, maybe two, and when he pulled back, there was a flicker of something tender in his gaze. Vulnerability, or maybe relief—it was impossible to tell. His fingers hovered near mine, not quite touching, as though acknowledging that we'd crossed a line that couldn't be undone. My heart was still hammering, betraying every attempt I made to keep my expression neutral, to pretend that this sudden closeness hadn't unraveled me entirely.

"You're too stubborn for your own good," he murmured, a faint smile curving on his lips, the type that always made my resolve waver.

"Stubbornness has kept me alive," I shot back, refusing to let him be the only one deflecting. "It's a good quality to have when you're surrounded by people who enjoy underestimating you."

"Point taken." He laughed softly, leaning back just enough to study me, his eyes searching mine with an intensity that made my stomach flip. "But there are other ways to stay alive, you know."

"Like trusting others?" I raised an eyebrow, my voice coming out sharper than I'd intended. Trust. Such a small word, yet it held more weight between us than any weapon we'd wielded, any barrier we'd ever put up.

The corner of his mouth twitched in that infuriatingly familiar way, the ghost of amusement mingling with something sadder, something that left a bitter taste on my tongue. "Trust is a luxury I'm not sure I can afford." His gaze drifted, focusing on a spot over my shoulder as if he could see through the darkness, through the trees, to some distant memory only he knew.

A quiet stretched between us, taut as a drawn bowstring, and I felt the ache of words I wasn't sure I could say. "You trusted me enough to fight beside me," I said softly, my voice barely carrying above the murmur of the wind rustling through the branches.

His eyes flicked back to mine, and there was something in them that made my heart skip a beat—a flicker of guilt, maybe, or recognition. "You're different," he replied quietly, almost to himself. "You see through things… through people, I suppose. Makes it harder to keep walls up."

I swallowed, feeling the weight of his words settle over me. It was true—I had a knack for sensing the cracks in his armor, the fleeting glimpses of the man he tried so hard to bury beneath bravado and silence. It was strange, really, how easily I'd begun to understand him, even as he tried to remain an enigma. "Maybe it's time you stopped trying to keep those walls up. Just a thought."

A spark of something dangerous, almost defiant, flashed in his gaze. "That's easy for you to say," he replied, his voice low, tinged with the hint of a challenge. "You've got your whole heart out there for the world to see. But some of us don't have that luxury."

I felt a pang of frustration, of wanting to shake him, to tell him that trust wasn't about luxury or convenience. But I stopped myself, biting back the words, knowing that he wouldn't hear them the way I wanted him to. Instead, I forced a small smile, one that I hoped hid the ache in my chest. "If I've got my heart out there, it's only because I don't know how to do anything halfway."

He laughed, a short, sharp sound that held more weight than any words could. "That's what I've always liked about you. Frustrating as it is."

The admission caught me off guard, and I felt my cheeks warm, a blush I could only hope he wouldn't notice in the dim light. "Don't go getting soft on me now," I teased, though my voice was softer than I'd meant it to be.

He rolled his eyes, but I caught the flicker of a smile tugging at his lips. "Soft isn't in my vocabulary. You should know that by now."

The playful glint in his gaze was like a balm, a reminder that, for all our jagged edges and scars, we had somehow found a way to exist in this strange, in-between place. And maybe, just maybe, that was enough.

Or at least, that was what I wanted to believe. But the truth was a more complex, thorny thing, one I couldn't quite grasp without feeling the sting of its barbs. Because the longer I looked at him, the more I realized how much he'd come to mean to me, and that kind of love—raw, unfiltered, almost frightening in its intensity—didn't fit neatly into the fragile peace we'd carved out. It was a wildfire, beautiful and destructive, and I knew that once it was unleashed, there would be no turning back.

He must have seen something shift in my expression because his own softened, his gaze gentling as he reached out, his fingers brushing mine in a tentative touch that made my pulse spike. It was such a small, insignificant thing—a simple gesture that held the weight of all the things we weren't saying.

And then, before I could lose my nerve, I turned my hand over, threading my fingers through his. The contact sent a thrill up my spine, a jolt of electricity that made my breath hitch. "You don't have to fight this, you know," I whispered, my voice barely audible. "Whatever it is... whatever this thing between us is, it doesn't have to be a battle."

He stared at our intertwined hands, his expression a mix of surprise and something else, something that looked almost like wonder. For a moment, I thought he might pull away, that he'd retreat behind his walls once more, but he didn't. Instead, he gave my hand a gentle squeeze, a silent acknowledgment of the tentative bridge we'd built.

"Maybe not," he replied, his voice a rough murmur, as if he were testing the words on his tongue. "But I don't know how to do anything without a fight."

A small smile tugged at the corners of my mouth, a smile that was both sad and hopeful. "Then maybe it's time you learned."

He let out a soft, self-deprecating laugh, shaking his head as if he couldn't quite believe what he was hearing. "You're asking a lot of me, you know that?"

"Probably," I admitted, feeling a flutter of nerves as I held his gaze. "But I think you're worth it."

The words slipped out before I could second-guess them, and for a heartbeat, the world seemed to stand still. He looked at me, really looked at me, his gaze piercing through every defense I'd ever tried to build. And then, without a word, he leaned in, his lips brushing mine in a kiss that was as gentle as it was devastating, a promise and a confession all at once.

When we pulled back, his eyes met mine, and for the first time, I saw the faintest hint of vulnerability there, a crack in the armor he wore so fiercely. "You're dangerous," he murmured, his voice a rough whisper that sent a shiver down my spine.

I smiled, my heart pounding in my chest, feeling the weight of all the unspoken words between us. "Only to people who think they don't need anyone."

He chuckled, shaking his head, but he didn't let go of my hand. And in that moment, as we sat there beneath the watchful stars, I knew that whatever came next, whatever battles lay ahead, we would face them together—two broken, stubborn hearts finding a way to mend in the space between.

The soft rustling of leaves surrounded us, the night cool and still, and for a while, we just sat there, holding onto a fragile peace I wasn't sure we deserved. The intensity of his gaze softened, and I found myself marveling at how unguarded he looked, almost vulnerable in a way I never thought I'd see. Part of me wanted to keep him in that moment forever, to cling to the impossible warmth that had blossomed between us like a wildflower in the cracks of a stone wall. But the other part, the part that knew all too well how fleeting these moments could be, was waiting for reality to sweep back in and rip it all away.

He broke the silence first, his voice hushed but steady, as if he feared to shatter whatever delicate thread held us together. "I don't know what this means," he murmured, his thumb tracing a light pattern across the back of my hand, sending tiny sparks up my arm.

I looked down, noticing how perfectly our hands fit together, how natural it felt to have his fingers intertwined with mine, and I struggled to ignore the quiet panic stirring in my chest. "Maybe it doesn't have to mean anything," I replied, though the words felt hollow. "Maybe it's enough that it just...is."

He gave a slight nod, his expression thoughtful, though I could see the doubt flickering in his eyes, a flash of hesitation that made my heart ache. "I've never been good at 'just is,'" he admitted, his voice so quiet I almost missed it. "I need a plan. A purpose. Something I can control."

My laugh was barely more than a breath. "You're the only person I know who'd try to strategize his way out of falling in love."

He raised an eyebrow, the hint of a smirk tugging at his lips. "If you think about it, love's probably the worst battle tactic there is. Gets you all sorts of distracted." He gestured around us, taking in the remnants of the night's chaos. "Doesn't exactly lend itself to survival, does it?"

"Maybe not." I bit my lip, letting my gaze drift over the darkened trees, the shadows that seemed to stretch endlessly beyond our little clearing. "But then again, maybe survival isn't enough."

He stilled, his hand tightening around mine. I could feel the weight of his gaze on me, the question that lingered just beyond his silence. I met his eyes, forcing myself to hold steady, to let him see that I meant it. "What if there's more to life than just getting through it? What if there's something worth fighting for that isn't just survival?"

A faint crease appeared between his brows, as though he was struggling to make sense of the idea, to see the world from my perspective for even a second. "That sounds suspiciously like hope," he said, his tone wry but tinged with something almost like reverence, as though he were studying a rare, delicate artifact.

"Maybe it is," I replied, smiling despite the tension that wound tight in my chest. "Hope can be a powerful thing."

He shook his head slowly, a reluctant smile flickering at the corner of his mouth. "You're more dangerous than I realized."

I smirked, squeezing his hand. "Good. Maybe you'll finally start taking me seriously."

His laughter was quiet, a soft rumble that filled the air between us, and for a moment, it was as if the world had shrunk to just the two of us. But the moment was short-lived. A low growl sounded from the darkness, sharp and guttural, sending a shiver down my spine. He tensed, his hand dropping mine as he reached instinctively for the dagger at his side. My pulse quickened, the warmth of his touch replaced by a cold dread that seeped into my bones.

"Did you hear that?" His voice was barely more than a whisper, his gaze scanning the shadows with the careful, practiced focus of someone who'd spent too many nights anticipating unseen dangers.

I nodded, keeping my voice low. "I thought it was just an animal, but..." I trailed off, not wanting to voice the possibility. Out here, in the wilderness, the usual rules didn't apply. Everything was twisted, more dangerous, more cunning. And it wasn't only animals lurking in the dark.

He caught my hesitation, his jaw tightening as he adjusted his grip on the dagger. "Stay close."

We rose slowly, moving in sync, our backs brushing as we positioned ourselves to face whatever lay beyond the edge of the clearing. The forest was quiet, too quiet, as though every living thing was holding its breath, waiting for something unspeakable to unfold.

Then, from the shadows, a figure emerged, draped in a tattered cloak, face obscured by the deep hood. My stomach clenched, dread pooling in the pit of my stomach as I struggled to make sense of it. The figure moved slowly, almost deliberately, their footsteps eerily silent against the forest floor.

I swallowed hard, trying to keep the fear at bay, but the presence of the stranger made it nearly impossible. I couldn't help but glance at him, noting the way his shoulders tensed, his posture defensive.

"Friend of yours?" I whispered, though I could already guess the answer.

He shook his head, his eyes narrowing as he studied the figure. "I don't have friends."

"Well, that's reassuring," I muttered, though there was no humor in my tone. "Any guesses?"

He didn't answer, and the silence stretched out, taut and brittle, until finally the figure stopped, standing just a few feet away. The stranger lifted their head, revealing a glimpse of pale skin beneath the hood, lips curving into a smile that sent a chill skittering down my spine.

"I thought I'd find you here," the figure said, voice smooth and unsettlingly calm. There was a familiarity to the tone, a softness that was almost friendly, which somehow made it worse.

His grip on the dagger tightened, his knuckles white, and for a brief moment, I saw something flicker across his face—recognition, maybe, or fear. "What do you want?" he demanded, his voice steady but edged with a barely concealed anger.

The stranger tilted their head, regarding him with a calm that bordered on disdain. "You know what I want," they replied, their gaze flickering to me briefly, a glint of something cold and calculating in their eyes. "And it's not just you."

A wave of nausea rolled over me as I realized what they meant. I could feel the weight of his gaze on me, a silent plea for forgiveness, for understanding, as though he'd known all along that this was inevitable. That our fragile peace, our whispered promises, had always been teetering on the edge of ruin.

"Don't do this," he said, his voice barely more than a murmur, a quiet desperation threading through the words.

The stranger's smile widened, a cruel, mocking thing that made my skin crawl. "Oh, but you should've known better. Nothing comes without a price. And I intend to collect."

I felt his hand reach for mine, a silent reassurance that was equal parts apology and promise, and my heart pounded as I braced myself, every nerve on edge. I wanted to believe that we could face this, that our bond, as new and fragile as it was, would be enough to see us through whatever lay ahead.

But as the figure stepped forward, a glint of steel flashing beneath the cloak, I knew, deep down, that this was only the beginning—that we were standing on the precipice of something dark and deadly, something that would test us in ways we couldn't possibly imagine.

And as the stranger raised their weapon, eyes gleaming with ruthless intent, I realized, with a sickening clarity, that we might not survive what was coming next.

Chapter 25: The Betrayer Among Us

I blinked, the rush of betrayal hitting me like a blade through my ribs. Darius's face was set in that cold way he reserved for enemies, and I realized, with a sickening certainty, that one of our own stood before us, an impostor in ally's clothing. The room, once filled with the soft glow of candles and the warm scent of firewood, now seemed to chill, the walls themselves turning sharp and unkind. We'd been careful—meticulous, even—in whom we trusted, pulling them in slowly, testing their mettle, watching their eyes for the glint of deception.

But we'd failed with Cassian.

His dark eyes flickered, but his stance remained firm, unmoving, as if he believed he could brazen his way through the storm of our anger. "This isn't what you think," he said, raising his hands, palms out in a way that might have been apologetic had it not been for the gleam of defiance in his gaze. He looked at me, a trace of mockery hidden in the curve of his mouth.

"What, then?" I demanded, a harsh laugh tearing through my throat. "Tell me what I'm supposed to think, Cassian. Because last I checked, allies don't hand over the plans to our enemies, no matter how well they plead innocence afterward."

A muscle in his jaw tightened, but he didn't drop his gaze. Darius stepped forward, his frame tense, and I could feel the restrained fury pulsing off him in waves. We both knew this wasn't simply a matter of broken trust. The relic we'd spent months tracking, the one artifact that could shift the balance of power in our fight, was now in the hands of people who'd sooner see us dead.

I remembered Cassian's loyalty—real or otherwise, he'd played it to perfection. The late-night conversations by the fire, the plans whispered in shadows, his laughter that had always felt genuine. I wondered if he'd laughed like that with our enemies, too, as he reported our every move. The betrayal tasted bitter on my tongue, and I swallowed hard against the growing ache in my chest. I'd vouched for him. I'd vouched for him more than once.

He moved as if to explain, but Darius cut him off, his voice a low growl. "Don't waste your breath, Cassian. The time for excuses is long past." He shot me a quick glance, the kind that said he was willing to let me take the lead on this, even though I could feel his rage simmering just beneath the surface. It was like an unspoken pact between us now, our loyalty the only thing left untouched by the poison of treachery.

Cassian dropped his hands, resignation setting into his face, but a trace of arrogance still clung to him, a kind of smugness I hadn't noticed before, or maybe had willfully ignored. "If you knew half of what I know," he sneered, his voice a pitch lower, "you'd have done the same."

"Then enlighten us." My voice was steady, though every nerve in my body was frayed, vibrating with the urge to scream or to lunge at him. I could see the gleam of his sword at his hip, a weapon I'd once seen him wield in our defense. The memory turned to ash, worthless.

Cassian's eyes narrowed as he looked between us, weighing his options. It was the briefest of pauses, but I didn't miss the flicker of fear that darted across his face. "It's bigger than us, all of us," he said finally, each word dripping with a certainty that only deepened my hatred. "You really think you're the only ones who understand sacrifice? Who fight for something worth dying for? The people you despise—the ones you call enemies—they believe they're saving this world."

"They're wrong," I replied sharply. "Their idea of salvation is nothing more than a bloodstained ruin. And you helped them bring us one step closer to it."

He smiled, a cold, humorless twist of his lips. "One step closer to it," he echoed, mocking me. "You're so wrapped up in your righteousness that you can't see the faults in your own cause."

A sharp pang of anger flared in my chest, mingling with a new, darker resolve. I wanted to strip him down to the hollow core of his intentions, expose him to the light he so clearly despised. "If you're so disillusioned," I asked, each word honed like a blade, "then why not just leave? Why go through all the trouble to betray us, to worm your way into our trust?"

His gaze darkened. "Because," he said, voice dropping to a near-whisper, "sometimes the only way to destroy something is from the inside."

The words fell like stones between us. The room seemed to shrink, each heartbeat loud in my ears as the weight of his betrayal settled into something heavier, something permanent. Darius and I exchanged a look, and I could see the fire burning in his eyes, a reflection of my own anger. We were outnumbered, and our advantage, already fragile, had just shattered.

"Then there's nothing left to discuss." My voice was steadier than I felt. "You made your choice, Cassian."

He laughed, a bitter sound that reverberated off the stone walls. "Don't look so shocked. You're both players in the same game, pretending you're any different from me. And in the end, you'll find yourself exactly where I am."

"Not a chance," Darius said, his voice hard as steel. And with a final, damning look, he turned to leave, signaling me to follow. I held Cassian's gaze for a heartbeat longer, searching his face for any sign of the man I thought I'd known. But there was only the sneer, the glint of satisfaction in his eyes as he watched us go.

Outside, the night air was cool, but it did little to wash away the heat of my anger. Darius and I walked in silence, each step grounding me, giving me the resolve I needed. Whatever came next, we'd face it together, even if it meant starting over with nothing but a broken faith and a grim determination.

I couldn't stop the flood of questions, the ones clawing at the edges of my mind. How deep had Cassian's betrayal gone? How many others had he fed our secrets to? But I knew I couldn't linger in those doubts. I couldn't change what had already been set into motion. All that mattered now was the path forward, however treacherous it might be.

As Darius and I continued down the darkened road, I felt a strange, fierce clarity take root in me, sharper and more certain than anything I'd felt in a long time. We'd been betrayed, yes—but we weren't defeated. Not yet. And as long as we had each other, as long as there was still a glimmer of hope, I'd fight like hell to see our mission through.

The silence between us was thick, stretching taut as we trudged down the narrow path leading away from the camp. Shadows from the trees spilled across the ground, their twisted shapes dancing in the flickering torchlight, casting everything in shades of deep, uncertain blue. I could feel the weight of the betrayal pressing against me, an ache that gnawed at my bones. But Darius was there, his presence steady, his gaze focused ahead, his steps deliberate. I wanted to say something, anything that could pierce through the silence, but words felt pointless against the tidal wave of emotions coursing through me.

We finally stopped at the edge of a rocky outcrop that overlooked the valley. The moon hung heavy and pale in the sky, casting a faint glow over the world below. Darius exhaled slowly, the sound rough and weary, and turned to face me, his eyes dark with thoughts I couldn't quite read.

"What now?" I managed, barely more than a whisper. The question hung in the air, and for a moment, it felt as if even the trees were holding their breath.

He gave me a long, searching look, his jaw tight. "Now," he said, his voice carrying a steely resolve, "we make sure we don't end up like Cassian. Selling pieces of ourselves to the highest bidder."

I laughed bitterly, shaking my head. "If he ever had a soul to sell." The words tumbled out before I could stop them, sharp and angry, but Darius's quiet nod was all the validation I needed. Somehow, just standing beside him, I felt a flicker of strength return—a reminder that not all our bonds were broken. Cassian had cut into us, yes, left us bleeding and exposed. But he hadn't taken everything. Not by a long shot.

"What do you think they offered him?" I asked, though I wasn't sure I wanted to know. The question felt like poking at a bruise, but I needed to understand. Needed to know if there had been something we'd missed—a hint, a sign.

Darius's eyes grew cold, his mouth set in a grim line. "More than we ever could. Wealth, power, whatever his greedy little heart could dream up. Men like him," he paused, a muscle in his jaw twitching, "they don't have the stomach for the kind of fight we're in. They think they do until they're staring down the consequences, and then they run."

He spoke with a calm, almost detached certainty that made me shiver. It was a side of him I'd rarely seen, and it reminded me just how far we were from the easy camaraderie we'd once shared with Cassian. The man I'd laughed with, trusted, was gone. Had he ever even been real?

A part of me wanted to scream, to rail against the injustice of it all, but instead, I let out a shaky breath, forcing the anger back down. "So, what do we do? If he's sold us out, then everything we've worked for is compromised. He knows too much—our strategies, our plans..." I trailed off, the realization settling in with a heavy thud.

Darius clenched his fists, his eyes darkening further. "We don't panic," he said, each word measured, calm. "Yes, he knows our plans, but he doesn't know us. Not really. He thought he could get the best of us by playing spy, but he underestimated what it means to actually have loyalty."

The statement was simple, but it settled something in me. Darius was right. Cassian might know our tactics, but he didn't understand the heart of what kept us going, the grit that bound us together even now, as wounded as we were. The more I thought about it, the more I realized that Cassian, for all his scheming, had never truly been one of us. He'd always felt a bit on the outside, watching, assessing. And now I knew why.

A sudden surge of resolve bubbled up in my chest, fierce and burning. "So, what's our next move?"

Darius's gaze shifted, studying the dark horizon as if it held the answer. "We go back to the beginning," he said, his voice low and steady. "Back to where we started this whole mess. If we can cut off their access to the relic before they even get close, we might have a chance."

I swallowed hard, the weight of his words sinking in. Back to the beginning meant stepping into the heart of enemy territory. It meant facing dangers we'd only narrowly escaped the first time. And it meant leaving behind the few safe havens we had left. But as terrifying as it sounded, there was a strange thrill in the idea—a spark of rebellion that made my heart pound with the thought of it.

"Risky," I said, a smirk tugging at the corner of my mouth despite myself.

"Extremely." His lips mirrored my smirk, a glimmer of that old, reckless humor shining through the cracks of his usual guarded demeanor. It was the first time I'd seen it since we'd learned the truth about Cassian, and for a moment, it was enough to push the betrayal to the edges of my mind.

"Then let's do it," I said, the resolve settling like steel in my bones. "I'd rather go down fighting than sit around waiting for them to come to us."

Darius nodded, his gaze steady on mine. "I knew you'd say that."

We set off again, the silence between us comfortable now, a shared determination replacing the tension that had weighed us down. The night seemed darker, the air colder, but the fear that had been gnawing at me had dulled, replaced by a fierce, reckless kind of courage. Whatever Cassian had planned, he hadn't counted on us fighting back. He'd thought he could break us, weaken us with his treachery. But he'd only made us stronger, more desperate to see this through to the bitter end.

After a while, Darius glanced at me, his expression serious. "You know, this is probably going to end badly."

I couldn't help but laugh, a sound that felt strange and foreign in the heavy stillness of the night. "Is that supposed to be a pep talk?"

He rolled his eyes, a smile flickering across his face. "Just being realistic. You're always asking me to be more honest."

"Fine," I shot back, grinning. "But next time, try a little less realism and a little more blind optimism."

He chuckled, a low, warm sound that settled something in me, the weight of our shared purpose anchoring me. For all the danger and uncertainty ahead, I realized that, strange as it was, I wouldn't want anyone else by my side.

By the time we reached the main road, the sky was beginning to lighten, the faintest traces of dawn spilling over the horizon. A new day, a new plan, and perhaps the faintest hope that, somehow, we'd come out of this in one piece. And for now, that was enough.

By midday, we'd reached the edge of what could barely be called a village—more a scattering of ramshackle buildings, crooked and leaning as though the weight of their own secrets pulled them to the ground. Darius and I stopped just shy of the first house, crouching behind a clump of overgrown bushes that hid us from view. The sunlight was dimmed by clouds, casting everything in a muted, gray haze. I pulled my cloak tighter, the chill settling into my bones as I scanned the place, looking for signs of life, signs of danger.

"What do you think?" I whispered, glancing sideways at Darius.

He studied the scene with narrowed eyes, mouth set in that familiar, grim line. "I think," he replied softly, "that if anyone here knows the relic's whereabouts, they're not going to tell us willingly. Especially not if Cassian's been running his mouth about us."

I felt a prickle of anger at the mention of Cassian, a reminder of his betrayal cutting through me like a shard of glass. But Darius was right. We couldn't afford to be anything but cautious now. We had precious few allies left, and anyone who claimed to be one would have to prove themselves before I so much as let them near my shadow.

"You're awfully optimistic today," I muttered, though there was a hint of a smile tugging at the corner of my mouth. We'd been through too much to lose our sense of humor now, as bitter as it sometimes felt.

Darius gave me a sidelong glance, his expression softening just a fraction. "I thought you wanted less realism and more blind optimism. Consider this me trying."

A laugh slipped out before I could stop it, but the sound died quickly as a figure appeared around the corner of the largest building, looking over their shoulder before ducking into a narrow alley. I sucked in a breath, heart racing. The person had been cloaked, their hood pulled low, but something about the way they moved felt familiar—too familiar. It was a sharp, purposeful stride, the kind that left no room for uncertainty. And I'd seen it a hundred times.

Darius caught the look in my eyes and followed my gaze, his own posture stiffening as he too recognized the shape of that walk. "It's him," he breathed, the words barely audible.

Without thinking, I took off, my body moving before my mind had even caught up. The world around me narrowed to that single, shadowed alleyway, the figure disappearing into it as I sprinted forward, Darius hot on my heels. I didn't care if he could hear me coming; if anything, I wanted him to know I was here, that I was hunting him down for answers he was going to give, whether he liked it or not.

The alley was narrower than I'd expected, forcing us to dodge around piles of discarded crates and broken barrels. A faint smell of rotting wood clung to the air, thick and heavy, but I barely noticed as I kept my eyes trained on the flash of Cassian's cloak ahead of us. He turned sharply, disappearing down another passage, and I pushed harder, my legs burning as I tried to close the distance.

Darius's voice came from just behind me, his tone urgent. "Careful. He's leading us somewhere."

"I know," I replied breathlessly, though I couldn't bring myself to slow down. I wanted answers. I wanted justice. And I wanted him to look me in the eyes and explain himself, even if the words tasted like poison on his tongue.

We burst out of the narrow alley into a small, abandoned courtyard, ringed by crumbling walls that seemed to lean inward, blocking out most of the light. Cassian stood in the center, his hood thrown back, watching us with that infuriatingly calm look he always wore. His hair was tousled, his face half-shadowed, but the gleam of satisfaction in his eyes was unmistakable.

"Took you long enough," he drawled, folding his arms over his chest. His gaze slid from me to Darius, a smirk playing at his lips. "I was beginning to wonder if you'd lost your edge."

My fists clenched at my sides, every ounce of restraint draining from me as I took a step forward, teeth gritted. "We haven't lost anything. But you might, if you don't start talking."

He laughed—a low, cold sound that scraped across my nerves. "Oh, I don't think you're in any position to be making threats. You don't understand the full picture, do you?"

Darius stepped up beside me, his expression hard as iron. "Enlighten us, then," he said, voice steely. "Because from where we're standing, it looks like you've sold your loyalty for a handful of silver."

Cassian tilted his head, studying us with an air of mild amusement, as though he were the one who had hunted us down. "Silver? Please. You think I'd go through all this for something so ordinary?" He shook his head, a condescending smile gracing his lips. "No. What I've gained is far beyond anything you could imagine. And all you had to do was walk right into it."

Dread coiled in my stomach, but I refused to let him see it. "We're not scared of you, Cassian. Whatever power you think you've found, it's not going to save you from us."

He laughed again, and the sound echoed off the cracked stone walls, filling the courtyard with a chilling resonance. "This isn't about fear," he said smoothly. "This is about inevitability. You two are playing the roles you were given, blind to the fact that you've been moving exactly as you were meant to. Every step, every sacrifice—predictable."

The words stung, twisting my anger into something darker, something I wasn't sure I wanted to name. "You think you know us that well?" I asked, my voice laced with a bitterness that even surprised me.

"I know enough," he replied, shrugging with an insufferable ease. "Enough to know that you'll both cling to each other, that your so-called loyalty will be your undoing." He shot Darius a pointed look, his smile growing sharper, crueler. "And you, you're not the only one who can guard secrets. In fact, I'd wager I know more about your past than you've ever told her."

Darius went rigid beside me, his jaw clenched so tightly that I could see the muscles twitching. My heart stumbled, fear clawing up my throat, though I refused to give Cassian the satisfaction of seeing it. But as I looked at Darius, at the tension straining through him, I couldn't help the prickle of doubt that took root in my mind.

Cassian's gaze flicked between us, his smirk widening as he sensed the crack he'd created. "Oh, don't look so shocked," he sneered. "Secrets are inevitable. You two, with your oh-so-trustworthy bond—you're just as flawed as the rest of us."

"Enough," I said, my voice trembling with barely restrained fury. But my mind was already racing, his words spinning through my thoughts like a dark, twisting thread. I didn't want to believe him, didn't want to consider the possibility that he could be right. But there was something in the way Darius held himself, something guarded, like a door slammed shut.

Cassian's eyes glinted with satisfaction, and he stepped back, hands raised in mock surrender. "Good luck," he said softly, his voice dripping with a malicious glee. "I'll be seeing you."

And before I could move, before I could shout or even react, he turned and vanished into the shadows, leaving us standing in that cold, crumbling courtyard with nothing but the silence, and a deep, gnawing uncertainty hanging between us like a blade poised to fall.

Chapter 26: The Path of Sacrifice

The air tasted of wet earth and secrets, a dampness that clung to my skin and sank deep into my bones. The cavern stretched endlessly before us, veiled in shadows that seemed to pulse with a life of their own. The relic lay on a stone pedestal at the far end, an unassuming trinket glowing faintly beneath a layer of grime. A simple thing, really, for something that could so ruinously upend lives. I could hear the soft drip of water echoing somewhere in the distance, and the chill made the hairs on my arms stand on end. It felt like a place time had forgotten. A place where sacrifices were measured in heartbreak, not blood.

Liam stood a step behind me, close enough that I could feel his warmth, even though he hadn't so much as brushed my shoulder. His breath was steady, too steady, and when I turned, I saw the determined set of his jaw, the intensity in his gaze as he stared at the relic.

"You're not thinking what I think you're thinking," I said, trying to keep my voice light, to keep the edge of fear from curling around my words.

He didn't respond immediately. Instead, he closed the small gap between us, his hands reaching out, stopping just shy of touching me. His fingers trembled, barely noticeable, but enough to make my heart stutter.

"We both know what needs to be done," he said quietly, his voice steady but low, as if he feared the cavern itself would hear and close in on us.

I shook my head. "Don't even think about it. There has to be another way. We just... we haven't thought of it yet."

He smiled, a sad, crooked little thing that twisted my insides. "If there was another way, you'd have found it by now. I know you, Evie.

You've been turning every possibility over in that brilliant mind of yours since we set foot in here."

I clenched my fists, the pressure grounding me, if only barely. "You think you know everything about me," I said, feigning a bravado that felt as thin as the light dusting the relic.

"I know enough," he replied, his tone softened by something achingly close to affection. "Enough to know you'd try to be the hero and take this on yourself if you thought you could get away with it."

The worst part was, he was right. I'd been racking my brain for an escape hatch, a loophole that didn't involve us standing here, in this damp cavern, on the edge of the abyss, bargaining with an ancient curse that didn't care about us or our sacrifices. But I couldn't tell him that—not with the self-sacrificing glint in his eye that made my stomach knot.

"Liam, there's no version of this where you go through with it," I whispered, hoping that somehow, saying it out loud would make it true.

He tilted his head, studying me with an intensity that made me want to look away, but I didn't. "There's no version where I let you do it alone," he said, so quietly it almost didn't reach me.

A shiver ran down my spine, and I was suddenly aware of every inch between us, every unspoken word hanging in the air. The relic's faint glow pulsed like a heartbeat, casting eerie shadows on his face, making him look like someone I barely recognized.

"Don't make this harder than it has to be, Evie," he said, reaching out to gently touch my shoulder, his fingers warm and steady against my chilled skin.

A pang of something like panic flared up, and before I could stop myself, I grabbed his hand, pressing it tightly to my shoulder, as if I could anchor him there, keep him from doing something reckless. "I won't let you," I said, my voice trembling despite the stubborn set of my jaw.

The ghost of a smile flitted across his lips. "You don't have a choice."

With that, he gently pulled his hand away, and I felt the absence of his warmth as keenly as a blade. He took a step closer to the relic, the faint glow catching the lines of his face, illuminating the shadows that lingered in his gaze. It was the look of a man resigned, determined, and utterly reckless.

My mind raced, grasping for anything that could change his mind. "Liam," I said, a pleading note slipping into my voice. "Please. We can find another way. Together."

He didn't answer. Instead, he turned to me, his gaze softer now, a kind of sorrow etched into his features that made my heart clench. "I'd do anything to spare you this," he murmured, almost to himself. "Anything."

It was in that moment that I knew I was losing him. Not to the relic, not to the curse, but to some choice he'd already made deep down. I took a step forward, desperation clawing at me, and wrapped my arms around him, pulling him close. I could feel his heartbeat, steady and unyielding beneath my cheek.

"You're not a hero, Liam," I whispered fiercely. "You're just a man. My man."

He stiffened at my words, and for a brief, electric moment, I thought maybe, just maybe, I'd gotten through to him. But then his arms tightened around me, holding me close as if he could memorize every detail of this moment, and I knew it was goodbye.

"I've never been much good at being anything else," he said with a humorless chuckle, brushing a thumb against my cheek.

With one final look, he pulled away, his eyes never leaving mine until he stood before the relic, his hand hovering over it, fingers shaking.

And in that heartbeat, time stood still. The relic's glow intensified, a fierce, unyielding light that seemed to swallow the cavern whole. It pulsed, hungry, waiting for his touch, for his sacrifice.

"No!" I cried out, lunging forward. But it was too late.

The second his fingers brushed the relic, the world shifted, a ripple of energy coursing through the cavern like an earthquake. A blinding light engulfed him, pulling him away from me, and I could feel the echo of his heartbeat, fading, slipping through my grasp like water.

The silence that followed was deafening, a hollow emptiness that sank into my soul. I dropped to my knees, gasping for air, for something, anything that would bring him back.

But he was gone.

And the relic sat silent, unmoved, as if it had never known him at all.

A hollow silence settled over the cavern, broken only by the soft shuffle of my boots on the damp, uneven ground. My pulse thudded in my ears, a desperate reminder that I was still here, still breathing, still clutching at hope like a fool. Liam had given himself up to the relic without hesitation, in that infuriatingly noble way of his. And now? Now the air felt heavier, the shadows longer, like the walls themselves had absorbed his presence and swallowed it whole.

I ran my hands over my arms, not because of the cold, but to remind myself that I wasn't dreaming. I was here, and he... he was somewhere I couldn't follow.

"Alright, relic," I muttered, the echo of my voice startling in the oppressive stillness. "You've had your pound of flesh. Now give him back."

The relic, of course, did nothing but sit on its pedestal, indifferent, unmoved. Its faint glow was gone, and all that remained was an ordinary, unremarkable hunk of metal and stone. Anger bubbled up in me, prickling at the edges of my composure. How could something so small, so mundane, hold such power? And how could it demand so much?

I kicked a stray pebble, sending it skittering into the darkness. "Come on," I said, my voice louder now, defiant. "I'm not leaving without him. Do you hear me?"

There was no answer. I knew there wouldn't be. Yet as the silence stretched, an idea took hold, a glimmer of desperation mingling with the anger simmering just beneath the surface. The guardian had spoken of a sacrifice, of something precious that could never be reclaimed. But it hadn't said the sacrifice had to be final. At least, not in so many words. There was a way—I knew it, even if I didn't fully understand it.

I knelt beside the relic, fingers hovering just above its dull, unremarkable surface. I didn't dare touch it, not after what I'd seen it do to Liam. But I could feel the pull, faint as a whisper, like the relic itself was mocking me, daring me to try.

"Well, you asked for precious," I said softly, feeling the familiar ache of longing stir deep within me. I knew what I had to give, what it would cost me. Memories, moments that defined me. I could feel them slipping through my fingers like sand, the realization settling heavy in my chest.

Closing my eyes, I took a shaky breath, summoning the image that hurt the most to part with. My mother's face swam into view, her warm smile crinkling at the edges, the way her laugh had filled every room we'd ever lived in. I could almost smell her favorite lavender perfume, hear her humming along to the old records she loved.

And then, just as I'd held it close, I let it go.

The cavern pulsed, the air vibrating as if the very fabric of reality were stretching, making room for my sacrifice. I opened my eyes, and for a moment, I saw nothing. Just empty darkness. Then, as if through water, a figure began to take shape, wavering and indistinct.

My heart pounded wildly as I leaned forward, hands clenching the edge of the stone pedestal.

"Liam?" My voice was barely more than a whisper, a desperate, fragile thing.

The figure solidified, and there he was—standing before me, his face a blend of confusion and disbelief. His eyes, those sharp, steady eyes that had always held just a hint of mischief, were wide as he took in his surroundings.

"Evie?" His voice was hoarse, like he'd been shouting or swallowed in silence for far too long.

A laugh, half-giddy, half-relieved, escaped me before I could stop it. I launched myself at him, barely noticing the way his arms automatically went around me, solid and real and exactly as I remembered. He smelled like the woods, like rain-soaked earth and pine, and I held onto him, refusing to let go.

"You came back," I murmured, the words slipping out before I could catch them.

He pulled back slightly, just enough to look down at me, brows knitted in confusion. "You're surprised?" His voice was gentle, a question wrapped in a half-smile that I could barely stand to look at.

For a long, shaky moment, we just stood there, holding onto each other as if the very ground beneath us might disappear. Then, a sharp pain began to edge into my mind, a hollow ache like a missing tooth, nagging and relentless. I frowned, trying to grasp at the fading memory, but it slipped away, leaving nothing but emptiness in its wake.

"Evie?" Liam's voice was soft, his thumb tracing gentle circles on my shoulder. "What's wrong?"

I blinked, shaking my head, forcing a smile that felt wrong, a fractured version of itself. "Nothing," I lied. "Just... happy you're here."

But he was watching me with that steady, too-knowing gaze, and I could tell he didn't believe me. "What did it take?" he asked, his tone somber, each word laden with unspoken understanding.

I tried to brush him off, tried to laugh, but it came out thin, hollow. "It doesn't matter. You're here. That's all that matters."

He looked at me for a long moment, eyes searching, his mouth pressed into a hard line. "Evie, I don't buy that for a second."

My chest tightened, the weight of the lie heavy, suffocating. "I gave it something precious, alright?" I said, my voice sharper than I'd intended, breaking the fragile spell of reunion. "That's what it wanted. A memory."

He stilled, his expression unreadable, and for the first time, I wished he would just argue, just do anything but look at me with that quiet resignation.

"A memory?" he repeated, his voice barely more than a murmur.

"Yes," I said, bitterness creeping into my words, though I didn't know if it was for him, the relic, or the hollow ache of something I could no longer remember. "One of the good ones. They wanted something that mattered, and I... I gave them one of the best."

Liam's jaw tightened, his gaze dropping to the ground. "You didn't have to do that for me."

Anger flared, hot and sharp, and I yanked my arm from his grip. "You would've done the same," I spat, every word edged with fury I hadn't even known I'd been holding onto. "You know you would have. You did, remember?"

He took a step back, the anguish in his eyes catching me off guard. "I'd rather lose my life than see you lose something that made you... you."

I opened my mouth, ready to argue, but the words caught in my throat, tangled in a mess of emotions I didn't know how to unravel. He looked away, his shoulders slumping in defeat.

In that moment, standing in the cavern's gloom with him looking at the ground as if it held the answers, I realized just how much I'd lost. Not just memories, but pieces of myself, chipped away, given freely for the chance to keep him here, alive.

And I had no idea if I could ever get them back.

The weight of the cavern pressed down on us, thick with unsaid words, unspoken promises, and the knowledge that neither of us would ever be the same. Liam had that look again—the one that made my heart twist, a blend of fierce determination and soft resignation, as if he'd come to some unchangeable decision I wasn't a part of. I wanted to reach for him, to shake him, to tell him that there was still something left to fight for, but a strange feeling rooted me to the spot, keeping me at arm's length.

He shifted, his gaze flicking over my face, as if he could read my every thought, every fear. "You're thinking too hard again, Evie," he murmured, his voice low and oddly gentle, like he was afraid of startling me.

"Is that so?" I replied, trying to inject a bit of bravado into my voice, though it fell flat between us. "I thought you liked that about me."

A flicker of a smile touched his lips, but it didn't reach his eyes. "I do," he said. "But I don't like seeing you hurt because of it."

I opened my mouth to argue, but his fingers found mine, warm and solid, grounding me in that moment. It felt like a truce, a tiny reprieve from the tidal wave of emotions threatening to drown us both. But the silence between us only thickened, charged with everything we weren't saying. And I couldn't shake the feeling that he was slipping away, inch by inch, even as he held my hand.

"Liam," I said, my voice barely a whisper, "we need to get out of here. Now."

He hesitated, his fingers tightening around mine for the briefest moment before he nodded, the tension in his shoulders easing just a fraction. "You're right. Let's get out of this hellhole."

We started walking, the dim light of the cavern casting long shadows on the stone walls around us. I could feel the weight of the relic behind us, as if it were watching, waiting, a predator in the dark. The further we moved away from it, the more I could breathe, the pounding in my chest easing with each step. I wanted to believe we'd left its curse behind, that whatever dark magic it held no longer had its claws in us.

But as we reached the edge of the cavern, something felt... wrong. I couldn't place it at first, just an odd prickling sensation along my spine, a whisper of something left undone. I glanced at Liam, but he seemed oblivious, his gaze fixed straight ahead, his jaw set with that steely resolve I'd come to know too well.

"Do you feel that?" I asked, my voice barely louder than a breath.

He paused, his brow furrowing. "Feel what?"

It was there, faint but unmistakable—a ripple, like a memory resurfacing, or a dream slipping back into view just as you wake. And then, just like that, I knew. The relic's curse wasn't just a demand for a sacrifice; it was a tether, binding itself to whatever it had claimed. Even now, it was pulling at us, reaching out from the depths of the cavern like a spider's web, trapping us in its invisible strands.

I tightened my grip on Liam's hand, feeling a surge of urgency. "We need to move faster. Now."

But just as I took a step forward, the ground trembled beneath us, a low rumble that sent a chill racing up my spine. The walls seemed to shift, closing in, the narrow passage tightening as if the cavern itself were alive, intent on keeping us within its grasp.

Liam shot me a look, one that spoke of a thousand questions and not nearly enough time to ask them. "Evie, what's going on?"

"I don't know," I admitted, panic creeping into my voice. "But I don't think the relic is done with us."

The rumbling intensified, loose rocks tumbling from above as the very earth seemed to shake, its fury unleashed. We broke into a run, sprinting down the narrowing path as the shadows loomed, stretching and shifting, a dark tide swallowing up the light behind us. The relic's curse was more than just a demand—it was a living thing, hungry, insatiable, and we were mere mortals trying to outrun a force older and far more powerful than we could comprehend.

Just as we rounded a corner, the passage opened up to another chamber, smaller but brighter, lit by a shaft of moonlight that filtered through a crack in the ceiling. Relief surged through me, a brief moment of respite, but Liam's grip on my hand tightened, his gaze fixed on the entrance we'd just come from.

"We can't keep running forever," he said, his voice calm, too calm, a dangerous sort of calm that set my nerves on edge.

I shook my head, refusing to accept it. "We don't have to. We just have to get out of here, and then we can... we can figure out what to do next."

But his eyes were already distant, his face pale in the cold, silvery light. "What if there is no next, Evie?"

His words hit me like a punch to the gut, and for a moment, I couldn't breathe. "Don't say that," I whispered, my voice raw and unsteady. "You don't get to give up now. Not after everything."

He looked at me, something fierce and almost broken flashing in his eyes. "I'm not giving up," he said quietly. "I'm just... preparing for the possibility."

"No." I shook my head, stepping closer, close enough that I could feel his breath, warm and steady, grounding me. "We're getting out of here. Both of us."

A slow, sad smile touched his lips. "You're stubborn, you know that?"

"And you're infuriating," I shot back, a spark of defiance flaring to life within me. "But that's not news, is it?"

He huffed a soft laugh, and for a brief, fleeting moment, we were just... us. Two people caught in the crossfire of forces we could barely comprehend, but still holding onto each other, refusing to let go.

But before I could say another word, a cold draft swept through the chamber, carrying with it a whisper that sent chills down my spine. It wasn't a voice, exactly, but a presence, ancient and unyielding, filling the air with an oppressive weight that made my heart stutter.

Liam's grip on my hand tightened, his knuckles white. "Do you hear that?" he asked, his voice barely audible.

I nodded, swallowing hard. "We need to move."

But as we turned to leave, a figure stepped into the moonlight, materializing from the shadows as if summoned by our fear itself. It was tall, cloaked in darkness, its features obscured, yet somehow... familiar, as if I'd seen it in a dream, or maybe a nightmare. My breath caught, and Liam's hand slipped from mine as he took a cautious step forward, his body tensed, ready for a fight.

"Who are you?" I demanded, trying to keep the tremor out of my voice, though my heart was racing, my skin prickling with an instinctive, bone-deep terror.

The figure tilted its head, a movement so slow, so calculated, it felt like a mockery of humanity. And when it spoke, its voice was low, echoing through the chamber like a roll of distant thunder.

"I am what you have summoned," it intoned, each word heavy with the weight of ancient, unbreakable truths. "And now, you must answer for what you have taken."

A cold sweat broke out over my skin, and I glanced at Liam, his face pale but resolute as he stared down the shadowed figure. There was no escape, no room for negotiation. And I could feel it, the truth settling over me like a shroud.

The relic's curse wasn't done with us—not even close.

Chapter 27: The Final Confrontation

The darkness felt almost sentient, as though it had drawn close just to mock us, curling into the edges of the room, thickening the air until it pressed like velvet against my skin. Shadows flickered at the edges of my vision, but the relic in my hand pulsed steadily, a heartbeat that matched the fierce thudding in my chest. I tightened my grip, feeling the strange warmth of the stone leach into my skin, and for a moment, I imagined that it was whispering something, something just beyond my grasp.

Beside me, Cade was a study in intensity, his jaw set, his gaze fixed unwaveringly on the figure before us. In the dimness, his eyes held a steely glint that might have been anger, or maybe fear—though he'd never admit it. Cade wasn't the sort to allow himself the luxury of fear, not when there was a job to be done, a fight to win. I'd known him long enough to understand that, but tonight, even his confidence seemed edged with something darker. I could feel it, simmering between us, heavy with the weight of all that had led us here.

Our adversary stood across the room, a mere silhouette against the wall of shadows, but there was no mistaking the power emanating from him. It rolled out in waves, like heat from a fire, twisting and curling around him, coiling around his figure in dark tendrils. He raised one hand, a slender finger pointing straight at me, and his lips curved into a smile that sent a shiver down my spine. This was no ordinary foe; this was someone who had waited for this moment as long as we had, someone who had built an empire on secrets and lies and would destroy anyone who dared to tear it down.

"Is that all you've got?" I taunted, voice steady despite the fear fluttering in my stomach. "I've seen scarier things in the junk drawer at my grandmother's house."

His smile widened, and a strange light flickered in his eyes—amusement, maybe. "You're brave. I'll give you that." His voice was soft, almost mocking. "But bravery only gets you so far, my dear. The relic belongs to me, and you know it. Give it to me, and I might spare you."

"How generous of you." I feigned nonchalance, though my pulse was racing. "But I think I'll keep it, thanks."

He took a step forward, and the air thickened, pressing down on us like a smothering blanket. I could feel Cade shift beside me, a subtle move, but I knew he was ready to spring into action at the first sign of a real attack. We'd come too far, lost too much to let this end with a simple exchange of words. No, this was going to be a battle, one that would test every ounce of strength we had left.

Our foe lifted his other hand, and with a flick of his wrist, a bolt of dark energy shot toward us. I barely had time to react, instinctively raising the relic in front of me. The energy collided with it, absorbed into the stone with a crackling hiss, and I felt the relic shudder in my grip. Its light flared, bright enough to sear through the darkness, and for a brief moment, I could see him clearly—the sharp angles of his face, the cold, calculating gaze, the twisted satisfaction lurking in his expression.

"Nice try," I muttered, more to myself than to him, though he heard it and his smile faded, replaced by a look of pure, unadulterated rage. Cade moved forward then, stepping between me and the advancing figure, his stance protective, unyielding. There was a brief flicker of something in the man's gaze—recognition, perhaps, or surprise at Cade's loyalty. But it vanished just as quickly, replaced by cold determination.

"I think you misunderstand," Cade said, his voice low, dangerously calm. "You're not walking out of here with that relic. And if I were you, I'd start praying for a miracle."

Our adversary sneered, but I could see the faintest hesitation in his stance, a crack in his otherwise impenetrable armor of confidence. Cade's words had rattled him, even if he wouldn't admit it. He glanced at me, his gaze flicking to the relic, and I tightened my grip, feeling the power within it pulse in response.

The room felt like it was holding its breath, the silence tense, brittle. And then, without warning, he lunged, his hand outstretched, reaching for the relic. Cade moved to intercept him, but the man was faster, slipping past Cade's defenses and seizing my wrist. His grip was like iron, unyielding, and I felt a surge of panic as his fingers tightened, pulling me toward him.

"Let go," I snarled, struggling against his hold. But his grip only tightened, his gaze fixed on the relic in my hand.

"It's mine," he hissed, his voice a harsh whisper in my ear. "I've sacrificed everything for it. Do you think I'll let a foolish little girl stand in my way?"

I felt a surge of anger, hot and fierce, and without thinking, I brought my knee up, connecting with his shin. He let out a grunt of pain, his grip loosening just enough for me to wrench my hand free. I stumbled back, clutching the relic to my chest, my heart pounding in my ears.

Cade was on him in an instant, his movements a blur as he tackled the man to the ground. They struggled, fists flying, the sound of their scuffle filling the room. I watched, breathless, clutching the relic, unsure if I should jump in or stay back. But before I could decide, our adversary let out a snarl of frustration and threw Cade off with a surge of dark energy that sent him skidding across the floor.

The man rose slowly, brushing himself off, his eyes narrowing as he looked at me. I could see the fury in his gaze, the desperation, and I knew he wouldn't stop until he had the relic in his hands.

But neither would I.

With a steadying breath, I raised the relic, feeling its warmth seep into my skin, its power humming through me. I didn't know how to use it, not really, but something inside me whispered that it didn't matter. All I needed was the will to fight, to protect what was mine, and the relic would do the rest.

The room seemed to shift, the air crackling with energy, and for the first time, I saw a flicker of fear in our adversary's eyes. He took a step back, his expression wavering, and I felt a surge of confidence, a fierce determination that burned away any lingering doubt.

This was it. The moment that would define us, that would decide our fate. And as I looked into his eyes, I knew—one way or another, this would end tonight.

The relic burned in my hand, its heat spiraling through my veins like fire, each pulse stronger than the last. It was as if it knew what was at stake, as if it was alive, sensing the fury in the air, feeding off it. Beside me, Cade's gaze was locked on our enemy, his face a portrait of sharp angles and steely focus. I could practically feel the unspoken promise between us, a silent vow to see this through no matter what. We hadn't survived countless battles, betrayal, and loss to lose here, to let him walk away with everything.

"You're getting desperate," Cade said, a hint of a smile ghosting across his lips. It was the smile he saved for moments of pure adrenaline, when the stakes were so high they scraped the sky, and he was ready to tear down anyone who stood in our way. "Never thought I'd see the day."

Our adversary's eyes narrowed, the flicker of a smile gone, his expression turning icy. He took a slow step forward, and the shadows seemed to cling to him, a living aura of darkness. "You think this is a game?" he asked, voice low and venomous. "You think a few tricks and bravado will save you?"

"Oh, I don't know," I replied, my voice as nonchalant as I could muster. "It's worked pretty well so far."

He sneered, but I caught the twitch at the corner of his mouth, the frustration breaking through his mask of control. There was something about that crack, about seeing him struggle to maintain his calm, that bolstered me. Maybe Cade and I weren't as outmatched as he wanted us to believe. Maybe he was afraid, too.

With a flick of his wrist, he sent another wave of dark energy slicing through the air. Cade dodged, quick as lightning, while I braced myself, lifting the relic instinctively. The wave collided with it, and the relic's glow flared, growing stronger, like it was feeding off his attack. I almost laughed, the rush of power, of hope, a dizzying relief.

"See?" Cade shot me a grin. "We've got this."

Our enemy's expression twisted, and for a moment, a flicker of doubt crossed his face. I could see it—tiny, but enough. He had planned for a victory, a smooth triumph, where Cade and I would be nothing more than stepping stones in his path. But that was before we'd had the relic, before he'd realized we weren't just going to hand it over. And now, here he was, facing the reality that maybe, just maybe, he'd miscalculated.

"Enough," he hissed, his tone icy, his face hardening into pure fury. "I've come too far to let you interfere. Hand it over, and I might show mercy."

"Mercy? I think we're past that," I replied, trying to keep the tremor from my voice, holding his gaze even though my hands felt like they were made of stone. "Why don't you drop the act? We both know you'd never let us walk out of here."

For a moment, he seemed taken aback, as if he hadn't expected me to see through him. But then he smirked, a chilling twist of his lips, and the glint in his eyes darkened. "So be it," he said, voice as cold and final as the blade of a guillotine.

With a roar, he lunged, faster than I'd anticipated, his movements fluid and deadly. Cade moved to intercept him, but a burst of energy knocked him back, sending him sprawling. Panic surged in my chest, but I forced it down, focusing on the relic in my hand. Its warmth spread through me, steady and grounding, and I felt its power thrumming beneath my skin, ready to be called upon. I raised it, channeling everything I had into it, and the air around us seemed to shimmer, charged with an energy that was almost electric.

Our adversary stopped short, his eyes widening as he took in the glow, the raw force emanating from the relic. I could see the fear in his gaze now, no longer masked, no longer hidden behind layers of arrogance. He was afraid, truly afraid, and that realization filled me with a fierce, blazing determination.

"I warned you," I said, my voice stronger than I felt. "You should have listened."

I poured everything into the relic, letting it surge out of me in a blinding flash of light. The room trembled, the walls seeming to bend and shudder as the energy exploded outward, a force of pure, raw power. I could see him stumbling back, shielding his face, his expression a mixture of rage and desperation.

But it wasn't enough. He wasn't giving up; if anything, the desperation only fueled him. With a snarl, he raised his hands, gathering his own energy, and I could feel the air shift, thickening with the force of his power. The room seemed to darken, the shadows pooling around him, wrapping him in a cocoon of darkness.

I braced myself, feeling the relic's energy waning, flickering like a candle in the wind. Panic clawed at me. We couldn't lose, not now, not after everything we'd fought for. I looked at Cade, who was pulling himself to his feet, his gaze locked on our adversary, unwavering, fierce. He gave me a small nod, a silent reassurance, and I felt a surge of strength, of resolve.

We stood together, side by side, facing the heart of the darkness, our determination a shield, our trust unbreakable. And then, with a sudden, desperate clarity, I realized what we needed to do.

"Cade," I whispered, gripping the relic tightly, feeling its warmth seep into my skin. "We have to combine our strength. It's the only way."

He glanced at me, his gaze intense, searching, and then he nodded, reaching out to place his hand over mine. The moment our fingers touched, a surge of energy shot through me, a current of raw, unbridled power. The relic pulsed between us, brighter than ever, its light spilling over the room, chasing away the darkness, burning through the shadows.

Our adversary let out a roar of frustration, his power faltering as he was forced to shield his eyes from the blinding light. I could see the fear in his gaze, the desperation, and I knew we had him. We just had to hold on, just a little longer.

I could feel Cade's strength flowing into me, merging with my own, and together we directed the power of the relic, pouring everything we had into one final, blinding surge. The light grew brighter, hotter, until it was all I could see, all I could feel. And then, with a deafening crack, the darkness shattered, dissipating like mist in the sun.

When the light faded, our adversary was gone, nothing but a faint shadow left on the floor where he had stood. The room was silent, still, the air cleared of his dark energy, and I felt a rush of relief, a weight lifting from my shoulders.

Cade let out a shaky breath, his hand still covering mine, and we stood there for a moment, just breathing, just taking in the quiet. I looked up at him, and he gave me a small, tired smile, his gaze warm, reassuring. We'd done it. We'd won.

But as I looked around the room, at the remnants of the battle, the shadows that lingered in the corners, I couldn't shake the feeling that this victory had come at a cost, one we might not fully understand. Not yet, anyway.

The stillness was unnerving, as if the air itself was holding its breath, waiting for the next tremor of chaos to shake it loose. I could feel my heartbeat slow, the initial rush of victory already fading into the hollow ache of exhaustion. Cade's hand was still on mine, grounding me, reminding me that despite everything, he was here. We had won, hadn't we? That should have been enough. But as I looked around the room, shadows still lingered, clinging to the corners like old regrets that refused to fade.

"What do you think?" Cade asked, his voice soft but carrying the edge of a challenge, as though he was half-daring me to say something hopeful. "You think he's really gone?"

I wanted to say yes. I wanted to believe it was over, that we could just walk out of here and leave the nightmares behind. But I couldn't shake the feeling that something was wrong, that the silence around us was more a warning than a respite. I forced a smile anyway, giving Cade a reassuring squeeze. "Gone? I don't know. But I do think he'll think twice before messing with us again."

Cade gave me a crooked grin, that rare, heart-stopping look of his that made him seem both untouchable and real all at once. "If he does come back, maybe he'll be a little less dramatic next time."

"Not likely," I muttered, rolling my eyes. "He's probably plotting his next grand entrance as we speak. Something with fireworks and maybe a few ominous fog machines. You know, because subtlety is clearly his thing."

"Ah, the villain's handbook," Cade said with a mock sigh, "always two steps away from a Broadway show. Where's the element of surprise?"

I let out a breath, laughing despite myself. "If he wanted us dead, he'd have just shown up at our door and gotten it over with. Instead, he lurks in shadows, throws out a few vague threats—he's in it for the theatrics."

Cade nodded thoughtfully, but I could tell he wasn't entirely convinced either. He'd felt it too—that crackling sense of something unfinished, something lingering just out of reach. He turned to me, his expression softening, and for a moment, I thought he might say something, something real and unguarded. But then, a faint rumble echoed through the walls, shattering the stillness and dragging us back into the present with a jolt.

"Did you hear that?" I whispered, pulse spiking as I scanned the room, trying to find the source.

Cade's grip tightened, his posture shifting into a defensive stance. "Yeah. And I don't like it."

The relic in my hand began to pulse again, slower this time, as though it was trying to warn me. But before I could process the sensation, a second rumble shook the ground beneath us, stronger this time, more insistent. The shadows in the corners shifted, coalescing into something darker, something almost alive. My stomach twisted as I realized that the victory we'd felt, the relief that had washed over us, had been nothing more than a cruel illusion.

"Run," Cade said, his voice barely more than a whisper, but it was all I needed. Without another word, we turned, sprinting toward the doorway. My legs burned, every instinct screaming at me to move faster, but the darkness was faster still, spreading across the floor in tendrils that seemed to reach out for us, each one tinged with a faint, eerie glow.

We burst through the doorway, the relic still warm in my grip, but the moment we crossed the threshold, the darkness stopped, retracting as if bound to the room behind us. I glanced back, breathless, and saw the walls shuddering, the entire space filling with shadow, swallowing every inch of light until there was nothing left but an impenetrable void.

"What... what just happened?" I managed, my voice sounding hollow and shaky even to my own ears.

Cade shook his head, his face pale but steady. "I don't know. But I don't think he was alone."

The words chilled me, the realization sinking in slowly, piece by piece. If he hadn't been acting alone—if he had followers, allies—then this wasn't the end. It was only the beginning of something much darker, something we hadn't anticipated.

A faint sound caught my attention, something soft, almost a whisper, and I turned, squinting into the shadows at the end of the hallway. There, barely visible, was a figure cloaked in darkness, watching us with an intensity that made my skin prickle. I took a step back, instinctively pulling the relic close, but the figure didn't move, didn't even blink.

Cade followed my gaze, his expression hardening. "Friend of yours?"

"Not one I'd care to introduce," I replied, keeping my tone light even as my pulse raced. "Let's go. Before they decide to be social."

We moved quickly, navigating the narrow corridors with practiced ease, but I could feel the figure's gaze following us, lingering like a shadow that refused to let go. Every step felt heavier, as though the relic itself was dragging us back, anchoring us to the darkness we'd just escaped.

When we finally reached the exit, I breathed a sigh of relief, the cool night air a welcome balm against the suffocating tension. But as we stepped out, I felt the relic pulse again, stronger this time, the heat surging through me like a warning. I stopped short, glancing down at the stone, its surface now etched with faint, glowing lines I hadn't noticed before.

"Cade," I said slowly, holding up the relic for him to see. "I think something's changed."

He frowned, studying it with narrowed eyes, and then his gaze shifted, catching on something behind me. His face went blank, all color draining, and I felt the blood turn to ice in my veins.

"Don't turn around," he whispered, his voice barely audible, but the terror in it was unmistakable.

I didn't need to turn to know that we weren't alone. I could feel it, a presence looming just behind me, the air thickening, tinged with the scent of something acrid, metallic. I forced myself to breathe, to focus, clutching the relic as though it could shield me from whatever horror waited in the darkness.

"Cade," I whispered back, my voice trembling, "if this is the part where you tell me to run, just know I'm already ahead of you."

But before he could respond, a voice drifted through the night, low and chilling, each word drawn out as though savoring the moment. "Going somewhere?"

I froze, my breath catching in my throat. The voice was familiar, achingly so, but wrong, twisted, as though warped by years of bitterness and malice. I clenched the relic tighter, feeling its warmth fade, replaced by a cold that seeped into my bones, numbing me.

Cade took a step closer, his hand brushing against mine in a silent show of solidarity, and I felt a faint surge of courage, a reminder that I wasn't alone. But as the darkness shifted, forming into a figure that seemed both familiar and foreign, my resolve wavered.

The figure took a step forward, emerging from the shadows, and my heart dropped as I saw his face—etched with lines of cruelty, his eyes gleaming with a darkness that had been buried, waiting, for far too long.

"Miss me?" he asked, his voice dripping with mockery, his gaze fixed on me with a cruel, unrelenting intensity.

And as the world tilted, as every hard-won victory turned to ash in that moment, I realized the horrifying truth. This wasn't just some enemy. It was someone I knew.

Chapter 28: Love's Last Stand

There was a stillness in the air, a sort of quiet that felt unnatural, as though even the wind was holding its breath in anticipation. I could feel my heartbeat hammering in my chest, each beat an urgent reminder of the moment's weight, the life-and-death stakes hovering like a storm cloud above us. I'd spent so much of my life running from things, avoiding attachments, and here I was, bound to this battlefield by a love that was fierce and wild—a love I hadn't expected and certainly hadn't planned for.

And then there was him, standing a few paces in front of me, looking at the cursed relic with a steady gaze, the kind of gaze one has when they've made peace with their choice. He was ready, prepared to offer himself to it, to give up everything, to protect me. I couldn't let him. I couldn't watch him do that. My heart felt like it was fracturing with each second that passed, knowing that he was about to sacrifice himself, and knowing that I would never be the same if he did. But how could I stop him? How could I take away his agency in this moment?

Still, the relic loomed between us, its ominous glow pulsing, as if savoring the tension in the air, feeding off the emotions that swirled like a hurricane around us. Its ancient curse was powerful, vicious, designed to consume those who dared to challenge it. And we were challenging it. The relic demanded a price, and it wouldn't let either of us go until it had claimed its due.

But I couldn't let him go.

Steeling myself, I moved closer to him, my hand reaching out, and without a word, I grasped his hand. His fingers curled around mine, strong and warm, and I felt an instant surge of calm, as though his touch anchored me, even as everything around us felt unsteady, on the brink of disaster. I looked up at him, ready to argue, to fight him if I had to, but he shook his head, a sad, gentle smile on his lips.

"You don't have to do this," he said softly, his voice barely more than a whisper. "This isn't your burden to bear."

"That's where you're wrong," I replied, squeezing his hand. "This isn't just your battle. It's ours. I'm not letting you sacrifice yourself—not when we finally have something worth fighting for together."

The relic seemed to throb with fury at my words, its light flaring, casting an eerie glow across the ground. Shadows stretched and twisted around us, as though alive, as though they could sense the defiance in the air. The curse was tangible, a dark, looming presence that seemed to hiss with anger, displeased with my refusal to let him face it alone. But I wasn't afraid—not of the relic, and not of the curse. What terrified me was the thought of losing him, of facing a world where he was nothing more than a memory.

As I held his gaze, I could see the conflict in his eyes, the battle between his own fierce desire to protect me and his reluctance to let me share this burden. But there was something else, too—a glimmer of hope, faint but undeniable. And in that moment, I knew we could do this together, that maybe, just maybe, we had a chance to break the curse without losing either of ourselves.

"Trust me," I whispered, stepping closer until there was barely any space between us. "We're stronger together. Whatever it takes, we'll face it side by side."

He nodded, his jaw tightening with determination, and then we turned, facing the relic, our hands still clasped, our resolve as one. The magic in the air intensified, swirling around us, a force as fierce and unforgiving as a storm at sea. I could feel its weight, pressing down on us, testing our resolve, as if it could sense our determination and was challenging us to prove it.

And then, as if in response to our defiance, the relic's light dimmed for a brief moment, a strange, almost eerie calm settling over us. I held my breath, wondering if perhaps we'd somehow subdued it, but then the light flared again, brighter and more intense than before, and I felt a surge of raw energy rush through me, binding me to him, to this moment, in a way that felt almost sacred.

The curse demanded a price, but as I looked at him, felt the strength of his grip in mine, I realized that the price was not something that had to be paid with one life or the other. It was a bond, a commitment, an unbreakable promise that we would stand together, that we would face whatever came our way, side by side. And so, without hesitation, I offered that promise to the relic, pouring every ounce of my love, my strength, my spirit into it, letting it feel the depth of what we shared, the power that came from standing together.

The relic pulsed, as though considering, and then I felt the magic shift, its grip loosening, its curse breaking, dissolving like smoke in the air. And in that moment, I knew we'd won, that our love had been enough, that we had broken the relic's hold over us.

But as the relic shattered, as its shards scattered across the ground, I felt a strange emptiness settle over me, a sense of loss that I couldn't quite understand. I looked at him, saw the same flicker of uncertainty in his eyes, and I realized that while we had won, something had changed, something fundamental that neither of us could fully grasp.

He reached for me, his hand finding mine, and as our fingers intertwined, I felt a surge of warmth, of reassurance. We had won, yes, but we had also paid a price—a price that we would only come to understand in time.

The dust settled around us in a slow, deliberate fall, like a reluctant snowfall over our heads. I stared at the remnants of the relic, the twisted shards littering the ground, glinting faintly in the low light. For something that had held so much power, so much darkness, it looked oddly fragile in pieces, like it could disintegrate into dust with just a puff of air. I couldn't tear my eyes from it, half-waiting for it to somehow pull itself back together, for another act, another price to reveal itself. But it lay still, silent, defeated.

His hand tightened around mine, pulling me from my thoughts. I looked up and saw that familiar softness in his eyes, the quiet relief tempered by that unshakeable resolve, the same gaze that had held me steady moments before. Yet behind that gaze, something was unraveling, a flicker of something raw that he quickly tried to bury. He looked away, jaw tightening, his fingers still interlaced with mine like he was afraid to let go.

"Don't look so relieved," I murmured, my voice shakier than I intended. "It's not like I'd let you be a martyr. That's not how we do things."

A hint of a smile tugged at his lips, but it didn't quite reach his eyes. "I figured you'd say that." He released a shaky breath, finally meeting my gaze again. "I wasn't exactly planning on making you watch me...go through with it."

"Oh, well, forgive me for interrupting your grand sacrifice." I shot him a look that I hoped read as annoyed, though I knew I wasn't fooling anyone. I had barely been able to breathe through my own panic. "Next time, maybe give me a warning so I can sit back and enjoy the show."

"Next time?" He raised an eyebrow, one corner of his mouth quirking up. "Sounds like you're looking forward to a repeat performance."

The joke, however faint, brought the tension down a notch, letting a small laugh escape my lips. But as quickly as the laughter had come, it faded, replaced by a silence thick with things unsaid. I could feel the air shifting between us, charged with something that was both reassuring and unsettling, like we'd crossed a threshold that couldn't be uncrossed.

"Tell me the truth," I said, breaking the silence, my tone firmer than I expected. "Did you really think sacrificing yourself would solve everything?"

He hesitated, glancing down at our still-clasped hands, his thumb tracing a slow, absentminded circle over my skin. "I thought... maybe it was the only way. Maybe it was the only way to keep you safe."

"That's a terrible plan," I said flatly. "One, because it doesn't work. And two—" I squeezed his hand, letting my words hang in the air between us, hoping he'd feel the weight of them without me having to spell it out.

His eyes lifted, a flicker of something vulnerable flashing across his face. "You think I don't know that?" he said, his voice low. "But sometimes... when you care about someone, you just—" He stopped, letting out a frustrated sigh. "It was the only thing I could think of. I wasn't willing to lose you."

"Well, then, it's a good thing you didn't have to." I tried to keep my voice light, though the lump in my throat made it hard to speak. "Because I'm not exactly looking for a replacement."

He let out a small chuckle, a breathy sound that seemed to surprise even him, like he'd forgotten how to laugh. And there it was again—that gentle, hopeful feeling that maybe, just maybe, we could be okay. That maybe we could find our way through this mess together.

But as I looked into his eyes, that glimmer of hope faded, replaced by a new unease. There was a shadow there, a heaviness I couldn't quite decipher, as if something was pulling him back, anchoring him to a memory or a regret I didn't yet understand.

"What?" I asked, my voice barely more than a whisper. "What's wrong?"

He shook his head, a haunted look crossing his face. "Nothing. It's... nothing."

I didn't believe him, not for a second, but I also knew him well enough to recognize that look, the one that meant he wasn't ready to talk. So instead, I leaned my head against his shoulder, letting the quiet wrap around us, the weight of everything that had just happened settling like a second skin over us both.

We stayed like that, the silence stretching between us, filled with words we didn't know how to say. And as we stood there, I felt the ground beneath us begin to shift—not physically, but in some intangible way, as though the very foundation of what we thought we knew was slipping from under us. It was as if the relic's shattered curse had left something lingering in the air, a reminder that not everything could be so easily mended.

Eventually, he broke the silence, his voice soft but steady. "You realize this isn't over, don't you?"

I looked up at him, studying the lines of his face, the seriousness in his eyes. "What do you mean?"

He sighed, raking a hand through his hair. "I mean... whatever that relic was, it was just a symptom of something larger, something darker. And we barely made it through this one. Whatever comes next... we have to be ready."

I nodded slowly, a quiet resolve settling over me. "We'll be ready. Whatever it takes."

He nodded, though his gaze remained distant, his hand slipping out of mine as he took a step back, a wall forming between us that I hadn't anticipated. The ache in my chest grew, but I swallowed it down, refusing to let it consume me. We'd come too far to let fear pull us apart now.

"Promise me something," I said, my voice stronger than I felt. "Promise me you won't do this alone. Whatever we face next, we face it together."

He looked at me, his eyes softening, that haunted look fading, replaced by something warm and fierce. "I promise."

It wasn't a grand declaration, but it was enough. And as he stepped forward, his hand finding mine once more, I felt a sense of calm wash over me, grounding me in the here and now. For the first time in what felt like forever, I wasn't looking over my shoulder, waiting for the next disaster. We had survived, somehow, and for now, that was enough.

But as we turned away from the shattered relic, I couldn't shake the feeling that something lay ahead, something that would test us in ways we couldn't yet imagine. I squeezed his hand, a silent reminder that whatever came, we would face it together. And as the sun dipped below the horizon, casting a long shadow over the path before us, I knew that our journey was far from over—but at least, for now, we had each other.

The night felt heavy, weighted with the kind of silence that comes after too much chaos, as if the world were holding its breath, waiting to see if we would shatter too. Every step away from the wreckage felt surreal, like waking up from a nightmare only to find it waiting for you just outside the door. His hand stayed in mine, an anchor in the darkness, but I could sense the tension in him, the unspoken question that lay between us, charged and unsettling. We were alive, yes, but I could feel the fragments of something unfinished lurking at the edge of our triumph.

"Do you think it'll ever stop?" I asked quietly, half hoping he'd have an answer I wanted to hear. But the second the words left my mouth, I regretted them; I knew there was no simple fix, no fairy tale ending that could be dusted off and handed over to us.

He paused, his gaze flickering over to me, thoughtful yet unreadable. "Do you?"

I could only shake my head. I wasn't sure what I believed anymore. Everything felt uncertain, like we were caught in the middle of some cosmic chess game, pieces moved by hands we couldn't see, couldn't control. And for all our talk about fighting together, there was a cold, creeping dread inside me that whispered maybe we'd only just begun.

He stopped walking, turning to face me fully, his hand still wrapped around mine, but there was a distance in his gaze that startled me. "You're right," he murmured, his tone hollow. "This isn't over. There's more out there, things that no one even knows about yet. We were fools to think it would be this easy."

I studied him, noting the subtle lines of fatigue around his eyes, the rigid set of his shoulders. I wanted to tell him he was wrong, that it was over, that we'd done enough, but the words felt hollow, forced. Instead, I held his gaze, letting the silence stretch between us like an unsteady bridge. And that's when I saw it—a flicker of something darker in his eyes, something I couldn't quite name, but it left an icy shiver down my spine.

"Are you... are you sure you're okay?" I asked, my voice barely more than a whisper.

A shadow of a smile crossed his face, thin and fleeting. "I don't know what I am anymore," he admitted. "I feel... like a part of me is still bound to that relic. Like it took something with it when it shattered, and I don't know if I'll ever get it back."

His words felt like a punch to my chest, the realization settling over me with an ominous weight. All this time, I had thought we'd broken free, shattered the curse that had held us in its grip. But now, looking at him, feeling the strange distance between us, I wondered if we'd only traded one kind of imprisonment for another.

"Maybe it's not about getting anything back," I said carefully. "Maybe it's about finding something new, building something that isn't tied to all of this." My words felt clumsy, insufficient, but I could see the faintest flicker of hope in his eyes, a spark that almost looked like relief.

"Maybe," he replied, but his voice was distant, as if he were already somewhere else. He dropped my hand, turning to look out into the shadowed landscape around us, his shoulders slumping. "But if it's true... if there's more out there..." He paused, the weight of the words hanging between us. "Then maybe it isn't something we can run from. Maybe we have to face it head-on."

"And by 'we,' you do mean the two of us, right?" I asked, forcing a note of humor into my voice to mask the worry knotting in my stomach.

He turned back to me, a real smile this time, though faint. "Of course. I'm not letting you off the hook that easily."

I laughed, the sound ringing out in the stillness, and for a moment, it felt like the world had tilted back into balance. But as quickly as the lightness came, it faded, replaced by that nagging unease that something wasn't right, that something dark and unseen lay just ahead, waiting for us.

We walked in silence, the weight of the unknown pressing down on us. The stars were faint above, obscured by clouds that seemed to gather with purpose, and I couldn't shake the feeling that we were being watched, that something was tracking our every move, waiting for us to make a misstep.

Then, suddenly, a faint sound echoed in the distance—a low, eerie whisper carried on the wind. I froze, glancing over at him, my heart hammering in my chest. He stiffened beside me, his gaze sharp as he scanned the darkness, his hand instinctively reaching for the weapon strapped at his side.

"Did you hear that?" I asked, my voice trembling slightly.

He nodded, his face pale. "We're not alone."

The words sent a chill through me, and I felt the hairs on the back of my neck stand on end. I couldn't see anything, couldn't make out any shapes or figures in the shadows, but the air felt thick, charged with an energy that was both familiar and terrifying. And then, just as suddenly as it had come, the whisper faded, leaving only silence in its wake.

But the feeling didn't leave. I could sense it, lingering just out of sight, a presence that was both threatening and watchful, like a predator waiting for the perfect moment to strike. I swallowed, forcing myself to stay calm, but I could feel the panic clawing at the edges of my mind.

"Keep moving," he whispered, his voice tight. "Don't look back."

I wanted to argue, to question him, but something in his tone made me obey, my steps quickening as I matched his pace. Every step felt like a countdown, like we were moving closer to something inevitable, something that had been set in motion long before we ever stepped foot in this place.

The silence grew heavier, pressing down on us, until I could barely breathe. And then, just when I thought I couldn't take another step, a sudden flash of movement caught my eye—a figure in the shadows, cloaked and silent, watching us with a gaze that felt like it could pierce through stone.

I stumbled, my breath catching in my throat, but he reached out, steadying me with a grip that was as reassuring as it was urgent. "Don't stop," he muttered, his gaze never leaving the figure.

We kept moving, faster now, the presence behind us growing closer, more menacing with every step. My pulse pounded in my ears, the fear coursing through me like wildfire, and for the first time since we'd shattered that relic, I felt truly afraid.

Then, without warning, the figure stepped forward, blocking our path, and the world seemed to close in around us, dark and unyielding. There was no way out, no escape from the shadows that surrounded us, and as I looked into the figure's eyes, I realized with a sickening clarity that this was only the beginning, that whatever curse we'd thought we'd broken had only led us here, to this moment, to this reckoning.

"Welcome back," the figure whispered, their voice a chilling echo in the darkness, filled with a malevolence that left me breathless.

And in that instant, I knew we were trapped.

Chapter 29: A New Dawn

The pavement beneath me was still damp, glistening under the first light of dawn as if the city itself was trying to wash away what had happened here just hours before. The air was sharp and cold, and I inhaled deeply, feeling the sting in my lungs—a reminder that I was still, somehow, gloriously alive. Next to me, Liam leaned against a crumbling wall, his shoulder slumped in a way that hinted at the true toll this night had taken. His clothes were torn, streaked with grime, and a faint line of blood trailed down from his temple. Yet there was that familiar flicker in his gaze, a determined spark that never seemed to fade, no matter how many battles we fought or how close we came to losing everything.

For a moment, neither of us spoke. We simply stood there, listening to the distant sounds of the city waking up. The soft hum of traffic, the low rumble of delivery trucks weaving their way through narrow streets, even the occasional bark of a stray dog—all of it felt impossibly normal, like a scene from another life. A life I had almost forgotten, one where I wasn't constantly looking over my shoulder or weighing my chances of survival against my sense of loyalty.

"You think it's really over?" My voice was quiet, barely more than a whisper. I hadn't meant to ask it, hadn't meant to admit that sliver of doubt that had lodged itself in my chest, stubborn and unyielding. But there it was, slipping out before I could stop it, exposing the raw nerve of my fear.

Liam's mouth twisted into a wry smile, and he shrugged. "Nothing's ever really over, is it?" he replied, his tone light, though his eyes told a different story. "But, yeah...for now, I think we've earned ourselves a little peace."

I tried to hold onto that thought, to let it settle like a balm over my racing heart. Peace. It was a strange concept, one I could barely remember from a time long before the curse, before the relic, before the endless, suffocating shadow that had swallowed up my life. But now, standing here with him, with the ruins of our battle scattered around us like some terrible mosaic, it felt like something more than just a dream. It felt real, tangible—a promise that I could almost reach out and grasp, if I was brave enough.

"You know," I murmured, letting my gaze wander to the horizon where the first sliver of sun was breaking through the clouds, "I can't decide if I should be excited or terrified. A future without...well, without all this. What's that even supposed to look like?"

He chuckled, a low, warm sound that curled around me like a lifeline. "Maybe it's just a bunch of boring things. Mortgage payments, grocery shopping, holiday dinners where nobody ends up throwing a curse across the table. You know, all the stuff people like us aren't supposed to want."

I snorted, glancing sideways at him. "You think you're ready for that? I mean, I hate to break it to you, but you're probably about the least qualified person to live a normal life. You'd get bored in ten minutes."

"Probably," he admitted, grinning. "But I've been told I'm a fast learner."

There it was—the teasing banter, the playful spark that had first drawn me to him all those months ago, back when he was just a stranger with a mysterious past and a knack for getting under my skin. And now, after everything we'd been through, I found myself wondering how much of me had changed, too. How much of that tough, guarded girl I used to be had softened, melted under his gaze, reshaped into someone I barely recognized. It was terrifying, exhilarating—a plunge into something unknown, and yet, somehow, it felt right.

The sound of footsteps pulled me from my thoughts, and I glanced up to see a figure approaching. It was Leo, his face as worn and weary as ours, but with a spark of relief dancing in his eyes. He looked us over, his gaze lingering on the various cuts and bruises, the disheveled clothes, the unmistakable evidence of the night we had just survived.

"So," he said, a trace of a smile quirking his lips, "am I interrupting something, or should I be congratulating you two on not getting yourselves killed?"

Liam shrugged, looking unapologetically smug. "We aim to please."

I rolled my eyes, feeling a strange mix of gratitude and exasperation. Leo had always been there, a steady presence even when I hadn't wanted him to be, his loyalty unshakeable in a way that had sometimes felt more like a burden than a blessing. But now, standing here with him, I realized that maybe I'd been wrong. Maybe his loyalty had been exactly what had kept me from slipping too far into the darkness.

"You look terrible, by the way," I said, arching an eyebrow at him. "Just in case nobody's mentioned it yet."

He laughed, a tired, genuine sound that warmed the cold morning air. "I'll take that as a compliment, coming from you. But seriously, what's next? Do we go back to pretending this was all some elaborate nightmare, or do we actually try to make something out of the mess we've left behind?"

It was a question I'd been avoiding, one that had lingered at the back of my mind through every fight, every close call, every heart-stopping moment when I thought this might be the end. And now, faced with the choice, I wasn't sure if I was ready for the answer.

But then Liam's hand brushed against mine, his fingers lacing through mine with a quiet certainty that steadied me, grounded me. And in that simple gesture, I felt a surge of courage, a fierce determination that pushed away the lingering shadows of doubt.

"We make something out of it," I said firmly, my voice steadier than I felt. "We don't get to walk away from this and pretend it never happened. We owe it to ourselves, to everyone who fought with us, to build something out of all this madness. Something better."

Leo nodded, his expression softening with something that looked almost like pride. "Then I guess we've got our work cut out for us, don't we?"

I glanced at Liam, a smile tugging at the corners of my lips. "Guess so. And you know what? I think I'm finally ready for it."

The city was slowly coming to life around us, pulling itself out of the night like a person stretching after a deep sleep. There was a peculiar beauty in the chaos of it—delivery trucks rattling down the narrow streets, shopkeepers rolling up metal shutters with bleary determination, pigeons squabbling over scraps left behind on the cobblestones. And there we were, planted in the middle of it all, an odd trio who looked as if we'd crawled out of some forgotten part of the world. To anyone passing by, I was sure we looked more like a bunch of reckless partiers than battle-worn survivors who'd just crawled through the darkest night of our lives.

Leo squinted at a streak of grime on his sleeve, trying to rub it away but only managing to smear it further. He shot me a look, one eyebrow raised in mock reproach. "Did you have to drag us through the sewer at the end there? I mean, really. A sewer?"

I shrugged, trying to look as nonchalant as one could when covered in a questionable layer of muck. "It was either that or an unmarked alley with a nice little nest of cursed rats. I figured sewer stench was the better option. Besides, you seemed to be handling it well."

Leo grimaced, giving his jacket a disgusted tug. "Handling it well? Please, I'll be smelling this for weeks."

Liam, who had been uncharacteristically quiet up until now, let out a soft laugh that made me glance his way. There was something different in his expression, a lightness that hadn't been there before. He looked almost...relaxed, as though the weight he'd carried for so long had finally slipped from his shoulders. And in a strange way, I realized that the same had happened to me. For so long, we had been bound by our shared burdens, each of us tethered to a relentless, unforgiving fight. But now, with the curse broken and the relic reduced to nothing more than dust and memory, I felt free. Lighter, even, as if the air itself had become clearer, easier to breathe.

"You two done bickering yet?" he asked, his tone teasing, though there was a warmth in his eyes that softened the jab. "Or should I give you a minute to fully appreciate the sewers?"

I rolled my eyes. "Don't start with me, Liam. Just because you were lucky enough to get away with only a smear of blood and a scrape on the cheek doesn't mean you get to act superior. Next time, I'm shoving you right into the mess and letting you see how you like it."

His smile widened, his gaze never leaving mine. "Oh, I'd expect nothing less from you."

There it was again—the familiar banter, the sparks flying in a way that had felt like second nature ever since we'd first met. But now, the stakes had changed. We had changed. And as much as I tried to keep things light, a part of me couldn't ignore the shift, the subtle undercurrent of something new weaving its way into every word, every shared look. The past few months had been a relentless blur of high-stakes battles, sleepless nights, and close calls that had nearly broken us both. But with the dawn painting the world in hues of rose and gold, I couldn't help but wonder if this was what we'd been fighting for—not just a future, but a chance at something real, something that had been growing quietly, unnoticed, amid the chaos.

"I suppose we should make ourselves presentable," I said finally, glancing down at the grime staining my own clothes. "It wouldn't do to walk into the Council looking like we just crawled out of the underworld."

"Too late for that," Leo muttered, earning a playful shove from me.

We turned our steps toward the safe house, a shabby little building tucked away in a part of the city where no one looked twice at odd comings and goings. Inside, the air was stale, thick with the scent of old wood and dust, but there was a comfort in it. Familiar, in a way that only a place of refuge can be after it's seen you at your worst. I made a beeline for the bathroom, eager to scrub away the remnants of the night, and heard Leo's disgruntled voice behind me as he realized I'd claimed it first.

"Don't take all day!" he called, knocking on the door for emphasis. "Some of us have dignity to salvage too, you know."

I stifled a laugh and turned on the tap, letting the cool water wash over my hands, then my face. As I looked at my reflection in the cracked mirror, I saw someone both familiar and unfamiliar. My skin was bruised in places, smeared with dirt and dried blood, but there was a glint in my eyes, a fierceness that hadn't been there before. For the first time, I looked at myself and saw a survivor—not a girl running from her past or desperately trying to keep up, but someone who had fought, who had won, and who was ready to start again.

When I emerged, Leo was leaning against the wall, his expression halfway between annoyed and amused. "About time," he muttered, pushing past me and closing the door with a dramatic sigh. I rolled my eyes and turned to find Liam waiting in the main room, watching me with that quiet intensity that had a way of making my heart stutter.

He took a step closer, his gaze holding mine. "You did good," he said softly, his voice barely more than a murmur. "I don't know if I've told you that enough."

For a moment, I felt my breath catch. It was a simple statement, but coming from him, it felt like more—like an acknowledgment of everything we'd endured, the unspoken understanding that had bound us together long before either of us had realized it.

"Don't get sappy on me now, Liam," I replied, my voice teasing, though there was a warmth in my chest that I couldn't quite hide. "You know I hate it when you go all sentimental."

He chuckled, a low, rumbling sound that sent a shiver down my spine. "Wouldn't dream of it."

And just like that, the moment passed, but something lingered, an unspoken promise hanging in the air between us. We both knew that our lives would never be easy, that the scars we carried were a permanent part of who we were. But now, standing here with him, I felt a glimmer of hope, a fragile, precious thing that I was almost afraid to acknowledge.

Leo reappeared, looking marginally more put-together, though there was still a faint line of dirt along his collar. "Well, aren't we a picture of elegance," he muttered, gesturing to the three of us with a sardonic grin.

Liam smirked. "Speak for yourself, Leo. Some of us manage to pull off 'post-battle chic' with a little more finesse."

I laughed, the sound filling the room, lightening the heavy silence that had settled after the events of the night. For the first time, I let myself imagine what might come next—not in vague, shadowed outlines, but in real, vivid colors. A future where we could rebuild, find peace, and maybe, just maybe, find a bit of happiness along the way. And as the sun rose higher, casting light through the cracked window, I knew one thing for certain: whatever came next, we would face it together.

The sunlight had a warmth to it that felt foreign, almost like it didn't belong here, in this gray city with its haphazard jumble of alleys and rooftops, stained brick and forgotten storefronts. It spread across the cracked sidewalk and filtered through the few green leaves clinging stubbornly to the branches above, casting a glow that softened everything. I could feel it on my skin, a reminder that the world was turning, that seasons were shifting, that maybe—just maybe—we could begin again.

But even with the light, there was a restlessness tugging at me, a prickling unease just beneath the surface. I glanced sideways at Liam, his face angled up toward the morning sky, that rare hint of peace softening his expression. Beside us, Leo was already getting twitchy, his fingers tapping a silent rhythm against his thigh as he cast a wary glance over his shoulder.

"Can you not look so...content?" Leo muttered, his voice laced with the kind of humor that barely masked his tension. "It's unsettling. I keep expecting the universe to take offense and lob a brick at your head."

Liam chuckled, the sound low and warm, his gaze never wavering from the horizon. "If the universe wanted me gone, it's had plenty of chances."

Leo huffed, crossing his arms. "Well, I'd rather not test that theory. What if this is all some kind of elaborate set-up? You know, to lull us into a false sense of security."

I shot him a sidelong look, an eyebrow arching. "You sound a little paranoid there, Leo. Maybe a few hours of sleep would do you some good."

He shrugged, but his mouth twisted into a smirk. "Hey, when you're right, seventy percent of the time, there's a little wiggle room for paranoia."

"And the other thirty percent?" Liam asked, an amused gleam in his eye.

Leo rolled his eyes, waving his hand dismissively. "Statistical outliers."

I laughed, shaking my head as we continued down the narrow street, weaving our way through the remnants of last night's storm—a few stray leaves, overturned trash bins, puddles that reflected the early light in fractured patterns. For a moment, the three of us walked in silence, the sound of our footsteps the only rhythm to mark the passing seconds.

But the quiet didn't last long. A faint hum caught my attention, a barely-there vibration that seemed to echo up from the pavement, winding its way into my bones. I slowed, frowning, my instincts flaring to life. I could feel it—something familiar, a ripple of the same energy that had twisted through our lives and led us to this point. It was subtle, barely detectable, but it was there, lurking beneath the city's skin like a secret waiting to be exposed.

Liam's hand brushed mine, a light touch that anchored me even as my senses prickled. He must have felt it too; his gaze was sharp, his body tense in that way he had just before a fight. Leo, ever perceptive, had gone still, his eyes narrowing as he scanned the street, the buildings, the rooftops.

"You feel that?" I asked, my voice low, careful not to break whatever spell had settled over us.

Liam nodded, his jaw clenched. "It's faint, but…yeah."

"What are the odds it's a harmless coincidence?" Leo whispered, though his tone suggested he already knew the answer.

"Zero," Liam replied, his voice steady but his posture braced.

The hum grew stronger, a soft, insistent thrum that seemed to reverberate through the walls, the ground, the very air around us. I could feel it building, coiling in on itself like a snake preparing to strike, and a cold dread twisted in my gut. I knew this feeling too well—the anticipation, the warning embedded in every beat of my heart. I had spent too many nights living with it, letting it guide me, trusting it even when it felt like madness.

We exchanged a glance, the unspoken agreement passing between us with the ease of habit. We didn't need words to know what had to be done. In a single, fluid motion, we slipped into the shadows, pressing ourselves against the worn brick of an old storefront, our breaths held as we listened.

The silence was heavy, taut, the kind of silence that pressed in on you, made you hyper-aware of every sound, every flicker of movement. But there was nothing—no footsteps, no whispers, no sign that anyone or anything was there. Only the hum, vibrating through the concrete like the distant rumble of an approaching storm.

Then, out of the corner of my eye, I saw it—a flicker of movement, just a flash, barely there. A figure slipping through the early morning haze, cloaked in shadows, moving with a grace that was both unsettling and mesmerizing. Whoever they were, they weren't alone. I could see two more shapes trailing behind, their forms indistinct but their intent unmistakable.

Liam's hand tightened on my arm, his grip a steadying force as he leaned in, his voice a whisper barely audible above the tension. "Stay close. We don't know what we're dealing with yet."

I nodded, my heart thundering in my chest. Every instinct I had screamed at me to move, to act, to confront whoever—or whatever—was lurking in the shadows. But we held our ground, waiting, watching, our breaths shallow as we strained to catch any hint of their purpose.

The figures drew closer, their steps almost soundless, their movements synchronized in a way that spoke of precision, of training, of something far more dangerous than a few common street thugs. My skin prickled, the familiar chill of recognition sliding down my spine. This was no random encounter. They were here for us.

I glanced at Liam, saw the understanding mirrored in his eyes, the quiet resolve that had become his trademark. He gave me a slight nod, barely perceptible, and in that instant, I knew we were ready, prepared for whatever came next. We had faced worse, after all. We had survived the impossible. But this time, there was something different, a shadow lingering at the edges of my mind, whispering that this fight would be unlike any before it.

The first figure stepped into the light, his face partially obscured but his eyes sharp, fixed on us with a predatory focus that sent a shiver of warning through me. He wore a faint smile, a ghost of amusement that didn't reach his gaze, and when he spoke, his voice was smooth, almost friendly.

"Well, well," he murmured, his tone laced with a mockery that set my teeth on edge. "Seems we've caught you at an awkward moment. Pity."

Liam stepped forward, his posture unyielding, his expression calm but deadly. "Funny, I was just thinking the same thing."

The stranger tilted his head, studying us with a detached curiosity that was almost more unsettling than open hostility. "Oh, I doubt that," he said, his voice soft, measured, as if he were discussing the weather. "You see, unlike you, we came prepared."

A chill ran through me as his words settled into the air, cold and final. There was something about him, something in the way he held himself, that told me he wasn't bluffing. And yet, there was no fear in me, only a sharp, keen awareness that left my senses humming, every nerve alight with anticipation.

Without warning, he raised his hand, and a wave of energy pulsed out, invisible but potent, slamming into us with a force that sent me reeling. I stumbled back, my vision blurring, my body fighting to steady itself against the onslaught. I caught a glimpse of Liam, his jaw clenched, his stance unwavering even as the energy swirled around us like a storm.

And then, in a heartbeat, everything shifted. The air went still, thick with a silence that was almost deafening. The stranger's smile widened, his gaze gleaming with a dark satisfaction as he took a deliberate step forward, closing the distance between us.

"Now," he murmured, his voice a soft caress, "shall we begin?"

Milton Keynes UK
Ingram Content Group UK Ltd.
UKHW030948261124
451585UK00001B/146